LYN
T

We hope you enjoy this book.
Please return or renew it by the due date.
You can renew it at **www.norfolk.gov.uk/libraries**
or by using our free library app. Otherwise you can
phone **0344 800 8020** - please have your library
card and pin ready.
You can sign up for email reminders too.

10/17

Also by New York Times bestselling author
Maria V. Snyder

The Chronicles of Ixia

The Insider series

Avry of Kazan series

www.miraink.co.uk

sea glass

MARIA V. SNYDER

Published in Great Britain 2011. This edition 2016.
MIRA Books, Eton House, 18-24 Paradise Road,
Richmond, Surrey, TW9 1SR

© Maria V. Snyder 2009

ISBN 978 1 848 45247 3

58-0913

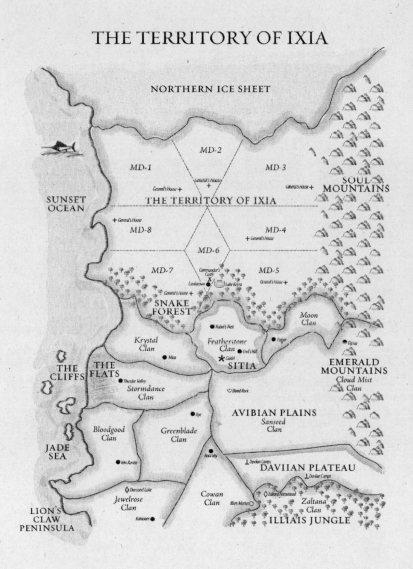

THE TERRITORY OF IXIA

NORTHERN ICE SHEET

MD-2

MD-1   MD-3

General's House   *General's House*   *General's House*   **SOUL MOUNTAINS**

SUNSET OCEAN

THE TERRITORY OF IXIA

General's House   MD-8   MD-4   *General's House*

MD-6

MD-7   *Commander's Castle*   MD-5

Castletown   *Lake Kayty*   *General's House*

General's House

SNAKE FOREST

Rubin's Nest   **Moon Clan**

Krystal Clan   *Featherstone Clan*   *Fulgor*

Mica   *Owl's Hill*   *Dawn*

THE CLIFFS   **THE FLATS**   *Gaids*   **SITIA**   **EMERALD MOUNTAINS**

Thunder Valley   **Cloud Mist Clan**

Stormdance Clan   ♡ *Blood Rock*

JADE SEA   *Rye*   **AVIBIAN PLAINS**   *Sanseed Clan*

Bloodgood Clan   **Greenblade Clan**

Vein Ravine   *Booruby*   ⊥ *Daviian Camps*   **DAVIIAN PLATEAU**

⊥ *Daviian Camps*

◇ *Diamond Lake*   ◇ *Zaltana Homestead*

JADE SEA

LION'S CLAW PENINSULA   **Jewelrose Clan**   **Cowan Clan**   *Illais Market*   **Zaltana Clan**

Kohaaan   **ILLIAIS JUNGLE**

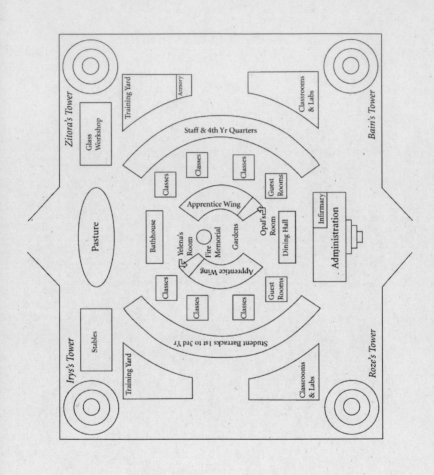

Zitora's Tower

Bain's Tower

Irys's Tower

Roze's Tower

Training Yard

Glass Workshop

Armory

Classrooms & Labs

Staff & 4th Yr Quarters

Classes

Classes

Classes

Guest Rooms

Pasture

Bathhouse

Apprentice Wing

Yelena's Room

Fire Memorial Gardens

Opal's Room

Dining Hall

Infirmary

Administration

Classes

Apprentice Wing

Guest Rooms

Classes

Classes

Classes

Stables

Student Barracks 1st to 3rd Yr

Training Yard

Classrooms & Labs

This one is for Chris Phillips,
for his unique perspective on life.
A brother to me in all ways and a true wizard.
In memory of Robert Phillips,
a great guy and wonderful father.

WORRY AND DREAD clawed at my stomach. I read the message again. The order was clear and concise. *Return to the Citadel immediately and report directly to the Council Hall.* The signatures of the entire Sitian Council and all three Master Magicians were scrawled under the missive. A bit heavy-handed, but I couldn't miss the importance nor doubt the seriousness.

"What does it say?" Janco asked. He plucked the paper from my fingers, scanned the short note and whistled. "This is major." Scratching the scar where the lower half of his right ear used to be, Janco squinted at me in concern. "You're not going to obey are you? 'Cause, if you do—"

"I know." No need to state the obvious.

"The Council will escort you straight to the Keep's dungeons where you will stay for a very, very long time," Devlen said in a matter-of-fact tone.

I glared at him.

"Did I say you can talk?" Janco asked him.

"I am trying to help," he replied, shrugging. His cloak covered his hands, which had been manacled behind his back.

"I don't want *your* help," I said.

Devlen opened his mouth, and Janco jabbed him in his solar plexus. As Devlen gasped to regain his breath, Janco threatened to yank out his tongue if he uttered another word.

We all knew it was an empty threat. Traveling with Janco, Devlen and two Ixian guards for the past twenty days had become an exercise in patience for me. Since Devlen's soul was currently living inside Ulrick's body due to a twist of blood magic, Devlen knew Janco couldn't harm him, so he needled Janco whenever possible.

We planned to escort Devlen to Moon Clan's lands in order to find his body with Ulrick's soul, and then have the Soulfinder Yelena switch them back. I had sent a message detailing this plan to Second Magician Zitora Cowan as soon as we reached the Sitian border.

"Opal," Janco said. "We need a decision. It's getting dark."

"Give me a minute." I drew in a deep breath. The Council wanted me to return. My new powers terrified them, and me, too, if I thought about it for long. The Council had an excellent reason to be nervous and want me safely contained. I could drain a magician of his or her powers. All I needed was a glass orb in my hands and I could extract their magic, transforming it into a physical substance—diamonds. A magician didn't even have to attack me as I had first assumed. Oh no, I could milk a magician dry without them doing a thing.

The Council's messenger hadn't waited around for a response. No one disobeyed a direct order from the Council. Certainly not a student glass magician who hadn't even graduated from the Keep yet.

"Well?" Janco asked with impatience.

Finding Ulrick was more important, and putting a stop to blood magic was vital. "We'll make a detour to Fulgor first. I'll send Zitora a message. She'll understand." I hoped.

However, my plans didn't go the way I had envisioned. Nope. No warning bells or strange portents would alert me that by the next day Devlen and I would be in the exact opposite positions.

Unaware of the coming storm, I ignored the Council's message. We hiked east through a thin forest. Dead leaves crunched under our boots. The cold season had stripped the trees and bushes, leaving behind bare branches. The warming season had started a few days ago, and the frozen ground had turned into a muddy mess as we traveled farther south. Glancing over my shoulder, I noted the beauty of the stark and simple woods against the wide swaths of colors in the sky. The cool air smelled damp and fresh.

"Should we make camp before it gets dark?" Janco asked.

This section of Sitia seemed familiar to me, and my

stomach knotted as I remembered when I'd been here before.

"Is your cabin nearby?" I asked Devlen.

"I was wondering if you recognized the area," he said with a faint smile. "The good old days."

I bit my lip to keep from contradicting him. When he wasn't trying to play with my mind and emotions, he enjoyed irritating me, too. For example, he had lapsed back into the Daviian pattern of speech instead of trying to mimic Ulrick. "How close?"

Devlen scanned the woods and met my gaze. An odd sensation rippled through me. Seeing his cold calculation in Ulrick's vibrant green eyes still unsettled me. Ulrick's long eyelashes, black hair and sharp features all remained, but I longed for Ulrick's tender smile.

"Quite close. Are you sure you want to go there?" Devlen asked.

I considered. "Better than spending another night in the open. Take the lead."

He led us to a small one-story cabin as all light fled the sky. Janco lit a fire in the hearth, then unpacked our travel rations.

"It's too dark to hunt. I'll search for a few rabbits in the morning." He placed a pot of water on the fire to cook his road stew.

At first, the ad hoc concoction of Janco's had tasted wonderful, but after twenty days, I longed for my mother's apple cobbler and bread pudding. Her roast pork alone would be worth the five-day journey to Booruby.

Homesickness and loneliness stabbed my chest. My parents must have been distraught when they learned of my disappearance. Despite knowing my mother would fuss over me and admonish me for hours, I longed for home.

As Janco stirred the stew, the two guards took turns bringing in more firewood. I grabbed a branch and made a torch. Devlen watched me. He had been manacled to the support beam in the living room. Last time we were here, I had been Devlen's prisoner.

I stepped into the kitchen to search for food, but the few scraps of bread and cheese had spoiled. Crossing the living room to check the bedrooms, I trod on glass shards, the *crackle-crunch* under my boots unmistakable.

"I did not get a chance to clean up," Devlen called.

I crouched. The shards reflected the torchlight. It had been one of the glass orbs the Stormdancers used to harvest a storm's energy. Another pang of loneliness touched me. Kade had remained behind in Ixia to calm the lethal blizzards blowing in from the northern ice sheet. Kade would fill a number of orbs with the killing wind's energy and save many lives. I closed my eyes, remembering his goodbye kiss. I would forgo my mother's cooking for another moment wrapped in his long, lean arms.

Janco announced the stew was ready. I opened my eyes and straightened. My saddlebags remained where

Devlen had tossed them in the corner with my sais still hooked onto them. Grabbing them, I returned to the fire, sitting down next to Janco.

Devlen groaned. "I should have hidden those."

Janco perked up, peering over his bowl. "What ja got?"

"My sais." I hefted the weapons. One in each hand. They looked like short swords except the main shaft was a half-inch thick and octagonal. A weighted octagonal knob at the top balanced the sai. It resembled a three-pronged pitchfork with a long center tine.

I held them in a defensive position. The metal shaft rested along my forearm. From this position I could block a strike, jab an opponent with the knob or switch my grip and do a temple strike with the shaft.

"Sweet," Janco said. "Can I try?"

I showed him a few moves and he was proficient in no time.

"These don't have the reach of a bow staff or sword, more of a defensive weapon. But in close..." He jabbed with both sais as if aiming at an invisible opponent's ribs. The weapons blurred with the motion. "In close, you have it made. I'm gonna get me a pair. A Sitian souvenir."

"She does not need to get close or even use those at all," Devlen said. "Not with the other goodies in her bags."

Janco stopped his attack and looked at me as if waiting for a treat. "Well? Spill."

I unbuckled the flaps and upended the contents onto the wooden floor. Glass spiders and bees rained out in a loud clatter. Janco exchanged the sais for one of the brown spiders. He examined it in the firelight.

"Trapping Warpers not enough? Have you moved on to trapping spiders now?" Janco asked.

"No. Tricky had attacked me with a magical illusion of big spiders. When I channeled his magic into the orb they transformed into glass." I suppressed a shudder. Those creatures had been a foot long.

"Why didn't they turn into diamonds?"

"He directed his magic at her in the form of spiders," Devlen said. "The magic only transforms into diamonds when she *steals* it." Anger fueled his words.

"From what you did with your magic, I don't blame her." Janco exchanged the spider for a glass bee. "In fact, I'd rather she steal everyone's magic. No power over another's mind. No stealing souls. No crazy or weird stuff. Diamonds are much better." He held the bee up to the firelight. The green-and-black stripes glowed. "Pretty."

I shivered. "Pretty scary. They're Greenblade bees. Their six-inch-long bodies are filled with lethal venom. Only I can crack open the glass and release the bee. One sting and you're dead."

"Cool." Janco's eyes lit with admiration.

Interesting how he could appreciate the killing power of a bee, yet he despised magical powers. I wondered if I should point out the inconsistency until I remembered

Janco could argue about any point, logical or not. I would get an hour-long lecture on how everyone knows bees sting, but a magician could hide their lethality until too late.

The next morning we resumed our journey. I planned to find a town in order to rent or purchase horses, but didn't know the surrounding area well enough. Unfortunately, Devlen was well acquainted. I hated to ask him for help, but the Council wouldn't hesitate to send a retrieval party once they figured out I disobeyed their summons.

"Do you know where the closest town is?" I asked Devlen.

"Why should I help you?"

"Do you want to walk all the way to Fulgor?"

"I do not mind. I enjoy your company. The longer it takes for us to get there, the more time I can spend with you."

"Watch it," Janco warned.

"How about I make a deal with you?" Devlen stepped closer.

My legs wanted to step back, but I held my ground. "You don't have anything to bargain with. We can just head east until we find one. Otherwise there's a good stable in Owl's Hill."

"You do not want to get that close to the Citadel and Magician's Keep." He shook his head. "I do have something to bargain with."

Unlikely, but I gestured for him to continue.

"Quartz and Moonlight." He watched my reaction and smiled.

"Who are they?" Janco asked.

"Mine and Ulrick's horses." And I missed Quartz almost as much as I missed Kade.

"I'll lead you to them and in exchange—"

"No way," Janco said.

"Let him finish," I said. And when the Ixian frowned at me, I added, "Please. They're Sandseed horses."

He nodded, but his expression made it clear to me he was unhappy.

"In exchange, I want you to remove the manacles."

"No way," Janco and I said together.

"I promise not to run. I have been cooperating with you the entire trip."

"You've been a pain in the ass the entire trip," Janco said. "I'm sure given the first opportunity you'd bolt."

"And I can't trust you at all," I said. "There is no reason for you to keep your promise."

Devlen sighed. "You know why I would not, Opal. Just look past the whole kidnapping thing and remember how you felt when we were together."

"The whole kidnapping thing? *You* might be able to dismiss it out of hand, but, to *me,* it's too big to look past."

"You just want to deny you loved me."

"I cared for *Ulrick,* whose body you stole. Not you!"

"Come on. You had to know I was not Ulrick. No one changes that much."

I almost laughed. He had done it again. Played with my emotions. It was like arguing with Janco—a no-win situation. Devlen had been trying to trick me into saying I had fallen for him well aware on some unconscious level of who he was.

The real reason he wanted me close was for the chance to reclaim his magical abilities with blood magic. The same illegal powers that Devlen had used to switch souls with Ulrick in the first place.

"Okay. Fine. Keep lying to yourself. I will take you to the horses anyway." Devlen led us to a large horse farm a few miles north of Robin's Nest in the Featherstone lands.

Peter Featherstone, the stable's owner, showed us to the pasture. Moonlight's mostly black coat stood out among the other horses. He nickered and ran to the fence with Quartz on his heels. Happy to see her, I threw my arms around Quartz's neck and hugged her. When she pulled away in impatience, I inspected her from nose to tail. Her reddish-brown and white coat gleamed. No mud or cuts marred her legs and her mane and tail had been combed free of briars and straw. Her hooves were trimmed and neat. No horseshoes, though. Sandseed horses won't let a farrier near them.

She nudged me with her nose, searching for treats. The only white on her brown face was a patch between her eyes. I probably imagined the sympathetic look she gave me, suppressing the sudden desire to pour my heart out to her.

I checked Moonlight. His sleek muscles enhanced his powerful build and he appeared healthy, too. The only white on him—the circle on his forehead and the reason for his name—shone as if recently washed.

"No doubt they're yours," Peter said.

"What do I owe you for their care?" I asked.

He looked at Devlen in surprise. "Nothing. He paid for two full seasons. In fact, I owe you."

"Perhaps we can work out a deal. I need three more horses."

"They won't be Sandseed horses. They're too expensive. It's been my pleasure to take care of these two. I've never seen such intelligence." Peter led us to the main stable.

The large wooden building smelled of earth and horses. Sawdust littered the floor and dust motes floated in the sunlight streaming through the big open doors. Two rows of stalls, sitting back-to-back, lined each side, creating three walkways. The main throughway was wider than the others. Ropes hung along the stalls to secure horses for grooming and saddling.

"Your tack is in the back room." He pointed. "I'll have my staff bring your horses and the rental horses. See what you think of them." He hustled back to the pasture.

I entered the tack room. My saddle hung on the far wall and I unhooked it. The leather had been cleaned. In fact, the bridles, reins and rest of our tack appeared to be in good condition. The neat and organized room reflected Peter's caring and professional attitude.

Which was why the crack of a whip surprised me so much. Laden with equipment, I hurried from the room.

Janco clutched his right hand. Blood poured from between his fingers. He dodged as a long leather whip snapped at him. His sword lay on the ground out of his reach. The two Sitian guards fought four men with pitchforks. Devlen stood to the side, grinning.

We were under attack.

2

I DROPPED THE TACK. My sais and glass spiders remained in my saddlebags. Right where I had left them with Janco. A brute of a man attacked him with a whip. Janco ducked and darted, trying to get to his sword. He was fast, but with each snap, the whip tore his shirt to rags. Blood stained the shredded material.

No weapons. No time. I charged the man wielding the whip, intending to knock him over or distract him long enough for Janco to regain his weapon.

I had forgotten about Devlen. He plowed into me before I reached my target. We crashed into the side of a stall. My breath whooshed from my lungs as his weight pressed me into the ground. Gasping and choking on dirt, I struggled to push Devlen off, to no avail.

"Gotcha!" a man's voice yelled.

The snaps stopped, but the ring of metal sounded for another minute until a furious round of clatters and curses ended in silence.

"What the hell is going on here?" Peter demanded. Good question.

"Contingency plan," Devlen said. He lurched to his feet with his hands still manacled.

I scrambled to grab him, but another man leveled his pitchfork at my chest. Our Sitian guards knelt with their hands laced behind their heads. Behind them two men pressed pitchforks into their backs. The man with the whip held Janco. The whip's leather strap wrapped around Janco's torso multiple times, trapping his arms.

The horse Peter had been leading shied away from the smell of blood, but he quieted the animal with a reassuring hand. "Explain now," he ordered.

I counted six men—seven if I included Devlen—against three. The fourth pitchfork man searched Janco's pockets and found the key for Devlen's cuffs.

Once freed of the manacles, Devlen rubbed his wrists. "Thank you." He turned to Peter. "As you said yourself, Sandseed horses are expensive. I am afraid these people here—" he swept his arm out, indicating me and Janco "—tried to trick you."

"He's lying—ow!" The pitchfork's sharp metal points jabbed into me.

"Do not be rude, Opal. You spun your story. Now it is my turn." Devlen smoothed his hair away from his face. "The reason I paid for two seasons is I planned to be gone for two seasons, but I had a feeling something like this might happen and confided in the stable manager." He inclined his head to the big man holding

Janco. "You see, Sandseed horses are prized in Ixia. These three are really Ixian soldiers."

The two Sitians guards tried to deny the accusation, but were pricked into silence.

"I am a horse trader and had business near the Ixian border," Devlen continued. "They disguised themselves as Sitians, kidnapped me and coerced me into bringing them here so they could steal my horses."

Protests erupted and pitchforks poked. My body felt like a steak being tenderized. Janco remained unusually quiet. A good or bad sign? I couldn't tell.

Peter's expression had turned from outrage to confusion. "But what about her? The painted mare wouldn't have let a stranger touch her. It took me three weeks to get her to trust *me*."

"My *sister*. Unfortunately, she was romanced by him." He pointed at Janco. "She is young and inexperienced. He used her." He clucked his tongue.

Outraged, I stepped away from the pitchfork. "We're not related. He's lying to you."

My guard glanced at Devlen, and I braced for the jab. Devlen gave him a dismissive wave. No holes for now. Yippee for me.

"I'm sorry," Peter said, looking from Devlen to me, "I don't know who to believe."

"You will want proof, of course," Devlen said. "Go ahead, Opal, prove your ridiculous story to Peter."

I opened my mouth and closed it. All I had on hand was the message from the Council and it would do more harm than good. The permission papers to travel through and leave Ixia had been collected by the border guards. The only way to convince Peter would be if he verified my story with one of the magicians in the Keep or with Zitora, which would alert the Council to my location. But better to be forced to appear before the Council and locked in the Keep's cells than be Devlen's prisoner again.

Devlen smirked as the silence lengthened. "She has nothing."

"Peter can contact Second Magician Zitora Cowan to verify my story," I said. The stable owner looked suitably awed.

"Name-dropping. Very impressive," Devlen said. "And it would take a long time, too. Extra points for creativity."

"Do you have any proof?" Peter asked.

"Of course." Devlen strode to Janco's pack and opened it. He turned it upside down and shook out the contents. "Ixian uniform. Ixian coins. Ixian weapons."

"It's a knife," I said. "Everyone uses a knife."

He yanked the blade from its sheath. "Not with Ixian battle symbols etched in the metal."

Real fear caressed my spine. Before, the whole situation was preposterous, but now I worried Peter would believe him.

"If you need more, I can saddle Moonlight. You know Sandseed horses are very particular about who can ride them."

Peter nodded.

"At least confirm my story with Master Cowan, before you do anything," I pleaded.

Devlen scoffed. "As if he has the time. How many mares are ready to foal?" he asked Peter.

"Too many." The stable owner sighed. "I don't have time for this, either. I'll send a message to Robin's Nest and have the authorities deal with it."

"Excellent idea." Yet Devlen frowned and rubbed his wrists.

Peter took the bait. "But?"

"Oh, it is nothing. Since Opal is not of age yet, my father will be summoned. And it is the warming season—a busy time for farmers. He will be furious with us both."

"I'm twenty," I said, but Devlen and Peter shared a yeah-right look. Turning to the stable owner, I appealed to his intelligence. "We don't even look like we're related. Please wait."

Peter chewed on his lip. "Horses have better sense than people. If he can saddle the black Sandseed horse, he's telling the truth. Then he can take you home to help your father." He turned to his manager, "Ox, secure those men. Use their manacles and lock them in the tack room. Bret, go fetch the authorities. You two—" he jabbed a finger at me and Devlen "—get your saddles and come with me."

The stable hands moved to obey. Ox kept Janco wrapped tight in the whip.

I met Janco's steady gaze. "Don't worry, I'll catch up," Janco said before Ox dragged him away.

With no other options, I grabbed my saddle and followed Peter to the pasture. My situation transformed from bad to worse.

Moonlight snuffled Devlen's hair, nudged him for treats and stood to be saddled without being tied to the gate. Yelena had told me Sandseed horses could sense magic. I had hoped Moonlight would balk at Devlen's soul in Ulrick's body until I remembered he had explained there was no magic to detect, and only the Soulfinder would know of his deception.

Peter saddled Quartz, but Devlen placed my saddlebags on Moonlight along with Janco's sword. Great.

He thanked the stable owner. "Now we can get home and help my father plow."

My panic must have reached my face. Peter touched my shoulder. "Don't worry too much. Your father'll be mad, but I'm sure he'll forgive you in time. Daughters hold a special place in their hearts. I know."

I tried to convince him of my honesty, but his stern frown warned me he'd had enough. Quartz felt my fear, but she nuzzled me as if to say, "Snap out of it." She snorted with impatience. Her desire for action was evident, but I remained on the ground, declaring I would wait for the authorities to arrive.

Peter glanced at Devlen. "I have rope and leather ties."

"No." The mere thought of being tied to the saddle

horrified me. I'd rather be free so I could escape as soon as we were out of sight. I mounted Quartz, feeling dazed over the speed with which my situation had changed.

Peter handed her reins to Devlen on Moonlight. With a final wave, he clicked and we left at a trot. I waited until the woods obscured the stable, then reached to unbuckle Quartz's bridle. The bone-jarring gait made it difficult to keep my balance. I almost fell. Not that I would care, falling and running was plan B.

"What are you doing?" Devlen asked. He stopped the horses.

"Enjoying the scenery."

"You have spent too much time with that annoying Ixian. Sarcasm does not suit you." He dismounted.

"And being a doormat does?" I swung my leg over, preparing to slide down and bolt.

He pulled the sheath with my sais from the saddle-bags. "No. You already proved you are not a doormat when you drained me, Tricky and Crafty of our magic. After I recovered from my surprise, I was quite proud of you."

"Proud?" Not the feeling I expected.

"Yes. What you did was ruthless and smart. You did not hesitate. Much better than the whimpering little girl at our first meeting."

I bit down on another sarcastic remark. I had been fourteen and a prisoner. He had tortured me—justified whimpering.

Devlen strode toward me with the sheathed sais. I

planned my next move. But instead of pulling the weapons and threatening me, he shoved the sheath and Quartz's reins at me.

"Here. Go. Do what you want." He returned to Moonlight and mounted.

I clutched the weapons to my chest.

He spun his horse around and laughed at my confusion. "Did you think I was going to drag you to a remote cabin so I can reclaim my magic from your blood?"

"Yes." Before I siphoned Devlen's Warper powers, he had used blood magic to help Tricky regain a bit of his magic by injecting my blood into Tricky's skin.

Good thing Tricky was incarcerated in an Ixian jail. And even better, Devlen didn't know he was protected by my blood. He was the only magician impervious to my glass magic.

"Ten days ago, I would have. But I am getting used to being without magic, and do not miss the hunger for more power that had consumed me. Right now, I am more intrigued."

Again, not what I expected. "Okay, I'll bite. Intrigued about what?"

"About your reaction when you find Ulrick."

"That's no mystery. I'll be happy."

"Even when he tells you he does not want to be saved?" He considered. "And his reaction after I inform him about our intimacies should be interesting. He cares for you and he will be upset you did not notice the change."

I suppressed the urge to correct him. Ulrick's behavior and attitude had changed, but I thought it was due to seeing his sister, Gressa. Her self-absorption and over-the-top ego caused him to realize how his own maudlin demeanor was being perceived as self-pity by those around him. It had made sense, and I liked his new confidence and boldness. Which could be why I didn't question the change. And why Devlen kept returning to the subject.

Focusing on the situation at hand, I pulled my sais. Devlen smiled. "What are you planning?"

"Take you back to the stable, and rescue my friend."

"That would not go well in your I-am-the-good-one defense with Peter. Besides, we have already proven your sais are no match for my sword."

He had a point. Last time we fought, he maneuvered past my defenses with ease, slicing my arms and legs until I was dizzy with exhaustion. If I returned to the stables, Peter would probably lock me up until the city guards arrived. But I couldn't let Devlen escape, either.

He watched my face. "Guess you are stuck with me."

Until I could recapture him. "Where are you going?"

"To Fulgor to find Ulrick."

Caught off guard, I paused, letting his words sink in. "Don't you already know where he is? You said—"

"I lied. At the time, I wanted you to think I held him. More incentive for you to obey me. After we switched bodies, he went one way and I went another. I keep telling you he consented to the exchange, but you refuse to believe me."

"You've just admitted to lying, and you wonder why I don't trust you."

He threw his hands up. "I guess finding him will end the argument. We need to hurry, though. I figure we have a day at most before your annoying Ixian is tracking us." Devlen spurred Moonlight into a gallop.

Lacking another option, I urged Quartz to follow.

Well after midnight, we stopped to rest for a few hours. Devlen had kept to the northern Featherstone forests, avoiding populated areas. Which was good and bad for me. Our passage through the trees left a clear trail for Janco to track, yet the isolation set my nerves on edge. He was armed. Granted, my glass spiders and bees were in my saddlebags on Moonlight, but I wouldn't use the bees, and the spiders were more effective when my opponent was surprised.

We collected firewood, and Devlen cooked a simple bread stew.

"We will need more supplies." He handed me a bowl of the steaming liquid.

I sniffed the contents.

He laughed. "You think I poisoned it."

"You could have put in a sleeping potion or goo-goo juice."

Devlen shook his head as if he couldn't believe my stupidity. I realized he had plenty of chances to escape or...what? Capture me? Why bother when I'm following him like a lost puppy?

Yet I flinched every time he moved, grabbed the hilts of my sais when he came too close and jerked when he said my name. I almost wanted him to attack so I didn't have to wait and worry anymore. Sleep would be impossible.

"We will leave at dawn and make a stop at the border market." Devlen unrolled his sleeping mat and squirmed into a comfortable position.

The small market was located on the borderline between the Moon and Featherstone clans. At our current travel rate, I estimated we would arrive at Fulgor in two days.

Devlen's breathing slowed. I contemplated rearresting him. He said he wanted to go to Fulgor, but he could have been lying. Perhaps I could grab his sword. The weapon lay in its sheath beside him. His hand rested on the hilt. I decided to make the attempt.

I waited an hour, hoping he would relax into a deeper slumber. Seizing the tip of the scabbard, I inched his sword away from him. He moved in a heartbeat, snatching my wrist and yanking me forward. I sprawled in an ungainly heap next to him.

"Opal, you should know better after all those nights we spent sleeping side by side." He released my wrist and snaked his arm around my waist, pulling me close to him. "I missed this."

I stiffened. "*You* would. Let me go."

"I do not miss the times after you knew who I was, but *before.* You did enjoy yourself."

Those memories were tainted with his deception. It

was difficult for me to recall them without feeling the fool, without feeling embarrassed and humiliated. If I removed him and concentrated on the time spent as being with Ulrick, then I could agree. But there was the doubt, too. Did I know in an instinctive way that he wasn't really Ulrick?

"I did," I said. "But what happened after has ruined any joy."

His muscles tightened for a moment. "I am sorry to have caused you pain. It was difficult for me to be so cruel, but I was obsessed and needed your help. I happen to be very good at finding those pressure points, and, if you think about it, there is no lasting damage. Once the pressure is released the pain stops. No bruises, no broken bones and no wounds to get infected."

"Should I be glad you tortured me that way?" Sarcasm spiked my words. I jerked away.

He sighed. "No. Just trying to explain."

"Don't bother. It's bad enough you tricked me and wanted to use me to find your mentor, but you planned to give me to Sir and Namir's men. I don't think they would have been as *considerate* as you and go for the no-lasting-damage torture." I shuddered, remembering Shen's hungry eyes and possessive touch.

"An empty threat. I hoped you would decide to stay with me and learn about blood magic once we freed my mentor."

I laughed. "Wouldn't happen."

"Why not? I will admit blood magic has a horrible history and reputation. But it does not have to be ill used. The blood I collected was freely given. I did not kill anyone to obtain it, nor did anyone die."

Creative lies. I didn't think he had it in him. "And the Kirakawa ritual…?"

"Would have been my first unwilling sacrifice."

"Uh-huh. So I'm to believe you never killed anyone."

He pushed up to his elbow. "No. I have been in battles and have defended myself. Even *you* cannot make that claim."

True. By my command, one of my bees had killed the leader of a gang of robbers, and two of Namir's men died at Icefaren station when I'd rescued Kade and stolen Devlen and Crafty's magic.

"But you still want to finish the Kirakawa, which is illegal and immoral. And requires you to release your mentor, who was imprisoned for a very good reason." A group of Daviian Warpers had used the Kirakawa ritual to boost their magical power so they could counter the Master Magicians. They'd almost gained control of Sitia.

The desire to rid Sitia of all knowledge of blood magic pulsed through my body.

He lay back, stretching out on his mat. "My priorities have changed." He stared at me. "I would rather focus on other things for now."

"Like what?"

"You."

3

THE TINY SMUDGE of light brightened, pushing the deep blackness of night away. While Devlen had slept, I transferred my bags to my saddle, tucking a few spiders and bees into my cloak and pants pockets. I couldn't use them against Devlen, but they could be useful for other situations.

Devlen awoke refreshed. I wished I could say the same. My single uneasy hour of sleep had been fraught with disturbing dreams of being hunted.

We packed our meager supplies and headed east. If Devlen had noticed my late-night efforts, he gave no sign of it. The morning air held a crisp scent of pine. No clouds tainted the bright sky. Except for my companion, the day promised to be a perfect one for travel.

I would have ridden right by the border market if I had been alone. The scattering of stalls and tables matched the brownish-gray color of the forest. Customers dressed in plain tunics and pants dyed in various earth tones shopped. It was as if the people had no desire to clash with their surroundings.

I fingered my new charcoal-gray cloak. Trading the Ixian one I had worn for this one, I'd also swapped the uniform Devlen had given me to wear while in Ixia. My cream-colored tunic and dark brown linen pants were suitably nondescript. In fact, with my brown leather boots, brown eyes and hair, I fit right in. My sister Mara's voice sounded in my mind, correcting me: *Golden-brown hair, Opal. Look at those streaks of gold.* And: *Mother named you for your eyes. Black opals are so elegant and reflect the light.*

I smiled, thinking about my younger brother's comments: *Mud brown and poop brown. Poor Opal, after Mother had Mara and Tula there was nothing pretty left.* My reply was to mention how deficient he was in intelligence, launching us into an argument with no winner.

Longing to see them erased my grin.

"How much money do you have?" Devlen asked. He dismounted and tied Moonlight to a nearby tree.

"Not much." I rummaged in my pack and found a few coins. Janco carried the bulk of the money.

"I will buy jerky and cheese, and you can get the bread."

We split up to purchase the food. A feeling of oddness settled on my shoulders. I felt as if I should seek help from the locals. Yet I knew any claims about my bizarre situation would be met with disbelief. Devlen's sweet-talking skills would negate any sympathy.

Fulgor would be the same. To prove my story, the authorities would have to contact Zitora for confirmation.

She would alert them to my status. I almost laughed at
the irony of trying to get Devlen arrested and instead
being the one locked up.

The best plan would be to find Ulrick and then bring
him and Devlen to Yelena. She could switch their souls
back to their right bodies. Devlen would then be incarcerated, I would report to the Citadel as ordered and
Ulrick...? Could do whatever he wanted.

Guilt squeezed my stomach. Ulrick and I had a relationship before Devlen interrupted. But now I had
Kade, and just the thought of the Stormdancer caused
a hurricane to blow around my insides. I would have to
tell Ulrick about Kade.

Devlen and I packed the items into our bags and
mounted. After spending another sleepless night in the
open, we arrived at Fulgor late the next afternoon.

Sitting across the table from Devlen, I felt unsettled.
He had done nothing to alarm me, but the atmosphere
in the Weir Inn's common room seemed charged. The
normal buzz of conversation was muted as if the others
were afraid of being overheard.

I glanced around. Town guards sat at tables and
leaned against the bar. More than usual or was I just
ultra-aware of them because of my situation?

I questioned Devlen on Ulrick. "Where did you
leave him?"

"We parted company at the Tulip Inn on the western
edge of town."

He stuck to his story and I had no way to force the truth from him. "I'll play along. Did he say where he planned to go?"

"I suggested he find a mentor to teach him how to use his new powers and to increase them."

"With blood magic?"

"Of course. You cannot add to your magical abilities otherwise."

I considered my own history with magic. At first, I had thought I possessed one trick—to capture magic inside my glass animals. But when Kade exhausted himself filling orbs with storm energy, I joined my essence with him and helped contain the lethal might of the tempest. Then I discovered the skill to harvest another's magic.

"Your magic was always there, Opal. You lacked the confidence and the knowledge to fully use it."

"You can read my mind?"

"No. Your face. Your expressions are easy to read. Despite your adventures with the sinister side of life, you remain an open and kind person."

I would call them my misadventures.

Devlen relaxed against the back of his chair. "You do not agree. Just because you are smarter and more cautious now, you are not jaded and suspicious. When you meet someone, you think the best of them until they prove you wrong. It is refreshing and a little frustrating, especially in Ulrick's case. He has not proven you wrong."

"Mind games and sweet talk. You're very good at those. You only know me through Ulrick's memories."

"And you have forgotten I was born a Sandseed and learned how to control my magic from the Story Weavers. Just because I chose to leave my clan to be a Warper does not mean I have forgotten my training. When I had magic, I scanned each person I touched. If they resonated with me, I had full access to the story threads of their life. Past, present and future." He leaned closer. "You resonated deep within me. More than any other."

He played with my emotions, conning me. I pushed aside his insinuations about knowing my life story. Focusing on the original topic, I asked, "Who would Ulrick seek out to teach him? According to the Sitian Council, all the Warpers are dead."

Devlen propped his elbows onto the table and rested his chin on his hands. "Why are you asking me questions when you do not believe my answers?"

"Perhaps I'm hoping you'll slip up and tell me the truth."

He huffed. "Okay, fine. I told Ulrick there were three other Warpers who had escaped. They might have moved on, but two were living in Ognap and the other was somewhere near Bloodgood lands. I assume Ulrick would head east to Ognap. If the two Warpers are still there, he would find them."

"How?"

"By their smell." Seeing my confusion, he added, "It

is not discernible by regular people or magicians. Only Warpers can smell it. Handy for a number of things, especially for finding spies in our midst."

Ulrick could be in Ognap by now. If he was, then it would prove Devlen's claims that Ulrick agreed to the switch. If he found the other Warpers, then they're all together and I would have to deal with three powerful magicians. But it would also mean I could drain and neutralize three more blood magicians. Which was fine with me. The sooner the better.

Before, Ulrick's skills were limited—his glass vases also trapped magic within them, but the magic transferred emotions rather than thoughts. Could he still use his own magic? Or had it remained with his body? I asked Devlen.

"No. Besides not knowing how to blow glass, all my own magic stayed with my soul."

"How does blood magic work?" I asked.

Devlen sipped his ale. "Everyone has a soul. Therefore, everyone has magic. But not all can access the power source and use their magic potential. Only magicians can link their magic to the blanket of power."

"I know all this. I studied at the Magician's Keep for the past five years."

"Humor me." His finger traced the wood grain on the table. "Blood magic binds a person's soul magic to his blood. It attaches energy to a physical substance. After the binding is achieved, blood can be drawn from the person and injected into another. The Warpers would mix the blood with tattoo ink and inject it into the skin."

Devlen rubbed his arm as if remembering the prick of pain. "For the first level of the Kirakawa ritual, only a small amount is needed. The blood gives the Warper a boost of magic, and instead of drawing a thin thread of power from the blanket, he could pull a thicker strand. If the blood...donor is not a magician, the boost is weaker than blood from a magician."

His gaze trapped mine. "This is where it becomes interesting. If the person receiving the blood is *not* a magician and the donor is *not* a magician, nothing happens. But if the nonmagical person injects blood from a magician, he gains the ability to connect with the power source. He becomes a magician. Think about it. Everyone could be a magician. Everyone would be equal. What is wrong with that?"

A persuasive argument, except for the one thing. "But it's addicting. No one stops at the first level. The first few levels are benign, but once you get to level nine—"

"Ten is when the killings begin. And at level twelve the heart's blood is harvested from the chambers of a heart. The final step reaps the most potent magic. Because the heart is where the soul resides."

I shuddered, remembering the bloodstained sand at the Magician's Keep. Sudden pride at my deeds during the Warper battle flared. Those who knew how to perform the last two levels of the Kirakawa had been imprisoned in my glass animals and hidden. Devlen had hoped to use me to find his captured mentor and finish the Kirakawa.

"What level were you on?" I asked.

"Eight."

The word hung between us like a dark cloud. I pondered his explanation and encountered an anomaly. "The magic blood is injected into your skin, but when you switched bodies with Ulrick the tattoos didn't go with you."

"Correct. The extra magic stayed with my body. When I entered Ulrick's, I only carried my original magic, which was strong." He tapped his mug on the table. "Interesting. The addiction clung to me even when I swapped bodies."

Horrifying was closer to the truth. If Devlen switched back to his body, he would have access to magic again and Ulrick would still be addicted.

He touched my hand. I recoiled. "When you stole my magic, you took away my greed for power. You could do the same for Ulrick."

Ulrick had been frustrated with his limited magical abilities. To render him without any magic at all would be devastating. "I'm not sure he would want me to."

"Does not matter what he wants. If you do not drain him, he will desire more magic and he has learned how to acquire it."

With blood magic. "How could you say it doesn't have to be ill used? Eventually anyone using it will advance to a point where he needs to kill in order to satisfy the hunger."

"The desire to increase your power does not influence what you choose to do with your magic. Once acquired, I could do good things like heal and help others with it. The Daviian Warpers believed Sitia needed stronger leadership. They used their powers to overthrow the Council because they felt Ixia was on the verge of invading us, and the current Council would be ineffective in repelling them."

"They were wrong."

Devlen shrugged. "For now. Ixia's Commander could always change his mind."

"I can't get past the fact of having to murder another to finish the ritual."

He considered. "You could find someone on the edge of dying and take his soul right before he passes."

"But then you deny him eternal peace in the sky."

"Only if he was headed to the sky. What if the fire world claimed him? Given the choice of eternal pain or helping another, I have no doubt he would choose to stay."

I almost agreed to the benefits of his scenario before I realized he had used his golden tongue to twist his words again. And I had fallen for it. Again.

His gaze slid pass me and a wry smile touched his lips. "Such a good boy. Right on time."

I turned. Janco and four Sitian guards hustled toward us.

Devlen spread his hands wide, showing he was unarmed, but his attention never left me. "I enjoyed our conversation."

Two guards rushed him. They jerked him to his feet and slammed him face-first onto the table. He offered no resistance despite being armed with Janco's sword, which Janco wasted no time in reclaiming. Frisked and manacled, Devlen was pulled upright. The amused smile remained on his now-bloody lips.

All the patrons in the room stared at the spectacle. The other town soldiers watched with interest, but didn't attempt to help their colleagues. Probably off duty.

"See you later," Devlen said as the guards escorted him from the inn.

Janco remained behind. He turned a worried expression my way. "Are you all right?"

"Fine. How about you?" I gestured to his face and neck. Angry welts and scabs striped his skin.

He rubbed his arm. "Lousy whip. Took me by surprise. Knocked my sword right out of my hand." His eyes, though, gleamed with appreciation. "Nasty weapon. I can't wait to try it out on Ari."

Janco's partner, Ari, was twice as broad. Powerful and smart, Ari wouldn't be easy to beat.

"Just don't let him catch the whip. If he grabs it, you're done." I righted the mugs on the table and sat.

Plopping into the opposite chair, Janco winced.

"Do you want to go to a healer?" I asked.

He was quick to respond. "No. Absolutely not. I'm fine." He waved down a server and ordered a meal. Moving with care, he leaned back. "Okay, spill."

I filled him in on what had happened the past two days.

"You didn't believe a word he said. Right?" Janco asked.

"Of course. I know better." I tried to sound convincing, but wondered if the effort was for Janco's benefit or mine.

"He's got to have another reason for being here."

He enjoyed twisting my emotions. Dismissing the thought, I said, "Your turn."

"That big oaf, Ox, must wrestle bulls. He's stronger than Ari and he wrapped me so tight in the whip, I couldn't move a muscle."

I suppressed a smile. Janco liked to exaggerate. This would be an interesting story.

"After waiting all day for the authorities to arrive, they wouldn't hear our side of the story. Just carted us down to Robin's Nest and dumped us in jail." He shot me a cocky grin. "Local yokels. They did a sloppy search. My lock picks went undetected. But then I was in a quandary." His grin turned sardonic. "I wished Ari was with me. He's good with planning. But then again he would have lectured me on getting whupped by a man named Ox. I would have never lived it down."

He swigged his ale and gazed at the liquid as if considering his near miss. Janco's mood matched the waves in the sea, constantly up and down.

"A quandary?" I prompted.

"Oh, right." He perked up. "If I escaped, the authorities would assume I was guilty and send soldiers after me. No big deal, except what to do when I caught up with you and Devlen? I couldn't have him arrested if I had a posse on my tail. But I didn't want to waste the night waiting for the town's guards to confirm my story. I've seen what he's done to you. It about killed me to decide."

Judging by the time of Janco's arrival with a team of Sitian soldiers, I figured he must have waited. "You did the right thing."

He downed his ale and wiped his mouth on his sleeve. "There is one problem."

Oh no. I held my breath.

"In exchange for help to rescue you, I had to promise to escort you to the Citadel."

I relaxed with relief, but my smile froze. A very un-Janco expression hardened his face. He was serious.

"I don't go back on my word," he said.

Bad news. I needed to find Ulrick. My mind raced. "What *exactly* did you promise?"

"I promised to take you to the Council. They're frantic for your return."

"Frantic? You could tell this from a message?"

"Yes. It read frantic." He crossed his arms. "And considering the torture I thought you were enduring, I wasn't going to waste time negotiating with them."

"Thank you for your concern."

He huffed, not mollified.

"Did you promise them a certain time? Like as soon as you rescued me or just that you would escort me home?"

A slow smile lit his face. "The time was implied. As in the sooner the better. But no. I just said I would bring you to the Council."

"Then we need to make sure you come with me when I return *after* we find Ulrick."

Janco ordered another ale to celebrate. "I like the way you think."

Locating Ulrick proved to be difficult. The next morning, Janco and I talked to the Tulip Inn's owner. He remembered Ulrick and Devlen because he had worried they would cause trouble. He thought Ulrick had been in a drunken brawl by the way he leaned on his companion and by the fresh blood on his face.

"They rented a room and I didn't hear a peep out of them all night. In the morning, they left," the owner said.

"Together?" I asked.

"Yep."

Devlen had said they parted company. Another lie. No surprise there. "Do you know where they were going?"

"Nope."

"Have you seen the big Sandseed since then?"

"Nope."

I thanked him for his time. We left.

"Now what?" Janco asked.

"Check the other inns. See if he stayed anywhere else. If that doesn't work, we can ask around town and hope someone has seen him."

Janco groaned. "This is going to take all day."

We searched the entire morning and half the afternoon. All to no avail. No one remembered seeing Ulrick or Devlen.

Janco gestured to the row of buildings. "He could have locked him in any one of these houses, and paid someone to care for him. I hate to give up, but I think we're searching for a raindrop in a storm. I vote we put the screws to Mr. Warper's pressure points and squeeze the information from him."

"You would have to hit the perfect spot," I said.

"I'm a patient man."

Dubious, I looked at him.

"All right, all right. So I have the patience of a two-year-old. Happy now?"

"No, but before we try Devlen there is one more place I want to go."

"Where?"

"Scene of the crime. Perhaps Ulrick had returned to his sister's glass factory. Gressa's his only family in the area. The rest live in Booruby."

"But you said she ran off when Ulrick confronted her about making those fake diamonds." Janco rubbed the place where the lower half of his left ear used to be.

"I'm guessing she's long gone, but maybe someone has seen him. Do you have any better ideas?"

"Yeah. Torturing Devlen. That's the best idea I've heard all day."

Janco followed me to Gressa's glass factory. I imagined the storefront would be boarded up or a new business opened in its place. A colorful sparkle from the window display greeted us. Rows of elegant glassware lined the shelves. Perhaps a new glass artist had bought her studio.

I peered at the vases and bowls. The excellent craftsmanship and intricate designs were the unmistakable marks of Gressa's vast talent. She had returned.

We entered the store. More of her pieces decorated tables and filled shelves. The centerpiece of her collection spanned over four feet—a delicate yet top-heavy, fan-shaped vase crafted with translucent orange glass defied gravity. The saleswomen wore silk tunics. Their serene smiles and sales pitch were as smooth as the glass they sold.

A tall woman glided toward us. Her expression didn't change after her gaze swept our dusty travel clothes. Bonus points.

"Can I help you?" she asked.

"I need to talk to Gressa," I said. No sense wasting time on niceties.

A tiny wince creased her saleswoman mask, but in a blink of the eye, it was gone. "I'm sorry. The Artist is on important business right now. Perhaps you would like to leave a message?"

"Do you know when she'll be back?"

"No. She is extremely busy. If you leave her a message, she might arrange a time for you to talk."

"Might." Janco huffed. "Which translates to not in a million years."

The woman strained to keep her polite demeanor.

"This is regarding her brother, Ulrick. It's very important," I said.

"Brother?" The woman's confusion appeared genuine. "She never mentioned a brother."

"Is she here? Or do we need to search the place?" Janco's threat was not idle.

The heart of the factory—the kilns and equipment needed to melt and work with molten glass—resided behind the storefront along with Gressa's office.

Flustered, the woman gaped at Janco.

He turned to me. "We should search anyway. Ulrick could be hiding in the back."

I led him to the door marked Employees Only. Alerted by the saleswoman's attempts to stop us, the rest of the sales staff turned their attention our way. Unconcerned, Janco barged into the factory, trailing a line of protesting women.

"Let me know if you see anyone," Janco said.

We wove through the heat surrounding Gressa's four kilns, annealing ovens and various benches. The workers glanced at the parade, but kept spinning their rods to keep the molten glass from sagging toward the ground. My hands itched to help. It had been a long time since I'd worked with glass, and the need ached inside me.

The familiar hum of the kilns vibrated in my ears. Not all of the factory employees were in the middle of a project. A large man grabbed a punty iron. The five-foot-long metal rod made a formidable weapon. He ordered us to leave the factory.

Janco continued his search, ignoring the man. Using his picks, Janco popped the lock to Gressa's mixing room and entered. I stayed by the door with my hands wrapped around the handles of my sais, keeping the man in sight.

Janco returned and headed toward Gressa's glass-walled office. After another order to stop failed to work, the man swung his rod. I yanked my sais from my cloak and deflected his strike. The clang of metal pierced the air. I switched my sais to a defensive position. With the shafts along my forearms and the knobs up, I could attack or defend, depending on the circumstances.

Two things happened. One good and one bad.

The noise created instant silence, but then the sales staff moved away to give their fellow worker more room to maneuver. A few disappeared.

Janco nodded at me. "Keep him busy."

Great. My opponent pulled back to bash me on the head. Perhaps barging in here hadn't been the best idea. I flipped my sais out and crossed them into an X-shape, blocking the head shot. The force of his blow vibrated down my arms.

He jerked the rod back, but I followed, closing the distance between us. I stepped to within a foot of him and jabbed him hard in the solar plexus with the sais's knobs. He stumbled, gasping for breath.

I caught a glimpse of another armed attacker and turned in time to stop a hit to my stomach.

Janco's voice cut through the din. "No sign of Gressa or Ulrick. Now what?"

The factory workers abandoned their tasks and armed themselves with rods, jacks and battledores.

"Time to leave," I shouted, but Janco was already engaged in a fight with two men. "Don't hurt anyone." I ducked a wild swing. The workers were strong, but unskilled at fighting. They also outnumbered us four to one.

Janco easily countered his opponents. He had almost cleared an escape path for us. Hope of a quick exit died when the town's guards burst through the door.

4

CONFUSION REIGNED. Between the town's guards and the factory workers, we were overwhelmed. Janco and I admitted defeat and surrendered our weapons. Explanations about why we had forced our way into Gressa's glass factory fell on deaf ears. It was obvious we didn't belong there. As we were led to the guards' headquarters, I hoped we would get a chance to tell our side of the story.

However, once we arrived at the station, we were stripped of our possessions, dumped into adjoining cells and left. The metallic clang of the lock echoed in my ears with a sickening familiarity. I counted the number of times I had been imprisoned and had to laugh.

"What's so funny?" Janco asked.

Three of the cell's walls were stone, but iron bars lined the door and front wall, allowing me to talk with Janco. "Just thinking about how this time is a legitimate arrest versus some of my other incarcerations."

"Ah, yes. I'm sure we'll be charged with trespassing, breaking and entering and attempted armed robbery. They'll probably add in resisting arrest and disorderly conduct for good measure."

"Sounds like you've had experience."

"Knowledge learned from my misspent youth. You gotta love the disorderly-conduct charge. It covers a wide range of behaviors, and, to my mother's horror, I was determined to test the boundaries." Humor laced his voice. "Speaking of bad behavior, I think I'll wait until dark to pick the locks."

"But they searched you and confiscated your picks."

He laughed. "Let me tell you a story about a beautiful seamstress in Ixia. Dilana has a fine hand with needle and thread and a fine smile, too—all warm and caring. Although she found my request to be a bit…odd, she acquiesced. With her clever stitchery, she has sewn lock picks into all my clothing. They're just a ripped seam away."

"I'm glad you're using your knowledge for good."

"My mother's ecstatic, and my new position earns enough money to pay for her hair dye." He tsked. "Poor woman went gray at a very young age."

Poor woman indeed.

"We should be here overnight," Janco said. "The guards know who you are and are probably contacting the magicians at the Citadel as we speak. If they decide not to press charges, we'll probably be escorted there. I don't think the Council will trust me again to bring you home."

"Who would press charges?" I asked.

"Gressa owns the factory, so it would be up to her." He paused. "I thought you said she was a fugitive."

"She was. Something must have happened." I considered. Gressa had been helping Councilor Moon's sister by crafting realistic yet fake diamonds from glass. The sister had been selling these fakes to finance her efforts to overthrow the Councilor.

The Sitian Council would honor a new Moon Councilor if she had gained her position through legitimate channels. The Moon Clan had a matriarchal government. The Councilor's oldest daughter inherited the position, but there had been times in the past when the Moon Clan's citizens had believed another sister was a better candidate for the job. They would stage a coup, and install their chosen with little to no bloodshed. The Council viewed this as the will of the people and accepted the new Councilor.

However, if the efforts to usurp the present Councilor originated from the dissatisfied sister, and if she used illegal means to purchase weapons and bribe the townspeople, then the Council wouldn't accept her and they would help the ousted woman regain her rightful position.

Master Magician Irys Jewelrose and Yelena had been in Fulgor to keep an eye on developments, to learn who led the unrest and to protect the Councilor. She had been convinced she was targeted for assassination, an illegal act according to the Sitian Council.

Irys's signature on my order to return to the Citadel meant she was no longer here. The crisis must have been averted. Otherwise, if the sister had gained power, the Council would have interfered. However, neither option felt right to me.

"Do you feel the…unease in the townspeople?" I asked Janco. "Or is it just my imagination?"

"It's not your imagination. The people around here are as tight as bowstrings. I could probably play a tune if I brushed up against enough of them."

"What about your interaction with the guards?"

"Wary and watchful. But that's typical behavior. I'm surprised by how civil they've been to me, considering I'm Ixian."

"It's because we don't automatically assume you're a vile magician intent on harm like you Ixians do when meeting a Sitian."

Janco harrumphed. "I don't assume *that.*"

"No?" Doubt colored my voice.

"I assume you're a vile magician."

"There's no difference."

"Yes, there is. I don't *assume* your intentions are harmful. I *know* no matter what your intentions are, magic causes harm to someone somewhere at some time."

"Oh, that's right. *You're* the expert on Sitians. *You* should have been the one appointed liaison between Ixia and Sitia instead of Yelena. Unless it's because the Commander and the Council have at least a crumb of intelligence between them."

"Nasty, Opal. I must have hit a nerve. Perhaps it was my 'magic causes harm' remark. You have plenty of experience with that."

"Shut up."

"As you wish."

I brooded in silence. Dozens of examples of positive results from using magic popped into my mind. Stormdancers tamed killer storms, healers saved lives, Story Weavers helped people and my glass messengers sped up communications between the clans. All good.

My thoughts drifted and without a window in my cell, I lost track of the time. I slept on the single piece of furniture in the room—a hard metal ledge. The jangle of keys woke me. A door slammed and two guards appeared in front of my cell.

"Come on," the guard on the left ordered. He unlocked my door.

"What's going on?" I asked.

"You're wanted for questioning." He swung the bars wide.

His word choice failed to hearten me. "By whom?"

"Councilor Moon's First Adviser. Turn around."

I hesitated and his partner stepped inside. The larger man held a pair of manacles.

Holding my hands up, I said, "They're not necessary. I'll cooperate."

"Good to know," the man with the cuffs said. "Turn around."

He loomed over me and I wondered if towns sought

bullies to hire as guards on purpose or were they naturally drawn to the job. Or perhaps the mean disposition was a side effect of the position. If I had to deal with guarding criminals all day, I would probably be surly, too.

"It's really not—hey!"

He spun me around and pushed me against the wall. Before I could draw another breath, my wrists were shackled together behind my back.

"Sorry. Orders." He pulled me toward the door.

He didn't sound sorry. I tripped over the threshold and the other man steadied me before I fell into the corridor. I glanced at Janco's cell. He stood near the door.

"What about my companion?" I asked.

"The Ixian..." The guard's mouth twisted as if he had a piece of gristle stuck between his teeth. "Stays here."

"But I'll be bored and lonely without her," Janco said.

"Not my problem. I have my—"

"Orders." Janco rolled his eyes. "Now I know where all the truly brainless Sitians can be found. Right here with all the wimpy Sitians."

The bully stepped toward his cell.

"Nic, stop," the guard warned. "He's trying to bait you."

"Listen to your friend, Nicky." Janco smirked. "He's going to save you from major embarrassment. You'll never live down getting beaten by an Ixian." He made shooing motions with his hand. "Now run along like a good little puppy dog."

I bit my lip to keep from smiling as I remembered a lesson learned from Yelena's brother Leif. Never underestimate the power of the pest.

Nic's body tightened, and a slight tremor traveled through his muscles as if he fought the desire to strike out. He turned his back on Janco and strode down the corridor. An impressive display of restraint.

Disappointment creased Janco's face.

Before the other guard could move, I said, "If you get too bored, think of a better ending to your quartz story. The rock-glowing-in-the-moonlight part didn't make any sense. And having a meeting at midnight is such a cliché."

"But that's my favorite part," Janco whined.

"Come on." The guard wrapped his thick hand around my upper arm and led me down the corridor.

I glanced back at Janco and met his gaze. He nodded, signaling he understood my hint. If I didn't return tonight, he would escape and meet me at Quartz and Moonlight's stable around midnight. I smiled at the irony.

Of course, my plan included my own escape—a more doubtful prospect. The next time Janco and I had a few minutes together, I would ask him to show me how to pick a lock. It was a skill I hadn't needed before my apprentice year at the Magician's Keep, but, by the way trouble kept finding me these past two seasons, my lack of knowledge could be fatal.

The Masters should add lock picking to the Keep's curriculum, but then again it could backfire on them. The Keep's cells were warded against any magical escape, but I didn't know how they protected against mundane methods. Guess I would know the answer in time. I shuddered, thinking about how upset the Council would be when I finally returned.

My escort believed I was cold, and he wrapped my cloak around my shoulders. Nic joined us as we exited the station and walked across the street to the Councilor's Hall. The white dome of the expansive building could be seen from most places in the city. Fulgor was the capital of the Moon Clan's lands, and housed all the government and military buildings for the Clan. Constructed from white marble streaked with green veins, the walls reflected the early-morning sunlight.

Wedged between the two guards, I could only glance at the quiet streets before we entered the Hall. There my companions handed me over to the Hall's guards.

The lobby's black-and-white tiles reminded me of a huge chessboard. I marveled at the glass chandelier hanging down from the dome high above the lobby.

Even though I had seen it before, the chandelier's delicate ice-blue panels and snowflake pattern still awed me. And Gressa had designed and crafted the piece when she was only fifteen. Unfortunately, her ego matched her talent.

My new attendants led me up the grand staircase to the first floor and down a long hallway that ended in ornate double doors guarded by two soldiers. They opened the door without uttering a word and ushered us into a huge reception room. Padded leather armchairs lined the walls, books rested on dark mahogany tables and a vast ebony desk filled the center and almost blocked the door on the far wall. My boots sunk into the plush carpet and I worried about leaving dirt on the pale pink floral design.

The desk dwarfed the blond woman sitting behind it. She wrinkled her nose in disdain, but waved us toward the far door, saying, "She's expecting you."

I turned to my guard. "I thought you said I was being questioned by the First Adviser."

"This is the FA's office," he said. "All our officials have offices befitting their stations."

I suppressed a whistle. If this was the FA's, what did Councilor Moon's look like?

The interior office was as ornate as the reception area and twice as big. In the far right corner loomed another expansive desk and another woman. She faced the large windows with her back to us. Sunlight highlighted her straight black hair and a feeling of familiarity tugged deep within me.

Stained-glass sun catchers refracted the sunlight, causing bright pinpricks of color to dot the walls and ceiling. Distinct glass vases decorated her neat desk.

"Gressa," I said.

Ulrick's sister turned around. Her resemblance to Ulrick was uncanny. Her long, graceful limbs, strong jaw, prominent cheekbones and eyes the color of grass on a sunny day matched his. Except this time, instead of being drawn to her because of the similarity, I was wary. Since Devlen switched bodies, seeing even a likeness of Ulrick's face triggered a flinch.

She studied me with a cold, unwelcoming expression for a moment, then gestured toward a chair. "Sit down."

I perched on the edge of an overstuffed maroon chair. She dismissed the guards to wait in the outer office without ordering them to unlock the manacles binding my wrists. At least she could have told them to remove my cloak. I sweated in the warm room.

Gressa picked up a glass letter opener and tapped it on her desk. "Why did you break into my factory?"

"I needed to talk to you."

"You could have sent me a message."

"I thought you might be in hiding."

"Really?" Her thin arched eyebrows lifted in surprise. "Why?"

"Because of making the fake diamonds and helping the Councilor's sister."

"Oh, that." She waved her hand in the air as if her past was as insignificant as the dust motes floating in the sunlight. "Obviously, it worked out. I offered my services and my knowledge of Akako's plans to Councilor Moon. After Akako was arrested, the Councilor offered me a position on her staff."

"Akako?"

Gressa sighed with dramatics. "The Councilor's sister."

That explained why Yelena and Irys left Fulgor, but didn't address the tension and worry emanating from the town's citizens. Perhaps it was due to Gressa being the First Adviser—the second most powerful position in the Clan. No doubt she would use her status for her own advantage.

She played with the letter opener. The clear glass handle tapered to a thin, flat blade. The edge had been sharpened with a grinding wheel. "What was so important you wouldn't take no as an answer, scaring my workers?"

"It's about Ulrick."

I didn't think it was possible, but her demeanor turned colder. "Were you planning to explain why you had him arrested?"

"Yes, and to explain about…" How best to state the situation? I considered my words with care. "Ulrick has been tricked—"

"I know."

"You do?"

"Of course. He's been tricked into falling in love with you. And now you're claiming he's really someone else. Oh, please." She jabbed the letter opener into the air. "You have no proof."

I closed my mouth. I knew this would be difficult, but I hadn't expected such hostility. "Have you talked to the Council?"

"Yes. They said you've disobeyed direct orders, and I should send you to the Citadel in chains if I have to."

"Have you communicated with Master Cowan?"

She leaned forward. "At length. Even she is doubtful."

Icy tendrils wrapped around my heart. Goose bumps prickled my sweaty skin. "But Janco and Kade can vouch for me."

"An Ixian and a missing Stormdancer?" She laughed. "I thought you were smarter than that."

"Kade's not missing. He stayed behind to calm the blizzards for the Ixians."

"Are you talking about the same Ixians whose Commander murders magicians, and has declared using magic within his territory illegal and punishable by death? Do you know how ridiculous your story sounds? Are you delusional?"

I drew in a breath. "Talk to Ulrick. Ask him to blow you a vase. Devlen may have read Ulrick's memories, but he can't duplicate the skill learned from years of working with molten glass. You grew up with him. Spend an hour with him and you'll know he's not your brother."

"There you go, Opal. *Now* you're thinking rationally. Except for one thing."

By the wicked delight flaming in her eyes, I knew this wouldn't go my way.

"I already had a long conversation with my brother. Your claims are a complete fabrication."

I hated it when I was right.

* * *

My guards escorted me to a "guest" room in the Councilor's Hall. With no windows, a small bed and one chair, the room felt tighter than my cell. The door closed behind me with a thump and the lock clicked shut, casting me into darkness. At least the guards had removed my manacles. I rubbed my sore wrists, then felt for the bed. My eyes adjusted as I lay there. Weak candlelight flickered through the cracks around the door.

Gressa had informed me Councilor Moon wanted to talk to me before they escorted me home. She had just returned from the Citadel. Again I berated myself for not taking advantage of my time with Janco and learning how to pick a lock. He would be free in no time. I wondered how long he would wait for me at the stable. Even though escaping would be horrible in my I'm-really-a-good-person defense, my determination to find Ulrick still burned strong.

Janco and I had hit a dead end in our search for Ulrick in Fulgor. If an opportunity to escape happened and I was successful, I would head to Ognap. Devlen had provided the dubious information, but it was better than doing nothing. Every day that passed meant another day the stain of blood magic would spread.

Time dripped. Each second hung as if it were on the end of an icicle, fattening until it grew too big to hold on. Then *splat*—another second gone. A preview of my future once I returned to the Citadel.

When two guards arrived to guide me to the Councilor's office, I didn't complain about the manacles.

As expected, her office suite made Gressa's seem ordinary in comparison. Instead of one assistant in the reception room, three women and two men bustled about. Soldiers stood at attention on each side of the double doors. They nodded to my companions. We entered the Councilor's office.

The ceiling was two stories above my head. Thin stained-glass windows spanned the walls from top to bottom on my left and right. The room was long and narrow. We passed an oval conference table and a sitting area with couches and armchairs. Straight ahead a huge U-shaped desk had been pushed against a picture window with the opening toward me. The Councilor seemed to prefer to face the view while working.

"Councilor Tama," my guard said.

The woman raised a hand, signaling us to wait. After a moment, she stood and approached us. With the late-afternoon sun behind her, her long blond hair appeared almost white.

Her smile died when she glanced at me. "Lieutenant, please release her." The Councilor's words were polite, but her tone said now. When the manacles came off, she said, "Leave us."

"She could be a danger to you," the lieutenant said.

Tama studied me. I suppressed the urge to squirm. She wore a white silk V-neck tunic embroidered with black half-moon shapes over a long skirt made from the same material. Delicate black leather sandals with silver crescents adorned her feet. My plain soiled clothes, bedraggled hair and muddy boots seemed an insult in comparison.

"Go wait by the door." She shooed them away. "Come. Sit." Tama pointed to a chair behind one of the long wooden tables of her desk.

I smoothed my hair, tucking the wild strands behind my ears before I complied.

"You don't look like a troublemaker," Tama said. She perched on the edge of the table. Her light blue eyes sparked with amusement.

I marveled at her pale skin. Her thin lips and tiny upturned nose resembled the Ixian people who lived near the northern ice sheet and not the darker skin tones of Sitia. She was also younger than I expected. I guessed her age to be around thirty.

"I'm not here to cause trouble, Councilor Moon," I said in my most sincere voice. "I'm here because—"

"I know why you came to Fulgor. And I know you've accused Gressa's brother of being a Daviian Warper in disguise. I read the order for your return before I signed it."

I had forgotten about the message from the Council.

She watched my expression. "Do you even realize the panic you caused in the Council chambers by not obeying the order?"

"I..." This time I squirmed.

"Master Magician Zitora Cowan defended you when

the news of your unusual kidnapping reached the Council. We weren't happy about the rumors coming from Ixia, but she was able to convince us of your integrity up until you failed to appear. Did you even think about Zitora before you decided to dash off to Fulgor?"

"I..." I slumped in my seat.

"I didn't think so."

Tama Moon's gaze rested on me and visions of being scolded by my mother rose. I refrained from hanging my head.

She crossed her arms. "Your claim about Ulrick was hard to believe before, but now it is impossible."

"Why? The Warpers used blood magic in the past, they—"

"Gressa has vouched for him. She *is* his sister."

"And she has admitted to helping *your* sister try to oust you. She can't be trusted." A subtle tightening of her posture and the increase of the tension in her arms warned me I had said the wrong thing.

"I trust her." A slight tremor of anger touched her voice.

I chose my next words with the utmost care. "I realize it is my word against theirs. I'm not lying, Councilor Moon. Please send a message to Yelena Zaltana and ask her to come back to Fulgor. She will be able to confirm my claims."

"The Soulfinder is in Ixia right now, dealing with the mess you left behind."

The protest died in my throat. It wouldn't help my case.

The Councilor settled in her chair. Piles of paper rested on the desk between us. She leaned forward, placing her elbows on the edge. "Opal, you're lucky I'm in Fulgor to attend to town business. I can give you a bit of advice. When you return to the Citadel, the Council will be hostile, but you have quite a bit of leverage."

"Leverage?"

Tama nodded as if expecting my confusion. "Gressa said you had no clue. Think for a moment. What invaluable service do you and *only* you provide?"

So focused on finding Ulrick, I needed more than a moment to understand. "My glass messengers."

"Correct. Do you realize how vital they've become to Sitia? To the Council? Almost instant communication with people far away. What used to take days now takes minutes. And only *you* can trap the magic inside them."

Unfortunately, I couldn't use them. Magicians with strong mental communication skills could "talk" to another magician through my messengers despite the distance as long as each held one in their hands. With use, the magic was depleted and a new one was needed.

The Councilor huffed. "*That's* your leverage. If the Sitian Council and Master Magicians decide to lock you away in the Keep's cells, then who is going to make more of those messengers?"

"We've been searching for another student."

"Pah!" She flung her hand out. "No one right now is able to duplicate your talent. And they've become so crucial to the Council and Sitia, the Councilors would agree to anything you ask to keep them in production."

"Oh! You mean, I could ask to be released or else I won't make more."

"Exactly! Now think about what you could do on a grander scale."

"Why?"

She sighed. "Opal, what are your plans once you graduate from the Keep?"

Visit my family and Kade, but I didn't think she referred to the short term. "I haven't really thought about it yet."

She gawked at me as if I were an idiot. I rushed to add, "It's been a busy two seasons."

Pressing her fingertips into her temples, she closed her eyes for a few seconds. "You're sweet, Opal. Even with me encouraging you, you still can't even contemplate selfish behavior." Her posture relaxed and she leaned back in her chair. "I'm going to give you a hypothetical situation. And I'm telling you this, not as Councilor Moon, but as Tama Moon, the businesswoman.

"Let's say I'm you in your current predicament. I would tell the Council and the Master Magicians to back off if they want more glass messengers. Then I would build a factory right here in Fulgor because I hear Moon Clan's Councilor is partial to free enterprise. And I would sell *my* messengers to the magicians."

"But..." I clamped down on reminding her about the Council's fears.

"It wouldn't be easy. The Master Magicians would worry about you, and send someone to bring you back to the Citadel where they could keep an eye on you. Frankly, I'm surprised the Masters even let you out at all. If you're killed…" She paused.

"It won't work. They won't just send 'someone,' they'll send a Master Magician and a whole platoon of soldiers. Besides, where would I get the money to build a factory?"

Her eyebrows rose a fraction and her lips curved into a small, knowing smile.

"Who told you?" I asked.

"Who do you think?"

"Devlen."

"Ulrick," she corrected. "He told his sister all about your new siphoning skills. The ones you didn't tell Master Cowan about. The ones that will protect you against an attack from a master-level magician. The ones that transform magic into diamonds. You can build a whole city with the diamonds hidden in your saddle-bags."

I had wanted to tell Zitora in person. The Council already knew I could transform magic into objects like spiders and bees, but I'd waited to tell them the whole story. Better to hear the news from me and see my honesty, my willingness to cooperate—I stifled a wild laugh. Guess I ruined that image by disobeying their orders.

Councilor Moon waited for me to process her

comments. The whole conversation with her felt unreal. She acted as if she wasn't a member of the Council.

"Why are you telling me all this? Aren't you afraid?"

"I'm not afraid of you. I have no magic for you to take, what can you do?"

I pulled a glass bee from the pocket of my cloak. Holding it between my finger and thumb, I showed it to her. "I could kill you before your guards could even react."

"All right. Go ahead." She laughed at my expression. "I know you won't do it unless your life is in danger, or the life of someone you love. You're a good person. I'm not scared of you, but I know the Council will lock you away, too terrified to see you as an asset. And I'm afraid you would let them!"

She drew a deep breath. "My opinions are in the minority. That's why I'm trying to get you to think about your future. Really think about it. You have such potential, and *Gressa* is willing to support you. I would need to remain uninvolved to keep the other Councilors happy. And there is no reason they need to be told about your *new* skills—only a few people know and we can keep quiet. Show up at the Citadel, tell the Council what you intend to do and come back."

Tama's argument had merit. Kade had also suggested I keep the information to myself. The notion tempted me, but I couldn't lie to the Council. If I trusted them and the Master Magicians to govern Sitia in a way that kept us all safe, then I would trust them to make the right decision regarding my own role in Sitia's future.

Councilor Moon should have the same trust in the government, especially since she was a major part of it. Perhaps her selfish attitude had been the reason her sister, Akako, had wanted to overthrow her.

I opened my mouth.

"Don't say anything right now," she said. "You're scheduled to leave for the Citadel tomorrow morning. You'll have four travel days. Promise me you'll think about it?"

I agreed, but as I was escorted back to the tiny "guest" room, I knew my decision wouldn't change. After all, I've had, since I left Kade in the north, almost twenty-six days to contemplate all the pros and cons. Like Tama said, I was a good person. I would do the right thing.

But it didn't mean I would do it *now.* Once I reached the Citadel, the chances of helping Ulrick would disappear. The guards hadn't manacled my wrists. My cloak remained wrapped around my shoulders. I clutched a glass spider in each fist, waiting for the perfect opportunity to surprise my guards and run away.

Unfortunately, people filled the hallways, rushing to finish their last tasks before going home. Shoved and locked back into the room, I rested on the bed. Later tonight, when the Councilor's Hall was empty, I would see if my spiders knew how to pick a lock. If not, there were other ways to trick the guards into opening my door.

I fell asleep plotting my escape.

* * *

A metallic snap invaded my dreams. Faint torchlight surrounded the figure of a man in the doorway. I sat up and prepared to crush the spiders in my palms.

"Come on," Devlen said with an urgent whisper.

I wilted. My spiders wouldn't work on him.

"You are not safe here." He hissed.

"Safer than with you," I said.

He muttered an oath, grabbed my arm and yanked me to my feet. His hand slid to my wrist as his fingertips found the pressure points. I braced as the memory of incredible pain replayed in my mind. Not again.

"Hell." Devlen released me. "Follow me or go on your own. Just do *not* stay here." He turned, peeked out into the hallway and strode away.

5

Not remaining locked in the "guest" room had been my plan all along. I'd been in the Councilor's Hall before, but I doubted I could waltz out the front door without raising any alarms. Instead, I followed Devlen.

The guard stationed at my door lay in a heap on the floor. I touched his neck. A strong pulse throbbed. Thank fate.

Stepping over him, I hurried down the hallway as fast as I could without making too much noise. Devlen disappeared around a corner. Only one torch lit the corridor. Its weak light struggled against the darkness.

When I reached the turn, I almost ran into him. He placed a finger to his lips and gestured for me to wait. A glow at the end of the hall brightened, illuminating an intersection. Faint voices echoed on the smooth marble walls. Two people strode into sight. One held a blazing torch. They conversed in tight whispers, arguing at low volume.

I steeled myself as they turned down our hallway.

Devlen grabbed my hand and pulled me back around the corner. We pressed against the wall. If they came our way, we would be seen. If they kept straight, we should be fine.

Their shadows arrived before they did, and snatches of the two men's conversation reached me.

"...doesn't matter. She's the Councilor..."

"...acting...we can't trust..."

We froze as they crossed the intersection, but the intensity of their argument claimed all their attention.

I relaxed until I realized Devlen hadn't released my hand. Before I could pull away, he drew me forward. Our connection made ghosting through the Hall easier. Whenever Devlen paused to listen or to wait for a late-night worker to clear an area, he signaled me by squeezing my hand.

We exited the building through the kitchen door, which led us to an empty alley. Our footsteps ricocheted in the silence, and I fought the urge to tiptoe. Devlen strode without stopping. He slowed after we traveled a few blocks from the Councilor's Hall, but kept my hand in his firm grip.

When I tried to yank it away, he said, "At this time of night, it would be better if we are seen holding hands, adding to the illusion we are lovers going for a moonlit stroll."

I snorted. "Who would see us? And why would they care?"

"The Moon Clan soldiers are out in force tonight. A prisoner has escaped from jail earlier this evening."

Janco. He probably had led the guards on a merry chase through the city just to pass the time. Or perhaps Devlen referred to himself? No. From what Tama said, no one believed me about the switched souls.

"When were you released?" I asked.

"Yesterday morning. In fact, you have spent more time in a Fulgor cell than I."

"Wonderful," I snapped.

We reached a main street. A few citizens hustled over the cobblestones. They kept their gazes down and shoulders hunched as if walking into a stiff wind. But the cooling air remained calm and the half moon's sharp edge gleamed in the clear night sky.

Guards patrolled the streets. We passed a few who squinted at us. Each time, Devlen would smile at me, pretending to be in the midst of a pleasant conversation.

"Do not stare, Opal. Your attention should be focused on me. We are having a lovely chat."

"Okay. Now you can tell me why I needed to leave the Councilor's Hall."

"My sister, Gre—"

"Gressa is *not* your sister." The words growled from my throat.

He held up his free hand. "No sense arguing. This is important. The Councilor told Gressa you had no intention of using your leverage with the Council."

"I promised I would think about it."

"I am sure you would. But we all know you will comply with the Council's decision."

"I disobeyed their order," I retorted. He had called me an accommodating doormat before. Although I had proven him wrong and freed myself and Kade, my current situation didn't support my argument. I avoided contemplating my current predicament. It wouldn't be good for my mental stability.

"I was quite proud of your defiance. But it is obvious that you will not turn rogue and stay in Fulgor. Gressa knows this, as well, and she is intent on keeping you here."

"It wouldn't work. She can't force me to make the glass messengers."

I wanted to ignore Devlen's expression. His raised eyebrow implied she damn well could. *He* would only need a few hours.

"How would she explain about my failure to return to the Citadel and the fact she has my glass animals?"

"For your disappearance, she will report you have escaped. As for the messengers, she could claim her brother has learned how to craft them, and that is why you are so intent on discrediting him...me." He shot me a sly smile.

"That's ridiculous." However, knowing Gressa, I'd bet she could pull it off. And Devlen hadn't released my hand. I scanned the street. Was he leading me to a place Gressa had prepared for my...stay? A vision of me chained to a kiln flashed through my mind. What happened to all those guards on the street?

Brilliant plan, yell for help from soldiers who work

for the Councilor and her top aide. I almost groaned aloud. The unconscious guard next to my room would be used as proof of my escape. This quiet late-night stroll wouldn't attract notice. I'd aided in my own kidnapping. *Idiot* wasn't a strong enough word for me.

Devlen chuckled. "Just figuring it out?"

"Yep."

"It would have been a neat trick."

Would have been? Confused, I remembered he had grabbed my wrist, planning to use force, but dropped my arm. Part of the act?

"Opal, look." He pointed to the end of the street. Quartz and Moonlight's stable was a block away. "Your Ixian is waiting inside." Devlen glanced at the sky. "Midnight, or close enough. Did you choose the time for dramatic reasons?"

"I improvised. How did you overhear our conversation in the jail?"

"Once the annoying Ixian escaped, the guards reported everything to the Councilor's Aide, with whom I happened to be at the time. I figured out your clues, but Gressa did not."

"Why are you helping me? You obviously intend to keep masquerading as Ulrick. With me...out of the way, it'll be easier for you."

He stopped and turned toward me. "Gressa is cunning and smart. She knows what happened to her brother, and has ensured my cooperation by threatening to expose and arrest me. Since I do not wish to be incarcerated, I *will* follow her orders." Releasing my hand, he stepped back. "If you are gone, then I will not be ordered to force you to make messengers for her. I do not want to hurt you ever again."

"You have to come with us," I said. "Once we find Ulrick, we'll need you."

"If Ulrick wants to switch back to his body, bring him here. I am working for Cressa. She has given me a staff position."

I muffled an hysterical cackle. Devlen a government employee while I remained a fugitive? At this point, I couldn't imagine how my life could get any more distorted and unreal. "Why would you stay here? Why not run away before she can arrest you?"

His gaze searched the street and he tilted his head back as if scenting the wind. "Something is...odd. I am worried you might be in more danger. If I stay here, I am in a better position to help you."

"You'll risk getting captured for a vague feeling?"

He shrugged. "I need something to do while you search for Ulrick."

"You're that confident he won't want to switch back?"

"Yes. And when you finally realize the truth, make sure you stop by Fulgor to apologize to me."

"Apologize to *you!*" I almost screamed the words.

"I already apologized to you. Travel safe, Opal. I am missing you already." Devlen spun on his heel and strode away from the stable. When he reached the end of the street, he glanced back, flashed me a smile and disappeared around a corner.

I hurried toward the stable as my thoughts whirled. Devlen was an evil Daviian Warper, who'd tortured, kidnapped and tricked me. Even though he could no longer access the power source, he remained dangerous. His limited knowledge of the Kirakawa ritual could be taught to another. Or he could try to reclaim his powers. I didn't know enough about my own new abilities to determine if anyone's blood would return his magic or if it had to be mine.

Ever since I drained him of power, he had been…different. No longer driven by his addiction to blood magic, he acted content. *Acted* being the key word. With his ability to sweet-talk his way out of any situation, and with his ease in living in Ulrick's skin, I would be a fool to trust him. Too bad being a fool was my best skill.

When I reached the stable, Janco had already saddled the horses. Quartz nickered and pushed her muzzle into my chest. I scratched her behind the ears.

Janco tied a couple of feed bags onto Moonlight's saddle. "How ja escape? I was all set to launch a rescue. A damsel-in-distress story is worth at least a couple of free ales at the pub."

"Sorry to disappoint you." Devlen could tell that tale, though I didn't think he would. If Gressa discovered he had helped me, he would be in serious trouble. An anonymous message to Gressa would complicate his new life. I grinned.

"Do you have juicy details?" Janco asked. "Do tell!"

"Later. Aren't you worried about riding out of here? They're searching for you."

Janco mounted Moonlight with one graceful movement. Impish delight lit his eyes. "They have me cornered on the north side of town. They believe I'm heading toward Ixia. We have another hour or so before the game is up."

"How did you manage that?"

"Oh, a little silver here, a little misdirection there. All fun."

After checking my saddlebags, I swung up on Quartz. Her ears perked up and the left one swiveled back to hear me.

"Where to?" Janco asked.

"East toward Ognap."

We directed the horses, walking through the deserted streets. Even without horseshoes, the thud of their hooves on the stones sounded loud.

Janco leaned forward and stroked Moonlight's black neck. "Quieter if you can," he whispered. Both horses slowed. "Thanks."

Surprised, I shot him a questioning look.

"Sandseed horses are very intelligent, and he's one beautiful, bright boy."

"And he allowed you to saddle him!" I said in an excited whisper. "How?"

He shrugged. "I introduced myself, and told him what was going on. Guess meeting the greatest swordsman in Ixia awed him into submission."

"A swordsman who can't handle a horsewhip. He probably felt sorry for you."

He tsked. "Low blow." Then smiled. "I've taught you well."

We spent the rest of the night in silence. The tight row houses of Fulgor soon transformed into clusters of buildings. I steered Quartz onto the main east-west road. When we reached farmland and marble quarries interspersed with forest, we stopped to rest.

As we set up a makeshift camp in the woods and hidden from the path, I explained my escape.

"Devlen? Why?" Janco asked.

"He said he didn't want to hurt me again."

"Ha! He's been playing the reformed man since we blasted him up on the ice. Don't believe him, Opal. I've seen criminals use it to be released, but most of them are back to their old tricks in no time."

"What about you? You're reformed."

"Not me. I just switched sides. I'm doing the same stuff—lock picking, sneaking around, tricking and spying. Except now I'm doing it for Valek and the Commander. And it has more…meaning. When I was a kid, it was just a challenge. I didn't steal, but I couldn't resist a locked door. And I wanted to get caught—just to see if I could escape the holding cells. Drove everyone nuts." He smiled at the memory. "I even broke *into* the jail, past five guards with none the wiser." But then his humor evaporated and he rubbed the scar spanning from his right temple to his ear. "Ended badly. That's how I have firsthand knowledge that you *don't* ever believe the reformed-man act."

He bustled about our small camp lost in his own thoughts. I yawned and shivered in the predawn air. The horses munched on their grain. I wondered if I could train Quartz to sound an alarm like Leif had trained Rusalka, who was also a Sandseed horse.

"Should we take turns guarding?" I asked.

"No." Janco checked on Moonlight, running his hand along the sleek coat. "Moonlight will let us know if someone comes too close. Right, boy?"

The horse nickered as if in agreement.

"That's seems too easy," I said.

"Not everything in life has to be hard. Horses are prey animals. If they notice anything strange, they'll alert the herd."

"And we're the herd."

"Yep. Their sense of smell and hearing are far superior to ours. So you can sleep in peace. No worries."

But what about the old worries?

"Who names a town Ognap?" Janco asked.

"It was probably named for a famous Cloud Mist Clan member." I tried not to sigh.

After sleeping most of the morning, we had saddled the horses and headed east toward the Emerald Mountains. Ognap was nestled in the foothills.

"Ixia is far simpler," he said. "Military Districts and

Grid Sectors for location names. No weird town names. No bizarre clothing or lack of clothing. We have uniforms, so when you meet someone new, you know *exactly* who they are and what they do. No guessing if they're going to zap you with their magic."

Janco's homesickness drove me crazy. He had been waxing nostalgic over Ixia the past two hours. The trip to Ognap would take another four days, and I didn't know if I could stand his mooning that long. If we cut through the Avibian Plains, we could shorten the trip. Being Sandseed horses, Moonlight and Quartz could use their special gust-of-wind gaits, which only worked in the plains, but the Sandseed Clan's protective magic would convince Janco we were lost and being watched.

I remembered the panic I had felt when I first entered the plains. My sense of direction failed and I knew warriors waited to ambush me. Leif introduced me to the protective magic. Since the Zaltanas were the Sandseed's distant cousins, Leif and his sister, Yelena, were welcome in the Avibian Plains.

If the protection recognized me, I would be fine, but Janco wouldn't. No sense risking it for a few days of peace.

"...Clan. Opal, are you listening to me?"

"Sorry. Could you repeat it?"

He slumped his shoulders in an exaggerated gesture of aggravation. "What's the Cloud Mist Clan like?"

"They have a few small towns along the foothills of the mountains, but most of them prefer to live either up on the mountain or under it."

"Under?"

"Mines. There are a ton of them. In fact, I'm surprised the whole mountain chain hasn't collapsed. They mine precious stones, jade, ore and coal, both white and black." I used the special white coal in my kiln. It burned hot enough to melt sand into glass and was cleaner than the black variety. It also cost more, but it was worth every extra copper.

"No diamonds. Not yet anyway," I added.

"Pity the only deposits have been found in the northern regions of Ixia," Janco said. "Otherwise that whole business with Councilor Moon's sister wouldn't have happened."

"That wouldn't have stopped her. Akako would have just found another way to finance her coup. Selling Gressa's fake diamonds as real was the fastest way for her to raise money."

Diamonds were expensive and hard to find in Sitia, and the Commander kept the imports to us to a minimum. Which made sense when I considered his aversion to magic. Diamonds held the unique property of being able to enhance a magician's power. Enough of them together could provide a significant boost, and since Sitia and Ixia's relationship remained on unstable ground despite Yelena's efforts, the Commander wouldn't want his potential enemy to increase their powers.

I wondered about the diamonds I had created. Would they augment a magician's magic or not? They didn't work for me. As my father would say, only one way to find out. The desire to be home, sitting in my father's laboratory and discussing glass, chewed my heart. Simpler times and simpler problems.

"How about the people? Are they friendly?" Janco asked.

The only Cloud Mist Clan member I knew was Pazia. She was Vasko Cloud Mist's daughter. Vasko had discovered a bountiful vein of rubies and was one of the richest men in Sitia.

I met Pazia during our first year at the Magician's Keep. Her powers had been the strongest in our class, and rumors she might become a master-level magician circulated even then. She hated me from the start and I endured four years of torment from the woman. In our fourth year, First Magician Bain Bloodgood assigned her to help with one of my magical-glass experiments. Pazia attacked me with an illusion of lethal Greenblade bees.

Channeling her magic into a glass orb in my hands, I transformed her illusion into glass bees and inadvertently drained Pazia of almost all her power. Despite the fact she aimed every bit of her strength at me, I should have stopped, but I was determined not to let her get the best of me again. My ego and pride had cheated Sitia out of a potential Master Magician. We only had three.

At least the incident hadn't been a total disaster. Pazia and I settled our differences and now she worked in the Keep's glass factory, creating intricate vases decorated with precious stones. Wealthy Sitians had been buying them as fast as Pazia could produce them.

"Opal, hello? Where ja go?" Janco waved a hand, snapping me from my reverie.

"Just thinking about the only Cloud Mist I know, and she's not representative of the entire clan. I've heard they're friendly if you're staying in one of their towns, but they won't let anyone visit the mines. The people who live up in the mountains tend to be very insular. They say they know a few routes across the Emerald Mountains. The Sitian Council sent an expedition with a Cloud Mist guide a few years back, but they turned around, claiming it was too cold and too hard to breathe. The high-mountain clan members also claim a vast desert is on the eastern side of the mountains. A wasteland with no end in sight. Has anyone in Ixia climbed over the…what do you call the chain in the north?"

"The Soul Mountains."

"Interesting *military* designation." I teased him. Not everything in Ixia had a number.

Janco frowned. "The mines have the proper codes." He scratched his goatee as he thought. "The Soul range is thicker in the north. We've had a few groups try to summit them, but they never returned. The winds are nasty in the higher elevations. Do you remember how strong an Ixian blizzard is?"

I nodded, remembering the horrible keening and bone-shattering cold.

"Well, it's twenty times worse in the mountains."

Shivering, I pulled my cloak tight. The late-afternoon sunshine warmed the land, but I hated being cold. All those years working in my family's glass factory had gotten me used to the heat. Eight kilns running nonstop kept the brick building steaming hot.

"Has anyone tried skirting them to the north?" I asked.

"Suicide. The mountains run right into the northern ice sheet. Between the icy temperatures and the snow cats you wouldn't stand a chance."

A finger of fear traced my spine as the image of bloodstained snow formed. Fierce, cunning and with heightened senses, a snow cat was impossible to hunt. They smelled, heard or saw a person well before the hunter spotted them. With their white coats blending into the ice sheet, the sole warning of an impending attack was movement. By then it was too late.

One man held the honor of killing a snow cat. The Commander of Ixia. Even Valek, the Commander's chief of security and assassin, couldn't make that claim. Yet he'd managed to hide the Fire Warper's glass prison in a snow cat's den. Interesting.

At least the prison would remain hidden. No one else would risk sneaking by seven snow cats to retrieve the Warper's soul. It would be suicide.

Four days of travel with Janco proved to be an extended exercise in patience. His curiosity focused on everything and everyone. Nonstop commentary about the strangeness of Sitia flowed from his mouth, and he enjoyed arguing. He found a fault with every issue, and we even debated on the merits or lack of merits of dust.

At least I learned a few self-defense tactics and he promised to teach me how to pick a lock in Ognap.

We reached the edge of the Emerald Mountains on the morning of the fourth day. The rolling terrain painted with lush greenery spread out before us like a rumpled quilt. Farms dotted the mounds, and clusters of buildings occupied the cracks. One large grouping extended along a narrow valley and climbed the hills to each side. Ognap, the Cloud Mist Clan's capital.

The snowcapped Emerald Mountains loomed beyond the foothills, stretching toward the sky. Impressive.

For once, Janco remained quiet. But as we drew near the town's limits, he stopped Moonlight. "With your glass messengers in every city, the details about our escape have probably been sent to each one. So there's a chance the town's guards will be watching for us. We could do one of two things. Either go in via the main road separately or circle around and find another way in." Janco glanced at the sky. "And we should go in after dark."

Although the thought of being alone tempted me, I decided we should stay together. My fighting skills needed to be much better for me to feel confident in them. Devlen had bypassed my sais with ease even though I had three years of lessons at the Keep. More emphasis on training and self-defense went into the final year of the curriculum. The final year I was currently missing.

We found an isolated glade to wait for the sun to set. To help pass the time, I challenged Janco to a match.

He jumped to his feet, his sword at the ready. "The glass warden isn't bor...ing. Her sais may sing, but I am the king."

"Warden and boring don't rhyme." I set my feet into a fighting stance with my sais in a defensive position. The guard was U-shaped and flared toward the weapon's point. I balanced one arm of the guard between my thumb and index finger, which lay along the hilt. The rest of my fingers curled around the other side of the guard.

"You try and find a word that rhymes with warden."

I tried, but Janco attacked and all my concentration focused on his lightning-fast strikes and quick parries. He won every match. Despite his tendency to lapse into extreme smugness, he guided my efforts to defend myself and I learned quite a bit from him.

During a break, he said, "Not bad. Not good, either. You need to practice every day for four hours."

"Four hours!" My arms ached and sides heaved after just an hour.

He grinned. "The Commander's soldiers run for two hours every morning, and practice drills every afternoon. When you're new, practice time lasts six hours and when you're an old soul like me, practice lasts about two hours. Keeps the skills sharp."

"Old soul." I laughed. "You're thirty."

He stroked his goatee. White whiskers peppered the black. "It's not the years, it's the experience." He paused. His eyes held a distant gleam as if seeing into his past. "My first practice was a shock. I was a cocky smart aleck—"

"Was?"

"Be quiet. I'm telling a story here. I easily bested my fellow trainees, but the trainers unarmed me in record time. And the Weapons Master was impossible to beat. He would just look at me, and my practice sword would fly from my hand."

I stifled my dubiousness over Janco's exaggerations.

He inspected the blade of his sword. "It irked me. Big-time. I started to practice eight hours a day and learned counterstrikes, attacks and strategies from anyone who would teach me. I trained with every sword we had. Broadswords, rapiers, short swords and sabers. Plus, I learned how to use a knife and unarmed combat."

"And?"

"He kept winning, but each match lasted a little bit longer. Until…"

He waited for me to prompt him. "Until?"

"I discovered my rhythm. My footwork was horrible, but one day it clicked and I started letting my instincts guide my actions. You know those little clues an opponent makes before they move?"

"No. I'm usually too focused on the weapon."

"A mistake. Here." He slid his feet into a fighting

stance and pointed his rapier toward me. "Get ready. Now watch my blade."

I concentrated on the silver shaft. He lunged. The tip of his blade stopped an inch from my chest before I reacted.

"Now watch my eyes."

I met his light brown gaze. Once again he shot past my defenses.

"Now watch my hips."

A slight hitch of movement alerted me and I stepped back. Countering, I blocked his blade with a clang and deflected it past my body.

"See?" he asked.

"Yes! Are there more?"

"A few. Those clues allowed me to concentrate more on my opponent's strategy and find their fighting cadence. Beginners are easy because they'll do the same series of moves over and over, while experts will keep changing it or will lull you into a rhythm and *bang!* Switch it up." Appreciation gleamed on his face as he stabbed the air. "It took me well over a year to discover the Weapon Master's dance. I had been making up rhymes in my mind to help me with my footwork, but for that last match with the Master, I recited them aloud. He hated that! Especially since my rhymes harmonized to his attacks. And anger makes you sloppy."

"You beat him?"

"Yep." He danced a victory jig.

"What happened after?"

He stopped. "I was transferred to the Commander's guard, where I met Ari." Huffing in amusement, he continued, "Since I beat the Weapons Master, I arrived with a cocky confidence." Janco held up a hand before I could comment. "I know, I know. Hard to believe. One match with the big brute knocked the swagger from my step as well as knocking me unconscious." He rubbed his jaw. "Then there was Valek with his super assassin skills and Maren with her bow staff. I had much more to learn. Endless practice ensued, and now here I am, just a humble average guy."

"Your humility is inspiring."

He ignored my sarcasm. "I endeavor to be a good role model."

"Shame your training didn't include fighting a big man named Ox armed with a horsewhip."

"Those are fighting words." He launched an attack and I scrambled to counter.

6

AFTER THE SUN SET, Janco and I packed our supplies and headed for Ognap. We found a small goat path south of the town and entered the city through a side street. About half the size of Fulgor, the town's business centered on gemstones. Once mined from underneath the mountains, the stones arrived in Ognap to be cleaned, faceted, categorized and polished before being sold or traded for goods.

Armed guards accompanied the caravans and watched the gemstone factories. Large barracks had been built on the east side of town to house them.

Torches blazed along the main boulevard as loud groups of citizens hustled between pubs under the watchful gaze of the town's security force. Shops and market stands buzzed with commerce. By the hum in the air, I guessed the evening's activities had just begun. Miners arrived for a few days' rest, bringing stories of rich veins and huge stones. They spent their wages, then returned to work.

Janco and I avoided the more popular areas and

checked into the Tourmaline Inn. The innkeeper, Carleen, rented us two single rooms—all she had left— and served us a wonderful beef stew and sweet berry pie. The explanation for the inn's name hung around her neck. A beautiful heart-shaped pink tourmaline rested on her broad chest.

She stroked the stone often, especially when speaking of her late husband.

"Pink." Janco spat in disgust when she left to help another customer. "I think I'm going to be sick."

The common room's decorations tended toward fluffy pink and soft. Hearts crafted from wood, stone and glass lined the shelves, and bright paintings of flowers hung on the walls.

I stifled a chuckle when Janco entered his room. His polite smile strained to hide his dismay at the mountain of pillows heaped on his bed.

"One of my favorite rooms," Carleen said. "It has a wonderful view of the mountains." Her fingertips brushed her pendant. She wrinkled her petite nose when she glanced at Janco. "There's a bathhouse across the street— you need to make use of it before retiring for the evening."

Carleen ignored his reaction and unlocked the next door for me. "It has my best mattress, sweetie." It was identical to Janco's. "Make sure you go along with your friend to the bathhouse." She waggled her fingers in farewell, and hustled back downstairs.

Janco leaned on the threshold of my door with his face creased in annoyance. "Did she just—"

"Yes."

"But I don't—"

"Yes. You do. We both stink."

"Well, I'm not—"

"Yes. You are."

He huffed. "You won't let—"

"No. No complaining. Let's go." I grabbed a clean shirt and pants from my saddlebags.

"Well, she could have handled it better," he grumped.

"No. She couldn't."

He settled into a sulky silence as we visited the bath-house.

Janco might not've appreciated the inn's excessive pillows, but after so many nights spent on the hard ground, I luxuriated in the bed, sleeping well past dawn. I snuggled deeper into the mattress until someone knocked on the door. Covering my ears failed to block the insistent rapping.

"Come on, Opal! We're burning daylight," Janco called through the wood.

I yelled for him to go away and the noise stopped. A moment of peace before the door swung open.

"Holy snow cats, did you sleep with all those pillows?" Janco asked.

Despite my cries of protest, he pulled them away and swept the blankets back. "Let's go."

With the utmost reluctance, I followed Janco outside. We walked from inn to inn, asking if anyone had seen

Ulrick or the two Warpers that Devlen spoke of. No one recognized the descriptions. We tried the pubs and taverns next and then the stables. Nothing.

"What's next?" Janco asked.

"The barracks. The Warpers could have gotten jobs guarding the gemstone caravans or even be working in the mines."

"They could. And Devlen could have lied and there is no one here to find."

I agreed. "Or they could have left. We need to make sure either way."

Janco rubbed his scar. "Asking questions won't work in the barracks. Guards for hire are usually ex-soldiers. They tend to stick together and protect each other. I'll wait until dark and do a little reconnaissance."

"And I can visit the pubs again and see if they show up."

"What if we don't find them?"

Good question. "We should check the mines, but they're off-limits and the security is impossible to breach."

"Nothing is impossible," Janco said. He practically drooled with gleeful anticipation.

"The Cloud Mist Clan has been mining precious stones for ages. Thieves and their own workers have been trying to steal them for ages. They have a complicated network of security. You can't just go in there and have a look around."

"Ah! A challenge."

Nothing I said dimmed his enthusiasm. In fact, it had the opposite effect. I hoped we found the Warpers before then.

After dinner, I suffered through Janco's lecture on safety.

"Make sure you have your spiders with you," he said.

"Janco, I—"

"Stay in well-lit areas, and, if you see the Warpers, don't confront them. Just follow them and we'll talk to them together. If you run into trouble, go to the town's guards. Better to be arrested than killed. Understand?"

"Yes, sir."

He remained stern.

"What? I agreed."

"Next time try it without the sarcasm."

We left the inn together. Wearing all black, Janco melted into the shadows. I continued along the main street. Torches blazed and groups of people strolled. Even at this hour merchants called prices and the rapid exchange of haggling filled the air.

Scanning faces, I wandered in the busy downtown area. I stopped to peruse one seller's glasswares, looking for Ulrick's unique style. He would need money to support himself. None of the vases popped with his magic. However, I found a beautiful statue of a Sandseed horse. A red heart nestled within its clear glass chest.

I held the horse in my hand. A faint throbbing pulsed

through my fingertips as if the heart beat inside. The cause of the vibration could be from magic or from my imagination.

"It's beautiful, isn't it?" the merchant asked.

"Yes. Do you know how the artist managed to keep the red glass's shape?" The first gather of molten glass could be shaped and colored, but, when another layer of glass is gathered around the shape, the heat would melt the shape, leaving the color behind.

"It isn't glass. It's a ruby."

That could explain the pulse. When I touched diamonds, they would either flash hot or cold and a vision of where they were mined filled my head. Perhaps rubies vibrated.

The merchant continued, "And not just any ordinary ruby. It's a Vasko ruby. The best of the best. Each stone comes with an authenticity seal from Vasko Cloud Mist himself!"

Perhaps only Vasko rubies throbbed. I thought of Pazia. Her family owned the Vasko mine. I would have to ask her if I could touch one.

"The horse is eight golds, but, for you, I'll sell it for six."

I shook my head. Too expensive for me. I only had one gold and a few silvers left in my pocket. "Do you have any more?"

"A few." The merchant bent under his table and brought out a swan, a dog and a cat. All with ruby hearts. All crafted by the same hand.

I examined the dog and felt its pulse. "Vasko rubies?"

"Of course. And since you seem so enchanted, I'll sell you the dog for five golds."

"Do you know who made these?"

A furtive expression settled on the merchant's face. "No."

"I don't want to bypass your business. I can't afford any of them. I'm a glassmaker." I pulled a few of my spiders from my pocket and showed him them. "I just wanted to see if I know the artist."

He scrutinized the spiders with reluctance. "I don't know his name or know if he is the artist. I buy the statues and the seals from him, then resell them. I'll give you one silver for each of your spiders. They're very lifelike."

"They're not for sale." I returned them to my pocket. So far, they broke open only for me, but there could be another magician with my skills. "Does the man come every day?"

"No. Every couple of days or so he stops by with a new batch."

"When's the last time he came?"

The merchant eyed me with suspicion. "Why is it so important?"

I downplayed my interest. "He could be a friend of mine. I haven't seen him in years and it's probably not him. He's a tall, muscular man with long black hair. His eyes are hard to forget. They're diamond-shaped with thick eyelashes. He also has a scar on his throat." I pointed to my neck below my left ear.

The merchant shrugged. "The guy looks like a Sandseed warrior to me." He huffed in amusement. "Don't know about his eyes. He'll probably be by in the next couple of days. Do you want me to tell him you're here?"

I thought fast. A Sandseed warrior could be one of the Warpers. "No. It's not him. My friend's from the Greenblade Clan. Thanks for your time." I hurried away.

Sticking to my plan, I searched the pubs and taverns for Ulrick and the Warpers. The unsanctioned Daviian Clan had been members of the Sandseed Clan before forming their own group. Called Vermin by the Sandseeds, the Daviians used blood magic to create powerful Warpers and they tried to take control of the Sitian Council.

The Council believed the Vermin and Warpers had been exterminated, but a few had escaped.

On my way back to the Tourmaline Inn, I stopped at various stands and looked for more heart-beating statues. A few merchants carried the glass animals. The general impression of the seller remained the same. A Sandseed warrior.

A pink sparkle flashed at me a block before the inn—another stand full of jewelry, and pink tourmalines dominated the display.

"Pretty, aren't they?" the merchant asked. "Three golds for any item. It's the best price in town." She held up a ring with a heart-shaped stone. In fact, multiple items contained heart-shaped tourmalines.

I glanced down the street. Carleen would have to walk this way to the market. "You know your customers."

She smiled. "The inn lady loves her pinkies. It matches her personality and gives her joy when she wears it. Each person has a certain gemstone that...calls to them. When they wear their special stone, they're empowered!" She thrust her fists into the air as if drawing strength from the sky.

Intrigued, I asked, "How do you know which one is for them?"

"Give me your hand."

Dubious, I held it out. She sandwiched it between her warm palms. Her smooth skin contrasted with my roughened and burn-scarred fingers. A ripple of heat traveled up my arm. She closed her eyes. The temperature inside me intensified. A red-hot finger pierced my heart. I gasped and yanked my hand back.

She studied my face with amazement. "My goodness, you have a conflicted heart. It's covered with storm clouds. But don't you worry." She patted my arm. "There was a flash of clarity and I saw your true stone." She rummaged around her table. "I only have one, but I can get more." Picking up a small pendant, she handed it to me.

The rich bluish-green color of the stone sparked with an iridescence. "What is it?"

"An opal."

I stared at her in shock. "But I thought opals were black."

"Some are, but they're other colors, too. Try it on." She threaded a silver chain through the loop of the pendant.

"Oh no. I can't afford—"

"Not to buy it. Wear it and you'll find the man of your heart." She linked it around my neck. "Perfect. And I'll sell it to you for two golds."

"I don't—"

"I'll include the chain."

"I'm sorry, but I really can't—"

"Sold," a familiar voice next to me said. He dropped two gold coins into the merchant's palm. "After all, it already worked. You were looking for the man of your heart, and now you've found him."

7

MY AUTOMATIC REACTION was to grab the hilts of my sais. I hadn't seen Devlen's face since he attacked me at the Thunder Valley market two seasons ago. But the big smile reminded me that Ulrick and not Devlen's soul resided within the body.

"How did you know I was here?" I asked.

"Word moves like lightning in these small towns." He hooked an arm around my shoulders and propelled me down the street. "One of the merchants sent me a warning that someone was asking about me. Or, rather, the new me." He squeezed me close. "I knew you would figure it out! Devlen claimed he would fool everyone, but I warned him he couldn't trick you."

Guilt flared. Caught off guard, I felt unbalanced. Our reunion was not how I had envisioned it. I thought I would have to rescue him.

"What's been going on? Tell me everything," he said.

I stopped and searched his face. "Did something else

happen to you when you switched bodies with Devlen? You seem…"

"Happy?"

"I was going to say different, but happy works. You never were the overjoyous type." He had been moody, sullen, protective and jealous, which made the times he had been in a good mood stand out. "Why are you happy? Do you have any idea what Devlen did in your body? What he did to me? If you consented to the trade, you're just as guilty as he is."

He sobered. "Let's find a quiet corner to talk."

He led me to a pub called the Emerald Eyes. Ulrick nodded to the owner and strode to a back table. I had been in here earlier and the owner claimed he hadn't seen anyone matching Ulrick's description.

After we sat, the man glided over to us carrying two mugs of ale.

"I see you found your friend," the proprietor said, setting a mug before me.

"No thanks to you."

The owner was unaffected by my comment. "Rick is my best customer. You're a stranger. Dinner?"

"Yes," Ulrick said.

"No," I said. When the owner left, I raised an eyebrow. "Rick?"

He squirmed a bit. "I couldn't use my real name. It didn't feel right, and I don't like the name Devlen. Rick worked."

"So you agreed to be Rick? It wasn't *forced* on you?"

He gulped his ale and set the mug on the table, placing it in the same ring of wetness. Avoiding my gaze, he fiddled with it.

"Why did you switch bodies with Devlen?"

"I couldn't resist."

"Resist what?" I prompted, although I had a good guess.

"The power." He looked up. "You know, Opal. Remember when everyone called your magic the One-Trick Wonder? How you longed to do more?"

"Yes, but I wouldn't—"

"Really? If someone gave you the chance, would you really have refused? If Pazia approached you, before she lost her magic, and wanted to change places? Think about it before you answer."

The temptation would have been strong, but I would have refused because of the blood magic.

Before I could speak, he said, "I went from Ulrick, the One-Trick Nobody, to Rick, The Magician." He laid his hands on the table with the palms up. The mug rattled, then floated into his hand. His lips curved into a satisfied smile.

"Didn't you think we might have just scratched the surface of your own magic? That you might be able to do more?" I clamped down on my next question. Didn't he think about me?

"He's a Sandseed Story Weaver. He read the threads of my life and said I possessed one ability—to infuse my glass pieces with a brush of magic so they could read a person's mood." Bitterness spiked his voice. "The only way to increase my power was to switch with him. He no longer desired his magical ability. Devlen wanted to be an average man. I'm sorry if he hurt you by leaving so abruptly..." Ulrick paused. "Is that how you discovered the switch? Because you thought I wouldn't leave you?"

Guilt warred with confusion. I replayed his words in my mind. "He was supposed to leave?"

"Yes. He was going to sever all contact with my friends and family...with you. I planned to learn all about my new magic, and then find you and explain."

"But didn't you know who he was?" Confusion won the battle.

"A Sandseed Story—"

"No. Who he *really* was?"

By his blank look, I knew he didn't. Devlen had possessed a strong mental ability and he could convince a weak magician of anything. Add his wordplay skills, and Ulrick hadn't stood a chance.

"He's a Daviian Warper. He attacked me twice. Didn't I tell..." No. I hadn't. The contents of my stomach churned with dread.

"Must have been during one of your secret magician meetings where I wasn't invited. No reason to tell a One-Trick Nobody." He swigged his ale and glared into the mug.

"It wasn't like that. When I explained about Sir and Tricky's kidnapping, you wanted a battalion of guards to watch me despite the fact I escaped on my own. If I had told you about Devlen—"

"We wouldn't be here."

"No. You would have never let me out of your sight."

"What's so bad about that?"

When I didn't answer, he continued, "Face it, Opal. You're dancing around the subject, but we both know the real reason you're upset."

"We do?"

"Yes. In switching my life for another's, I gave up on us. With his Story Weaver ability, Devlen replayed our times together. Watching you from a different perspective, I realized you never loved me." The distance in his eyes faded. He leaned forward as if excited by a new idea. "But you're here now. When he left, you must have realized your true feelings, tracked him down and discovered the switch." A hopeful tone lit his voice.

A conflicting array of emotions rolled through me. Guilt dominated, and I needed to tell him…everything. "Ulrick, Devlen didn't leave."

"Oh?" A quizzical expression crinkled his eyebrows.

"He was a Daviian Warper—"

"*Was.* He doesn't have any power—well, unless he can blow glass—because I have it."

Unable to form words, I shut my mouth. Devlen had convinced him the switch included magic. And from his words, Ulrick didn't know about blood magic.

"What?" he asked. "He couldn't have hurt you. With

your glass spiders and bees, sais, and surrounded by Leif
and that Stormdancer, you were well protected."

I pieced together Ulrick's comments. Devlen had
spun a story using Ulrick's own fears and disappoint-
ments. No magical power. No love, and, since his sister
did hit him over the head, no family support. If they
switched bodies, Ulrick would have his desire, and
Devlen would sever relations with Ulrick's friends and
go his merry way. If his argument hadn't worked, Devlen
could have used his magic to persuade him.

"It appears Devlen lied to you and tricked you, too,"
I said.

A stubborn conviction settled in a hard line across
his shoulders. "I guess it's easier for you to believe he
tricked me than think I left you."

A rush of fury pulsed in my veins. How many more
people would accuse me of lying to myself or others? I
suppressed the urge to bash him on the head.

The arrival of Ulrick's dinner allowed me a few
minutes to cool down and collect my thoughts. He ate
with abandon, as if concentrating on his food would
keep me from commenting.

"Let me tell you a story while you eat," I said. I
related how Devlen used his disguise as Ulrick. Sticking
to the facts, I kept an even pace even when I admitted
to letting him seduce me. "You acted different yet the
same. Bolder and more confident." I gestured to him.
"I hadn't realized that was what I needed from you to
go to the next step in our relationship. At the time, I

thought your change was due to being tricked by Gressa. You…Devlen told me you realized you no longer needed your family's approval. And I rationalized the change to you finally moving past your disappointment over your magic."

He had stopped eating and looked at me in either horror or pain. Both cut through me, exposing my guilt.

"And perhaps in a deep level of my consciousness I knew you were different. In order to be honest, I have to admit the possibility. I'm sorr—"

"Go on," he said. His voice was rough, and his food forgotten. "What else happened?"

I explained how Kade's capture forced me to admit I had feelings for the Stormdancer, and how my need to help Kade unwittingly revealed Devlen.

Ulrick flinched. "Go on."

I told about the torture and how I tricked Devlen into going to Ixia's northern ice sheet to meet up with Sir and his gang. They had caught Kade spying on them and planned to coerce him into harvesting the killing energy from Ixia's blizzards into glass orbs. "Devlen wanted me to find his mentor's prison. He didn't care about Sir's scheme. He knew I could locate the imprisoned Warpers in my glass animals through my nightmares."

Ulrick gripped his chair arms, but said nothing. I continued the story, finishing with Kade's and my escape.

"You drained Devlen? No magic left?" he asked.

"None."

"Without him attacking you?"

"Yep. I stole his magic."

He sat in stunned silence, which continued as all the information sank in. The tavern owner hustled over to inquire if everything was all right.

"Fine, fine." Ulrick pushed his plate away. He tapped the mug. "I need a refill and a shot of whiskey." He rubbed a hand over his face. "Where is Devlen now?"

"In Fulgor."

"In prison?"

"No. He's working for your sister."

"Say that again."

"No one believes me. If they do, they're pretending they don't like Cressa. She's using Devlen." A bone-deep weariness soaked into my body.

"For what?"

"I don't know. She's Councilor Moon's first adviser now. Do you remember what happened when you went to her factory and confronted her about the fake diamonds?"

Ulrick raked his fingers through his hair. He had let the black strands grow past his shoulders—surprising considering he always kept his own hair short.

"She seemed impressed we had discovered her work," he said. "I tried to convince her to fess up to the authorities and perhaps earn a lighter sentence. After that..." He quirked a rueful smile. "She bashed me on the head. When I regained consciousness, Devlen was helping me."

"She did follow your advice. She told the Councilor of Akako's plot and gained her trust." Which didn't quite add up, unless Tama had other reasons to keep Gressa close. "What have you been doing since then?"

"Devlen instructed me how to increase my powers. He claimed there were two Story Weavers in Ognap who could guide me, but I haven't found them. Instead, I've been earning money by helping a local glassmaker. I guess he lied about the Weavers, but…" He tapped his chest. "A part of me still believes him, yet with my magic, I can sense you're telling the truth, too."

"The Sandseed clan was decimated five years ago by the Daviian Vermin. No Story Weavers survived. The two he mentioned are Warpers." Before he could contradict me, I said, "Not many people know because the Sandseeds don't want it to be made public. Yelena is helping them until one of their children develop the ability."

The owner returned with Ulrick's order, placing the drinks on the table before hustling off. While we talked, the room had filled with people.

Ulrick downed the whiskey in one gulp. He played with the empty glass. "You kept many things from me, but you gave Devlen, and that Stormdancer, much more. I don't want to be with you anymore." He tossed a few coins on the table and stood.

"I understand, but you need to come with me to Fulgor. We'll find Devlen, and Yelena can switch you back to your own body."

He looked at me as if I had spoken in a foreign tongue. "Switch back to a magicless body?"

"You'll still have your glass magic. Despite what Devlen told you, your own magic stays with your soul. The added magic you have now is from blood magic, which I haven't even explained to you yet. It's—"

"Another one of your secrets? No more, Opal. I'm done with you." He turned away.

I leaped to my feet, grabbed his arm and pushed his sleeve to his elbow, exposing the tattoos. "Blood has been mixed with the ink. It's the real reason you have more power. It's illegal."

He yanked his arm free. "I don't care. I have magic and I have freedom. *You* can't force me to go to Fulgor."

"Yes, I can."

"How?" He crossed his arms and straightened to his full height.

"I can drain your magic, leaving you with nothing." I bluffed. I wasn't sure if I could steal blood magic. Tricky had kept his, but it was my blood, not another's. And I didn't know how it all worked.

He laughed. "You don't have an orb with you."

I picked up the shot glass. "Any glass will work." Another bluff.

He knocked the glass from my grip. It shattered on the floor.

"Oops. Nice try, Opal."

"I don't have to be close to you. I can pull your magic from a distance."

He appeared unimpressed. "A few feet? A mile?" He shrugged. "I can sense you from that distance. Besides, I have no intention of letting you get that close." His gaze hardened and an invisible force pushed me into my seat. "I have my own defenses."

"There are other ways to counter you."

"But first you have to find me."

The tavern owner appeared by his side. "Something wrong?"

"Yes," Ulrick said. "She's causing trouble. Call the authorities and have her arrested for drunk-and-disorderly conduct." He slipped the man a coin.

"Yes, sir."

Ulrick strode to the door, but I couldn't stand until he left.

The owner remained next to the table. He blocked my way. "Can I get you a drink while you're waiting?"

"No thanks. I'm leaving." I stepped around him and encountered two tank-size men with flat expressions. My sais would probably bend around their large shaved heads. Sighing, I returned to the table. "I'll have a glass of wine."

The owner inclined his head as if to say, "Wise move," and headed toward the bar. He spoke with a young man who then sprinted from the tavern. Probably to report to the town's security force. With the two musclemen hovering nearby, I stayed in my seat. Digging two handfuls of my little glass spiders from the pockets of my cloak, I kept them hidden in my palms. I waited for the perfect moment.

When a server passed me carrying a full tray, I tripped her. The poor girl flew forward and the mugs of ale splashed all over the next table. Amid cries of dismay, I crushed the spiders in my hand, hoping no one noticed the huffs of air and the flashes.

About a dozen spiders appeared on the table. "Crawl all around the tavern," I ordered, sending them a mental image of what I needed them to do. They scurried to obey. I smiled. Handy little guys.

Shrill shrieks and screams followed gasps of horror as the spiders dashed and scuttled through and over the tavern's patrons, providing me with an excellent distraction. I left without trouble and, after a fruitless search of Ognap for Ulrick, I returned to the Tourmaline Inn.

While waiting for Janco to return, I reviewed my conversation with Ulrick. The whole encounter felt surreal, and not as I expected. His reaction to me had been justified, but his desire to remain in Devlen's body must be part of the addictive nature of the blood magic. Yeah, right, Opal. Better to blame blood magic than to blame yourself. Or Ulrick.

Devlen claimed the exchange had been mutual, but Ulrick hadn't been given all the facts. Plus, the magical persuasion made the whole endeavor suspect. I would need to track Ulrick down and capture him somehow. Perhaps Janco would have a few ideas on how to accomplish that.

Then what? Escort him to Yelena? She was the only person who could corroborate my story. Janco's word didn't count, as far as the Sitians were concerned.

I stretched out on the bed, but sleep eluded me. My thoughts whirled out of my control, matching my life. If I was caught by the Council now, they wouldn't hesitate to lock me in the Keep's cells. Better to stay free and sort this mess out on my own.

The bang of a door woke me from a light doze.

Janco rushed into the room. "Wake up! We need to leave. Now!" He shoved my stuff into my bag.

I pushed up to my elbow. "Why?"

"The local guards have been...ah...alerted to our presence."

Hopping out of bed, I grabbed my clothes. "How?"

"Minor...miscalculation. I'll explain later. Move!"

I tossed my saddlebags over my shoulder and followed him into the inn's hallway. He skidded to a stop at the top of the stairs. Janco put a finger to his lips as Carleen's irritated voice reached us.

"...indecent hour. My customers won't be happy."

The glow from a lantern brightened the staircase. We backed away as Carleen and a large group of soldiers mounted the steps.

AS THE SOLDIERS stormed up the stairs, Janco and I backpedaled to his room. He locked the door.

"Do we pelt them with pillows when they break in?" I asked.

"Cute." He crossed to the window and opened the shutters. "I hope you're not afraid of heights."

"You first."

He hung a leg out and turned so his stomach rested on the sill. "Watch the landing—there's a puddle about a foot to the left." Janco dropped from sight.

Fists pounded on the door and a loud voice ordered me to open up. All the incentive I needed. I tossed my saddlebags toward the right side of the window, then followed Janco's example and lowered myself down. Hanging by my hands, I let go. After a second of stomach-buzzing free fall, I hit the ground hard.

Voices shouted from above. A figure leaned from the

window. Janco grabbed my hand and yanked me to my feet.

"Come on. Come on." He pulled me down the alley.

Dark shapes appeared ahead of us. Janco changed directions, whipping me around. He stopped. More soldiers blocked the other end.

"How important is it to stay free?" he asked.

"Important, but not enough to seriously hurt anyone."

He nodded and pulled his sword. "Choose an opponent and rush him," he instructed. "Don't stop. Use your momentum to break through the barricade and keep going. Step on the person if you have to. Just keep going."

He charged the line of soldiers, yelling a battle cry. I kept pace beside him. They flinched back. Interesting strategy.

Hindered by my saddlebags, I couldn't grab my sais. Instead, I palmed a few spiders. When we drew close, I crushed them. The flash helped to confuse the soldiers, and I ordered the spiders to bite their hands. It's hard not to drop your weapon when a large eight-legged creature sinks its teeth into you.

I rammed my free shoulder into a man who swatted at his clothes. He rocked back and I spun around him, stumbling for a heart-cramping moment.

Yelps of pain and cries of confusion surrounded me, but I listened to Janco's instructions and kept going. We broke through the line. Janco flashed me a huge grin and a thumbs-up.

We ran through dark streets and stayed in the shadows. My bags kept sliding down my arm, throwing me off my stride. The weight dragged on me and my chest heaved with the effort to suck in air.

"Horses?" I huffed.

"Being watched." Janco sprinted with ease. He wasn't even out of breath. "You need to get more exercise."

"And...you need...to not...make...miscalculations."

"And ruin the fun?"

I glared, but it failed to diminish his obvious glee in being pursued by a pack of soldiers.

We zigzagged through Ognap until I lost my sense of direction and we lost the most dogged pursuer. My companion moved as if seeing the surrounding buildings with a second sight.

Eventually we slowed as the tight rows of factories broke into single dwellings and dwindled into farms, stopping only when we reached the relative safety of the forest.

I dropped my saddlebags and collapsed onto the ground, panting for breath.

Janco sat next to me. "We should wait a few hours before returning for the horses."

"Guarded, remember?"

"Oh yes. I can't forget that. It's what started this whole adventure in the first place."

"Your miscalculation?"

"Unfortunately. I went to check on Moonlight and Quartz and make sure no one had come around asking questions about them. Two Sandseed horses in the same stable—heck, in the same town—is a rare occurrence. In fact, I thought it was rather stupid of us to stable them together and I wanted to correct our mistake." Janco lay on his back, staring at the sky. Stars dotted the blackness. No moon. "I hate it when I'm right in a bad way. Even though I circled the stable a few times, two of the town's guards had found a perfect place to wait."

"Perfect?"

"A sweet blind spot with a clear view of the stable. The game was up the second they marked me. Good thing I'm fast."

"How are we going to get the horses? Won't the guards wait in that same place again?" I asked.

"Heck no. They'll probably confiscate the horses and stable them right next to their headquarters."

"That helps us how?"

"It's a better place for a distraction."

"Do I want to know what you're planning?"

"No. It's better you don't." He paused. "Do those Greenblade bees of yours have to sting?"

I crouched in a shadow. Exhaustion clung to me and I wished Carleen's soft pillows surrounded me instead of my glass bees. Torches blazed near the station house, and activity teemed inside and outside the building despite the late hour. Janco had gone to fetch his distraction.

Dozing lightly, I woke to bawdy ballads.

"...she closed her knees, not one to please..." A drunken voice sang out loud and off-key.

The rumble of a team of horses shook the ground under me. Four horses, pulling a loaded wagon and an equally loaded driver, entered the bright torchlight. Livestock crates had been haphazardly piled inside the wagon, but it was too dark to see what type of animal the crates contained.

The drunk's horrible singing drew the soldier's interest and a few of them stepped outside to investigate.

"...oh please go down on your knees and let me ease—"

"Hey, buddy," one soldier called.

"Whoa!" The drunk stopped the horses.

"The harness isn't secured," the soldier said. "You're going to lose your team."

"Well, I'll be a pile of sugar near an anthill!" The drunk muttered and tried to step down from the wagon. He slipped and ended up sprawling on the ground.

Only Janco could make a pratfall look graceful. He swayed to his feet and tried to fix the harness, making it worse.

"Sir, you shouldn't be driving a team in your condition." The soldier pulled the straps from Janco's hands.

"Ah, hell, man. The horses drive themselves. I'm just here for entertainment. Hey, did you hear the song about the one-breasted woman finding love with a one-

armed man?" Janco launched into the song as he retrieved the reins and attempted to secure the horses.

A significant look passed between two soldiers. They
bookended Janco and offered to help him, pulling him
away from the team. He staggered over to lean on his
wagon.

By this time, more soldiers had joined their colleagues. And it was my cue to circle around to the back
of the wagon.

"Mighty decent of you fellows," Janco said. "While
you're hooking them up, I'll get you some of my home-
brewed honey."

"Are you a beekeeper?"

"Yep. The best of the best. No one has bees like me."
He giggled. "Bee like me. That rhymes." Janco slapped
his thigh.

The soldiers unhooked the team.

"We'll guard your horses and goods," a soldier said.
"Lieutenant Hunter will escort you inside to sleep it
off."

"Mighty nice of you fellows, but I have a schedule to
keep. Let me get you some of my honey. This stuff has
quite the kick to it."

When I reached my position, Janco climbed and fell
into the wagon, crashing into one of the crates. It broke
open underneath him.

"Whoops. That's not good."

I cracked open eight glass bees and instructed four
of them to buzz by the horses' ears and swing around

the soldiers a few times without stinging anyone. The other four I sent inside the building to harass the soldiers within. I repeated the order that they do not sting.

As predicted, the horses panicked and the soldiers scattered. I crept toward the stables and sent a few more bees to chase out the ambush Janco said waited for us. Sure enough, three men bolted from various hiding spots.

Janco joined me as I opened Quartz and Moonlight's stall doors. Unease twisted in my stomach as I mounted Quartz. I hadn't ridden bareback before. Janco hopped on Moonlight and spurred him toward the back fence. The black horse leaped the barrier without trouble. I urged Quartz to follow. I hadn't jumped a horse, either. Heck of a time to find out if I could do both together.

I held her mane and pressed my legs against her sides. The fence grew taller as we neared. I closed my eyes and let Quartz take control. She launched and we sailed. The landing almost jarred me loose, but she jigged to the side and I regained my balance.

We caught up to Janco and Moonlight. He was all smiles. "Never a dull moment with you, Opal. Did you see the size of those bees?" He whistled in appreciation. "I swear, one guy wet himself. And I never knew a man could scream at such a high pitch."

While glad to have the horses back, I worried about our distraction. "You better hope no one was stung. Otherwise, a murder charge will be added to our arrest warrants."

We returned to our makeshift camp to pick up our bags and headed north. With each stride, I knew the chances of finding Ulrick again diminished. He could be anywhere, and every city had been alerted to watch for us. After I'd paid for new saddles and tack with the last of my coins, I realized it was time to admit defeat.

"I could always steal—"

"No, Janco. We're in enough trouble. It's time for me to return home."

For once, I wasn't tempted to go through the Avibian Plains. I wanted to prolong our trip back to the Citadel.

After nine days on the road, sleeping on the ground and eating nothing but rabbits and berries, I was ready to return. I missed my friends, my sister, Zitora and working in the glass shop. I wished Kade could stand with me when I faced the Sitian Council.

We had no trouble sneaking into the Citadel even with two horses. Janco's knowledge of the backstreets and shortcuts through the Citadel aided our ease of travel, but caused me to wonder.

"I thought Ixia stopped sending people to spy on us," I said.

"Oh…well…I did spend a great deal of time here during the Warper Battle." Janco's grin widened.

"Uh-huh. That's not very neighborly. Does Yelena know?" I asked. As the liaison between Ixia and Sitia, Yelena worked to keep the peace.

"Know what?" He feigned ignorance.

I let the subject drop. With plenty of time to contemplate my return to the Citadel, I had decided to go to the Magician's Keep first and seek out Zitora before turning myself in to the Council. I wanted to explain if she'd allow me.

Constructed with green-veined white marble, the Citadel's outer walls encased a complex maze of residences and businesses. It also housed the Sitian government buildings and the Magician's Keep.

By the time we arrived within sight of the Keep's main gate, it was well after midnight. I hoped Zitora was still awake.

Janco handed me Moonlight's reins and hugged me tight. "I kept my promise to escort you home safely."

"Aren't you going to come in with me? I need you as a witness."

"Don't worry, I'll be at the Council's interrogation to lend my support. I just don't like staying in the Creepy Keepy. Too many magicians." He shuddered, then waved goodbye.

I eyed the guarded gate. Would the guards detain me or let me through? I leaned my head against Quartz. The task of proving my good intentions and my word loomed before me like the Emerald Mountains. An impossible summit with unknown and potentially dangerous terrain on the other side.

Summoning my nerve, I mounted Quartz. Moonlight followed us as we approached the Keep's gate. A

small barrier had been drawn across the entrance. Easy
to jump if we wanted.

I laughed at the guard's shocked expression. The
magician on duty blinked at me several times.

"Hello, Cole." I waved to the magician. "If she's
awake, could you tell Master Cowan I'm back, please?
Tell her I'll see to the horses before I report in to her
office. Jerrod, can you move the barrier, please?" I
used Janco's advice to act as if I were in charge.

It worked. Jerrod rushed to lift the gate.

"Thank you." I urged Quartz forward.

Zitora's office was located on the second floor of the
Keep's administration building, which was straight
across from the entrance gate. Built with peach-and-
yellow blocks of marble, the smooth walls appeared dull
in the torchlight. Right now the Master Magician would
be either in her office or in her tower. Four massive
towers had been built at each corner of the Keep's
square-shaped campus. A two-story-high marble wall
connected them and marked the Keep's borders.
Zitora's tower occupied the northeast corner of the
Keep.

I bypassed the administration building. Catty-corner
to the back of the admin on each side were the two guest
quarters. Directly behind it was the dining hall, where
all the students, staff and magicians had their meals. A
few lanterns glowed from the massive kitchen's
windows.

Quartz trod through the formal gardens located in

the center of the Keep's grounds. She liked to rub against the lilac bushes. Usually I steered her away from the grass, otherwise the gardeners would yell at us, but at this time of night they were asleep. A few students hustled between buildings, paying us no attention.

The apprentice wings curved around the garden on each side. From above, they resembled parentheses. My quarters were at the end of the east wing, next to the east guesthouse. The desire to crawl into my own bed tugged at my heart. I suppressed it along with all my other wishes. They lumped together and sat in my stomach like a wad of sour cheese.

We passed the amber-colored statue that marked the spot Yelena had defeated the Fire Warper. Many magicians had died during the Warper Battle. It was the place where I had worked with molten glass, rendering the prisons. Yelena used her Soulfinder abilities to send the Warpers' souls through me and into the glass. And just like my other glass creations, I remained connected to those evil souls. They haunted my nightmares.

I yanked my unpleasant thoughts to the present. The memorial statue had been carved to resemble flames from a campfire. In the sunlight, the yellowish-orange colors flickered as if real. It sat atop a gold-colored pedestal. Plaques hung on each of the four rectangular sides. The front plaque listed the names of those who had died. A side plaque listed the names of the defenders, including Valek, Ari and Janco, as well as the Sitians who had helped. I smiled, remembering Leif complaining that he was listed second to last.

The one on the back recited the danger of craving magic and warned of how the best intentions could have disastrous results. Yelena Liana Zaltana's name and title filled the final side and below hers, in smaller letters, was my name. Opal Cowan, glass magician. We were credited with defeating the Daviian Vermin and the Fire Warper they had released.

I had protested when they installed the statue. My part in the battle was minor compared to most, but Yelena had turned and looked at me with those beautiful green eyes.

"Opal," she said, placing a hand on my arm. "Without you, I would not be here. I would be existing in the underworld, spending an eternity guarding those evil souls. I made sure your name was with mine."

I hadn't been able to argue with her logic. My nightmares didn't occur every night and were worth enduring to have her here with us.

The bathhouse beyond the formal garden was the identical size and shape of the dining hall. My skin itched and I smelled like a horse. I added another wish to my growing list, trying to ignore the stiff feel of dried sweat on my shirt.

The small pasture occupied the back section of the Keep. Situated between the stables and the glass shop, it was used for limited grazing. Quartz headed left without being signaled. She knew where the fresh water, clean straw and sweet hay could be found. And the Stable Master's famous milk oats.

Glad the Stable Master was asleep, I rubbed both horses down, fed and watered them before treating them to his homemade milk oats. They both trotted to their stalls. Quartz sighed with sleepy pleasure as I secured the door. She fell asleep before I left the stable.

The hulking dark presence of Third Magician's Keep tower pressed down on me. I should go straight to Zitora's office in the administration building, but a warm glow from the east side of the pasture beckoned me. The distinct crisp smell of burning white coal filled the air, drawing me near. Light beamed from the windows of the glass shop. I would just poke my head in for a second, see who manned the kiln and make sure all was well with the equipment.

Entering the glass shop, I paused. I soaked in the roar of the kiln, standing still until I felt the rumble deep in my bones. Dropping my saddlebags, I shrugged off my cloak and tossed it to the side. I let the heat press against my skin like a comforting blanket. Home.

Piecov, a first-year student, bent over a table, writing on a piece of paper. He startled when I called his name.

"Opal, you scared me!" He rushed to me with his arms wide. Wrapping me in a hug, he squeezed. "Thank fate you're back. We missed you, and your sister has turned into a tyrant."

"A tyrant?" I cocked a dubious eyebrow. My beautiful sister Mara made honey seem bitter in comparison. She was incapable of being mean. Jealous? Who, me?

"She's worried sick about you and has been grumping at us for months. You should have sent her a message," Piecov admonished. "We've been hearing a ton of crazy rumors about you and Ulrick and about a Stormdancer and a Warper. What's been going on?"

I slumped on a stool. It would take days for me to explain everything. Piecov was right; I should have sent Mara a message once I returned to Ixia and decided to disobey the Council's orders.

"It's a long story. I'll fill you in later. Where is Mara? Is she still staying in the east guest quarters?"

"No. She's living with Leif in the staff quarters."

Good news. Perhaps they decided to make a formal commitment. Our mother would be thrilled over the possibility of grandchildren.

"Do you want me to fetch her?" Piecov asked.

"No. Don't bother her." I inspected the equipment as Piecov launched into what the glass artists had been doing since I left over forty-two days ago.

"You should see Pazia's newest project. She made a bowl and ringed the edge with diamonds."

"It sounds gorgeous." I adjusted a valve, thinking about the significant expense of the diamonds. Imported from Ixia, they were of limited quantity. I jerked, remembering diamonds stored magical energy and could be used by magicians to boost their power.

Perhaps Pazia attempted to augment her small magic with the bowl.

Then another thought rocked me. Buried and hidden in my cloak and saddlebags were enough diamonds to fill a foot-wide orb. What would happen if I placed a charged diamond in one of my glass messengers? Would another magician be able to recharge the magic inside the glass?

Besides being the only person who could trap magic in glass, the other limit to my messengers was their short lifespan. Once the magic was used, it no longer worked. But what if it could be used over and over again? I would lose my leverage. No longer be indispensable.

"Opal!"

Mara's cry jolted me from my thoughts. She plowed into me, pushing me against the back wall. Her hands clamped on my shoulders and her face creased with a medley of emotions.

"I want to hug you and shake you all at the same time." She dug her fingernails into my skin.

"Make up your mind before I start to bleed."

She pulled me toward her, then released me. I stumbled back.

"How did you know I was here?" I asked.

"Leif smelled you. He woke me up and said Quartz was in the lilac bush."

Yelena's brother had unusual powers. His magical ability to smell a person's intentions and their past deeds remained unique among magicians. He was frequently called in during criminal investigations to aid in determining guilt.

"Why didn't you send me a message? What's been going on?" Mara demanded.

"Didn't Leif tell you?"

She waved a hand. "You know Leif's aversion to politics. Besides, they're keeping a tight lid on what happened to you in Ixia. All I know is you were kidnapped again! And taken to the northern ice sheet. Oh, Opal, you must have been so frightened." Her arms enveloped me and she stroked my back as if she soothed a child.

The events on the ice sheet seemed frozen in my heart. Distant, as if I watched through a glass sheet. Only the time spent with Kade in Ixia could warm my insides. I remember being scared, but now I felt numb.

I pulled away from Mara. "It's a heck of a story. Most people don't even believe me. Yes..." I rushed to assure her. "I know you will, and you *make* sure to be at the Council's interrogation so you can hear it all. I'm too exhausted to repeat it now."

"Council's interrogation? It's that bad?"

"Oh, yeah." I picked up a pontil iron. "How's the kiln been running?" I asked, changing the subject.

She clutched her skirt and released the fabric over and over. "A little hot. It's the warming season. With the temperatures heating up during the day and cooling so fast at night, it's hard to find the right balance of coal, but we will."

"How's the cauldron? Any signs of cracking?" Glass was very acidic and would eventually eat through a ceramic bowl.

I slid the kiln's door open a crack. Bright orange light seared my vision. I squinted and poked a pontil iron in the molten glass-filled cauldron, spinning the metal rod to check the consistency of the melt. Molten glass gathered on the end of the rod like taffy and I removed the iron. Turning the rod to keep the glass from drooping and dripping onto the floor, I studied the slug. It glowed as if alive, pulsing with a deep orange light.

If Mara answered my question, I didn't hear her. It felt wonderful to hold such potential in my hands again. It had been so long. I sat at the gaffer's bench and picked up metal tweezers to shape the glass before it hardened. Since I hadn't used a hollow blowpipe, I couldn't insert magic inside. But maybe I could try—"

"Stop right there," a voice called.

Mara sat on the edge of the table with her hands over her mouth, staring at the door. A moment passed before I realized a guard aimed a crossbow at me. Piecov had spread his arms wide to show he was unarmed.

"Step away from the bench," the man ordered.

I abandoned my piece and moved a few feet away.

"Hands where I can see them."

I raised my hands. Interesting how annoyance pulsed through my veins instead of fear. His alarm was evident by the sweat staining the fabric under his arms. What did he think I was going to do?

He called out an all clear over his shoulder, and moved aside. The arrow remained pointed at me. Irys and Zitora entered the shop. By this time, anger had replaced my annoyance.

"Make sure you have a null shield in place. I might try to escape." I didn't bother to cover my sarcasm or fury.

Zitora and Irys exchanged a look. They *had* erected a null shield. As Janco would say, holy snow cats!

"Opal, why didn't you report to my office when you finished with the horses?" Zitora asked.

Aha! Understanding dawned. My stop in the glass shop looked suspicious if they believed I had turned rogue. My anger cooled and disappointment twinged deep in my chest. How could Zitora believe I'd turned rogue?

"I couldn't resist. I figured it would be a long time before I would be allowed to come here."

"Allowed?" Mara recovered from her surprise. "Why wouldn't she be allowed?" Outrage fueled her words. "Without her, you wouldn't have—"

"Mara." I drew a breath and released it. "They have a good reason." I stepped forward and a loud pop pierced the air. A force slammed into my shoulder, knocking me to the floor. Dazed, I stared at the shattered glass next to me. The piece I had left on the rod had cooled too fast and cracked off.

Unfortunately, the noise startled the guard and he'd shot me with an arrow.

9

PAIN RADIATED FROM my left shoulder, shooting down my arm and ringing my neck. Legs appeared, voices queried and my vision blurred. Hands helped me to stand and I stumbled until an arm wrapped around me. Supported, I lurched to the infirmary with no real memory of the trip.

Healer Hayes's mouth moved, but I didn't understand his words. My sister squeezed my hand. I blinked at her in surprise. Nice of her to come along, I opened my mouth to thank her, but Healer Hayes touched the arrow's shaft and my world turned black.

An insistent poking jabbed my shoulder, each thrust a painful burning spike as if a hot needle gouged my skin. I swatted my torturer with my right hand because my left arm was stuck.

"Stop it, Opal, or I'll tie down your other arm," Healer Hayes said.

I peered at him through slits in my eyelids. He fussed with white bandages stained red.

"It hurts."

"The arrow head went deep, damaging tissue, muscle and bone. I hope you'll regain use of your left arm."

I gaped at him. The pain was a mere inconvenience compared with the prospect of a useless arm. How would I work with glass?

"There." He finished wrapping my shoulder and helped prop a few pillows behind my head. "Are you hungry?"

My stomach felt as if I had swallowed a bucket of sand. "No."

He sprinkled a white powder into a glass and poured water over it. Handing it to me, he said, "Drink this for the pain, and make sure you consume plenty of liquids today. Tomorrow you *will* eat." He set the water pitcher down on the wooden table by my bed.

"How long will I have to stay?" The utilitarian room reminded me of when my sister Tula had been murdered over five years ago. She had been so close to a full physical recovery when her attacker returned to the infirmary to finish the job.

"Until I say you can go." He patted my hand. "You're going to need your full strength to face the Council."

His reminder inflamed my injury. I gulped a few mouthfuls of the bitter water. When he left the room, a guard outside the door moved aside to let him pass. Great. I tried to laugh but it hurt too much. Of all the scenarios I had imagined about my return, being shot by an arrow hadn't been one of them.

I dozed off and on. Without a window in my room, I couldn't tell the time. Mara's strident voice pierced the fog of my thoughts.

"...her sister and if you don't let me in, I'm going to—"

Her threat was cut off by Hayes's soothing voice. Then the door flew open and Mara swept into the room laden with a basketful of...stuff. Hayes was two feet behind her. She demanded a prognosis, firing questions at Hayes until she was satisfied.

"Right now, rest is the—" he tried.

"She'll get plenty of rest," Mara assured him. "*I'll* make sure of that." She shooed him out the door, then unpacked books, a blanket, biscuits and the glass fox Tula had crafted for my birthday. Mara placed the fox on the table and bustled about with the other items. I studied the little guy. I'd never been able to achieve the same exquisite details with my animals. Those lifelike touches made Tula's statues sought by collectors.

"Leif sent Yelena a message to return. Healer Hayes is a dear, but you need her healing powers to fix that shoulder," Mara said.

"Mara—"

"I have given Zitora strict orders that you not be questioned unless I'm there."

"But—"

"And I've sent a message to Mother and Father. The more supporters you have around you the better."

I gaped at her as if she'd grown wings. "Wow, you *have* changed. You're more—"

"What?" She crossed her arms, waiting. She had pulled her long, curly hair into a bun, exposing more of her heart-shaped face.

"Bossy."

She sighed. "I had to be. You disappeared and no one would tell me what was going on. I badgered Zitora until she caved. But then she still only gave me vague snippets of information." Frustration laced her voice. She paced in the small room. "I wanted to help you, but I didn't know where you were." Mara halted and glared at me. "It was a nightmare for me, a repeat of when Tula was kidnapped. I didn't want to stand around waiting to be told you had died, but I was forced to. Just like with Tula."

The truth of her words hit me. I had been so focused on finding Ulrick, I hadn't even thought about her. "I'm sorry I caused you so much grief. It was very inconsiderate. But you shouldn't have bothered Yelena, and this is the busy season for Mother and Father."

"Nonsense. Strength in numbers, my dear." And just like that she forgave me.

She settled on the single chair by my bedside, wriggling into a comfortable position. Her intention to stay clear, Mara laid a warm hand on my forehead. "No fever for now. Good. Go to sleep, Opal. I'll be here to watch over you."

My protest died on my lips. When Tula had been recovering from Ferde's assault, Mara had stayed home to work in the factory with our brother, Ahir, while I was whisked to the Citadel by Master Jewelrose. Yelena had wanted my help in "waking" Tula. Her trauma had been so severe, her mind had retreated to a fond memory. With Yelena, I traveled through her thoughts and convinced her to return to consciousness.

Tula and I had always been close. Being about eighteen months apart in age, we had been inseparable. We either idolized Mara or were jealous of her. She was the oldest and could do no wrong, acting more like a mother than a sibling. Her beauty and the constant flock of admirers didn't help our feelings. Our brother received attention because he was the baby.

As I drifted to sleep, I realized Tula and my actions growing up had isolated Mara. I promised I would try to rectify the relationship.

Janco's complaints woke me. "'Bout time. I've been here for an hour."

I cracked an eye open. Janco lounged in the chair with his feet propped on my bed.

"Can't leave you for one night." He tsked. "Shot by friendly fire. It sucks to be you."

"How nice of you to spare my feelings. Any other little joyful nuggets you care to comment on?"

"Sheesh, you're grumpy in the morning." He sulked. "Where's Mara?"

"Probably sleeping. I gave the poor woman a break—she's been here for two days straight."

Two days already. I rolled my shoulder—all I could do with my left arm wrapped tight to my body. Darts of pain radiated.

"I don't blame her for wanting to stay with you. That was a heck of a homecoming even for the Creepy Keepy." He brightened a bit. "But she trusts me. She wouldn't let anyone else stay with you."

"She's being a bit overprotective," I said.

"With good reason. Leif's been running interference for you, but the Council demanded you report to them tomorrow." He dropped his feet and sat up. Wincing, he rubbed his side. "Yelena's here already. We had an early workout, but she's planning on seeing you later this morning."

My stomach flipped with mixed emotions. Happy Yelena had arrived and terrified about the Council session.

Healer Hayes entered the room and shooed Janco out so he could change my bandage. He frowned and hemmed as he worked.

"What's wrong?" I asked him.

"It's healing. But it's slow." His lips pressed together as if he chewed on a thought. "You need to know why."

My heart beat a faster rhythm. The news had to be bad. I waited as he struggled to find the right words.

"I couldn't use magic to heal you," he said.

"Why not?"

"The Masters have erected a null shield around you. No one can work magic through a shield, so your shoulder will have to heal on its own. Sorry."

I didn't have the energy to be upset. It wasn't a surprise. It felt more like a betrayal. I've been living in the Keep for five years, working with the Masters on various projects and risking my life. Couldn't they even give me the benefit of the doubt?

"And sorry about this." Hayes sliced my bound arm free.

Pain exploded as the weight of my arm dragged on my shoulder. He worked fast and placed my elbow into a sling, but not fast enough to prevent tears from flooding my vision.

He brushed my hair from my eyes when he finished. "How about some good news?" He smiled. "You can go back to your own quarters this afternoon."

I worried when Yelena didn't visit, but, as promised, Hayes discharged me. My return to my own quarters should have been a relief, except for my entourage. Two guards, Mara and Janco followed me to my rooms.

Mara fussed about, opened the shutters, changed the linens and dusted. Janco sat on the couch and muttered about the audacity of the guards who remained outside my door.

The apprentice quarters were all identical a bedroom and living area with a stone hearth. One simple armchair and small couch faced the fireplace on the left side of the room. A wooden table and two chairs occupied the right side of the room, and the bedroom contained a single bed, an armoire and a desk.

"Where are my saddlebags?" I asked Mara.

She stopped for a moment as if deciding. "Confiscated along with your cloak. Sorry, I tried to reason with them."

I fumed silently and it was a respite when Mara and Janco finally left. Pacing my rooms, I wanted to... What? My shoulder throbbed. I couldn't work with glass. Zitora hadn't visited me. I'd been ordered to remain in my quarters until my hearing tomorrow.

The Council session would be my chance to prove myself. I rummaged around my desk for parchment and ink. Good thing I wrote with my right hand. Sitting, I detailed everything that had happened, including conversations. Tama Moon's hypothetical situation of using my talents as leverage didn't seem so wrong to me now.

Reviewing the talk with Tama, I realized the actions of the Master Magicians were extreme. If they didn't know about my ability to siphon magic, then why would Zitora and Irys bring an armed guard with them to the glass shop? Why did they have a null shield around me? Because they knew. And there was only one logical person who could have told them. Councilor Tama Moon.

After a sleepless night caused by worry—where was Yelena?—and pain—the whole left side of my body ached—I reported to the Council as instructed, entering the cavernous great hall in the Council Building. I apologized to the eleven Council members and three Master Magicians for not following a direct order. I attempted to explain my actions, but from their hostility, I knew they had formed their own conclusions and nothing I said would change their minds.

I expected the harsh reprimand. I expected the fear and the comments on my character or lack thereof. I anticipated the disbelief about the Warpers and the blood magic.

What I failed to expect was Zitora and Yelena's silence, and Councilor Tama Moon's ruthless undermining of my credibility.

Tama claimed, "Ulrick was working undercover to infiltrate the illegal operations on the northern ice sheet. And to save the Stormdancer." Her voice resonated with authority in the vast room. "Opal was unaware of this, so her reactions to Ulrick's cover story would be genuine. Unfortunately, he played his role too well, and she is unable to believe the real story."

As the silence in the great hall thickened until it clung to my sweaty skin like syrup, I glanced at Yelena and Zitora, appealing to them to correct Tama, to leap to my defense, to do…something. Anything.

Zitora stood. "Councilor Moon speaks the truth."

EVERY SINGLE PART of my body reacted as if I had been doused by the ice-cold runoff from the Emerald Mountains. Blindsided and ambushed, I sat in front of the Councilors and Masters unable to speak or even draw a breath.

"I'm sorry to have put you through that." Zitora spoke to me for the first time since I was shot by the arrow. "But it was vital to the mission." She turned to the Council. "Opal's determination to help Ulrick, even though he didn't need it, should be noted in her favor."

The atmosphere in the great hall changed. A sense of relief permeated the air as the Councilors nodded and gave me sympathetic looks as if to say the poor dear had no clue, no wonder she disobeyed our orders to return. Their belief that all the Warpers were dead had been restored, and the whole nonsense about blood magic and switching souls had been explained away as a mere cover story.

Somewhat recovered, I opened my mouth to protest, but an invisible hand snapped my jaw shut. Yelena's gaze met mine. With a slight shake of her head, she warned me to keep quiet. The force on my teeth released.

The Council launched a battery of questions about my new magical ability to siphon magic from another magician. I answered, but realized the outcome no longer rested in my hands. A bigger conspiracy lurked behind this meeting. I would either be told or not, and I ceased to care. I knew the real story and no matter what happened here or how long it took, I vowed to expose Devlen and put a stop to blood magic.

The debate raged around me, but I tuned them out. Instead, I focused on my surroundings. The great hall's narrow windows stretched to the ceiling three stories above my head. Sunlight striped the marble floor and the Councilor's U-shaped table, casting Councilors Greenblade's and Zaltana's faces in shadow. Five Council members sat along one long section of the U-shape while the remaining four Councilors lined the other side. Yelena and the three Master Magicians occupied the short end.

I studied the long silk tapestries hanging between the hall's windows. One for each clan, and I noted with pride the representation of an intricate glass vase on my clan's banner. My hometown of Booruby was famous for glassmaking.

Shifting my position, I tried to find a comfortable spot on the hard wooden stool set before the Councilor's table. Two guards kept close watch. The wooden benches along the marble walls remained empty. The public, including Mara and Leif, had been barred from attending this session and since my parents would not arrive in time—my mother refused to ride a horse—they decided to wait to hear the Council's decision and make plans then. Janco had been sent back to Ixia. His grumpy goodbye had come with an offer to return if I needed him whether the Councilors wanted him or not.

Yelena's voice slashed through my numbness. "You can't ban her from working with glass. Who will craft more messengers?"

Good to know Yelena remained on my side. Unlike Zitora, who wouldn't meet my gaze. The words *null shield* and *supervised* caught my attention, but otherwise I allowed the conversation to flow. In my mind, I replayed my last time with Kade, remembering his kiss and the feel of his strong hands on my back.

Many horrible things had happened to me, except Kade. He was worth enduring for. I could bow to the Council's wishes, play the obedient student and pretend I had been duped by Ulrick's undercover story to gain trust and freedom. And real answers. The Council would know the truth eventually.

Yelena's approval pulsed in my chest.

"...and let's not forget the diamonds, Councilor Krystal," Councilor Jewelrose said. "We wouldn't have to rely on imports from Ixia anymore."

"Only at the cost of a magician's power, which is too high," Krystal replied.

"We don't know if she has to take all their magic. We could experiment—"

"Absolutely not! Remember what happened to Pazia Cloud Mist…"

Again I ceased to listen to the debate. The strips of sunlight moved across the floor and climbed the opposite wall. When the light faded into a gray semigloom, the Council adjourned for the day. I was escorted to the holding cells in the basement of the Council Building. I laughed when they served me dinner. What else could I do? Cry? Scream? Rage against the injustice? No point. The reason for my humor was the wooden cup filled with water. No glass. No magic. No need to put me in the Keep's special cells.

I tried not to compare this cell with all the others I had been in. Or with all the times I had been confined by ropes or chains. But my mind refused to obey me. My memories drifted back to when Alea had kidnapped me to get to Yelena. The Daviian wanted me to trick Yelena, so she used a masked Warper to coerce me into helping her. It worked. I would have done anything to make him stop. Imagine my horrified surprise when Devlen explained he had been the man behind the mask.

Shuddering, I forced my thoughts on more pleasant memories to survive the night.

As the Council's discussions dragged on for days, I discovered one good thing about spending my evenings in the Council's jail. I learned who supported and believed me. Mara's encouragement hadn't surprised me, but Pazia's frequent visits did. She even testified on my behalf. A few of the glass-shop workers stopped to entertain me with tales of their efforts.

Zitora failed to visit and Yelena took her sweet time. She finally came by on the third day with Leif. I slid from my bunk, but she put her finger to her lips, then pointed to her ear.

Leif stared off in the distance for a moment. His short muscular build, square face and brown hair were the complete opposite of his sister. Striking green eyes were the only feature they had in common. "I blocked the snoops," he said. "So how's my favorite glass wizard?" he asked me.

"Peachy. I just *love* it here!" Sarcastic and bitter, I'd outdone myself. Of course, I regretted it as Leif jerked back like he'd been slapped. "Sorry," I said.

Leif glanced at his sister. "This isn't good for her. We should bust her out."

I snapped. "Why would you do that? According to the Council, I'm a danger to myself and others. I'm just a poor, deluded, brainless girl who believed in the impossible, who—"

"Opal, that's enough." Yelena's stern tone stopped my tirade. "I've talked to Kade and Janco. I believe you."

"Then why haven't you said—"

"Because we were outmaneuvered."

"But you would know Devlen is in Ulrick's body. Right?"

"I hope so."

"Hope?" Not the answer I wanted to hear.

"It's a unique situation, Opal, and there aren't any other Soulfinders around that I can ask."

True. "But you can vouch for me, testify that switching souls is possible?" The pained grimace answered my question.

"I can assure the Council of your integrity. Without Devlen or Ulrick here, I can't *swear* they switched. I know you're telling the truth, but the Council can argue that the men are very good actors and have tricked you." Yelena flicked her long black braid over her shoulder.

"Couldn't you read Zitora's mind and tell the Council she's lying?"

Leif made a strangled sound. "Accuse a Master Magician? Ho boy, you really need some fresh air."

Yelena frowned at him. "I can't read her mind. Her mental defenses are too strong for me. And if I rifled through Councilor Moon's memories, it would be a major breach of the Ethical Code and I would be arrested."

"What about reading their souls?" I asked.

An odd expression gripped Yelena's face before she covered it. "Zitora felt she did the right thing. As for Tama, ever since her sister tried to overthrow her, she has hired a magician to cast a protective null shield around her when she's in public." She fidgeted with her sleeve. "The other Councilors believe it's a wonderful idea and are in the process of doing the same. I have…mixed feelings about it."

"A null shield is becoming a weapon like Curare," Leif said. "Before the Warper battle, only the Sandseed Story Weavers knew how to create one. Now the knowledge is spreading." He shrugged. "It's smart to protect the Councilors from a magical attack, but, on the other hand, it can mask deceptions and be used against us."

I agreed with Leif. In order for Sir to capture Kade, the strongest Stormdancer in Sitia, a null shield had been intertwined with a net. Yelena knew all the details, but she decided the Council should only be told Kade had been neutralized by a null shield. No sense giving anyone ideas.

"However…" Gazing down at her hands, Yelena laced them together.

Not a good sign. I braced for the bad news.

"However, the diamonds found in your saddlebags are the real problem." She raised her head and leaned toward me. "You scare them more than I do."

I laughed. At this point, what else could I do? If I looked on the bright side, I finally had done something better than Yelena. The fact it would keep me locked up didn't stifle my manic mirth.

"Opal," Yelena warned. "This is serious. They're not picking on you. They have an excellent reason to be scared. Think about it from the Council's point of view. Your ability to transform magic into glass is concerning, but Master Magician Zitora vouches for you. Then you disappear and claim you were tricked by blood magic and kidnapped to Ixia. The Council is distressed, and orders you to return so they can hear the whole story, but you run off to Fulgor.

"Now they're alarmed. When Councilor Moon reports you have escaped and tells them about your new powers, they become frightened. Plus the fact you used the power without consulting them or without any due process. In their eyes, you have become unpredictable and unreliable. A rogue. Zitora can no longer vouch for you because if she didn't know about your siphoning power, what else doesn't she know. Why didn't you tell her?"

No longer able to keep still, I paced. "I thought it would be better in person. I wanted to discuss it with her first. But now she's avoiding me."

"She's keeping her distance in an effort to remain impartial."

"Swell."

"Opal, sarcasm will not help you," Leif said. "I know."

"Nothing *will* help me."

Yelena moved closer to the bars. "Tomorrow you *will* be honest, you *will* be remorseful, you *will* be respectful, and you *will* abide by the Council's decision no matter what. They need to see you are not a threat. They need to feel they can trust you."

"Would *you* do all that?"

"I already have. If I can earn their trust, so can you."

I slumped against the wall. My shoulder burned as fatigue settled over me. The task of gaining the Council's trust felt equal to being ordered to climb over the Emerald Mountains. Impossible.

"It's not impossible," Yelena said.

"Reading my mind?"

"No. Your posture."

"Now what?" I sank down to the floor. At least I had a clean cell. Amazing how the small things become important.

"We wait," Yelena said. "It's a trick I learned from Valek. Let them think we believe their story about Ulrick. Let them get comfortable and relax their defenses. All the while I'll keep an eye on them and, hopefully, discover what they're up to."

"What about me?" I gestured to the bars between us.

"I think the Councilors are leaning toward letting you continue your work for the magicians. If that's the case, you need to be on your best behavior, and you'll need to pretend Ulrick fooled you. You're not to tell *anyone* a different story, as they will have someone watching you."

"How long do I have to pretend?" I asked.

"It may be seasons. I need to return to Ixia to help Kade convince the Commander to allow him to tame the blizzards. Don't worry." She held her hand up. "I'll assign…someone to keep an eye on Councilor Moon and Devlen." She studied my face. "You've been through worse. Just hold on and we'll figure this one out."

She glanced at the main door, then turned to me as if she had made a decision. "Irys will have a fit, but it's cruel to let you suffer." Yelena crouched and reached through the bars, pressing her hand on my injury.

"What—ow!"

Her magic held me immobile. Pain flared, then dulled to a throb, changing into a bone-deep itch. She pulled away and closed her eyes. Blood spread on her shoulder, soaking her tunic.

The door to the cells flew open. Master Jewelrose sprinted into the room followed by a bunch of guards.

Without opening her eyes, Yelena said, "Wait."

Irys scowled, but kept quiet. When my mobility returned, I scratched my newly healed skin.

Yelena rolled her shoulders and met Irys's unhappy gaze. "Her wound was infected." Her statement sounded like a challenge.

My cell felt colder after they left. I wrapped a blanket around my shoulders—part of a huge care package Mara had brought me. The whole Council session, being locked in a cell, the lies and backroom dealings had left a rancid taste in my mouth. I had trusted the Council, had believed Zitora would defend me, not betray me. Not anymore. Time to stop wallowing in pity and act. Time to trust no one and stop relying on others.

I reviewed Tama Moon's comments about my glass messengers and leverage. Her advice didn't strike me quite the same way this time. Before I thought them selfish. Perhaps I needed to be a little more selfish. I would wait and bide my time as Yelena requested, but I would also prepare. I'd proved to Devlen I wasn't a doormat, and I would prove it to the Council, as well.

As Yelena had predicted, the Council released me with a number of conditions. I could craft my glass messengers, as long as another magician remained in the workshop. No experiments with my magic were allowed. I could leave the Magician's Keep if I had permission and a Council-approved escort. In other words, I continued to be a prisoner, but without the bars. They kept my glass bees, spiders and the diamonds in my saddlebags. They returned my cloak and bags.

At least I wouldn't be monitored by magic. With a null shield around me at all times, no magic could penetrate it. However, I would have escorts anytime I left my room. Swell.

The Council session had lasted six days. Yelena left for Ixia and said I should return to my studies. Except Zitora had taken me out of my classes so I could concentrate on the glass factory and experimenting with my powers.

It was the middle of the warming season. The Keep's current session would finish at the end of the heating season—approximately one hundred and fifty days away. The time loomed over me like a prison sentence. Would I be allowed to graduate?

One way to find out. I dressed in my usual glassmaking clothes—a pair of brown pants and a plain khaki short-sleeved tunic. I wrapped a leather belt around my waist so the end of my shirt wouldn't interfere with my work. Pulling on my worn leather boots, I smiled, remembering how they had filled with water when I tried to climb out on the sea rocks to talk to Kade.

After pulling my hair into a ponytail, I swung my cloak around my shoulders and paused. I wondered if the Council had inspected the garment before sending it back to me. Fingering the hem, I felt a line of odd-shaped bumps. Janco's habit of sewing lock picks into all his clothes had given me an idea. I had hidden a handful of my diamonds and my glass spiders in my cloak.

I debated removing them and hiding them in my rooms, but decided to keep them in place for now. Working up the nerve, I headed toward Zitora's office, ignoring the man shadowing me. Even though Zitora had avoided me throughout the Council's interrogation, she remained my mentor.

A few students hustled along the Keep's walkways. The cold morning air blew through the campus as if the temperature held no regard for the time of year. I entered the Keep's administration building and dodged the surprised and suspicious glances cast my way.

Zitora's office was located on the second floor. I raised my hand to knock on her door, but it swung open. First Magician Bain Bloodgood hustled out.

"Come, child, we have much to discuss." He linked his arm in mine and led me down the hallway at a fast pace.

I glanced back. Zitora's office door clicked shut. The

sound mimicked the tight feeling in my chest. When I almost stumbled on his navy robe, my attention returned to the First Magician.

"Master Bloodgood, why—"

"Not out here." He pushed open his door and ushered me into his office. All the Master Magicians had an office in the administration building.

The room smelled of parchment and ink. Bookshelves covered all the walls. He cleaned off a chair, adding more height to the mountains of files and texts on the floor.

"Sit down." Bain settled behind his desk. Small metal contraptions littered the surface and dark ink stained the wood. He peered at a slip of paper. "You have completed four years of course work, but your studies have been interrupted this year."

"I was helping—"

"In order for you to graduate, you need to finish the apprentice's curriculum."

"But Master Cowan said—"

"Opal." His voice warned me to keep quiet. "I'm well aware of your special arrangements with Zitora. However, she is no longer directing your education. I am." He handed me the paper. "You will start tomorrow morning."

I scanned the schedule of classes. Two in the morning, two in the afternoon and a session in the evenings with Master Bloodgood followed by one hour in the glass shop.

"Any questions?"

About a thousand, but I swallowed most of them. "Why isn't Master Cowan my mentor anymore?"

"She does not have enough experience to handle your... unique situation. Anything else?"

I tapped the paper on my leg. "I already attended Magical Ethics and Famous and Infamous Magicians Throughout History."

"Consider it a refresher."

His words stung like a hard slap on the wrist. I studied his expression, searching for the real reason. His gray eyes showed nothing but polite interest. A stark contrast to his wild hair. Of all the Master Magicians, Bloodgood, with his long, flowing robes and lack of concern over his personal grooming, matched my imagination for someone with a Master title.

"I will see you tomorrow evening." Bain dismissed me.

Remembering my promise to Yelena, I nodded and left. Without conscious thought I arrived at the glass shop, only to be stopped by a Keep's guard stationed next to the door.

"Sorry, miss, you're not allowed inside without a...companion," the man said. He fingered the hilt of his weapon and glanced about as if nervous.

Scared of me? I suppressed a laugh, knowing if I let it go, the humor would transform into sobs. "I'm not going to work with the glass. I just want to talk to my sister."

"Sorry. No." The young man puffed up his chest as if expecting a fight.

"Can you tell her I'm here?"

He deflated. "Er...I guess. Don't move." Opening the door, he leaned in and called for Mara, then resumed his position.

Mara hustled out. "For sand's sake, why don't you just come in? I have a vase on the rod."

"The General here won't let me." I pointed to the guard.

She balled her skirt in her fists, heating up to blast the poor man.

"It's not his fault," I said before she could let loose. "He's following orders. Can you stop by my rooms when you're done for the day?"

Aiming a tight nod at me, she returned to the glass shop. An afternoon without plans loomed. Freedom... sort of. After taking a few moments to decide, I walked toward the stable.

Quartz's delighted whinny banished the dark cloud around me. I tossed my cloak over a stall door and immersed myself in the simple pleasure of grooming her. When her coat gleamed, I hopped onto her back and practiced riding her without saddle, reins and bridle.

The midday sun warmed the air. We trotted in the training ring, doing figure eights. Remembering our close escape in Ognap, I steered her with my knees toward a series of low wooden barriers. Her muscles bunched under me as she skipped over the hurdles, landing with nary a bump. The next set of obstacles was two feet higher than the first.

Quartz flew over them with ease. I matched the rhythm of her gait, moving my body with hers. The power from her muscles soaked into me and I felt as if we no longer existed as two separate beings.

We turned to the last series of jumps. About six feet high, the four barriers seemed a mere nuisance to our heightened senses. We increased our pace and launched, landed, took four more strides, then another jump. Losing track of the time, we circled the ring until fatigue broke us apart and we returned to horse and rider. I dismounted and we walked a few more laps so she could cool down.

She matched my pace, her soft steps in the dirt the only sound. The Stable Master leaned on a fence post, watching us in silence.

Back at the stable, I rubbed her down as the Stable Master ran his hand along her legs, checking for hot spots.

"You found the zone," he said. "That state where you and Quartz united and became one. Makes up for all those hours of shoveling horse manure. Doesn't it?"

"Yes. Does it only happen when riding bareback?"

"Bareback helps. Physical contact is important. You can find the zone when using a saddle, but it's much harder." He fed Quartz a milk oat. "She's a good jumper with strong legs. You were flying over those expert hurdles after only a short warm-up." He scratched behind her ears and she closed her eyes with a grunt of bliss. "I was going to yell at you to stop, but it was fun seeing you take on those jumps."

When the Stable Master left, I returned Quartz to her stall. Empty of students, the stable's earthy scent and peaceful atmosphere beckoned, increasing my desire to find a hay bale and sit. But my past adventures had exposed all my weaknesses, so I searched for the Weapons Master.

I found Captain Marrok in the armory, sharpening swords. Waiting for him to finish, I examined the various weapons hanging on the walls and stacked on tables—an impressive collection. I fingered the hilt of a switchblade. My sais worked well for defense, but they couldn't be hidden. I needed a smaller offensive weapon.

"Hello, Opal! Welcome back," Marrok said. He sheathed the blade and set it into a bin. He had cropped his gray hair to a bristle. Tall and tanned like leather, he reminded me of a wooden practice sword—nicked, well-worn, yet still strong.

Marrok pulled off his gloves. "The rumors about you have been rather spectacular."

"And they're all true." I didn't want him to repeat them, preferring to remain ignorant.

He laughed. "Don't worry, I'm an old soldier. I don't believe anything unless I'm ordered to believe it."

"Good to know."

"What can I help you with?"

"I want to get back on a training schedule."

"With your sais?"

"With my sais, self-defense, knife fighting…" I swept my hand out. "Everything."

He whistled. "You might make a few people nervous."

"They're already nervous. Have you been ordered not to?"

"Nope. But you're going to have to dedicate a lot of time each day."

"How much?"

"You'll have to build up to at least four hours a day. Six would be better."

"Six, then."

He considered. "Don't you have classes?"

"In the afternoon. I'm free all morning." I would skip the two refresher classes Master Bloodgood assigned and deal with the consequences when they arrived.

"When do you want to start?"

"Now if possible."

I soaked in the hot water, letting my bruised muscles relax. Captain Marrok had started my session by sparring with me. No weapons, just hand-to-hand combat to gauge how much I knew. Not a lot, but not beyond hope, either.

Taking my time, I washed the horse hair, sweat and grime from my body, luxuriating in the Keep's bathhouse. When I finally returned to my rooms, Mara had already arrived.

We chatted about the glass shop for a while, but Mara sat on the edge of the couch, causing me to wonder why she couldn't relax.

"I received a message from Mother," Mara said.

A bite of annoyance nipped me. Since Mara moved to the Keep, I never received letters from our parents anymore, though a message meant my mother had used one of my glass animals through the magicians stationed in Sitia's major cities. With my encounter with the Council, my parents had gotten special permission to send messages via the relay station in Booruby. "And?"

"Well…" Mara fiddled with the hem on her shirt. "They're worried about you and want you to know you can come home anytime."

I could just imagine the look on my mother's face when she spotted my entourage trailing behind me. However, from my sister's discomfort, I knew there was more. I waited.

"They're planning to come for your graduation." Mara plucked at her sleeve. "Ahir is coming too."

"It will be great to see them," I said.

"Perhaps you can talk to Mother about…you know." She made a vague half wave with her hand.

"No. I don't know. Come on, Mara, what are you dancing around? You can tell me, we're sisters."

"Really?" She finally met my gaze. Ire pulled her lips taut. "So why do I have to hear about your…adventures from Leif? Why do you always change the subject when I ask what happened to you in Ixia?"

"It's difficult to talk about…Ulrick. Answer all the same questions." Weak. "Leif knows…" Weaker. I rubbed my shoulder. Even though the wound no longer remained, my muscles ached.

The real reason I avoided the subject with Mara became clear. I hadn't wanted her to believe I was a simpleton for falling for Devlen's lies.

"Mara." I held her hand. "I'm so sorry. I've been and am an idiot. The whole thing with Ulrick…I was such a fool."

She squeezed my fingers. "You were used. That bastard, tricking you and making you believe his lies. It's not your fault he played his role so well. If I ever see Ulrick again, I'm going to chop off a certain body part of his with Leif's machete!"

"Ulrick—"

"Should have told you he was on an undercover mission." Mara tsked.

I paused in shock. Yelena had made Leif and me promise not to tell the truth about Devlen and Ulrick to anybody, but I had thought he would be honest with my sister. I hoped to eventually confide in her, but I couldn't break my promise.

"At least you helped rescue the Stormdancer. I heard he was rather grateful. Did you two melt any snow?" She leaned back. All was forgiven.

I detailed my relationship with Kade for Mara, but

in the back of my mind I wondered what Yelena planned to tell him about the other situation. Would she confide our strategy to pretend I was fooled? Would he then doubt his feelings for me? Or would he instinctively see through the ruse? Either way, my desire to see him flared and simmered in my chest.

The next morning I arrived for my training session, pushing as far as possible without exhausting myself. My afternoon classes of Money Management and Societal Trends were more interesting than I expected. Concentrating on the topics helped me to ignore the rather pointed stares and gawks from my fellow students.

As graduating magicians, my class would be assigned positions throughout Sitia. We would be living on our own and earning an income for the first time.

I gained new insight during the lecture on message priority in the Societal Trends session with Professor Greenblade. The ability to send a message over long distances almost instantly created a new department in the Sitian government. A few of my classmates would be appointed to work the relay stations. The government was in the process of drafting a series of protocols for those wanting to send a message to another town.

The Master Magicians and high-ranking officials, like Leif and Yelena, all had their own glass animals for communication. The Council members held priority status. Their messages were sent without question or delay. Business owners and the public wanted to use them, too. Their demands increased as knowledge of the relay stations spread throughout Sitia.

"More and more people will want access." Dax Greenblade's sea-green eyes scanned the students. "How will they put this new magic to use?"

"Family emergencies," Mary said. "Messages can be sent to family members to return home."

"Suppliers!" Steven said.

"Explain," Dax urged.

Steven pulled on the brown hairs growing from the bottom of his chin. "A person could order supplies through the relay stations instead of traveling to another city to buy them."

"Or," Chelsi said, "factories could collect orders first before manufacturing goods." Her curls bounced with her enthusiasm.

"Criminals could be caught faster," Rebekah said. "Information about them could be sent to all the towns and all the guards could be searching for them."

"Already happening." The words slipped from my lips without thought.

She spun on me. "How do you know? You just make them. You don't decide what the Council does with them."

Dax answered for me. "For special circumstances, the stations are used for distributing information. However, that could become the norm for all criminals."

He continued with a list of other possible uses, but

my mind had snagged on Rebekah's comment for two reasons. One, the students didn't know about my defying the Council's order. Amazing, considering how fast gossip and speculation shot through the Keep's campus.

And Rebekah made an excellent point. I wasn't involved with the decision-making process for how to use my glass messengers. Why not? A faint memory of Zitora mentioning the committee rose to the surface of my mind. At the time, I had no interest in being a part of it, trusting the Council to decide. Another mistake.

Dax's voice interrupted my musings. "Think about how these stations will affect society." He held up three long fingers. "Give me three changes we will see."

"They will eliminate the need for long-distance messengers," Steven said. "People will lose their jobs."

Chelsi agreed. "Less travel means the demand for horses will drop."

"But," Rebekah said, "the need for caravans will increase."

"Explain." Dax kept one finger raised.

"If it is easier and quicker to order goods, then more merchants will place orders for merchandise from factories all over Sitia and the items will need to be delivered."

"The demand for horses would increase then and all those out-of-work messengers can get employment from the caravan owners," Mary said.

"Good. Do you think the government should charge people to use the relay stations?" Dax asked.

The answer was unanimous.

"Of course," Steven said. "The stations cost money to run, and you have to pay the magician."

Another snagged thought. The stations didn't have to pay for the glass.

"You've all been focused on business and commerce. How do you think the stations will affect Sitians?" Dax asked.

Chelsi jumped in. "Arguments over priority. Some people always think their message is more important than everybody else's."

"Arguments over the cost. I'm sure someone will argue emergencies should be free," Mary said.

"I'd bet a few wealthy business owners would want their own station. Pay for all the costs so they could use them anytime they wanted."

"Ahhh.... Now you're thinking." Dax beamed at Rebekah. "Which creates another problem. Anyone?" When no one spoke, Dax looked at me. "Opal, you've been too quiet. What do you think will be the biggest problem?"

"Supply."

"Explain."

"As the uses for the glass...messengers increases, demand will increase. However, the supply is limited."

"Exactly!" Dax shouted.

He kept the debate going, but my mind filled with a horrible vision. I saw myself twenty years in the future, working at a huge glass factory. Workers crafted glass messengers and I made an endless circuit, blowing magic into each one, creating hundreds a day. Since society couldn't function without my glass messengers, I couldn't leave for fear I would be hurt or killed, and would spend the rest of my life imprisoned in the factory.

11

"OPAL?" Dax's soft voice held concern.

I glanced up. The other students had left. "Sorry." I grabbed my books and stood.

"I hope I didn't upset you."

"Not at all," I lied. "You just gave me a lot to think about."

"Good. You're in a unique position. You should be considering all the possibilities. This extends beyond the Keep and the Council."

His words haunted me throughout dinner. My future vision wouldn't dissipate no matter how hard I tried to focus on another topic or memory or my food. What would happen if I stopped making my glass now before it became ingrained in society?

Could the Council force me? Of course. All they needed to do was threaten harm to my family or Kade or threaten to invite Devlen to help change my mind.

Would the Council stoop to such measures? If they believed it was vital to society, I guessed they would.

I arrived at Master Bloodgood's office at the appointed hour. Worry gnawed on my ribs like a hungry tree leopard. He called me in before I even knocked.

"Please sit down." First Magician sat behind his desk, all traces of a friendly grandfather gone. He studied me as if I were prey. "How were your classes?"

I wouldn't play this game. Not anymore. "Master Bloodgood, please don't pretend. Do me the honor of acknowledging the fact you already know how my classes went and everything I did and said today." Suicide. I braced for his reply.

"Very well. What I do not know is why you skipped your morning classes."

"I already earned high marks for them. Saying I need a refresher is an insult to my intelligence. What is sorely lacking in my education is the ability to defend myself. My...ah...adventures in the field have taught me I need to improve my fighting and self-defense techniques." And picking locks.

"Are you saying you know better than *me?*"

"Yes, sir." Double suicide. Was that even possible?

The silence pressed on my skin, sending darts of fear through my chest. I resisted the urge to squirm under his scrutiny. To apologize. To beg his forgiveness.

"Good for you. I approve your new schedule."

I needed a few seconds to recover. Master Bloodgood didn't wait. He launched into a lecture about examin-

ing the past to predict the future. At the end, he assigned
me a research project.

"Go through the history books and search for any
mention of another glass magician."

An odd request, considering he knew more about
Sitian history than most history professors. "Wouldn't
you have remembered reading about one before?"

"Yes and no. If one was mentioned by name or by
direct reference, I would have remembered. However,
many times bits of information are scattered throughout and I do not think they are important because I do
not know enough about the subject. You have the experience, and will be able to pick up on those subtle
facts." He swept an arm out. "You're welcome to read
the books here or take them along. Make sure you are
careful with them. Many are very old."

"Yes, sir." I pulled a few dusty tomes from the shelves
and carried them back to my rooms before I reported
for my hour in the glass factory.

The magician assigned to "watch" me waited outside
the door with ill-concealed dislike etched into his large
forehead. He had been an apprentice when I started my
studies at the Keep. I couldn't remember his name and
he didn't bother to introduce himself.

"The null shield is down," he informed me in clipped
tones. "If you deviate from what you are supposed to do,
I will have it up in an instant."

"Do you know anything about glass blowing?" I
asked.

"Doesn't matter. I know about magic and am quite powerful. That is all I need to know."

Of all the people the Masters could have assigned, I had to get him. I stifled my frustration. "Okay, Skippy, let's get started. I only have an hour."

The thick, roaring warmth embraced me as I entered the shop. Hot smells of glass and the dusty scratch of sand filled my nose. Mara worked at a bench, shaping a bowl with Piecov assisting. A young novice heated the end of a blowpipe. Her hands left sweaty smudges on the metal.

Mara introduced Emilie as my new assistant. Emilie's blond hair clung to her neck and she shrank back when I extended my hand in greeting. Wonderful.

"Thank you for the consideration, Mara. But you know I'm quite able to work on my own. I'm sure Emilie has homework to do."

Before my sister could voice her protest, Emilie dashed out with hurried thanks. It was bad enough to have Skippy hovering; I wasn't going to endure the girl's frightened flutterings. Cranky? Who, me?

I pulled the blowpipe from the heater and blew through the pipe, checking to make sure nothing blocked it. The far end pulsed with reddish light. Hot glass only stuck to hot metal. I opened the kiln and gathered a slug of molten glass onto the pipe.

Using metal tweezers, I shaped the glass into a dog. When I reached the step where I should channel magic from the blanket of power and into the heart of the dog,

I skipped it. Instead, I cut in a jack line and cracked the dog off the pipe. He went into the annealing oven to slowly cool.

Magicians would know he lacked magic. The dog wouldn't glow with an inner fire, and they would see what everyone else saw when examining my sculptures. An ugly cocker spaniel.

Usually in an hour, I could make a dozen animals. This time, I ended up with five. None of them glowed with magic.

Skippy peered at me. His close-set brown eyes pinched together with suspicion. "I didn't feel you draw magic."

I shrugged. "I didn't. I've been surrounded by a null shield for the past ten days. Perhaps I'll be able to do it tomorrow."

When I reported my lack of usable glass messengers to Mara, she tapped a finger on her desk. As the glass-shop manager, she ordered supplies, scheduled workers and maintained the kiln.

"Every day I've been getting orders for more," she said. "The supply you left me is almost gone." Her voice remained neutral, yet a question lurked.

"I'll try again."

"If you need help just let me know. You have my *full* support."

We confused Skippy. He might be a powerful magician, but I suspected he lacked basic common sense.

He announced the return of the null shield with

sneering glee. I ignored him, returning to my rooms to delve into history for Master Bloodgood. The project intrigued me and I scanned for information about glass magic as well as diamond magic.

I wanted to explore the possibility of using diamonds in my glass messengers. They might be useful someday when I reached an understanding with the Council. Until then, I would keep it quiet.

After a week of going through the motions at the glass shop and not producing any usable glass, Master Bloodgood questioned me in his office.

"What is the problem, child?"

"The null shield." I flipped through an old book, seeking a reference.

"It should not be up when you are at the shop."

"It isn't."

"Hale has reported that you have not accessed the power source."

"Hale?" I thought. "Oh! Skippy."

"Opal." First Magician's voice sliced the air. "He is a magician and your elder. You must show him respect."

"I'll show him respect when he earns it." I marveled at my audacity. This refusal to back down and be a good little girl had bubbled from deep inside.

"Is he the reason you are not producing the messengers?"

"No. It's the null shield." The penetrating way Master Bloodgood looked at me sent warning vibrations along my spine. If he wanted, he could lift the null shield and read my mind. He could force me to craft my glass if the Council granted him permission. The Ethical Code didn't apply to convicted criminals.

"I see." A shrewd gleam shone in his eyes. "I will talk to the Council. However, if they agree, Hale might be assigned as your almost constant companion."

"He shouldn't hinder my work." An annoyance, but I could deal with his presence. One thing at a time. First the null shield.

The Council granted my request after a week-long debate. By this time, the shortage of glass messengers had reached a critical level. I increased my output and filled orders. Skippy and his friends, Junior and Buddy, took turns babysitting me.

At the beginning of the warm season, I invited Pazia to my rooms after my shift in the glass shop. Fifteen days had passed since I won my concession.

As soon as my door closed, she asked, "Why do you think babysitters are better than the null shield?"

"I'm hoping to outwit the babysitters."

"Good luck." She pulled her golden hair out of a ponytail, letting it cascade past her shoulders. Even dressed in stained work clothes, her slim waist and petite build were enhanced. She could wear a burlap sack and still have Piecov follow her around like a dog in heat.

"Tea?" I offered.

"Sure." She glanced around my living area. "You could use a few pretties to brighten up the place."

"I'm not allowed to have glass in here."

"Oh."

I placed a couple chunks of wood on the banked coals, prodding a fire to life for the teakettle.

"Mara would flip if she knew you had her coal." Pazia grinned. "How about you do my mathematical assignment and I won't rat you out?"

"Nice try. I'd rather endure Mara's lecture than do pages of equations."

"Me, too. I used to be able to get out of doing those assignments."

I poured the hot water into two mugs. "How?"

"Most of my instructors were weaker than me. I just convinced them they had seen my homework."

A reminder of how powerful she had been. She'd had the potential to be a Master Magician if it wasn't for me. I handed her a steaming mug.

"Don't start," she said, correctly reading my expression. "You defended yourself." She sipped her tea. "I'm sure you didn't invite me here to reminisce."

"No. We could only do that if we had good times together."

"Well, visiting you in jail was fun for me," Pazia teased.

"And saving you from those thugs at the jewelry store was fun for me," I countered.

"All right. Point taken."

We drank our tea in silence. I then asked her about her diamond-edged bowl. "Where did you get the idea?"

"The cobalt glass reminds me of sapphires and I love sapphires with diamonds. Blue and silver."

"Where did you get the diamonds?"

She shot me a shrewd look. "You're going someplace with this. Right?"

"Right."

"I bought them from Elita. And, yes, she's still in business. She helped to capture Mr. Lune, so was only slapped with a huge fine and probation for selling black-market diamonds."

"Could the diamonds give you a power boost?"

"From hardly anything to barely something?" Sarcasm rendered her voice sharp. She drew in a breath, held it and released it. "Sorry. At a quarter carat, the diamonds are too small to hold any usable power. Maybe if I had put carat-size or larger on the bowl, I could enhance my magic."

"How about if you put the diamond inside the glass?"

"Why would you do that?" The idea dismayed her.

I explained about the glass animals in Ognap with their ruby hearts.

"Odd. Most people who own jewels want to be able to touch them."

"I felt a vibration, but I thought that was just me." The animals had pulsed in my hand as if their hearts beat.

"It is you. *Normal* people feel a connection to the

stone. More an affection than an actual buzz. To encase it in glass would…frustrate me. I would never do it."

"I guess your father doesn't mind. The sculptures had Vasko certificates."

Pazia thumped her mug on the end table. "My father would *never* allow anyone to put his rubies in glass. Are you sure the certificates were genuine?"

"No. They could have been fakes. But how can your father control where his rubies go? Once he sells them, they could be resold without his knowledge."

A humorless smile spread on her face. "You'd be surprised how easy it is to get your way when you have a lot of money and power. My father has contracts with his sellers to ensure they are sold properly. He hires auditors and undercover investigators to keep track of them.

"Hell, he tracks his rubies from the moment they are mined. *No one* steals from Vasko. He probably already knows about the fake certificates, but I'd like to send my father a message just in case."

A reasonable request. "Sure. But before you go, do you think you could access magic from, say, a two-carat-charged diamond encased in glass?"

"I don't know. We could experiment."

"*You* could. *I'm* not allowed to experiment with glass."

Understanding lit her face. "Who is going to pay for the diamond?"

"Wait here." I retreated to my bedroom. Digging through the pockets of my cloak, I felt for an appropriate-size lump. When my fingers touched the smooth gem, an ice-cold pain pierced my hand. An image of Crafty filled my mind.

My arm turned numb as I rejoined Pazia. "Is this big enough?" I dropped the gem into her palm.

She pinched the diamond between her thumb and index finger. Holding it up to the firelight, she examined it. "It's already charged with magic." Awe filled her hushed voice. "Who's magic is this?"

"Doesn't matter. Keeping this quiet is all that matters right now."

"Why?"

"Just testing a theory."

"Opal…"

"It could be nothing. Just trust me on this."

"You will explain it to me sometime?"

"I promise."

"All right." She pocketed the diamond. "I'll let you know what happens." She walked to the door and paused. Grinning, she yanked it open. Skippy tumbled into my room, landing in a heap on the floor.

Pazia tsked and stepped over him. "How rude, listening through the keyhole. Have you forgotten already?"

He untangled his legs and stood. "Forgotten what?"

She rapped on the open door. "Thick mahogany wood to protect the students. Almost soundproof. I hope the splinters in your ear don't get infected." Pazia turned to go, but glanced over her shoulder. "I take that back. I do hope the splinters get infected."

* * *

I played the good little girl for another two weeks, then stopped making the messengers again. Called into Master Bloodgood's office, I explained how the constant surveillance of Skippy and his crew had distracted me.

"He listens at my door when I have company," I said. "I've no privacy. I'm sure after demonstrating my willingness to cooperate after a month and a half, the Council can relax. I'm in the Keep after all, surrounded by magicians."

With an amused half smile, Bain Bloodgood said he would present my...ah...request to the Council.

"Are you making any progress on your assignment?" he asked.

"No. I've gone through ten history books and haven't found anything." I couldn't be the only glass magician. Then again, I hadn't known about my powers until Yelena's visit, when she saw the inner glow in my sculptures. Perhaps another possessed the same ability, but hadn't realized the significance. "Master Bloodgood, I need to go to the market."

He studied my face. "You have an idea. Wonderful. Of course, Hale must accompany you."

"I'd be lonely without him."

The next day between my morning workout with the Weapons Master and my afternoon classes, I headed west toward the Citadel's market. Skippy trailed behind and I ignored his complaints about missing lunch.

Located dead center of the Citadel, the market was open every day until the hot season. Then it only opened one day a week. Many of the inhabitants left when the heat baked the Citadel's marble walls, turning the whole place into a giant oven.

Businesses and factories radiated from the market like rings around a target. The residences of the citizens occupied the northwest and southwest corners.

The buzz of vendors and shoppers reached me first. Turning a corner, I stepped into the energy-filled market. After living a rather quiet existence, the smells and shouts threatened to overwhelm me. I hovered on the edge, watching the flow of commerce.

Soon a member of the Helper's Guild appeared at my elbow. "Lovely lady, can I assist you today?" The young girl wore an eager expression. Her bright green sundress matched the color of her eyes.

"Yes. Can you please tell Fisk that Opal Cowan would like to speak to him?" I slipped her a copper.

Her demeanor stayed the same. "Master Fisk has trained me and I can help you as well as he can."

"I know, but I'm a friend of...Master Fisk's and I would like to talk with him." I stifled a giggle over calling Fisk master. At fifteen, he was five years younger than me, but he founded the Helper's Guild, creating jobs and income for poor and abandoned children. I reconsidered. The title of master suited him.

She told me to wait before disappearing into the crowd.

Skippy's loud sigh and tapping foot grated on my nerves. "You know she's not coming back. I'm sure Fisk has better things to do than chat with you."

His sneering tone almost caused me to kick him. Almost. I jabbed a finger at a smoking market stand. "Why don't you get a beef pie for lunch? My treat."

"No, thank you."

He reminded me of Pazia before she lost her powers. Cocky, snobbish and entitled. He hadn't experienced the ugly side of life where people deceive you and hurt you and lie to you. He would probably soil himself if threatened.

Fisk arrived and wrapped me in a bear hug. "Lovely Opal. It's been years!"

My reply was muffled by his broad chest. He laughed and released me.

"It's only been a few seasons. Although you've grown a foot taller and a foot wider since I last saw you!"

No longer a gangly young man, Fisk had filled out. Almost six feet tall, he gazed down at me. A few light brown hairs jutted from his square chin.

"Now you're exaggerating." He linked his arm in mine. "What can I do for you?"

"I need a book merchant. One who can uncover hard-to-find books."

"And she's in a hurry," Skippy said.

Fisk turned his attention to the magician, and I introduced them.

"I can hire you a better bodyguard," Fisk said. "One who is not so impatient."

"I'm not her bodyguard," Skippy said. "I'm her—"

"Babysitter." I supplied. "The Council worries I might cause trouble."

Skippy's face reddened.

Fisk laughed with a deep chuckle. "I wouldn't use the word *might*. More like when."

I punched him on the arm. "You're not helping my reputation."

"From the rumors I've been hearing, your reputation is beyond help."

"What have you been hearing?" I asked.

Fisk slid his gaze toward Skippy, then waved a hand in the air. "Oh, you know. The standard gossip. Now, let me show you to Alethea's. She's the best book finder in Sitia."

Alethea proved to be knowledgeable and promised to hunt down books about glassmakers throughout history. While we browsed Alethea's shop, two kids burst through the door. They argued about a silver coin one of them had lost. Just as they passed Skippy, they came to blows, knocking into the magician.

Fisk drew me into a back room. "That should keep him occupied for a moment. What's going on?"

"It would take me days to fill you in."

"I can distract your companion long enough for you to escape."

"Another time that would be great."

"How can I help?"

"I would like to purchase a set of lock picks without Skippy knowing about it." I handed Fisk a gold coin.

"Too much." He dug for change.

"Keep it. I also would like a switchblade. The Weapons Master believes they're the tool of dishonorable thieves."

"And you don't agree?"

"No. I lean more toward the vital-to-my-survival type of tool."

"There will still be plenty of money left over."

"That's for when I'm at the market with my babysitter, and I do this." I pulled my hair into a ponytail.

"My signal for a distraction?"

"Yes."

His light brown eyes sparked. "My favorite kind of job. Haggling for housewares has lost its appeal."

"I'm surprised Yelena hasn't recruited you for her missions," I joked.

"Who says she hasn't?" He winked.

Skippy barged into the back room. "What's going on?"

"We're looking at the books." I swept my arm to indicate the shelves.

"Didn't you hear the fight? Why didn't you help?" The short black hair on his left side stuck up and dirt stained his gray pants.

"Help a powerful magician like you?" I asked, all innocence and wide-eyed. "Why, I'd just get in the way." I breezed past him and called goodbye to Alethea. "Send me a message if you find anything."

Fisk left to assist his other clients and I led Skippy back to the Keep.

* * *

For the next two weeks, I trained an extra hour with my sais each night instead of making my glass messengers. According to Master Bloodgood, the Council wasn't pleased with my new...request. He warned the discussion had turned ugly at one point and a few Councilors wanted to force my cooperation.

"How?" I asked.

"You do not seem surprised. You have already considered this possibility." He leaned back in his chair. "Your sister lives and works at the Keep. She would be the most logical target."

"They threatened to harm her?" I grabbed my chair arms to keep from jumping to my feet.

"No. But they can consider firing and evicting her. See if that is enough."

"They'll risk upsetting Leif."

"A calculated risk."

"Is this official?" I asked.

"Not yet, but I would suggest you meet them halfway. How about a reduction in the number of hours you are watched when you are in the Keep?"

"That would work. For now."

He tapped a finger on his long nose. "You have a plan. I take it this will not end here?"

"I'm sorry, Master Bloodgood. I didn't mean for you to be caught in the middle."

"Nonsense, child. I applaud your efforts to stand up for yourself. Just watch you do not get too greedy or too stubborn."

"Yes, sir."

He dismissed me. Before I left, I pulled a few more texts from his shelves. I searched for history books reporting on the more mundane aspects of life instead of those focusing on the magical marvels.

With my arms full, I negotiated past his office door and down the empty hall. Most of the administration workers were gone for the day. Only a few industrious souls and the Master Magicians remained.

The musty smell of mold and dust emanated from the stack I held. I sneezed and almost dropped the pile onto the floor. Sitting down, I shuffled the volumes to build a steadier heap.

As I worked, familiar voices reached me. Zitora's office was nearby. Her murmur reminded me of the time I had fallen asleep while she lectured me on diplomatic negotiations. I inched closer. Skippy waited for me in the lobby downstairs.

A man's garbled voice answered her. I put the books down and scooted next to the doorknob. The conversation continued without interruption. She had to know I crouched outside her door. No one could sneak up on a Master Magician.

Perhaps she didn't care. Or she felt the topic of their discussion was safe for me to overhear. Perhaps she wanted me to listen. Yeah, right. I guess if I convinced myself she wanted me to eavesdrop, it would make me a better person than Skippy.

I collected my books and stood. Pathetic. I wouldn't stoop to underhanded spying.

"...Ulrick...convinced her...Devlen...poor girl," Zitora's muffled voice said. "She could use...under-standing..."

I couldn't move. She talked about me. Even muffled, her words still stabbed me.

"...do all...I can...help," was the reply.

I recognized the man's voice and staggered. My stack of books tipped over as I tried to catch my balance. They crashed to the hard tile floor as I slipped and fell. Together we caused a smashing sound to echo down the empty hallway. Loud enough to draw Zitora and her visitor from her office.

12

AT THAT INSTANT, I wished I could turn gray and melt into the grout on the floor. But no such luck. Zitora and Kade peered down at me. She showed no surprise. Kade, on the other hand, lit up as if I was an unexpected gift.

He knelt next to me and gathered me in his arms. "Are you all right?"

I pushed him away. I hadn't seen him in three months and the first thing he did was go to Zitora's office.

"Don't let me interrupt your *important* meeting with Master Cowan," I said. I stood and wiped imaginary dirt off my pants. Stacking the books, I hefted them in my arms.

"We were just finishing," Zitora said. "I'll leave you two alone."

"That's what you do best," I said, "leave."

"Opal," she warned.

"What? Are you going to punish me for my insolence? I hope you're creative about it. As far as bad things, there's not much left that I haven't already endured."

She exchanged a glance with Kade. One of those see-what-I-mean type of looks, before retreating to her office.

I continued down the hall without bothering to see if Kade followed or not. Bad enough he stopped to see her first, but to fall for her lies about Ulrick...

Kade fell into step beside me. "Did it ever occur to you I was on my way to see you in Master Bloodgood's office when Zitora stopped me?"

I slowed.

"I thought not."

"But she was telling you about Ulrick and—"

He squeezed my arm. "Yes, I know all about it. *Yelena* told me in Ixia."

I had forgotten she went to the Commander's Castle. She believed me and Kade knew the true story.

I stopped. "I'm sorry."

Even in the flickering lantern light, Kade's brown hair shone with yellow, gold and red highlights. His hair had grown past his shoulders. The ends curled slightly.

He cupped my face in his hands. "You're forgiven."

Pulling me toward him, he kissed me. The books in my arms prevented us from doing more.

"Here, let me help." Kade grabbed a handful of texts.

When we reached the lobby, Skippy trailed us. Kade stiffened.

"He's my babysitter," I explained.

"At least you're not in a cell."

"True. And I'm not surrounded by a null shield."

The details of my negotiations made him laugh. "I guess Yelena didn't tell me everything." He gave me a pointed stare. "You've changed. We'll have to catch up back in your quarters."

No eavesdroppers there, but Skippy or one of his pals would be hanging around. However, once we arrived at the door to my rooms, Kade turned to Skippy and told him to go home.

"I'll keep Opal safe tonight," Kade said.

"I have my orders." Skippy crossed his arms. "Unless you're a Councilor or a Master Magician, I'm in charge."

"Skippy's a *powerful* magician," I said.

"Really?" Kade acted impressed. "Can he block a force-eight gale?"

"I'm sure he can. Show him, Skippy." I gestured.

"My name is Hale. Stop calling me Skippy or I'll have you arrested. Would you rather spend the night in the Keep's cells instead of your boyfriend's arms?"

"You're bluffing," I said.

"Try me."

"Skippy can only have me arrested if I use my glass magic."

The magician kept his temper, but he must have pulled power because Kade responded with a restless breeze.

"I'm staying," Skippy said.

Kade touched my arm, cutting off my reply. "Fine.

But you can watch the door from over there." He pointed across the courtyard.

A whoosh of air hit Skippy, pushing him backward. His clothes flapped and dirt swirled around as he fought against the narrow wind. The nearby trees and bushes hardly moved. The wind forced him to the spot Kade had indicated and died. When Skippy tried to walk closer, the blast hit him again. He glowered at us, but stayed put.

"Interesting. What do you call that?" I asked.

"Technically it's a microburst, but if anyone official asks, he was caught by an errant wind. The poor guy." Kade tsked. "It came from nowhere."

We entered my quarters. I lit the lanterns while Kade stirred a fire to life. Evenings during the warm season tended to be chilly. Although... I watched Kade as he added logs to the flames. The flickering soft light illuminated his long eyelashes. He kept his mustache and thin anchor-shaped goatee with its line of hair growing along his strong chin. He wore a tan tunic and dark brown pants tucked into calf-high boots. Scuffs and stains marked the leather; he would need a new pair soon.

Kade tossed more firewood until the hearth blazed with heat.

I stopped him from adding another log. "It's hot enough."

"I'm making sure you're not cold. I know how much you hate it." Kade wiped the sawdust from his hands and stood.

As he was five inches taller than me, I gazed up at him.

"I had other ideas about keeping warm." I leaned into him.

"Blankets?" he asked, feigning ignorance.

I unbuttoned his tunic.

"Sweaters?"

I removed his shirt and ran my hands down his shoulders and around his back. Hard muscles clung to his lean frame. Too lean. He had lost weight.

"A hot bath?" He yanked at my clothes.

My fingers sought his waistband. In a matter of seconds, our clothes piled onto the floor. I drew him close. Skin against skin, igniting desire and hunger. Everyone had been so cold and distant. I needed him, wanted to join him inside his skin.

We kissed, sinking to the ground until we were prone.

"Any more guesses?" I asked.

"No." He covered my body with his. Between kisses he said, "*I'll* keep you warm."

Sparks of heat raced through my blood, and fire burned in my heart as Kade kept his promise.

I didn't want to move. But when the fire died down and the cold floor sucked our remaining warmth, we transferred to the couch. Wrapping a blanket around us, we nestled together.

"What's been going on?" Kade asked.

"You said Yelena told you."

"She told me the facts, but not how *you* were dealing with it."

I searched his gaze. "Facts?"

"I believe you."

I sagged against him as pure relief melted my muscles. If he had doubted me, I would have shattered. "You're the only one."

"Yelena and Leif—"

"Want to believe me, but aren't one-hundred-percent certain."

"But can't she read your mind?"

"Yes, but if I've been fooled to think Devlen stole Ulrick's body, then my memories are true."

Comprehension smoothed his face. "Zitora claims the trauma of being tricked has made you cling to Ulrick's story, but she said you were slowly getting over it and I should encourage you to put it all behind you."

I huffed with derision.

"Opal, she stressed how important it is for you to move on. I think she's worried you're still in danger."

"In danger of what?"

"Of being locked up for your own good. Or if you press the matter, perhaps those who are part of the larger conspiracy will decide to silence you."

A shiver raced along my skin. Kade pulled the blanket over my shoulder.

"You need a hot cup of tea. Let me get—"

"No. Stay." I clutched his arm.

"Yes, sir." He settled back on the couch.

"Don't worry about me. I'm cooperating. Even Mara thinks I've been duped." I remembered my stall tactics for more freedom. "Well, I'm being good enough. I haven't said anything about blood magic."

Kade raised an eyebrow. "Good enough? What about the extra hours of training? The negotiations with the Council? Didn't Yelena advise you to cooperate fully? What happened to your determination to abide by the Council's decisions?"

"I would have been more obedient if they played fair."

"Life is rarely fair."

By Kade's wistful tone, I knew he meant his sister Kaya. She had been killed when an orb shattered while she danced. The Stormdancer orbs had been sabotaged, rendering them too brittle to hold the storm's energy.

"I know that *now*," I said. "Parents teach their children to share, to play fair, to be honest. But...surprise! Life isn't fair. And it takes a while to transition from the childhood lies to the adult reality. I probably clung to the part of me that still expected fairness longer than most."

Kade considered for a moment. "Zitora was right about you."

"Don't believe her, Kade. I don't trust her or the Council."

"She's a Master Magician—"

"So what! Roze Featherstone was a Master Magician and she unleashed a Fire Warper on Sitia. Her rationale was twisted. She convinced herself her actions

were best for Sitia. Even at the end she believed." My
stomach churned, remembering Roze's corrupted soul
as it passed through me and into her glass prison.

"You don't think Zitora is trying to protect you?"

"No. I think she's trying to protect herself."

Kade remained silent for a few heartbeats. "My
mother taught me to think the best of someone until all
the evidence was collected."

A fancy way of saying don't jump to conclusions. But
it wasn't a jump when Zitora supported Councilor
Moon's claims. It was evidence. "Parents do their
children a grave disservice, protecting them from the
truth and raising them in a fairy world of fairness and
lies."

Kade moved back and studied my expression. "You
weren't this bitter when we were locked in that store-
room on the northern ice sheet. Tricked and tortured,
yet you remained optimistic."

"Optimistic? I told you to kill me along with Sir and
his gang. How is that optimistic?"

"Maybe that's not the right word." His gaze swept the
room as if he searched for the proper inspiration. "You
still had…faith…trust in people despite the situation.
Who do you trust now?"

"Mara—"

"Besides family members."

I sorted through the people I knew. "I trust you and
Janco."

"A rather short list."

"Here's a longer list for you. Alea, Pazia, Tricky, Tal, Devlen, Ulrick, Gressa, Councilor Moon and Zitora."

"And they are...?"

"All the people who either lied, tricked or used me."

He remained quiet. Probably thinking of a counterpoint, but I didn't want to discuss it anymore. Kade was here. With me. Yet I still grasped his arm as if I clung to a rock while waves tried to knock me off. I relaxed my grip and wrapped my arms about his torso.

"You lost weight. Didn't they feed you in Ixia?" I asked.

"The Commander was very generous, but I ate most of my meals with Yelena. Seeing her pick through her food as if everything contained poison, I lost my appetite. Plus, I was worried about you."

Before he could change the subject back to me, I asked him, "What did the Commander decide about the blizzards? Is he going to let you dance in them?"

"The Commander is rather stubborn about magic. I had planned to stay on the ice sheet to calm the storms until the warming season, but Janco's partner, Ari, arrested me and escorted me to the Commander's castle."

"But a cell can't hold you!"

"If it's strong enough it can, but, even though Ari is built like a tank with curly hair, he couldn't hold me without a null shield. I could have escaped at any time. But I cooperated with him. No sense angering the Commander. And I was treated like a guest when I arrived at his castle." He poked the fire. "He's intelligent and adamant. I wasn't able to convince him to allow a group of Stormdancers to harvest the blizzards next cold season, but he did agree to watch a demonstration."

"Did you impress him with your superior skills?"

Kade laughed. "I don't think Commander Ambrose is impressed by much. I didn't get a chance to show him. By the time he agreed to the demonstration, I needed to leave if I wanted to spend time with you before the heating season's storms."

"Getting the Commander's approval is more important than me," I said.

"I see your sense of self-worth hasn't changed."

I straightened, pulling away. "Those blizzards kill people every year. Saving people's lives versus spending time with me? Even if I was the Queen of Sitia, the choice is obvious."

"That's why I'm going to be on the northern ice sheet with the Commander during the first blizzard of the next cold season. It will be a more effective display than taming a warm-season thunderstorm. Also Commander Ambrose grew up in Military District 3 and knows by experience just how much damage they can do."

"Oh."

"See how you shouldn't jump to conclusions?" Smugness oozed from him.

"It wasn't a jump. More of a leap. No. A skip. Definitely a skip. No jumping involved."

"Really?" He doubted me.

"Yes. You don't know what a jump is."

"I don't?" Confusion replaced his dubiousness.

"Yes."

"Care to tell me?"

"No. I'll show you." I pounced on him, dragging him to the floor. Smothering his squawk with my lips, I pinned him under me. When I had regained my breath I said, "*That's* a jump."

"I'm still a little fuzzy on the definition." He snaked his arms around me. "Please continue your demonstration."

I pressed my body against him, but a nagging thought hovered. I wouldn't have been this bold before. Dismissing the notion, I turned my full attention to the man below me, certain he would agree that change, in this case, was for the better.

Sometime during the night we transferred to my narrow bed. I woke with Kade curled around me as the morning sun's rays shot through the cracks in the shutters. Groaning, I peeled the covers back and yanked at Kade's anchoring arm on my hip. But he wouldn't move.

"Blow it off," he muttered half-asleep.

"I can't. I'm in training. I'll skip my afternoon classes. Hell, I'll even skip lunch for you, but training is too important."

He lifted his arm. "Are you worried about being attacked?"

"Not at this moment, but I need to be able to defend myself just in case." I slipped out of bed. The cold air raised the hair on my arms and I quickly dressed in my training uniform—loose, comfortable gray pants and a white sleeveless tunic. The day would warm in a hurry. I brushed my hair, pulling it back into a ponytail.

Leaning on one elbow, Kade watched me. His tousled hair shone in the sunlight and his amber-colored gaze beckoned.

Tempted, I looked away. "Besides, the activity helps me burn off my frustration."

"There are other ways to…exercise."

I smiled over his word choice. "I don't want to hurt you."

"Thunder and lightning, girl! How much frustration do you have? I would think after last night…"

"It helped, but ignoring the snide remarks and slights from my fellow students, and suffering through the delicate and cautious way my teachers treat me every day, I need to punch something. I ruined one training bag already imagining Skippy's face on the black leather."

"That bad?"

"Imagine Raiden convinced you a storm was coming and you ran and told all the other Stormdancers to prepare for a big nasty blow. But they don't believe you. When Raiden shows up, he tells everyone he lied to you and you fell for it. Fell for it so hard you still think a big nasty is coming despite being told otherwise. How would the others treat you when you try to warn them?

How would you feel, knowing you're right but unable to prove it?" I gripped my arms, to stop from saying more.

This past season had been wasted time. Devlen and Ulrick could be anywhere by now, teaching blood magic to anyone. When the Council finally believed me, they might have a whole army of Warpers to deal with instead of a few.

"You have a good point." Kade threw back the rest of the blankets. "While you're busy, I'll go submit my official request to the Masters."

"Request?"

He paused on the edge of the bed. "I guess I should ask you first. You might want to stay here and train." He teased.

"Kade." A mock warning rumbled through my voice.

"We have about thirty days left until the next round of storms. Although they're milder than the cooling season's, the heating season has produced a few rogue nasties in the past. We don't have any orbs and we need to teach the new glassmakers how to make them all in the next month."

I understood. "And only one person knows the sand recipe for the orbs."

"You never told Zitora?"

"Didn't have time and now she avoids me."

"Then tell me. Not knowing worked when that group held me up on the ice sheet, but there is no reason to stay ignorant," Kade said.

"Forty percent—"

"Whisper it." He tapped his ear. "Just in case Skippy's nearby."

"Nice try, but I know you'll just grab me."

He feigned innocence, but I ignored him.

"Am I that predictable?" he asked.

"Like a hot-season thunderstorm."

Groaning, he flopped back on the bed. "It's too early in the morning for a weather analogy. Go." He shooed. "Tell me later when I'm awake enough to remember it."

I left my quarters, and when Skippy fell into step behind me, I didn't care. My thoughts dwelled on Kade and the possibility of leaving the Keep.

My opponent lunged, shot through my defenses and jabbed me in the solar plexus. I expelled all the air in my lungs in one harsh whoosh.

"You're dead. Third time today." Captain Marrok leaned on his wooden practice sword as if it were a cane.

Doubled over, I struggled to breathe. My sais grew heavier in my hands with every gasp.

"What's going on? You're better than this." He pointed at me with his sword. "Since I've been the Weapons Master, I haven't had a student work as hard as you or improve so much."

"Sorry..." I puffed. "I'm...distracted."

"Then get undistracted. You're not going to get a second chance in a real fight. Treat every practice bout as the real thing." He tossed the weapon down. "Go work with Sarn on self-defense tactics. Maybe that'll help you refocus."

I suppressed my groan. Sarn outweighed me by a hundred pounds. Thick barrels of muscle bulged from his arms, legs and chest. He was easy to outrun, but, if he clamped his oversize hands on me, my chances of winning went from slim to none. He wouldn't let go unless forced and he felt no pain. Muscles even covered his fingers. Who had muscular fingers? The man was a mutant.

The one sliver of brightness in working with Sarn was, if I broke free from him, I could get away from anyone. No success so far, but not for lack of trying.

"Hiya, Opal! You back for another session?" Sarn asked.

"I wouldn't miss it."

Unfazed by my grumbled reply, he grinned. "Great! What do you want to start with? Stranglehold? Choke hold? Ground pin? Armlock? Leg lock?"

"Such choices. You really know how to spoil a girl."

"You know me, the King of Smooth. There! I made you smile." He beamed as if he'd just passed a final exam.

Mutant he might be, but he was the nicest mutant I knew. However, all kind thoughts vanished when he wrapped his hands around my throat. My own fingers instinctively pulled at his before I remembered it would be a waste of time. With my hands free, a number of other moves remained.

I tried a palm strike to his chin. No effect. I used hammer fists down on the crook of his arms and then slammed my forearms up into his elbows. Nothing. My vision buzzed with white-and-black spots. Time almost up. I needed a weak spot within reach.

Without thought, I pressed my fingers and thumb into his right wrist. He dropped to his knees with a cry of pain. Confused at first, I stared at him as he yelled for me to stop.

Understanding what I had done, I let go and knelt next to him. "I'm so sorry. Are you all right?"

"Whoa. That was intense." He rubbed his wrist.

"I'm sorry, I shouldn't—"

"Don't apologize. I don't say sorry when I choke you." Sarn inspected his arm. "Wow, what a move. No bruising or anything. Can you teach me it?"

"No. I don't…" I stood. Bad enough that I had found one of Devlen's pressure points and used it to inflict pain, but the thought of teaching it to another sickened me. Horrified, I bolted to my quarters.

13

CURLED UP IN BED, I shook under the covers. Who was the mutant now? Me. All that time Devlen had tortured me to get his way, I had been learning, remembering the locations of all those horrid spots on the body. I instinctively knew where steady pressure would cause relentless pain. Pain so bad, I had agreed to do terrible things. And I'd used it on Sarn.

By the time Kade arrived, I had decided to stay under the blanket. Safe. No students. No teachers. No babysitters. No Devlen. No Ulrick. No Council. The list was quite long.

The bed creaked under his weight. "I'm guessing your training session didn't go well." He pulled at the blanket, but I held it. "Opal, talk to me. What happened?"

When I wouldn't let him remove the cover, he crawled underneath, worming his way next to me. His warmth seeped into my skin, calming the tremors. He said nothing for a while.

"I talked to Master Bloodgood," he said.

I tensed.

"Relax. I asked for permission to borrow you for a few weeks."

"What did he say?" I asked.

Encouraged by my reply, Kade wrapped an arm around my waist. "He said he would query the Council and the other Masters."

"Good luck with that. By the time they come to a decision the storm season will be over." Bitter and jaded. Who, me?

"I did stress the importance of a quick answer. Master Bloodgood seemed to think they would let you come with me. With concessions of course."

"Let me guess. Skippy has to come along and I have to make a hundred glass messengers before I can go."

"You're right." Surprise laced his voice. "How did you know?"

"Because I'm starting to think like them. I'm beginning to agree with them. I'm too dangerous. I can't be trusted. They should lock me up where I can't hurt anyone."

"Opal, what happened?"

"If I tell you, you'll be disgusted and leave."

"If your self-pitying behavior and being suffocated by the blanket hasn't driven me away, I doubt anything else would."

"I'm not indulging in self-pity." I scooted away and bumped against the wall.

"Then what are you doing?"

"Being realistic."

"I see. Well…actually, no, I don't. It's too dark under here to see."

"I know too much." I sighed. How best to explain? "Right now I can tell you the location of all those hidden glass prisons. I can find a pressure point on your body and cause you pain. And if I held an empty orb, I can drain you of all your powers. I can't…*un*know all this. Can't turn it off. And when forced into a desperate situation, I'm going to use this knowledge automatically and hurt someone."

"The trail of bodies in your wake is concerning," Kade said.

"I'm serious."

"So am I. All right, so you know the locations of the prisons. Why aren't you going around collecting them? Selling them off to the highest Daviian bidder? Don't answer. Just listen," Kade said. "You know where the pressure points are. Why aren't you using them on Skippy, threatening him with them? And why aren't you going around draining magicians of all their power? You'd be the richest person in Sitia with all those diamonds."

"Can I talk now?" I asked.

"No. I'm not done. You haven't done all those things because you know they're wrong. And yes, when forced into a desperate situation, you will defend yourself with the weapons available to you. Think about it. The reason your back's against the wall is due to someone attacking you. Not the other way around. Unless you've been picking fights?"

"I did grump at a dining-room server for spilling hot water on me."

"Did you knock her out with one of your sais? Clamp down on one of her pressure spots?"

"Point taken."

"Good. Can we pull the blanket off now? I'm dying under here."

I pushed the cover off and squinted in the bright light. Kade's hair clung to the sides of his sweaty face and hung in his eyes. Smoothing the loose strands behind his ear, I remembered when he had lectured me before.

We had been standing on The Cliffs and he encouraged me to have more self-confidence. At the time, saying I was an all-powerful glass magician had been a joke. Now, it seemed like a nightmare.

"Where did you go?" Kade asked.

"Back to The Cliffs when you said I was too young to understand."

He laughed, and I marveled at the way the gold flecks in his eyes sparked.

"I remember the situation being rather dire and here comes this…this twelve-year-old to save us. She looked as if a stiff breeze could knock her over. I thought we were sunk." He slapped his hand on his thigh. "Then I have to fish the girl from the sea. You resembled a drowned puppy."

"I'm twenty, and Nodin didn't warn me about the slippery rocks or the monster waves," I said.

He shook his head. "All hope was gone until you held Kaya's orb. Then you transformed before my eyes. When you have glass in your hands, you are confident and powerful. I knew then you would solve our problems."

"Is that when...let me see if I remember it right...I 'arrived in your life like an unwelcome hot-season squall'?" I asked.

"That line is golden. And you didn't melt." He tsked.

"Golden?"

"I'm a Stormdancer. The weather controls my life."

Before he could launch into more weather analogies, I said, "You didn't answer my question."

"I can't pinpoint an exact time, but when I heard you had been kidnapped by the traitor and his gang, I realized how much I cared for you."

"I thought you came to the inn because you were worried about your Stormdancers."

"I was. Tal had betrayed us. But the real reason was so I could see for myself that you were all right."

My thoughts returned to that night. After dinner I had gone to the stable to check on Quartz. Kade followed me. We were alone, and his actions seemed as if he wanted to say something important, but we had talked about grief over our dead sisters. If he had confessed his feelings, I wouldn't have gone with Ulrick, and Devlen wouldn't have used Ulrick to get to me.

A useless train of thought. Devlen would have gotten

to me regardless. His addiction to the blood magic would have driven him to find another way.

"How about you?" Kade ran his fingers along my arm. "When you handed me Kaya's orb."

"I thought you were overcome by the orb's song."

"I was, but when you knelt next to me in concern... There was an energy... A spark."

"Ah, yes." He inched closer. "Drove me crazy."

"Drove you away."

"Not anymore." He pulled me against him.

When Kade and I finally emerged from my rooms, the sun hovered above the horizon. I had missed my afternoon classes.

"Too late to go to the market?" Kade asked.

"Yes."

"Food then?"

"Yes. I'm starving."

After we ate, Kade tagged along as I reported for my riding lesson with the Stable Master. Quartz grazed in the pasture, but galloped to the fence as soon as she spotted me. Moonlight followed.

"Beautiful." Kade stroked Moonlight's neck. Named for the white moon on the all-black stallion's face, the Sandseed horse's gaze held intelligent curiosity.

"Figures," the Stable Master grumped at Kade.

"Excuse me?" Kade kept a neutral tone, but a breeze stirred.

I introduced him to the Stable Master.

He glanced at Moonlight snuffling Kade's shirt. "Stormdance Clan? Are you a—"

"Yes."

"Figures!" Scowling, the Stable Master fed the horses his special milk oats.

"Do you have a problem with Stormdancers?" Kade asked him in the same flat tone.

"No, son. I'm having a problem with this spoiled-rotten horse." He pointed a callused finger at Moonlight. "I tried to match him up with a few students, but he's bucked everyone off. I thought he might be waiting for that Ixian fella or that glass fella to come back."

"How do you know he won't buck Kade off?" I asked.

The Stable Master just looked at me as if I were an idiot. Moonlight let Kade scratch him behind the ears. His whole body leaned toward the Stormdancer.

"Oh. That's good then since we need to travel to The Cliffs and I wanted to ask you if we could borrow a horse."

"Ask! Glory be! Someone's actually gonna ask me this time?" The Stable Master clutched his heart. Then he disappeared into the barn and returned with a strange saddle. "Here." He thrust it into my hands. "I want you to try a jumping saddle on Quartz." He turned to Kade and hooked a thumb toward the stable. "If that brat of a horse allows you to saddle him, you can join us for practice jumps."

Quartz and I finished a series of hurdles when Kade and Moonlight joined us in the training ring.

The Stable Master swore. "Lousy spoiled horse.

Okay, let's see what you can do with him." He shouted instructions and put us through a grueling hour of jumping, trotting and turning maneuvers.

The horses' coats gleamed with sweat by the time he ended the session. I peeled the fabric of my tunic away from my skin to help dry off as Kade and I walked the horses to cool them down.

"Phew! I used to think riding a horse was easy," I said. "Watching a rider from the ground, it looks like the horse is doing all the work."

Kade agreed. "I rode for travel purposes only. This felt different. As if I had a connection...like riding a wave. If you align your body just right, you can ride a wave to shore. It's fun, but takes effort."

"I'd rather ride a horse than a wave." If Kade hadn't saved me, my first encounter with the sea would have been my last.

"Sounds like I need to teach you how to surf."

"How about I watch you from the beach?"

He laughed. "After the orbs are ready, I'll take you to Sunfire Cove. It has gentle waves and no rocks. I did promise you a day on the beach."

"It won't count."

"Why not?"

"You promised me a day of languishing in the sun. I imagined napping and relaxing and other activities that involve lying down. No surfing lessons and no Skippy."

He glanced at the fence. Our ever-present watchdog

peered at us. "He'll be outnumbered at The Cliffs. A little sandstorm should take care of him for a day."

A pleasant thought. "But he'll tell the Council and the small bit of trust I've gained would be lost."

We rubbed the horses down and made sure they both had fresh water and hay in their stalls. The Stable Master stopped by as we cleaned tack.

"You don't have much finesse with a horse, son. Practice and a good instructor should fix it. But I've a feeling you two are heading out soon?"

"As soon as we can," Kade said.

"Figures. Always rushing off!" He poked me in the shoulder. "I expect you to continue your training when you get back."

"Yes, sir."

Even though my tired arms ached, I needed to spend a couple hours in the glass shop crafting messengers. It would take me a few days to finish a hundred.

I introduced Kade to my sister. Mara sized him up with a lingering and suspicious gaze. "Is he the Storm-dancer you and Ulrick rescued?" she asked me as if he wasn't standing in front of her.

I cringed, but she didn't spare a glance for me.

"I owe *Opal* my life," Kade said.

"But not Ulrick? Did Ulrick fool you, too?" she asked.

"Mara—"

"Ulrick did not fool me." Kade's voice turned icy.

"Why didn't you tell Opal then?" Her tone flared into an accusation.

"Mara, that's enough!" Her hostility surprised me.

"No, it isn't." She fisted her skirt in her hands. "I want an answer. He let you believe that blood-magic story." She rounded on him. "Do you know she's been sulking in her rooms for the past two months? Avoiding her friends and family?"

She was right. I avoided her. I didn't want to lie to her.

"My sulking isn't Kade's fault," I said. "He tried to tell me. I didn't listen to him, either." More lies. Wonderful. "I'm not avoiding you. I've just been busy with my classes and training." Liar.

"But you have no trouble finding time for *him*."

She sounded jealous and hurt. I had wanted to be closer to her, but I did the opposite. "He needs me to help with the Stormdancer orbs."

"I need you too." Her soft voice filled with pain.

At that moment, I would rather be with Devlen than standing here. I would rather endure the agony of a pressure point than say what I had to say. "You don't need me, Mara. You have Leif and Mother's messages and the glass shop to run."

"Is that what you really believe?" Her words punctured my heart.

No! "Yes." I turned away. "I have work to do." Groping for a pontil iron, I managed to pick one up and gather a slug of molten glass despite the tremors in my arms. With single-minded determination, I worked on sculpting the glass and blowing magic inside.

I kept up a fast pace, concentrating on the glass. This used to be enjoyable, turning fire into ice. Not anymore. When I finally glanced up, Mara and Kade were gone. Only Skippy remained. After my little performance, Skippy was the only company I deserved.

I soaked in the bath until my skin wrinkled. Reluctant to leave the bathhouse, I lingered while changing and combing my hair. All those hours spent training in the sunlight had streaked the brown strands with gold, reminding me of Mara's curls. Guilt pierced my stomach. I would apologize to her for my harsh words when I resolved this mess. Perhaps I should write her a note explaining everything in case something happened to me.

Pessimistic thoughts. I really needed to escape the Keep. Walking through the campus, I searched for fond memories of my time here. The glass shop used to be a safe haven, the memorial garden rekindled my connection with the glass prisons and the student barracks reminded me of the lonely years I spent there. My fault for keeping everyone away, but no warm remembrances to grasp.

Skippy's shift had to be over because Junior followed me. A quiet man, he seemed intent on his duty and he kept his opinions of me and the situation to himself. I slowed, waiting for him to catch up.

He hesitated, swiping his black hair from his eyes. Confusion creased his thick eyebrows together. "Something wrong?" he asked.

"No. I..." What? "I wondered what you'd be doing if you didn't have to watch me."

"Oh." He blinked at me. "I'd be helping in the infirmary."

"You're a healer?"

"Not a strong one, but enough to help." He shrugged.

"Then why did they assign you to baby...er...guard me?"

"I can erect a null shield pretty fast. But I volunteered for this job."

"Why?" I asked in surprise.

He searched my face as if seeking a sign of sincerity, then glanced away. "Not everyone believes you're a danger. In fact, a few think the Council is being too harsh on you." He pulled at his sleeve. "I thought I could..." He smoothed his shirt. "Help out...be a counter to Hale." He fiddled with his cuff button. "Besides, if I wasn't here, I'd be assigned to guard a Councilor." He quirked a smile at me. "They're all worried about a magical attack."

"From me?"

"No. From anyone with magical powers. Councilor Moon has made them uneasy with her constant null shield. This—" he swept his hand out to indicate me and the campus "—is actually a much better task."

Interesting. And I didn't make it easy for him, either. "What's your name?"

"Jon."

We walked together to my quarters. I opened the door and invited Jon inside.

"No, thanks. You already have a guest." He smiled and crossed the courtyard, settling next to a tree.

I closed and locked the door. Kade lounged on the couch. A bright fire crackled in the hearth. I warmed my hands before joining him.

"I'm a horrible sister," I said. The flickering flames of the fire matched the pulse of regret in my chest.

"You had no choice." Kade wrapped an arm around my shoulders and pulled me close. "No worries, though. I told Mara everything."

I straightened. "You... But... The Council." Sagging back, I closed my eyes.

"*I* didn't promise to keep quiet. And I couldn't stand to see her suffer. Guess I have a soft spot for sisters." Grief touched his voice.

I glanced at him.

He gave me a lopsided smile. "Mara understands. Well... she's a bit furious about not being in the loop. I don't envy Leif tonight." He tugged at his collar. "Is he as good with that machete as everyone claims?"

"I'm sure you can handle him with one of your microbursts." I laughed just imagining Leif's outraged expression.

"Unless he used a null shield," Kade said.

The light mood evaporated. "How are your fighting skills?"

"Rusty. I should probably train with you tomorrow."

His gaze turned distant as he stared at the fire. "I wish I had known about null shields *before* my fight with Tricky and Sir. When they threw that net, it severed my connection with the atmosphere. The shock alone paralyzed me for an instant and the fight was over. I hadn't realized how much that connection was an unconscious part of me—like breathing—until it was gone. Ever since I was a teen and made my first sand devils on the beach, I've been able to access the power source. With a null shield around me, I'm rather useless."

"Oh, I wouldn't say that."

He focused on me. "Why not?"

"I'm sure you can be very useful."

"How so?"

I leaned against him. "Keeping me warm, for one."

After a demanding session in the training yard with Captain Marrok the next morning, Kade and I cleaned up and changed. Despite his claims of being rusty, Kade's skills with a sword were good enough to counter the students and a few instructors.

We decided to eat lunch at the Citadel's market. Kade needed to purchase supplies for our trip to The Cliffs and I wanted to stop by Alethea's to inquire about my book order.

"Don't forget to shop for new boots." I pointed to his scuffed ones.

He glanced down in surprise. "I guess I do. And I'll need to buy a sword."

"Thinking of null shields?"

"Unfortunately."

Skippy trailed us through the crowded market. I tried to include him, even called him Hale, but his superior demeanor made it impossible for me to interact with him. Besides, if he snubbed me one more time, I sensed Kade would try out his new sword on him.

Alethea's bookshop bustled with people. While waiting for her to finish with a customer, I browsed the shelves, scanning the titles. A sudden influx of patrons filled the room and I ended up in the small back area alone except for Fisk.

"I don't know how you managed this," I said. "I didn't even see you come in."

"My special magic," he said with a wide smile. "Here are all the items you requested." He handed me a book-shaped package.

"Books?"

"Knowledge is power." He winked.

"How much do I owe Alethea?"

"It's taken care of."

"Thanks."

"Anytime. Do you need me to distract your companions? Alethea has a back door."

"Not today." I laughed at his disappointment. "You're a scoundrel."

"I can be a prince for the right price."

I swung at him and he danced back before slipping

through the bookcase. The design of the shelves concealed an opening. Good to know.

The front room remained packed. Poor Kade stood in a corner and two heavyset women pinned Skippy between tables. I gestured for them to go out and tried to weave my way through the store. My companions reached the door, but the two women now blocked my way. After a few minutes, I gave up and returned to the back room to use the clever exit. I would loop around the building.

Crates and trash containers littered the alley. The ripe smell of garbage drifted from burnt-orange-colored pools. A few pigeons pecked at crumbs. All normal except the quiet. After the buzz of the bookstore, the silence felt odd.

Tucking my package under an arm, I kept my hands near my sais as I hurried down the alley. A flash to my right side startled me. I swung around. Sunlight winked off a glass jug. I laughed. The first time alone in weeks and I was a jittery mess. I should enjoy this moment of peace before plunging into the market's chaos.

I drew in a deep breath and relaxed until a rat the size of a small dog skittered across my boots. Jumping back, I yelped in surprise. So much for my peace. I turned to go. Another large rat ran past me. Two more circled my legs. The whole alley filled with them—a dark moving carpet. Their chittering and squeaks drowned out my panicked gasps.

I bit down on the desire to scream long and loud.

One rat climbed my pants, and I knocked him off with my sais. My package dropped as I swung at rats. During one of my frantic jigs, I spotted a hooded figure at the end of the alley. Magic.

The rats were an illusion. Though knowing the swarm existed in my mind didn't stop the attack. The pain from their sharp teeth still hurt. The thuds as I swatted them away didn't sound any less solid.

My sais wouldn't deter them, so I searched for another weapon. The glass jug. Wading toward the jug, I grabbed it and concentrated on the feel of the glass. Potential throbbed under my fingers. Magic coursed through the alley. I channeled it into the jug. Pings sounded. But I controlled the flow, creating a three-foot-wide rat-free zone around my feet.

The thread of magic linked back to the magician. With glass between my hands, I could siphon all of his magic.

I waited. The pings slowed as the rats kept their distance.

The attack stopped and the magician bolted. Relief coursed through me. I leaned on a building, catching my breath. About twenty glass rats filled the jug. I spilled one in my hand. Shrunk down to an inch long, every detail of the rat was perfect. I found my package and dumped the rest of them into it.

Debating about the jug, I hesitated. What if the magician came back? I returned the container to where I found it and pocketed a few of the mini rats just in case.

Not wanting to be a standing target, I hustled down the alley, searching for a way to return to the main street. I rounded a corner and bumped into the magician.

14

I BACKED AWAY, grabbing the glass rats. Why didn't I check around the corner before rushing around it? Because I was an idiot.

He seized my wrists before I could crush the glass. "Relax, Opal. It's me." He released me and yanked his hood down.

Skippy. My emotions flipped from terror to anger. "What the—"

"Congratulations," he said. "You passed."

My hands remained in fists as I sorted out his comments. "The attack was a—"

"Test, yes."

"I could have drained you of power."

"That's why Master Bloodgood was nearby. I'm not a simpleton."

"So the whole thing was a setup? How did you... Fisk."

"Handy fellow. Good thing he's on our side."

I thought he was on *my* side. "Why test me?"

"To see what you would do when ambushed. The Council ordered it. They wanted to gauge your reactions before agreeing to your trip to the Stormdance lands."

My anger settled into annoyance. I wanted to be upset about the ambush, but I passed the test. We returned to the market. Kade and Master Bloodgood waited for us.

"Did you know about this?" I asked Kade.

"Not until we reached the bookshop." He peered at me. "Look on the bright side. You can come with me." He tried a smile.

I still wasn't happy.

Skippy held out a hand. "I'll take the glass rats now."

"No."

He glanced at Master Bloodgood.

"They're mine. You can't do anything with them. In fact, I want my spiders and bees returned to me," I said to the First Magician. I almost laughed at Skippy's appalled expression.

"Why?" Master Bloodgood asked.

"Just in case I'm attacked on the road. They're good weapons to have. And I should have an orb, too."

Skippy sputtered.

"I will present your request to the Council. When do you plan to leave?"

"As soon as Opal's finished her messengers," Kade said.

They all looked at me. "If I can work in the glass shop this afternoon and evening, I'll have them done today."

"We'll head out tomorrow morning," Kade said.

"I will have an answer for you then." First Magician

paused, then placed a hand on my arm. "You did well, child. Keeping control of your powers despite your panic. Those were huge creatures."

My skin crawled just thinking about them. I stayed close to Kade as we finished our shopping. Although I scanned the crowd for Fisk, I didn't see him. No surprise. I fingered one of my rats. Someday I would thank him for tricking me.

When we returned to the Keep, I dumped my packages in my room and hurried to the glass shop. The student helpers seemed glad to see me. They finished their projects so I could use the kiln and work-bench.

Piecov stayed to assist me. His skill with molten glass had improved so much I asked him to shape the glass once I trapped the magic inside.

"Try blowing," I instructed. "Think about pulling a thread of power and sending it into the glass."

He blew through the blowpipe. Only air reached the slug. No magic. It occurred to me that we could test all the magicians in the Keep to see if they could perform glass magic. The Master Magicians searched for another, but they had been screening young magicians. No one had thought to try established magicians.

But then I wouldn't be the only glass magician. My leverage would be gone. Piecov handed me the pontil iron with a fresh glob of glass and I turned my attention to creating another messenger.

About an hour into the session, I realized Skippy hadn't followed me into the shop. A first. Perhaps being tested wasn't so bad after all.

The shop emptied around suppertime. Piecov shoveled white coal under the kiln and waved bye. My stomach grumbled. I put the finishing touches on my last piece and cracked off the seagull. My sculptures tended to match my mood and thoughts, so all the messengers I crafted today were either seashells or shorebirds.

Pazia entered the shop as I cleaned up.

"Did you ditch your babysitter?" she asked.

"He ditched me."

"I see you're still good at driving people away," she teased. "Even Piecov bolted."

"Funny. As much as I enjoy your attempts at humor, I need to get something to eat." I hovered by the door.

"Hold on a minute." Pazia strode toward the annealing ovens. Mara had bought a second oven to handle all the finished pieces. Glass needed twelve hours to slowly cool to room temperature or else it would crack or break.

"Number two is cooling. The other is done. Piecov forgot to put the sign up."

"That boy." She tsked. "I keep telling Mara we need a checklist." Pazia opened the oven and gasped.

The door blocked my view. "Something break?" I asked. Even with the ovens, breakage occurred.

She pulled back and a bright light filled the room. I

squinted at the round glowing object in her hands. Pazia gawked in amazement.

"What's in there?" I asked.

"Your diamond."

"You're kidding." I stepped closer.

"Not this time."

"Did you add any magic when you inserted it into the glass?"

"No. The diamond was fully charged. I just spun a globe around it."

I glanced at the windows, hoping no one noticed the unusual glow. "Can you feel the magic?"

"It's buzzing in my hands." The white light shone on her face and her eyes sparkled with excitement. "This is a…super messenger! A hundred times more powerful than your animals."

"Then try using it."

"Don't you want—"

"I can't use the magic in that form." A source of frustration, but not important at the moment.

She closed her eyes as her body stilled.

"No Greenblade bees," I said.

A quick grin before she fisted the ball and concentrated. The tools on the gaffer's bench floated into the air. She spun them in a circle and set them down. A pile of rags erupted into flames. Pazia opened her eyes. The blaze died. Her gaze unfocused and she appeared to be lost in her thoughts.

After a few minutes, I called her name in concern.

"Wait," she said.

Easy for her to say—she wasn't dying of curiosity. I fidgeted until she "woke."

"Wow. That was..." She bounced with exhilaration. "I talked to my father. He's coming to graduation!"

"Your father?" He lived over nine days away. "Was he near one of my messengers?"

"No. He's a magician. He's been so angry with me, but he promised he would come."

"He didn't need a messenger to hear you? You went directly to him?"

"Yes! I surprised him when I tapped on his mental defenses."

I considered the implications. "I don't think Yelena could reach him from here without a messenger."

Pazia exposed the glass ball in her hand. It no longer glowed. In fact, black streaks crossed the center and cracks fractured the surface.

"The diamond has shattered. When I used up the magic, it broke," she said. "They're the hardest substance in the world." She spun the ball. "Incredible."

"And not very useful," I said, taking the broken sphere. The diamond had splintered and couldn't be recharged. A failed experiment.

"They're good for onetime use. Could be useful for emergencies." She snagged her lower lip with her teeth. "But the cost to produce them would be steep. Prohibitive for all but the very rich. My father would be able to buy a few super messengers. He would love to own the regular messengers, too. He gets so frustrated having to send a request to the station downtown and waiting for approval."

A familiar story. However, Vasko Cloud Mist had money and political influence. "How powerful is your father?"

"He tested for Master level, but failed."

He would be an excellent ally. "I can make a few extra messengers for him."

"Are you allowed?"

"Why not? They're mine. I used to sell them in a store before Yelena discovered how to use them." I retrieved three of the ones I made yesterday and wrapped them for her to take. I could replace them tonight.

Piecov returned that evening to help me finish the messengers. The annealing ovens were loaded with them. My arms and wrists ached from the long hours of work. I arrived at my quarters with no memory of the trip.

I almost groaned out loud when I spotted my empty saddlebags on the floor, but clamped a hand over my mouth so I wouldn't wake Kade. He slept on the couch. I tiptoed to my table. Fisk's package remained unopened. Tearing the paper as quietly as possible, I removed the outer wrap, uncovering two books.

The first title, *The History of Glassmaking in Sitia,* made sense, but the other, *Infamous Assassins,* didn't until I opened it. Fisk had a warped sense of humor. From the outside, it looked like a regular book. Inside, sections had been gouged from the pages, creating a nice hiding place for a switchblade and a set of lock picks.

I grasped the black handle of the weapon and triggered the blade. It shot out with a satisfying snick. Kade bolted to his feet. Air swirled around the room, then died.

"Your sais not enough?" he asked.

"No. Too easy to disarm, while this—" I brandished the blade "—is easy to hide and to surprise." I had quoted Janco. He would be proud and obnoxious at the same time.

"Aside from any more Council-ordered tests, you won't be in any danger."

I'd heard that before. "It doesn't hurt to be prepared." I closed the knife.

"It won't do much against a sword."

"I know. But it'd be great against a null shield net."

He flinched, conceding the point. "I'm done." He pointed to his backpack. "I filled Moonlight's saddlebags with feed and a few camping supplies in case we can't find a travel shelter." He stretched and yawned. "Once you're packed, we'll be ready."

I dreaded packing. I'd rather be crawling into bed with Kade.

He sensed my reluctance. "Do you want help?"

"How about I just buy everything I need on the road and skip this?"

"You must get a generous student stipend."

I didn't. In fact, I had spent my last gold coin for the knife and picks. All I had left were a few silver coins, which should be enough to get me to the coast and back. Dragging the saddlebags to my armoire, I sorted through my clothes while Kade watched from the bed.

The next morning, we saddled the horses while the Stable Master muttered and fussed. Skippy scowled. I knew he wasn't happy about the trip, but he refrained from complaining. He only snapped at me once, when I checked over his supplies.

"How many trips have you taken to The Cliffs?" I asked him. No reply. "My point. You're going to need your cloak. If the breeze is coming off the sea, it'll be cold."

"We do have fire pits, Opal," Kade said. "I think the sea breeze is refreshing. Not everyone hates the cold," he teased.

"I'm not fond of it, either," Leif said behind me.

I jerked.

"Sorry." Leif's smirk countered his apology. He dropped his saddlebags on the ground. "Do you want to check my supplies, too? I packed my stuffed bear and wool undergarments. Do you think I'll be warm enough?"

Ignoring his joke, I asked, "Are you coming with us?"

"Wouldn't miss it."

I studied his neutral expression. "Did the Council order you?"

"Nope. I volunteered. Especially since a certain Stormdancer sent me my own personal thunderstorm." Leif shot Kade a pointed glare.

Kade busied himself with adjusting the stirrups.

"Mara hasn't given me any peace because of a certain bigmouthed dancer, so I figured I'd come along," Leif said. "Here, this is from Master Bloodgood." He pulled a leather sack from his bags and swung it at me.

I caught it and pulled it open, pouring my glass spiders and bees into my hand. Sunlight glinted from the pile. "No orb?"

"Not yet. Bain said the Council can only handle one step at a time."

Fair enough. "Since you're coming, does that mean Skippy can stay here?" I asked, trying not to let hope taint my voice.

"No," Skippy said. "I'm still your Council-approved guardian."

Guardian. Interesting word choice. "What about Jon or...the other guy?"

"They're the relief. The responsibility is mine." He puffed his chest a bit.

"So if you lose me during the trip, you'll get in trouble?" I tried to tease him, but his reaction remained cold.

"You won't lose me."

Leif snickered. "Hale always had delusions of grandeur even in school."

"Better than a goof-off with bizarre powers," Skippy retorted.

I guessed they had attended the Keep together.

Leif grinned. "Bizarre is always better than boring. Always. However, your confidence of not losing Opal is misplaced. I'm sure you would try very hard, but if she took Quartz into the Avibian Plains, you'd lose more than her."

"That's ridiculous. She wouldn't go in there. It's suicide."

"That's a nice mare you have there, Hale. What's her name?" Leif asked.

Confused by the change in subject, he said, "Beryl."

"She's well bred and in perfect health." Leif ran a hand along her neck. Her brown mane and tail matched the small brown specks splashed all over her tan coat. "But she's not a Sandseed horse like Quartz or Moonlight. They're welcome in the plains anytime and it doesn't matter who is on their back. They even have their own special gait while there that would leave poor Beryl behind in a cloud of dust." Leif clucked his tongue.

"Special gait?" Kade asked.

"Ah, yes! Their gust-of-wind gait, which *you* need to experience sometime." He poked Kade in the arm. "Maybe after I pay you back for ratting me out to Mara."

The Stable Master returned from the pasture. "Get moving, you're burning daylight! And, even worse, you're in my way."

Leif retrieved his saddle from the tack room and whistled for Rusalka.

A russet-and-white horse jumped the pasture's fence.

"All the Sandseed horses can do that," Leif said. "Kiki can even unlatch the door to her stall."

Skippy huffed in annoyance and led Beryl outside to wait for us.

"You're a horse snob, Leif," I said.

"I like messing with Mr. Perfect." He secured his bags and put a bridle on Rusalka.

Kade watched him. "Why don't the Sandseed horses run away?"

"'Cause they're spoiled rotten. We groom them, feed them and shelter them. They can't get that in the wild. They choose to stay with us and even give us pet names when they first meet us."

"Really?" I studied Quartz. She shifted her weight as if impatient to go.

"Yeah. A first impression is very important to a Sandseed horse. Yelena is Lavender Lady. Irys is Magic Lady. General Cahil is Peppermint Boy much to his chagrin. Janco is Rabbit and Valek is Ghost."

"Do you know my horse name?" I asked Leif.

"No, but Yelena should. She's the one they talk to."

"What's your horse name?" I asked Leif.

"You'd never guess it."

"Silly Boy?"

"Not even close." Leif finished saddling Rusalka.

"Goof-off?"

"Nope."

"Irritating one?"

"Watch it," he warned.

"What is it then?"

"Sad Man."

"You're right. I'd never guess that. How... Why?"

Leif sighed. "It's a long story."

Kade swung up into Moonlight's saddle. "Well, we have seven and a half days on the road ahead of us. Plenty of time."

Plenty of time for Leif to embarrass me in front of Kade. And it didn't take him long. The first night we stopped at a travel shelter located along the main western road. This route followed the border between the Krystal and Stormdance Clan lands.

As Leif cooked dinner, we attended to the horses, settling them into the stable next to the shelter. We ate a delicious beef stew while Leif regaled us with stories. Unfortunately, most of them included me. We sat in a semicircle around the hearth. The shelter was empty except for us.

"...remember the storm thieves?" Leif asked me.

"I'm trying hard to forget." I glared my displeasure at Leif.

"Storm thieves?" Kade asked.

I groaned as Leif launched into the tale of how a group of bandits had used storms to sneak up on unsuspecting travelers.

"...Opal's turn to guard us and the horses, but the wind blew the rain sideways, masking all sounds and smells."

"Speaking of guarding," I interrupted, "should we set a watch schedule for tonight?"

"No need," Leif said. "There's no danger this time. No one is after you."

When I failed to look reassured, he added, "Rusalka will sound a warning if she smells anything. You know how loud she can be."

I couldn't forget the shrill sound.

"Of course, with the storm, Rusalka was as surprised as Opal..." Leif resumed his story.

I ceased listening, having no desire to remember my failure to warn Leif and Ulrick. Instead, I gazed at the fire and tried to think of events with happier endings.

"...she almost killed me!" Leif cried, snapping me from my musings. "I thought she didn't pick up on my hint to crush her spiders and bees. The leader—"

"I'm going to bed." I stood with sudden purpose. "Good night." Heading to the row of bunk beds that occupied the bulk of the shelter, I found a decent mattress in a lower bunk and unrolled my sleeping mat. Using my cloak as a blanket, I lay down and palmed two glass spiders just in case. A couple of glass rats nestled inside my cloak's pockets within easy reach.

Why would Leif think that story was funny? I had released a Greenblade bee from glass and it stung the leader, killing him. My actions caused his death. He was the first. A few men had died when Kade released the energy from Kaya's orb, but their demise seemed unavoidable, while the leader... If I had been smarter, his death could have been avoided.

Kade's dark silhouette appeared in the semigloom as he walked toward me. He sat on the edge of my bed. "Are you all right?"

"Fine. I just didn't want to hear any more."

"You've certainly encountered a wide range of trouble." His voice held concern.

"Now do you understand why I've been training so hard?"

"Yes. Please keep it up. At least, for Leif's sake."

"Leif?"

"He enjoys telling stories, and they're even better when they have happy endings."

Aside from spending one night in the open, the next five nights on the road resembled the first. We arrived in Thunder Valley around midafternoon on our sixth day. By this time I was sick of Leif's stories and looking forward to spending a night alone with Kade. We paid for one night's lodging at the Sea Breeze Inn on Kade's recommendation.

Disdain pulled at the corners of Skippy's mouth. He didn't voice his objection to rooming with Leif, but he insisted on conjoining rooms.

Kade needed to contact the other Stormdancers and the new glassmakers. He ran errands while Leif, Skippy and I shopped in the market. With only a day and a half left of our journey, we didn't need much. Though that didn't stop Leif from drooling over the food vendors.

"As long as you like seafood, you won't starve," I said with a laugh.

Leif grimaced. "I'm not big with that slimy, smelly stuff. I'll take travel rations over fish any day."

"Then you better buy a pound or two of jerky."

"How long will we be there?"

"A day or two at most," Skippy said. He glanced at the sky with a worried frown.

I copied him, seeking storm clouds but finding only a wide expanse of brilliant blue. "Six or seven days at least, and a *month* at most."

"You don't need that much time to teach the glass-makers," Skippy said with a surly tone.

Taking a deep breath, I counted to ten, containing the desire to send one of my spiders to bite him.

Skippy hadn't said much during our trip, preferring to sit at the edges of our conversation as if he wanted to distance himself from us common folk. His snide comments still aimed to provoke me. I remembered his remark after the test about not being able to annoy me enough to lash out at him. Perhaps the Council had ordered him to continue his unpleasant behavior.

"You're showing your ignorance about glassmaking and stormdancing," I said to Skippy. "We'll need to wait for a storm to make sure the orbs have been properly made before we can leave."

His gaze shot to the sky again, giving me an idea.

"And it needs to be a big storm." I threw my arms wide. "One that produces giant waves and howling winds. Where the seawater crashes into The Cliffs and we have to evacuate up to the storm cave."

The color in his face whitened with each sentence, leaving behind a pale mask of fear. "What about the horses?"

"We let them loose on the beach. Beryl can swim, can't she?" I asked.

"Swim? I don't know." He laced and unlaced his fingers. "Is that a Sandseed-breed skill?"

At this point, Leif lost it. He laughed so hard tears flooded his cheeks. "Some…magician," he said between gulps. "Can't…even tell…when she's…pulling your leg."

Skippy snapped his mouth shut and glared at Leif. The color rushed back, pooling in a bright red flush on Skippy's cheeks.

"It's hard to be rational when you're afraid," I said in Skippy's defense, feeling bad about teasing him.

"You should know. You're the expert on being irrational and afraid," Skippy said.

"What do you mean?" I stepped closer to him.

"How rational were you when you stole those magicians' magic? How logical were you when your own boyfriend managed to confuse you so bad, you *still* believe he's a Daviian Warper in disguise?"

I drew my arm back, preparing to punch him. It wouldn't be a sucker punch. Oh no. I wanted him to know my intentions.

"That's enough." Leif wedged himself between us.

"Let's finish our shopping." He hooked his arm around mine.

I fumed in silence as we searched for a jerky vendor. Weaving through the stalls, I scanned the tables of goods. Leif spotted a smoky pit and hurried off. Skippy stayed with me.

Sparks of sunlight drew me to a stand selling glassware. The colored drinking glasses and bowls had a simple yet elegant design. They appeared sturdy and functional, too.

The stand's owner noticed my interest. I peered at the woman, remembering when I had been falsely accused of theft and arrested. She wasn't the same woman who had helped frame me.

"Beautiful, aren't they?" the owner asked. "Just two silvers each. Perfect for newlyweds."

I laughed as Skippy stiffened. She probably thought he was being protective instead of wary.

"Here…" She handed me a plate. "Feel how light they are. And they're all handcrafted."

Tiny silver diamond shapes decorated the blue-green glass. "Isn't all glass handcrafted?" I asked.

She pulled her long brown hair behind her shoulders with a dismissive flick. "No. A few factories have molds now. They just pour in the molten glass and wait. It's cheating." The woman's hands moved as she talked.

"You're the artist," I said.

She nodded. "Which is why I can guarantee they're genuine."

"Do you have any vases or sculptures?"

"Yes, but they don't sell as well. The local customers are usually looking for practical." She rummaged under her table and pulled out several vases, then disappeared again. Muffled sounds emanated from below.

I reached for a red bud vase, but Skippy laid a hand on my arm.

"You can't be serious," I said. "Do you really think I'm going to do something?"

He hesitated, then released his grip. I picked the vase up and examined it. The thin neck widened into a series of three round shapes as if they were beads on a necklace. She would have had to blow into the glass, then pinch it tight with her jacks before blowing again. Well crafted but still under my fingers—no magical potential.

"Skippy, lift the null shield," I said.

He narrowed his eyes. "Why?"

"So I can siphon all your magic." When he flinched, I wanted to punch him again. "So I can assess her skills. She might be a prospective glass magician."

"Oh."

The glass throbbed, waiting for me. I concentrated on the vase. It didn't pop like Ulrick's. The woman reappeared with her hair mussed and dirt on her tunic. She placed a small crate on the table and opened the lid.

Skippy jerked when she unwrapped a bundle, revealing a miniature person. I almost dropped the vase. She set the statue down and dug in her crate for another.

With care, I picked the girl up. The exquisite and exact details made the piece lifelike as if the young girl would hop with glee. Created with colored glass, the four-inch-high statue was a true work of art.

The glassmaker lined up six more people. She sighed. "I can't sell these."

"Why not? They're gorgeous." I passed the girl to Skippy and examined a swordsman.

"They're expensive. In order to be compensated for my time and the materials, I need to sell them for half a gold each. Most folks around here can't afford to spend that much on trinkets."

"Trinkets! They're collectibles," I said. "How did you manage to work with these? Even the thinnest pontil iron would be too big."

She grinned. "I knew it. You work with glass, too." Then a shrewd look replaced the smile. "Why do you want to know?"

"Don't worry. I couldn't reproduce your level of detail."

"She can't. Opal's animals are crude, a child's effort compared to these," Skippy said with a touch of awe in his voice. He twirled the little girl as if willing her puffy skirt to spin around her.

The woman's face lit up, so I swallowed my nasty comment. Skippy was right, although I wished he'd used another descriptor than "child's effort."

"I make colored glass sticks, then melt them over a flame instead of using a kiln. I use small tweezers and hold the glass on with a thin metal stick."

"How do you make a single flame hot enough?" I asked.

"Trade secret," she said. "And with working that small, I can craft glass beads and other miniature figures."

"You shouldn't have trouble selling the beads."

"I don't. They go to the jeweler's for necklaces and bracelets."

Her enthusiasm was contagious and rekindled my love for the craft. All too soon, Leif arrived with a heavy package of supplies.

"I've been looking all over for you," he said with exasperation. "Let's go before my arms break."

Disappointment filled the woman's face. I would have loved to purchase the statue of the little girl, but my purse contained only a few silvers of my own. The other coins would be needed to pay for lodging on the way back to the Citadel.

"What's your name?" I asked her. "I'll make sure to recommend you to others."

"Helen Stormdance." She held out a hand.

"Opal Cowan." I shook it.

Helen gazed at me for a moment. "The glass magician?"

My normal reaction would have been to flinch. For someone in this remote town to have heard of me would have caused me discomfort or even fear. But she was my peer. "Yes."

She gazed at me with frank appraisal as if judging the quality of a glass vase. "Are you here to teach the new orb makers?"

"Yes."

Helen waved me closer and leaned toward me. "Keep an eye on them," she whispered in my ear. "They claim to be experts, but *we* don't know them. I'm willing to help if needed. As you can see—" she swept a hand over her wares "—I'm highly qualified."

By the way she emphasized the "we," I knew she meant the glassmaking industry. Most tradesmen exchanged information and kept up with the competition.

"Thanks. I'll keep it in mind." I considered her information and wondered how the Stormdancers chose their new glassmakers.

Skippy handed Helen a gold coin. "I'll take these two." He pointed to the little girl statue and one of a farmer.

She wrapped them with care as I recovered from my shock over his sudden purchase. I didn't know Skippy at all and suspected his nasty disposition toward me could all be an act.

That evening, when we were alone in our room, I asked Kade about the new glassmakers.

"The orb makers were a family business for...ever," Kade said. "The parents would pass the knowledge and skills down to their children, who pass it on to their children. This is the first time since the very beginning we had to select a new family. Raiden was in charge of picking them. I trust him."

Raiden was the camp manager at The Cliffs, making

sure the Stormdancers had enough supplies and food to last through the storm season.

"Do you know how he selected them?" I asked.

"No. Why?"

I explained about Helen's comments. "It could be sour grapes because she wasn't picked to make the orbs, but then again she might have a genuine concern. In my hometown of Booruby, I either know of or have heard of all the glassmakers."

"We should keep an open mind and see how they do," Kade said. He pulled me close.

"Think the best until proven otherwise?"

"Exactly. You should adopt it as your motto."

I liked my way better. Assume danger and be pleasantly surprised when proven wrong.

Our last night of the trip started bad and ended bad. No travel shelters had ever been built on The Flats. The wide expanse of shale spread out for miles before stopping at The Cliffs' edge. Sheets and sheets of the stuff, sometimes smooth, more often broken into uneven steps or ground into gravel. Uncomfortable to ride on and sleep on despite a mat.

Kade stood with the breeze in his face. He inhaled. "Smells like home."

Leif tried to light a fire. "Smells more like a cold supper," he grumped.

Skippy glanced at the sky. "Does it smell like a storm?"

"No. Just a fresh sea wind. In the warm and heating

seasons, the ground heats faster than the seawater."
Kade used his hands to demonstrate. "When the sun
sets, the warm air rises and the cold air sinks, creating
a breeze." He crouched next to Leif. "I can redirect the
breeze until bedtime."

A bubble of calm engulfed us. Leif's pile of wood
ignited.

"Sweet," Leif said.

After dinner, we arranged our sleeping mats. I
dozed on and off. Once Kade fell asleep, the wind
picked up speed, keening through the cracks. Blankets
flapped and needles of cold air poked. I shivered in my
cloak, wishing I could huddle with the horses. Perhaps
I could ask them to lie down upwind and create a wind-
break. The four horses leaned together with their
rumps to the wind.

An almost full moon hung above us, casting a white
light on The Flats. Everything shone as if frozen, including me.

Rolling closer to Kade, I tried to snuggle with him.
He didn't move. How could he sleep on rock-hard
ground with all this noise? His blanket was half-off his
body. I sat up to fix it. His open eyes stared into the clear
night sky.

"Kade?" I shook him hard. "Kade!" His blanket blew
away, revealing his neck. A black dart jutted from his
throat. I yanked it out and sniffed the blood-covered tip.
No scent. The damn wind blew too hard. It didn't matter.
Only one poison would render him like this. Curare.

I checked Leif and Skippy. Both paralyzed. I touched my own neck, but found nothing. The horses resembled statues. Panic flushed through my body, replacing the cold. Yanking my sais from their sheath, I armed myself and scanned The Flats. Nothing. Yet.

Should I use Kade's sword or Leif's machete? Leif's arm reached for his bag and I remembered he always carried the antidote to Curare in his pack. I scrambled to open it, but movement caught my attention.

Downwind, a dark shape rose from the ground. One more joined it and two more stood on my left. Swords glinted as they advanced.

15

FOUR AGAINST ONE. I waited with my sais held in a defensive position. My companions had all been shot with Curare-laced darts, the horses, too. No help from anyone.

The black-clad figures approached with their swords pointed at me. I couldn't fight four at once. Not with my sais, but my pocket held my glass bees and spiders. I would need a free hand.

"Surrender," a man's voice called. "Put down your weapon."

I threw my sais at the two closest ambushers. One clanged on a sword, the other flew past a head—just missing it. But now my hands held glass.

"Leave now, or die," I called over the wind.

They hesitated and glanced at their leader—the farthest from me. The leader motioned them to continue. "Play nice, Opal," he said.

I recognized his voice. Ice filled my veins and coated my heart. Tricky. How did he escape from Ixia?

"Don't come any closer," I said. "I have Greenblade bees. One sting and you're dead."

"Go ahead. Crush them." Tricky joined his friends, forming a semicircle around me. A black hood covered his head.

Sensing a trap, I considered. I didn't want to kill anyone, and had hoped to scare them off. Perhaps bees with instructions to buzz around would chase them away.

Tricky didn't want me dead. At least, not yet. I knew what he wanted. My blood. No Curare for me. Curare paralyzed muscles and magic, and would neutralize any power in my blood.

Kade's comments about being in a desperate situation flashed through my mind. I had warned them. My hands, though, wouldn't move to break the glass. Since I hadn't been pricked, it left one explanation. Magic held me immobile.

Tricky sheathed his sword and strolled over to me. He grabbed the glass from my useless hands, pulled my cloak off and searched me for more weapons. Revulsion churned in my chest at his rough touch as he emptied my pockets. More bees and spiders joined the others. He tossed my possessions to the side.

"Len and Aubin, keep watch. Boar, my pump." Tricky called out orders. "You, sit." He pointed to me.

A force pushed on my shoulders and my knees bent on cue. Once down, Tricky's magic continued to hold me as if bandages wrapped around my body.

I studied the man unpacking supplies. He handed an unfamiliar device to Tricky and pushed his sleeves up. The firelight illuminated the tattoos on his arms.

Blood magic strikes again. Only one person was needed to spread the plague. Frustration pumped in my heart fueled by fear and anger. If the Council had only believed me about Devlen, this wouldn't be happening.

When all looked ready, Tricky knelt next to me with a knife in his hand. Sweat rolled down his face and he grunted when his magic released me.

"Don't try anything." He warned. "I can immobilize you again." He ripped off my left sleeve and wrapped a thin rope around my upper arm, pulling it tight. "Lie down. Stretch out your arm and make a fist."

No choice, I did as instructed. As I unfolded my legs, I felt a lump at the base of my spine. I tucked my free hand under my back. Tricky tapped the underside of my forearm. He tried to hide his fatigue from me, but I kept my gaze on him. If he was too weak to use magic, I might be able to get to my glass bees piled nearby.

"I dreamed of killing you for stealing my magic," Tricky said. "Then I wanted to torture you for ruining our plans and having me arrested in Ixia." He stroked my neck with his fingers, rubbing his thumb over my windpipe. "But you did me a huge favor. I should be thanking you."

I shrank away from his touch. "Favor?"

He leaned close to my ear. "You didn't tell the authorities I still had magic. That you couldn't take it from me," he whispered.

Horror splashed through me. "But I told..." Kade, asking him to tell Janco. But with all the cleanup and other explanations, my message must have been forgotten. I should have made sure. "It was such a small amount."

"It was enough to fool the guards and escape." Tricky traced the blue vein down the inside of my arm with the tip of his blade. "One little problem. I can't increase my powers unless I use *your* blood."

The desperate thumping in my chest filled my ears. About halfway between my wrist and elbow, Tricky drew his knife across the inside of my forearm. A burning pain sizzled and blood welled.

He covered the wound with a rubber suction cup and held it in place. A slurping noise came from behind him.

"It's working," Boar said. He squeezed a rubber ball attached to the tube. Red liquid filled a glass container in his lap. "It's slow."

He untied the rope around my arm, and instructed Boar, "Use your healing magic, but instead of stopping the flow, encourage her blood to gush. Draw strength from me." Tricky's face creased with effort. He rubbed my arm. "Relax. It'll be over in a minute. No pain. You'll just go to sleep."

I felt light-headed and realized he planned to suck me dry. I couldn't just lie here and let him. Fuzzy thoughts tried to plan. Glass container. Rubber tubing. Lump in my spine—my switchblade.

Pulling the weapon from the small of my back, I yanked it free and triggered the blade. Snick. Tricky's gaze switched to my right hand. I jabbed him in the shoulder before he could draw power. He scrambled back in surprise, dropping the tube. I scooped up a handful of glass—spiders and a bee—crushing them.

The noise and flash stunned Boar for a second. Recovering, he gained his feet, cradling the container of my blood. The two other guards rushed toward me with their weapons drawn, but I pointed to the single Greenblade bee, hovering in midair. "Stop right there!"

They paused next to Boar. "Tricky, help," Len cried.

No response. Tricky didn't move. A lesson I learned from Yelena—treating my blade with Curare.

"Give me the jar," I said.

"Aubin!"

A blur of motion and a knife skewered the bee. It fell to the ground, too heavy to fly. I ordered my spiders to attack them. A moment of confusion created a distraction while I found another bee. I sent this one to break the jar, but the glass was too thick. My last bee hovered for a mere second before being impaled with a knife.

"Don't move. Or the next one goes into your heart," Aubin said, aiming a dagger at me. "Drop your weapons and keep your hands where I can see them."

I released the spiders and turned my palms out.

"Boar, can we finish the job?" Aubin asked.

"Not without Tricky. My magic is too weak."

"Give me the jar. Help Len carry Tricky." Aubin tucked the container under his arm.

With Boar's help, Len draped Tricky over his shoulder.

Aubin gestured to me with his knife. "Come."

"No." Tricky wanted me alive. They could harm me, but probably wouldn't kill me until after he woke. I hoped his goons didn't know how to counter Curare.

Aubin considered. "We can force you. You'll be hurt."

"Doesn't matter." I swept a hand out. "My companions will wake well before Tricky. You won't be able to get far carrying him and dragging me along. Once they can move, you'll have a Stormdancer and two powerful magicians after you. I'd give you a twenty-percent chance of living through the encounter." I tapped my finger on my lips. "Hmm…I changed my mind."

"You'll come with us?" Aubin asked.

"No. I think twenty percent is too high. I forgot Curare doesn't last as long on Stormdancers…something with the electrical charge in the atmosphere neutralizing the drug. I think a ten-percent chance of survival is more accurate. It *is* the storm season."

I kept my gaze steady as Aubin studied me. Dizziness spun behind my eyes, but I ignored it.

"Then I'll kill your companions so there is no need to worry about them following us."

My heart flipped. I used every bit of energy to keep my voice calm. "Zero chance of survival."

"Why?"

"One of the magicians is the brother of the Soulfinder. If she doesn't scare you, then her heart mate, Valek, should. Not only is he the Commander's assassin, but he's immune to all magic. Plus, you'd have every Stormdancer after you, and the Master Magicians, as well."

"Let's just go," Boar said. "We have enough blood."

"We can't leave her here. She'll send her bees after us," Aubin said.

Boar muttered and searched the ground. He found my sais and grasped them by the shafts. He strode toward me. "Do you know how to fight with these?"

Confused, I glanced at Aubin.

"Answer his question."

"Yes," I said.

"Do you know the soldier's honor code for a fair fight?" Boar asked.

"No."

He stepped closer and held the sais out. I automatically reached for the hilts, but he snatched them away.

"Neither do I." Boar swung one of the sais, aiming at my temple.

Pain pulsed in my head, waking me. I shaded my eyes from the searing reflection of sunlight off the shale ground. My body ached and my arm stung. I stayed prone for a while, chasing fuzzy memories. When I remembered the attack, I scrambled upright, searching for Tricky and his goons.

No one except Kade, Leif, Skippy and the horses. They all remained paralyzed by Curare and would be immobile for another... I checked the sky. A few hours past dawn. From my unfortunate experience with the drug, I knew they would be incapacitated for almost a full day. At least my companions could hear, see, breathe and swallow.

A hiccuppy laugh bubbled. Kade and the others had heard the whole fight. I wondered what I would get in trouble for. Falling for Boar's honor-code trick or for letting them get away with my blood.

I needed to focus before the shakes came or I passed out again. Stumbling over to Leif's pack, I found the Theobroma lumps. The wind had died down and a few half-burnt branches had survived last night's flames. One good thing about being unable to light fires with magic was I kept matches in my saddlebags.

I coaxed the meager firewood into a small blaze and melted the Theobroma. Once the brown liquid cooled enough not to burn skin, I spooned the antidote into each of my companion's mouths, guessing how much was needed. For the horses, I coated my fingers with it and rubbed my hands on their tongues.

My arms shook by the time I finished. Shivers racked my body. I wrapped my blanket around me and lay next to Kade, pulling his blanket over us both.

Leif woke me an instant after I fell asleep. At least, that was how it felt to me. I blinked in the light, cursing the brightness. My heavy limbs refused to move. I didn't have enough energy to stand.

"Drink this," Leif said.

He tipped a mug toward my lips. A foul-smelling liquid sloshed. I tried to pull away, but he put his hand under my head, dripping the yellow substance into my mouth.

"Swallow or I'll hold your nose closed until you do," Leif threatened.

I gulped and winced. It tasted like dirty wash water.

"It will help your body produce more blood. Make you feel stronger so we can get off this horrid rock and down to the soft sands of the beach."

"Go on without me." I shooed halfheartedly. "It's not like you need me to save you or anything... Oh, wait. I did save you."

"And you took your sweet time, too. Although I give you major bonus points for your...ah...very creative arguments about why they shouldn't kill us."

I shivered at the memory as Leif urged me to gulp more of his potion.

"I meant it, don't let me keep you from the beach."

"Nice try, but you're going to drink all of this. Besides, if I tried to leave, a certain Stormdancer would probably zap me with lightning."

"Where is Kade?" I sat up, feeling better.

Leif looked past my shoulder. "Walking the horses. They weren't happy about being paralyzed. Once we calmed them, they let Kade work off their stiffness." He met my gaze. "I'm sorry, Opal. We should have posted guards, but I thought the horses would warn us of any intruders. I never thought someone would use Curare on them."

"Curare plus the wind. Tricky's gang probably stayed downwind where they couldn't smell them."

"I notified the authorities in Thunder Valley with my messenger. Hopefully they'll be caught, but we should take you home—"

"No. I'd love to chase them down, but the Storm-dancers need orbs."

"What if they come back?"

"They won't. Tricky has what he came for." And the spread of blood magic continued. For now. I would stop it. I promised.

"What happens when he runs out of your blood?" Leif asked.

"We'll use me as bait and go fishing."

"I'm serious, Opal."

"So am I."

Of course, my bravado didn't last long. When Kade arrived with the horses, I wanted to melt into his arms and forget the whole nightmare. He held me in a tight embrace.

"You did well last night," he said with pride in his voice. "I wanted to shout with joy when you regained consciousness. Until then..." His body stiffened as he struggled to find the right words. "Until then, it was hell. Not as bad as watching you be tortured by Devlen, but rather horrible. And here I've feared null shields, not knowing that...this...Curare is a million times worse."

I agreed and Kade stepped back to search my face.

"You've been hit by it, too?" he asked.

I realized Kade didn't know much about my history. Every time we were together we had a specific problem to deal with. Since he had returned from Ixia, we hadn't spent too much time talking.

"Yes. Unfortunately, I have a lot of experience with Curare."

"When?"

"It's a long story. I'll tell you later." I leaned against him.

He wrapped an arm around my shoulders. "Will the... strangeness go away? I can use my magic, but I still feel vulnerable. Fragile."

"That's the antidote," I explained. "Theobroma opens a person's mind to magical influences and destroys a magician's mental defenses." I gestured to Leif and Skippy. "If a weaker magician like Tricky attacked them now, they wouldn't be able to counter him. It doesn't last as long as Curare. You should be fine by nightfall."

"Is it true Curare works differently for Storm-dancers?"

"No. I lied to them, hoping to give them an incentive to leave without killing anyone." I hugged my arms to my chest. Tricky's goons had just started using blood magic, and hadn't reached the point when the all-consuming desire to gain magical power overruled logic. Otherwise, they would have killed without a second thought.

"Opal," Leif called. He crouched next to the remains of the fire.

I joined him.

He pointed to the two Greenblade bees. "They look like good knives, but I'm not crazy enough to pull them out."

Interesting. The bees were dead, but hadn't disappeared. I reviewed last night's attack and realized I hadn't given them a task.

"Rest in peace," I said. The knives clattered to the ground. Their clean blades shone in the sunlight.

"And I thought Yelena had eccentric powers," Leif said. "Finding lost souls seems normal compared to commanding dead bees."

"Not funny." I collected the glass spiders that had been scattered during the fight and found my sais. "Have you seen any of my bees?"

"After Boar knocked you unconscious, Aubin ordered him to take them."

"Why? They can't use them."

Leif picked up Aubin's weapons and stood. "I'm guessing Aubin has excellent knife-throwing skills. It's a good way to attack from a distance and to attack without being seen. Just like your bees." He met my gaze. "Just how far can your bees travel? Could they find someone out of sight?"

"I don't know."

"Neither does anyone else. Theoretically, you could send a bee to assassinate the Commander in Ixia without leaving the Keep. Valek would no longer be the most infamous assassin. Perhaps Aubin was on to something."

As Leif's words sunk in, fingers of ice brushed my skin. I had used my spiders and bees for self-defense, never once considering other possibilities. Why? As Devlen had said, I was too nice. If I wanted to stop Tricky and blood magic, I needed to start thinking like them.

Quartz seemed more than happy to continue our journey. We arrived at the top of The Cliffs by midafternoon. A hundred-and-fifty-foot drop-off ended at a sandy beach. Waves capped with white foam crashed along the shoreline and around the strips of rocks, pointing toward the horizon. Sunlight glittered on the sea's blue-green surface.

The tangy smell of the salt water reached us. I inhaled a deep breath. No matter how strong the storm, I would always feel safe here. The cries and squawks of seabirds combined with the shushing of the waves—a welcoming sound.

"You have got to be kidding me," Leif said.

Mounted on Moonlight, Kade waited for the rest of us to join him at the start of the trail.

"That's not a path, that's...suicide." Leif hunched

over his saddle. "That's not wide enough to fit a sheep, let alone a full-grown horse."

"The horses fit fine," Kade said. "We use them to haul supplies to the caverns."

"Caverns?" Skippy asked. His pale face reflected his queasiness. He hadn't said more than two words since last night's attack.

"You'll see." I dismounted. "Unless you're a Storm-dancer or a mountain goat, it's better to walk down. Concentrate on the trail and don't look past the edge. Go on, Kade. We'll meet you on the beach."

He clicked his tongue, urging Moonlight down the steep path. Show-off. Good thing Sandseed horses refused to wear shoes or else he would have skated the whole way at that speed.

I glanced at Beryl's hooves. "You better go last. In case she slides."

"Slides?" Skippy turned whiter.

Since I was the only one with experience, I led the rest. The trail snaked back and forth, cutting through ripples in the rock face. Wind and water had sculpted The Cliffs. Wings of rock jutted and caves pockmarked the wall. The path crossed natural bridges and skirted around columns.

When we reached the beach, Leif fell to his knees with a dramatic cry. "Solid ground! I'll never take you for granted again."

"Are you going to kiss the sand?" I asked.

"Don't be ridiculous."

"Now *I'm* the one being silly?"

"Yes."

I led them to the beach stable. Made of bamboo and thatch, the stable could house five horses. Kade rubbed down Moonlight.

Skippy scanned the building. "You were serious about the horses swimming."

Kade snorted. "If a storm approaches, we'll take the horses up to the storm cave. For now, it's more comfortable down here."

When everyone had unsaddled their horses and settled them in stalls, I showed them the main cavern the Stormdancers used. Big and bright with lanterns, it was at beach level. Raiden stirred the contents of a large pot over a cook fire. Various people lounged about on cots or chairs, but a woman and man jerked to their feet when they saw us approach.

"'Bout time," Raiden said. He straightened and shook hands with Leif and Skippy. His skin had tanned to a rich brown and more gray flecked his short black hair. The wrinkles on his face were a lighter tan color as if he always squinted while in the sun.

"A wide-brimmed hat would help with that raccoon look," I teased. Even though I knew his age to be around forty, he appeared a lot older than the last time I visited. Perhaps the stress of the glassmakers' murders and having his strongest Stormdancer kidnapped had aged him.

"At least I don't look like a ghost," he said. He

beckoned to the couple hovering nearby. "This is Ziven and Zetta, brother-and-sister glassmakers. And—come on, you lazy bums—our other Stormdancers, Prin, Wick and Tebbs."

Another round of introductions was made. The Stormdancers didn't bother to shake our hands. They waved hello from their seats. I knew Prin and Wick. Prin matched my size and age, though her silver-colored eyes gave her an exotic air. Bearded and burly, Wick grunted a greeting.

Tebbs had pulled her brown hair into an intricate knot on top of her head. Her gaze swept us with sharp interest, but she glanced away as if bored when I tried to make eye contact. She appeared to be near Heli's age of sixteen, but she acted like an older woman, copying Prin's mannerisms and gestures.

"Where's Heli?" I asked Raiden. Heli's youth and enthusiasm tended to energize those around her.

"Out searching the beach for treasure," he said.

"Treasure?" Leif asked.

"What Heli considers treasure." Raiden sighed. "Shells, odd driftwood shapes, stones and coral. Her cave is full of junk."

"She has a few beautiful pieces," I said in her defense.

Raiden snorted and returned to his stew. The smell of steamed clams wafted from the pot. Leif wrinkled his nose, but couldn't resist following Raiden to peek under the lid.

The glassmakers talked to Kade. I joined them, much

to Zetta's dismay. She shot me an annoyed frown and a warning flared in her brown eyes. Kade, however, made room for me.

"...just need the sand recipe and we should have melt by tomorrow," Ziven said. His black hair had been twisted into long ropes that hung over his shoulders and back.

"Then the kiln is hot?" I asked.

He glanced at Kade as if seeking approval.

"Opal is our glass-and-orb expert," Kade said. "She knows the proper sand mixture and will instruct you on how to proceed."

Zetta's ill humor deepened into outrage. "She's not a Stormdance Clan member. It violates all traditions that she knows the secret recipe."

Zetta's hair matched the length of her brother's except she had small braids instead of ropes. Colorful beads decorated the ends of the braids. The beads clicked together when she jerked her head.

Kade stared at her until she calmed. "Opal figured out the sand recipe just by examining the mix. Can either of you do that?"

They hemmed and shuffled their feet.

"I didn't think so. As I said before, she's in charge. I won't use any orbs unless she approves them first. Now, I believe Opal asked you a question."

"Yes, the kiln is hot," Zetta said. She kept her voice even, but she clutched her arms.

"Is the cart near the stockpiles?" I asked.

"No. We used it to bring coal up to the kiln," Ziven said.

More tradition. To keep the kiln safe from the water and weather, it had been installed in a high cave with a natural chimney to vent the smoke. It was also far away from the stockpiles on the beach. Crafting the orbs off-site and sending them to the coast just wasn't done, either.

"Get the cart. I'll meet you at the piles."

They left but not without Zetta treating me to another glare when she thought Kade wasn't looking. How childish. I suppressed the urge to stick my tongue out in response.

"Thanks for the vote of confidence," I said to Kade.

"Do you need my help with the orbs?" Kade asked, but his gaze sought the sea.

"No. You go."

"Go where?"

"Out onto the sea rocks."

"How did—"

"You're swaying with the surf. Go commune with the waves and air currents." I shooed him toward the beach.

"I get a better sense of approaching storms when I'm near the water," he said in defense.

"Isn't that what I just said?"

"You made it sound…absurd."

"I didn't mean to. That's important, unlike surfing the waves. *That's* ridiculous."

"Not once you try it."

I shivered, thinking about the cold water. "No, thanks."

"It's going to be fun changing your mind." Kade waved and ran down the beach with an unconscious grace and hopped onto the black rocks. He stepped from one to another, traveling farther out. As the waves crashed into them, spray and foam erupted around him, but didn't slow him down.

My attempt to cross them had ended with a wipeout and a gash on the head. When Kade reached the final rock, I waited for the glassmakers near the stockpiles.

Four wagons covered with tarps rested along the back wall of the stables. I uncovered them, checking their contents. Glittering in the sunlight, the bright white sand from the Krystal lands filled the first wagon. Both the black lava flakes and the grains from Bloodgood's red beach were in the second wagon. A wooden divider separated them. Lime packed the next wagon and the last contained soda ash. All the ingredients needed to make glass.

I found shovels and trowels, but couldn't locate a few important items. Ziven joined me, pushing the wheelbarrow.

"Where's Zetta?" I asked.

"She's waiting back at the kiln." He grabbed a shovel. "What's the recipe?"

"I could tell you, but it won't do you any good."

"What?"

I gestured. "The scale isn't here, or the drum mixer.

How are you going to weigh out the ingredients and blend them together?"

He considered. "We brought them to the cave. It doesn't matter. We can mix and weigh up there."

"What if you don't bring enough of one ingredient? You would need to make another trip. It's better to have those down here."

Ziven grumbled and complained about transferring the scale and mixer. When he returned, he and Zetta made a big production out of moving the heavy equipment. I ignored them by examining the glass ingredients for any foreign substances or contaminants. Dipping a trowel full of lime into the water, I checked for Brittle Talc. It would turned purple if tainted. No change.

When the glassmakers finished, I told them the sand recipe. "Forty percent Krystal's white sand, forty percent local sand..." I scooped a handful of coarse yellow-and-brown grains from the beach. Compared to the tiny white granules, the beach sand appeared oversize. "Fifteen percent Bloodgood red sand and five percent lava flakes."

Ziven and Zetta didn't move. I handed a shovel to each.

"How do we measure out percentages?" Ziven asked.

I blinked at him. He asked about a fundamental skill. "By weight. The kiln can hold one hundred pounds of mix. After you put in the lime and soda ash, the sand ingredients will balance out the rest."

Comprehension failed to light their faces.

"You'll need eleven pounds of lime and fourteen pounds of ash, which is twenty-five pounds. So to figure out how much Krystal sand, you'll need to take forty percent of seventy-five pounds, which is thirty pounds."

"Why didn't you just say thirty pounds of white in the first place?" Ziven asked.

"She's showing off," Zetta said.

As they shoveled and weighed the sand, I calculated the rest. "Eleven and a quarter pounds of Bloodgood red and three and three-quarters pounds of lava flakes." I pressed my lips together before I could say more. My father taught me how to calculate percentages into weights before I could read. All his recipes used percentages, as did most glassmakers', since kilns were built in different sizes, depending on the need. If the Stormdancers bought a kiln that could hold a hundred and fifty pounds, then the ingredient weights would all change.

I worried about their qualifications, remembering Helen's comments about these two. At least they knew to mix the substances together. The drum mixer resembled a metal barrel laid on its side. Inside the container were fins to help stir. After securing the lid, a handle turned the drum to blend everything.

But when they began pulling the wheeled cart, I couldn't conceal my amusement. By their fury, I knew any chance for a civil relationship was gone.

"You could help. Or are you too valuable?" Ziven asked.

"Experts don't get their hands dirty," Zetta said.

She'd pushed me too far. I'd had enough verbal abuse.

"Do you want to keep your jobs?" I asked them.

They shared a glance.

"It's an easy question even for you. Either yes or no."

"Yes," Ziven said.

"Then shut your mouths and listen to me. Making the orbs is vital. Screwing up means killing Stormdancers. Right now, I'm the only person in the world who knows how they're made." I stepped closer and lowered my voice. "I don't care if you like me or not. But if you utter one more snide comment, you're both fired."

"You can't—" Zetta clamped her mouth shut when her brother slapped her arm.

I waited, but they remained silent. Good. "Now think. Wheeling a hundred pounds is doable on a flat surface, but what happens when you try to pull it up a slope?"

"It's harder?" Ziven answered.

"Right. How did these wagons of supplies arrive?"

They both looked at the stable. Quartz's and Moonlight's heads poked out.

"They're not our horses," Ziven said. "Ours go home after we bring all the supplies in."

"All you need to do is ask."

"The owners?"

"The horses." I found a harness hanging in an empty stall. "Quartz, will you help us?"

She nickered and I secured the leather straps and attached the cart. Within minutes, we arrived at the kiln's cave. After we unloaded the sand mixture into the kiln's cauldron, I suggested they blend another batch and store it up here. They had plenty of time as the melt wouldn't be ready for another eight to twelve hours.

They agreed to my idea and I helped them prepare and deliver a second batch. Once we finished, I led Quartz back to the stables. I rubbed her down and fed her a few treats. My stomach rumbled. The sun hovered above the horizon, painting the sky with yellow, orange and red streaks.

I headed to the main cave. Kade wasn't on the rocks. I found him talking with the other Stormdancers. They sat around the cook fire with Leif and Skippy. All held bowls of steaming white liquid. Even Leif.

"I thought you didn't like seafood," I said to him.

He slurped the juice straight from his bowl. "Fish. I said I didn't like fish. This is soup."

"There are clams in it," Raiden said. He ladled a bowl for me.

"Clams aren't fish." Leif helped himself to another portion.

"I can cook fish so it tastes like steak," Raiden said.

"Really?" An avid glow lit Leif's eyes. He and Raiden launched into an intense discussion about cooking.

I found a seat next to Kade. He draped an arm around my shoulders but didn't pause in his conversation. Prin looked at us in surprise. She continued to study us with a speculative frown. Wick leaned back in his chair with his eyes closed and an empty bowl in his lap. Tebbs perched on the edge of her seat, listening intently.

"...a few big storms are forming out at sea, but nothing will come close for a few days," Kade said.

"Then why do we have to come here so early?" Tebbs asked. She had tried to catch Prin's gaze, but gave up when Prin wouldn't glance at her.

Tebbs's rookie question confirmed my guess at her young age.

"There have been early season storms in the past, so it's always prudent to be prepared and ready early," Kade said. "Hopefully, the first storm will be mild and you can dance with Prin." He smiled at Tebbs. She blushed and glanced down.

"Is this your first storm season?" I asked her.

"I was supposed to start my training last time, but with the orbs breaking and..." She played with the hem on her linen tunic. "Well. You know." She cleared her throat. "Anyway, my powers came in much later than most of the others. Mother said I purposely ignored them before." At this point Tebbs realized she babbled. "Yes. This will be my first time." She settled her expression, trying to appear mature.

"Do the Stormdancer powers begin at puberty, too?" Usually, magical ability flared to life at the same time as a child's body matured to an adult. For most, the transition complicated an already difficult time period, and a person's power could be overlooked at first. It was one of the reasons for Irys Jewelrose's annual trip to find and assess potential magicians. The threat of a young magician becoming uncontrolled and flaming out was another reason for her trip. Flameout would damage the power source, creating trouble for all the magicians.

"Yes, but there are exceptions," Kade answered. "Heli could make a dust devil when she was ten and Tebbs, here, didn't realize it was *her* mood affecting the weather instead of the other way around until she was eighteen."

I thought of Master Jewelrose's annual task again and groaned. Everyone looked at me. "Why didn't I think of it before? Kade, you can use one of my glass messengers to find new Stormdancers."

"That's a great idea!" He beamed.

I suppressed the impulse to kiss him. "I'll make you a bunch when we're done with the orbs."

"You don't need a special glass mixture?" he asked.

"Nope. Any glass will do."

"You can't do that," Skippy said.

I noticed he had been listening ever since Kade mentioned the storms out at sea.

"Why not?" I asked.

"The Council has set up protocols for obtaining a messenger. He'll have to put in a request to the local station, who will pass it on to Councilor Stormdance, who will present all requests to the messenger committee, who then decides who to approve," Skippy explained as if I should already be aware of this chain of command.

And he was right. I should be informed about what the Council did with my messengers. No wonder Vasko Cloud Mist was so happy to have his own; by giving him three I had bypassed a season's worth of paperwork. It explained why Pazia had asked me if it was allowed.

The other Stormdancers peered at us in confusion, except Wick, who snored. Kade enlightened them about my messengers.

"...if you see the glow inside, then you have magical power."

"But aren't they the things that let you communicate from far away?" Prin asked.

"Yes. They have many uses." Unmistakable pride filled Kade's voice.

Prin blinked at me. "*You* make them? *You're* the glass magician?"

"Why are you so surprised?" Kade asked.

"I...it's just that...I never made the connection before. She was here only a few days." Prin sounded aggrieved. "No one told me."

"Not too many people know," I said. "It's *safer* that way."

Everyone remained quiet for a moment.

"In any case," I said, "they are my creations and I can give them to whomever I want."

"The messenger committee isn't going to like that," Skippy said.

"I don't care."

"You should. I can prevent you from making them." Skippy straightened.

"It's not part of your assignment."

"Doesn't matter. It's the right thing to do."

"I don't agree."

"That doesn't matter, either," Skippy said.

"Yes, it does," Kade said. "Opal's opinion matters to *me*."

"We're away from the Keep, Stormdancer. I can erect a null shield at my discretion."

"You're outnumbered. There are five of us. Seven if you include Leif and Opal. And a null shield isn't going to stop me from dumping you in the ocean." Kade remained relaxed in his seat, but a dead-serious expression touched his face.

Skippy wisely kept quiet. Prin and Tebbs exchanged a look. Wick snorted and mumbled in his sleep.

The glassmakers arrived and hesitated by the cook fire as if scenting the tension in the air.

"How's the melt?" I asked.

"Good, good," Ziven said. He poured soup into two bowls, handing one to his sister. "We should be able to make orbs tomorrow morning."

"Excellent," Kade said.

The friction eased a bit. Conversation resumed. I wanted to ask Raiden about the glassmakers' experience, but would wait until we could talk in private. few of the Stormdancers had their own caves to sleep in; others collapsed on cots around the main cavern's fire.

When I visited before, I slept with the others. I wondered if Kade's cot was big enough for two. Despite being the leader of the Stormdancers, he had chosen a small cave with only enough room for a cot and a brazier. He claimed the room was a nice respite from the vastness of the sea.

The soft yellow firelight lit his profile. His straight nose widened just a bit at the end. Grains of sea salt clung to his long eyelashes. He had tucked his hair behind his ear. The sun-streaked strands resembled gold threads. Kade caught me staring and smiled.

Darkness pressed against the cave's entrance, and I was going to suggest we retire for the evening, when I realized Heli hadn't returned.

"Is Heli always gone so late?" I asked Kade.

He glanced around in dismay. "Ray, did Heli come back yet?"

Raiden jerked as if slapped. "Haven't seen her all day. I'll check her cave. Maybe she's sorting her junk." He lit a lantern and hurried out.

Kade lit a few more lanterns as we waited. Unable to sit still, I hovered near the base of the trail. By Raiden's worried expression, I knew Heli's room was empty.

"The sea's calm today," Kade said. "No rogue waves or riptides."

"Maybe she fell and broke her leg or hit her head," Prin said.

"Which way did she head out?" I asked Raiden.

He shrugged. "She's always going out. This is the first time she's been gone so long."

"She's alone. Maybe she was attacked," Prin said.

No wonder Heli had called Prin Ms. Doom and Gloom.

We split into two groups. Raiden, Prin and Tebbs headed north, while Kade, Leif and I turned south. Skippy stayed behind with the still-sleeping Wick just in case Heli bypassed us.

"Signal if you find her," Kade had ordered.

"How?" Prin asked.

"Send a blast of air and I'll do the same."

We marched down the beach. The sand crunched under our boots. Waves shushed in a steady rhythm. We checked caves, inspected shadows and called Heli's name.

"I keep forgetting how young she is," Kade said. "She's been dancing for four years, but she's only sixteen."

Leif stopped. He closed his eyes and drew in deep breaths. "Is she...springy? Enthusiastic?"

"Yes," I said.

"Then she came this way." He paused. "It's been a while. No bad scents."

We continued. The moon crested The Cliffs, casting a pale light over us. Eventually our lantern sputtered and died.

"Now what?" Leif asked.

"We keep going," Kade said. "Are you still... smelling her?"

"Yep."

"Let me know if anything changes."

"Will do."

My eyes adjusted to the weak moonlight. As I searched for a sign of Heli, I worried she might have drowned. Would the sea deposit her body on the shore like one of her treasures? Did Kade know the currents well enough to trace her through the waves? Now who was being Ms. Doom and Gloom?

"Heli!" Kade cried with delight and ran to a figure up ahead.

By the time I reached them, he had picked her up and swung her around.

"Where have you been?" he demanded when he set her down. She looked like a little girl next to him.

"Out collecting," she said. "I kept finding these wonderful bits of sea glass." She held up a bulging mesh bag. "More and more of them all scattered along the beach and well...I guess I went too far. But I couldn't stop picking them up! The time flew and the next thing I knew, it was too dark to see the glass." She gave Kade a wry smile. "Just my luck *you* returned today." Heli noticed me. "And you brought Opal." She jumped with glee. "Opal, just wait until you see these pieces. You're going to die!"

"I nailed it," Leif said. "Springy."

I introduced him to the young Stormdancer. Even

though she had been busy all day, Heli still had energy to relate to us all her adventures. Before we headed back to the caverns, Kade signaled the others, sending a strong burst of wind up the coast.

Although they chastised her for being gone so long, the others were relieved Heli was safe. She pulled a small table next to the fire and dumped her treasure on it.

Sea glass of different shapes, sizes and colors glittered and winked. The pile beckoned. The desire to hold the pieces and claim them filled me. We were all drawn to the table. The sand and movement of the water had smoothed and polished the bits of broken glass. I picked up a blue piece.

Magic burned my fingers, jolting up my arm and shocking me. I dropped the piece with a cry, but the others grabbed at them, fighting over them. Raiden and even Wick—when did he wake?—clutched pieces as if they were children with candy. Heli scooped a bunch in her hands, yelling at everyone the sea glass was hers.

The arguments turned nasty. Voices grew louder. Soon fistfights would break out.

I pulled at Kade's sleeve, and shouted for him to stop. But he shoved me away, protecting his hoard. I landed on the ground hard, staring at the horrible scene before me. The violence escalated and I guessed why.

The magic in the sea glass had enchanted them.

16

IF I DIDN'T do something and soon, there would be bloodshed. The magic in the sea glass forced everyone to crave it. They all desired the shiny pieces for themselves. Even I had felt the pull. However, as soon as I touched one, I...woke. That didn't work for the others, who fought and grabbed for the pieces.

The fight bordered on a melee, with Kade and Wick wrestling and Prin punching Raiden. I blocked the ruckus from my mind, and concentrated on what Heli had said about collecting the sea glass. She couldn't help herself from gathering them until dark.

I glanced at the fire. If I doused it, would the ensuing darkness work? A null shield would be perfect. Unfortunately, Skippy struggled with Ziven. However, Leif knew how to erect one.

Leif crawled on the floor, picking up the dropped glass. I pounded on his shoulders and screamed in his ear. He batted me away as if I were an annoying fly. In desperation, I straddled his back and cupped my hands over his eyes, pinching his nose tight, too. Leif's magical senses involved smells. If he couldn't smell, perhaps he wouldn't be influenced by the sea glass's magic.

He bucked and cursed and rolled, slamming me into the side of the cave. I held tight despite the pain radiating up my spine. He smashed me against the stone wall again and again, then stilled. My ribs ached, but I kept my hands clamped to his face. Pressed between him and the wall, I waited.

"Opal, why are you covering my eyes?" Leif asked. His voice sounded funny.

"Magic in the sea glass has made everyone insane with desire. I need you to build a null shield."

"I'll need to see, and breathe."

"Don't look at the sea glass," I instructed. "Put the pieces in your pocket."

He emptied his hands and I removed mine.

"I'll be a date for a necklace snake," Leif said as he surveyed the chaos. "All this for a...pretty...sparkle..."

"Leif!" I yanked his head around. "Don't look."

"Oh, sorry." He shook his shoulders. "What did you need?"

"Null shield."

"Oh, yeah." He blinked.

"Now! Before the Stormdancers start sending tornadoes at each other."

"Oh, right." Leif focused on the ceiling.

I thought about asking him to move his weight off me,

but decided to stay quiet for now. The sounds of
fighting diminished. I risked a peek over Leif. The
others stood panting and looking at each other in confusion.

Long scratches on Prin's right cheek bled, Wick's eye
puffed, Raiden rubbed his arm, Kade pushed Skippy's
hands away from his neck, and Heli gaped in horror.

"Leif?" I asked.

"Hmm?"

"Move, please."

"Oh, sorry." He rolled away.

I sucked in a deep and painful breath. It felt like I
might have cracked my ribs. "Keep the shield in place
until we put all the glass away." I staggered to my feet.

No one said a word. Heli's mesh bag had fallen to the
floor, landing under the table. I picked it up and noticed
one piece of sea glass remained on the table. All the
others had been snatched and fought over, yet no one
desired the milky blue triangle.

I examined it. Was it the one I had touched?

"Leif, where is the shield's boundary?" I asked.

"Past the fire."

I handed the mesh bag to Heli. "Collect all the sea
glass."

She blinked at me as if I'd asked her to fly.

"Go on," I urged. "Make sure you get them all." I
carried the little blue piece past the fire, bracing for the
burning pain of magic. Nothing. Its magic was spent
and it didn't even sparkle as much as before. In fact,

scratches marred the piece, rendering it ugly and ordinary. I put it into my pocket.

When Heli had gathered all the glass, she handed me the bag. Leif dropped the shield and the Stormdancers swayed in relief. Everyone suddenly found something to do, righting the chairs and cleaning up the mess made by the fight. No one wanted to talk about what happened, but we would have to.

Raiden stirred the fire, adding logs. Flames leaped toward the ceiling. I collapsed into a chair and Kade saw my wince of pain. He was beside me in an instant.

"Do you need a healer?" he asked.

"No."

Leif poked me in the side. I yelped.

"How about you answer that question again?" Leif's smug expression wilted as I glared at him. He hurried to his saddlebags.

Kade knelt next to me. "I pushed you down. I'm sorry—"

"Not your fault." When tears flooded Heli's eyes, I added, "Not anyone's."

"I'll fetch a healer," Kade said.

"I don't need one. Does anyone else?" I asked.

No one spoke up. Leif returned with a variety of first-aid supplies. "If her ribs are broken, she'll need a healer. But if they're cracked, she can heal on her own without danger." He sorted through his collection of herbs. "I'll brew you a tea to help with the pain, but first I want to assess the damage."

"Assess how?" I asked.

He gave me a grim smile, then turned to Kade. "Is there a private place where I can examine her?"

Despite my protests, Kade carried me to his cave. I grabbed the bag of sea glass, knowing better than to leave it behind.

After being tortured by Leif's examination, he declared two ribs on my left side were indeed cracked. He wrapped a bandage tightly around my middle. I dressed as he hurried off to make tea and to check on the others. If the brew was anything like the horrid stuff he fed me after Tricky's attempt to bleed me dry, I planned to dump it onto the ground.

Kade tucked me into his cot. He started a fire in the brazier, then promised to return after helping Leif. I squirmed, trying to find a comfortable position. A sharp point jabbed me in the leg and I remembered the blue piece. I pulled it out. Leaning over the cot and ignoring the pain, I opened the brazier's door. In the firelight, I examined the glass. So much trouble for such a little thing.

The scratches seemed random until I flipped it over. It could either be my overactive imagination or someone had carved a letter into the glass.

Kade returned carrying a steaming cup. I showed him the glass before he could force me to swallow the tea. He flinched as if burned.

"Relax. This one is spent. No magic."

He took the sea glass and handed me the mug. "Drink up."

"Ugh." The liquid smelled like a wet dog. "What do you think?" I pointed to the glass.

"I think you should drink your tea and go to sleep."

"About the scratches?"

He waited.

"Fine. Look, I'm sipping." I slurped loudly. As usual, Leif's medicinal concoction tasted horrible.

Kade examined the piece in the firelight. "The markings on this side resemble the letter S."

"I thought so! We should look at the others."

"And go crazy again?" Kade asked.

My elation died. "Have you discussed the...incident with the others yet? Are they all right?"

"Minor injuries only. Leif applied poultices and dispensed tea. Everyone was so exhausted I sent them all to bed. We'll discuss it in the morning." He sat on the edge of the cot. "You know, the tea tastes worse when it's cold."

I downed another gulp. "You should go to bed, too."

"I'll sleep in the main cavern. I don't want to bump your ribs."

"No need to worry." I scooted over.

"Opal, you should—"

"Finish my tea first. Good idea." I drained the cup. He still looked unconvinced.

"Please stay. The last two nights have been horrible." First Tricky, then the sea glass. With all that had happened, I had forgotten about the wound on my arm. In fact, even the pain in my ribs had dissipated. Leif's tea worked. I would thank him, but he would be obnoxious about it.

Kade slipped into the cot next to me. Once his arms wrapped around my waist, I fell asleep.

"I didn't see anyone," Heli said. She concentrated on the empty bowl in her lap, spinning it around. "I was in the middle of nowhere."

The early-morning sunlight touched the horizon. The beach remained in The Cliffs' shadow, casting twilight into the main cavern. Everyone gathered around the cook fire. And everyone avoided each other's gaze.

My ribs ached, but I wasn't about to ask Leif for more of his tea.

"A magician had charged the sea glass," Kade said. "Either he scattered them on the beach for you to find, or they were deposited there by the current."

"Why?" Heli asked. She sounded like a little girl.

"To sabotage us or as a joke," Kade guessed.

"Heck of a cruel joke," Raiden said.

"Maybe someone really wanted you to find them," I said. "Maybe they were trying to send you a message." I pulled out the blue piece.

Ten people flinched, including Kade, who should have known better.

"This one is safe," I said, handing it to Leif. "Looks like someone scratched the letter *S* on it."

Leif turned it over in his hands. "Why is it safe?"

I thought back. "When I touched it, it...sparked, waking me. After all the...craziness last night, it was the only piece not claimed."

"Let's assume you're right and it's a message," Kade said. "How do we examine the other pieces without going insane with desire?"

"Opal can spark them," Leif said. "In a place where we can't see."

It was a reasonable step in logic. However, I dreaded the prospect, remembering the burn and shock of pain from just one piece.

I pulled Leif aside. "Can you brew me more of your tea?"

"Which one?"

"The wet-dog one you gave me last night."

"Are your ribs hurting?"

"Yes." Which was the truth.

I returned to Kade's cot and dumped the sea glass onto the blanket. A mug of Leif's potion was within reach. Steeling myself, I drank the entire mug, then reached for the first piece.

By the time I finished, my numb hands could barely hold the glass. Pain burned along my skin from wrist to shoulders. My bones ached. I wrapped my arms around my waist and curled up on the cot.

Kade woke me with a hard shake. "Opal, what happened? We thought you'd be back by now."

My body throbbed. My arms and hands tingled as if they'd fallen asleep.

"Is it your ribs?" he asked in alarm.

"Yes. No. Leif. Dog." The room dimmed and Leif appeared next to Kade. A hot liquid burned my lips. I choked on the taste of dirt mixed with mint.

"Drink it. It'll help you," Leif said. "Trust me."

I wanted to make a sarcastic comment, but the pain eased and I drifted into a relieved sleep.

The next time I opened my eyes, Kade hovered above me with an anxious expression.

"I'm fine," I said, although I didn't have any energy.

"You slept for two days. That's *not* fine."

"Two days? But the melt, the orbs..." I tried to sit up.

Kade held me down. "No. You are to stay in bed until Leif gives you permission to move."

"Who made Leif boss?"

"I did when he saved your life."

"Pah! I would have been fine." I couldn't believe Kade had fallen for Leif's dramatics.

Kade sighed. "Opal, why didn't you tell us?"

"Tell you what?"

"About the pain. You didn't have to spark all that glass. You could have done a little at a time."

"Heli felt so bad... I wanted to help."

"She'll be fine. She's been sorting the sea glass, trying to decipher the message."

I tried to push up to my elbow, but Kade refused to budge. "Has she gotten any of it?"

"Not yet. One side of the glass has a letter and the other has a number code scratched on it. Once she figures out the code, she'll be able to assemble the letters in the right order."

An interesting puzzle. I longed to join her and to check on the glassmakers. "Can you ask Leif to come visit so I can get up?"

"Will you promise to stay in bed?"

"Yes."

Kade left. I fidgeted and thought of a bunch of questions I wanted to ask. A little of my energy returned— enough so I regretted promising to stay prone.

Leif arrived carrying a mug. "How's my favorite glass wizard today?"

"Wonderful. Can I move now?"

"Not yet." He handed me the drink.

I wrinkled my nose. Another foul-smelling brew. This one reminded me of mushrooms and moldy store-rooms.

"It's a restorative. You're to finish every drop and eat a full meal before you're allowed to walk among the living."

"Why do all your potions taste so bad?" I stalled for time.

"They're all made from plants and fruits grown in the Illiais Jungle. My father is an expert on herbal remedies, and, since I'm not the super healer like my sister…" He gave me a wry smile. "I have to make do with using leaves and spoors and roots and seeds."

Leif's clan, the Zaltanas, lived in the jungle. Their homestead had been built in the tree canopy, blending in with the surrounding greenery.

"Are you going to drink it? Or do I need to hold your nose and force it down your throat?"

I sipped the potion. It tasted better than it smelled. Swallowing a few more sips, I noticed deep scratches on his nose and cheeks. "Are they from me?" I pointed.

"I think so."

"Sorry."

"No problem. You sliced my face, I cracked your ribs. Let's call it even." His tone remained light, but his expression was uncharacteristically somber. "If you hadn't broken the spell...just imagine." His hand touched the hilt of his machete. "If I had thought about it before you went to neutralize the glass, I would have stopped you. The magic on them was strong. Maybe even master-level strong."

"Really?"

"It's hard to say for sure. I couldn't examine them while they were charged, but most magicians keep mental defenses in place so they don't fall for illusions and magical suggestions. The Stormdancers don't because their magic is...different. But the rest of us do. And for the sea glass's magic to break through mine and Skippy's defenses, it had to be strong."

"Skippy's?" I found that hard to believe.

"He may be a prick, but he's a powerful prick."

"Good to know." I thought about Leif's comments.

"The magician who charged the glass was either desperate or deranged." I drained the rest of Leif's brew and upended the mug. "Can I get up now?"

"Nope. You still need to eat."

"I'm sure Raiden has a savory dish on the fire." I pushed the blankets away. How did I get so many? Swinging my legs over the side, I stood, using the little energy I had collected. My legs buckled under me and I plopped down on the cot.

Leif watched me with an aggrieved expression. "It would be refreshing if, *for once,* I helped someone who actually *listened* to me."

"I drank your tea."

He harrumphed.

Kade arrived with a tray full of food.

"Make sure she eats it all," Leif said, shooting me a warning glare before he left.

I consumed a large serving of Raiden's special fish stew, bread and seaweed. The salty green leaves crunched between my teeth.

"What have the glassmakers been doing?" I asked Kade.

"They made a few orbs. But Heli's getting closer to figuring out the code. She thinks there may be missing pieces. Once you're feeling better, she wants to take us back to the spot where she found them."

I squinted at him in suspicion. He had changed the subject from the glassmakers rather fast and now he avoided my gaze. Yet I couldn't help being intrigued by the prospect of going to find more sea glass.

When I finished every bite as instructed by Leif, Kade put the tray on the floor. Instead of feeling energized by the food, I felt sleepy. My eyes kept drifting shut. Movement roused me as Kade pulled the blankets over me.

"Want to…" I muttered.

"Later." He kissed my temple.

It was hard to stay mad at Leif for spiking my food with a sleeping potion when I felt so much better. The early-morning twilight shone through the cracks in the curtain. Kade slept on a pile of blankets on the floor. He looked exhausted, so I tiptoed from the cave without waking him.

I felt bad about slipping out, but I didn't want to have to drink one of Leif's potions before I could go anywhere. Hiking up the trail, I checked on the kiln. The glassmakers had been busy. A handful of orbs filled a table. I picked one up and brought it out into the light.

A purple iridescent film coated the outside of the round translucent glass. It resembled a bubble of soap. A small neck and lip for the opening ruined the perfect sphere shape. I ran a finger along the inside of the hole. The orb could be any size as long as it wasn't too heavy for a Stormdancer to hold, but the opening had to be a specific diameter or else the rubber stopper wouldn't fit.

Once a Stormdancer filled the orb with the storm's energy, the stopper sealed the energy inside. When the orb arrived at one of the Stormdance Clan's factories, a glass tube was inserted through the rubber to transfer the energy from the orb to the machinery.

I hefted the orb. This one weighed about eight pounds and felt solid, but so had the ones that shattered during the last storm season. Carrying it back to the table, I tried to ignore the hum of potential vibrating through my fingers.

I stopped short. Why couldn't I use an orb to siphon the magic from the sea glass? Because at the time the melt wasn't ready, and Skippy would have had a fit—not that I cared. If we found more sea glass, I would have to try it.

The rubber stopper fit perfectly. Impressive. In fact, it fit all the orbs on the table with the same snugness. Incredible. My opinion of Ziven and Zetta increased by a factor of ten. All were a beautiful round shape and their sizes matched. Wow.

Only one test left. I found a hammer and pounded on the orb. It broke with a solid crack.

"What are you doing?" Ziven asked with a sharp and accusing tone.

I startled and spun around. "Good morning to you, too."

He strode into the cave, scanning the equipment as if he'd caught me stealing. "Why did you destroy that orb? It was—"

"Perfect. So far." I took one of the broken pieces out to the light and inspected it. Ziven followed me.

The thickness of the glass was consistent throughout the section. Good. "Do you have any orbs left over from the previous glassmakers?" I swallowed a sudden lump in my throat. Sir had murdered the three siblings for the orb's recipe.

"Why?" Again the suspicious tone.

"To compare the density. I just want to be sure these match those before I give Kade my approval."

"Oh. Okay." He strode to the back of the cavern and returned with another orb.

I smiled when he handed it to me. It was egg-shaped. One of Nodin's. He always had trouble shaping the orb. With reluctance, I broke it and evaluated the cross-section.

"Your orbs are wonderful. They should work well for the Stormdancers."

Ziven beamed and it transformed his whole face. He looked years younger.

"Zetta will be happy to hear it," he said.

I collected the broken pieces and dumped them into the cullet barrel. One of the joys of working with glass was being able to reuse it. The cullet would be melted in the cauldron and made into new orbs.

On my way down to the main cavern, I checked in on Kade. He was still sound asleep and I wondered how late he had stayed up the night before. Most of the people who slept around the cook fire remained motionless in their cots. For a second, I panicked, thinking they had all been hit with Curare. But then Leif rolled over and Wick snored.

I scanned the sleepers, searching for Skippy. Not the type to rub elbows with the masses, he must have taken a cot up to one of the empty caves for privacy. Since we arrived at The Cliffs, he had been keeping a low profile. I didn't mind. It was a nice break not having him by my side all the time.

Not wanting to bother anyone in the common room, I headed to the stables to check on the horses. I found Raiden filling their buckets with fresh water.

"Good thing we have this spring back here," Raiden said. "Otherwise, we'd have to cart in a tankful of drinkable water every season."

I helped him feed the horses and muck out the stalls. Quartz nuzzled my ear before eating her breakfast. They all needed exercise. I would ask Kade about riding them to the location where Heli found the sea glass. It would save time and energy.

"Has Heli discovered anything more about the glass?" I asked Raiden.

"No. And she's obsessed about it. It caused enough trouble, so I told her to toss it back into the sea."

"It's harmless now."

Raiden shot me a dubious look.

I changed the subject. "Your new glassmakers have made some beautiful orbs."

"Will they work?"

"They should."

"*Should* isn't an encouraging word."

"There's always a possibility something may go wrong." A lesson I learned from experience, yet each time there was an element of surprise.

"Would you stake Kade's life on it?" Raiden asked. "Because you know he'll want to be the first one to test the new orbs out."

I knew. "Yes, I would."

Raiden stared out to sea for a moment. "That's more encouraging. Especially since it's obvious you two are a couple."

"He hasn't said anything to you?"

"I've hardly spoken to him since he returned. He's been gone since the end of the cooling season, when he chased after the bastards who murdered Indra and her brothers." Raiden kicked a rock into the sea. "He sent me a message explaining what happened, but it was basic facts." He gave me a sly smile. "He's happier now. And I don't have to worry too much about him taking unnecessary chances and risking his life. We don't have many Stormdancers."

"How many are there?"

He gestured toward the cave. "What you see is what you get."

"Five! That's all?" And one was in training.

"We lost Kaya and Gian during the last storm season, and the year before a rookie lost control and drowned. Then with the glassmakers' deaths, I'm surprised Tebbs even admitted she had the power."

"She probably heard about the fabulous location and posh accommodations," I teased.

"Hey! When I was younger, the dancers slept on the beach and cooked for themselves. Now they have cots and privacy screens and a cook. They're spoiled."

I laughed. We finished cleaning the stalls and headed back to the common area.

"We must be doing something right," Raiden said. "When the word spread that we needed glassmakers, we were overwhelmed with applicants."

"How did you decide to hire Ziven and Zetta?" I asked, glad for this opportunity.

"I wanted to invite you back to help us since you know the orb-making process, but Councilor Stormdance said you were busy."

Busy disobeying the Council's orders and hunting down Ulrick. No need to tell Raiden that.

When I didn't say anything, he continued, "I whittled the field down to two families based on experience and knowledge, but, before I could announce my choice, Councilor Stormdance arrived with Ziven and Zetta. He claimed they were perfect for the job and hired them."

"You must have been livid."

"*Livid* is too tame a word." He scowled. "The Councilor gives me the responsibility and doesn't even ask my opinion. It was a big waste of my time."

"Look on the bright side. They produced a high-quality orb. That's the most important thing."

"Yeah, yeah. Silver lining and all that, but I just wish those two had—" he waved his hands as if trying to pull the right word out of the air "—more personality. They're too serious and suspicious. They always think you're trying to trick them or tease them. We're here four months a year, living together. I hope they relax now that they have the orb recipe."

We returned to the main cave. A few people had roused. Raiden stirred the fire to life and I walked over to Heli. She bent over a table, moving the sea glass around with her fingertips.

"Anything?" I asked.

She startled.

"Sorry."

"Don't apologize," she said. "I should be apologizing to you. To everyone, but no one will listen. They tell me it's not my fault."

"It isn't—"

"Bull. Put yourself in my place. How would you feel?"

I considered. "Lousy."

"At least you didn't die."

"Heli, don't listen to Leif. He exaggerates and revels in drama."

"Really? Because two days ago when you were still comatose, he was alarmed. And I watched him have many serious discussions with Kade, who looked distressed." She cocked her head to the side, peering past my shoulder. "Sort of like he looks now."

I turned. Barefoot and with sleep-tousled hair, Kade

strode toward me. His unbuttoned shirt flapped behind him. I braced for his lecture.

"As much as I enjoyed thinking all kinds of horrible possibilities about your whereabouts, do you think the next time you disappear, you could leave me a note?" Kade asked. "We can even make up a form. I'm gone because of A, Tricky, or B, Devlen, or C, fill in the blank. You can just circle a reason and leave it for me."

"Wow. That's some impressive sarcasm," Heli said. "I'm glad I'm not on the receiving end this time."

Considering all that had happened to me since I'd known Kade, I couldn't blame him for being upset. "I'm sorry. I'll try not to do it again."

An eyebrow spiked. "Try?"

"Since your *suggestion* of making up a form actually is a *good* idea, I'd say try is the best I can do. I have no control over a whole list of things, but what I can control, I'll make sure to let you know."

His anger dissipated as he conceded the point. "You liked my form idea?" A hint of a smile played at the corners of his mouth.

"It could use a little work. I think we should put check boxes next to the list—circling the reason might take too long. With a box, I can just check and go."

"I'll get right on it."

Despite my assurances that I felt fine, Leif wouldn't approve my request.

"Rest today and you can go tomorrow," he said.

Kade agreed. "You can help Heli with the code. Maybe find out more about the sea glass."

I grumped, but listened and even drank a cup of Leif's wet-dog brew with breakfast.

Heli welcomed my aid. We sorted the glass by color, by number and by letter, hoping to see a pattern. Nothing. The numbers weren't consecutive. We tried matching the pieces like a jigsaw puzzle, but none of them fit together.

"What can scratch glass?" Heli asked. She held a translucent green one.

"Diamonds can and other hard gemstones. Glass cutters have bits of diamonds on the wheel, but they're not the nice ones used for jewelry."

"So anyone could have done it?"

"The scratches, yes. The magic, no."

"Did you get any sense of the magician when you neutralized them?"

Heli looked so hopeful, I hated to disappoint her. But all I felt was burning pain. "No."

All our attempts to decipher the markings failed. Heli was determined. She had the trip back to the sea glass's location all planned out, enlisting help from Leif to form a null shield before we reached the destination to keep everyone safe.

We would ride the horses. Heli with me on Quartz. Raiden insisted on coming along, so Kade offered to share Moonlight. Though not happy about the prospect, Skippy would tag along, too.

Unfortunately, we never had the chance to execute

Heli's plans. As we gathered around the fire to eat dinner, Leif arrived and pulled me aside. He held one of my glass messengers in his hand. "Opal, we have to leave. Now."

17

"WHY?" I ASKED LEIF IN ALARM. "What happened? Mara—"

"She's fine. Nothing bad happened. I just received a message from Irys...Master Jewelrose." He hesitated. "You're not going to like this, but it makes sense."

"What? Tell me." I gripped his arm.

Leif glanced across the fire. The others talked and ate dinner, ignoring us, but Kade watched in concern.

"The Masters have detected a wild magician in the Bloodgood lands. This person is on the verge of flaming out. They've ordered us to get down there and stop him—or her."

"How?"

"This is the part you're not going to like. The Masters want you to siphon the wild magic into an orb."

Shock rendered me speechless.

"You'll save a life and stop the power source from warping. It's a win-win situation for everyone."

When put that way, he had a point. "Does the Council know? Did they give permission?"

"Yes, it's all been approved. We need to leave tonight."

"Do you have a specific location?"

"All they know is, the person is near the coast, maybe out on the peninsula."

"Rather vague."

"Don't worry. When we get closer, I'll be able to smell the power."

Our whispered conversation went on long enough to draw Kade over to us.

"Something wrong?" he asked.

Leif explained about the message.

"Take one of the orbs and any supplies you need," Kade said.

"I guess we'll have to tell Skippy," I said. The thought of traveling with him so soon was an unappealing prospect. "Unless we ditch—"

"No," Leif said. "As much as I would love to sneak out without him, the Council would be upset."

"And think about how this *errand* for the Masters will gain you more of the Council's trust," Kade said.

Another good point. Though the more I thought about this mission, the greater my annoyance. The Council treated me as if I were this dangerous entity until a situation arose where I might be beneficial to them.

Kade helped me collect supplies and pack my saddlebags. Ziven fussed about giving up one of the orbs until

Kade reminded him that the glassmakers worked for the Stormdancers. Not the other way around.

I joined Leif and Skippy at the stable. Bamboo torches burned, casting a flickering yellow light.

"We'll leave Moonlight here for now," Leif said. "We can pick him up on the way back."

Skippy scowled and muttered as he saddled Beryl. Quartz's and Rusalka's ears perked forward. They surged out of their stalls as if excited for another trip. I gathered their tack and we readied the horses.

Kade arrived with a handful of salted fish. "It's not much, but it'll get you through a couple days."

"Thanks." Leif packed them into his bag. "Good thing I still have all that jerky, and a few new recipes from Raiden." He finished tightening the girth straps around Rusalka.

I hefted the saddle onto Quartz's back. Kade helped me center it.

"I guess your surfing lessons will have to wait," he said.

Finally, one good thing about this unexpected trip. I tried to look disappointed, but couldn't maintain it for long. "Darn."

"If it's any consolation, we'll have time when you get back. And by then, the storms will have fueled the waves. They'll be bigger and stronger and more fun."

"Wonderful." I loaded the word with as much sarcasm as possible.

Kade failed to be disheartened. "You're going to love it. Trust me."

By the time we finished with the horses, the moon crested The Cliffs, coating the sand with a weak light. Stars peppered the night sky. No wind stirred. Calm waves rolled onto the beach with a soft hiss-slap.

"Wear your cloak," Kade said. "It's going to be cold tonight."

We had already said goodbye to the others. Prin seemed happier than the glassmakers over my departure, which surprised me. Heli asked me to keep an eye out for more sea glass and Raiden wished us clear weather.

Leif and Skippy mounted, waiting for me. I wrapped my cloak around my shoulders. Kade pulled me into a tight embrace.

"Please be careful," he said in my ear.

"I will." We kissed.

"We're wasting time," Leif said.

After another quick hug goodbye, I swung up on Quartz. Leif urged Rusalka into a gallop, heading south. Skippy and I followed.

I enjoyed riding on the beach. The scrunch of sand under the horses' hooves, the tangy salt air and the sparkles of moonlight on the surface of the sea all combined into an exhilarating experience. Of course, the novelty wore off as my energy waned. The beach looked inviting. Soft sand and the rhythm of the waves lulled me. I dozed in the saddle.

When the sun rose, we stopped for breakfast. Leif agreed to a few hours of sleep, but set a watch schedule.

"I don't want to be surprised again." He rubbed his neck. "I'll take the first shift."

Skippy collapsed on his mat and fell asleep in no time. Even though exhaustion pulled at my body, my mind raced.

"How long will it take us to get there?" I asked.

"Seven to nine days, depends on how far south the magician lives. We'll stay on the beach most of the way. Master Bloodgood said it would be the fastest route."

"What about the horses? They'll need fresh water and more grain."

"There are a few coastal towns along the way. We'll stop there for supplies and sniff around." Leif smiled.

His comment led me to wonder about the magician's wild magic. "How do the Masters know someone is out of control? The Bloodgood peninsula is a long way from the Keep."

"They flash. Without any control over what they're doing, they'll grab power and use it all at once. It sends ripples in the power blanket, alerting the Masters. It usually takes a few flashes for the Masters to pinpoint the location of the wild magician." Leif's gaze grew distant. "It's how Irys found Yelena. She flashed while Irys worked undercover in Ixia. Yelena learned how to control her power, but if she had been too close to flameout, Irys would have killed her."

And now Irys and Yelena were good friends. Interesting. "Have the Masters killed many people?"

"Six in the last fifty years." He dug his fingers into

the sand. "I was there for three of them. My abilities helped the Masters find the person faster. Fortunately, that is a rare event. They usually find the magician before it becomes necessary. And now with your glass animals and their inner glow, Irys has a foolproof way to identify those who have power. This is the first person she missed in five years."

"Why didn't the Masters sense this person before now?"

Leif played with the sand, letting the grains pour off his palms. "This one is...different. He or she has flashed twice in the past season. The first one was minor and didn't cause too much concern. But the second was huge, bordering on flameout. That's why we're scrambling to find him or her." He wiped his hands on his pants. "But this time, we won't have to terminate the person." Leif's excitement lit his face. "Your ability to siphon the magic will solve the problem."

Despite my annoyance at the Council, I was glad that my strange glass magic would help someone.

The days and nights blurred together as we set a fast pace. We slept on the beach during our short breaks. The Cliffs turned into hills, then smoothed into dunes. On the fourth—fifth?—day we stopped at a small seaside town. Faded paint peeled off wooden buildings and crushed seashells paved the streets.

As we rode through the two blocks of downtown, the residents gawked at us. By the way the children chased after us and pointed, I figured the place didn't get many visitors. Windows had been boarded up. Only one inn remained open for business.

We rented a room. First thing I did was order a bath. Sand filled my boots and stuck to my skin. I decided I liked it much better melted as glass.

The town's sad state wasn't unique. During the next two—three?—days of our trip, we rode past other settlements. All weathered and lacking vitality.

But on the day Leif turned serious about sniffing out the wild magician, the beaten-down buildings changed into well-cared-for dwellings. Shoppers bustled in the market. Residents smiled and commented on the weather.

During dinner that night, I asked Leif about the difference.

"Oysters," he said. "We're getting closer to the oyster farms. Lots of jobs and money associated with harvesting oysters and selling the pearls. Since these pearl-growing oysters were discovered off the Bloodgood peninsula, business has been booming."

Our pace slowed as we rode through the clusters of oyster farms. Leif combed through the streets, searching for the wild magician. He talked to various townspeople. When a person started to display signs of magic, gossip and speculation would spread.

However, no one had heard rumors and most residents seemed surprised. After three days of nothing, Leif speculated the magician might be inland. He contacted the Master Magicians, but they insisted we stay on the coast.

"It's been ten days. How much longer?" Skippy asked.

"As long as it takes," Leif snapped. "If you ask that question again, I'm going to punch you."

On the eleventh day, we met with one of the town's leaders. He didn't know of anyone with powers, but he had some suspicions.

"There's a group living on the tip of the peninsula. They keep to themselves, so anything is possible with them. About twice a season, they send the same three men to sell their pearls and buy supplies." He adjusted his straw hat. The wide brim blocked the sun from his gray eyes. "They built a wall, blocking access to the tip. We've gotten the hint that visitors aren't welcome. But if you're here as representatives of the Master Magicians and the Council, they have no *legal* recourse to block you."

That was the kicker. Legal versus illegal.

"How far from here?" Leif asked.

"About four hours on horseback. There's not much between our town and the tip. Heck, I'm surprised they can harvest oysters on that rocky point. The currents whip around there, making it dangerous to swim."

We all glanced at the sea as if we could see the tide. The sun dipped into the horizon, sending ripples of color.

"We'll wait until tomorrow," Leif said, then thanked the man.

Renting a room at one of the local inns, we dumped our bags on the floor and discussed strategy.

"If you notice, I never say wild or uncontrolled magician," Leif said. "People know those words can get someone killed and they'll lie to you. New magician is a better descriptor."

"Why are you telling us?" I asked. "You've been doing all the talking."

"This situation could be trouble. The leaders may be suspicious. They may separate us in order to question us alone—make sure our stories match." He stretched out on one of the four beds. "I've dealt with isolated groups of people before. They don't like strangers and authority. We'll need to tread carefully. And follow my lead. Go along with anything I say, even if it doesn't make sense."

"And how's that different than normal?" I teased.

He threw a pillow at me. I caught it and plopped it on my bed.

"Did you bring your switchblade?" Leif asked.

"Yes. Why?"

"They'll probably confiscate our weapons, claiming they don't allow violence within their territory, but promising to return them when we leave."

"Yet, they'll be well armed. Right?" I asked.

"Yep. And they'll have a justifiable reason as to why. Don't believe everything they tell you, either. Otherwise, you'll want to join them."

"It's a good thing I have Skippy here."

The magician didn't even bother to correct me. He glared, but his heart wasn't in it.

"I'll bite. Why is it good he's here?" Leif asked.

"I'm sure he has orders to make sure I return to the Keep. If I decide to go native and dive for oysters, he'll save me."

"You're right. Wow. He's actually going to be useful. I need to write home about it." Leif searched through his bag as if looking for paper.

Skippy ignored him. He gathered a few items and left for the washroom. I noticed he walked with a slight limp. We'd been on horseback for a week and a half. Skippy started bugging Leif about travel time a few days into our trip. Standoffish and snide remarks were expected, but not whiny.

When Skippy returned, I kept an eye on him as he prepared for bed. His stiff movements and little winces confirmed my suspicions.

I stood and stretched, groaning a bit over my aching ribs. "Phew. I'm saddle sore. Do you have any barbasco yams, Leif?"

"Of course." He dug through his supplies, pulling out an orange lump. He sliced a section off and handed it to me. "I could use some, too." Cutting a few more pieces, he popped one into his mouth. Then he reached over with a casual motion and gave one to Skippy.

I looked away before Skippy caught me staring. Arranging my pillows, I chewed on my yam, then slipped into bed.

* * *

"That's a heck of a wall," Leif said.

As we traveled toward the peninsula's tip, the land narrowed until the sea was visible on both sides of the trail—more like a goat path. Black rocks and sand dominated the landscape. A few bushes and trees clung to life, but, other than the occasional gull swooping above, the area was barren.

I agreed with Leif. It was an impressive barrier. Boulders had been stacked together, forming at least an eight-foot-high wall. Sitting on Quartz, I still couldn't see over it. The barricade spanned the entire length of the peninsula. Continuous except for a sturdy iron gate.

"I bet the gate's locked," Leif said. "Any takers?"

"No. Go on," I urged. "Knock."

Leif dismounted and strode up to the gate. "Hello?"

A well-armed man appeared on the other side. "What do you want?" he demanded. His manner oozed hostility and contempt.

"Good morning to you, too," Leif parried with sarcasm.

The man's deadly gaze would have sent most people running.

All pleasantness dropped from Leif's face. He stepped forward, his nose an inch from the gate. "I want to talk to the person in charge. Now."

"Why?"

"Not your concern."

The big brute towered at least a foot over Leif. Stubble

covered his cheeks, chin and the top of his head. "Request denied."

"Fine. I'll come back with the authorities." Leif turned to us. "Do you think we should tell Bain? Perhaps he would want to join us."

"Oh yes," I said. "First Magician is a Bloodgood. He'll want to visit his family, and the sea air would be healthy for him."

"Who are you?" the guard asked.

"I am Leif Liana Zaltana, a representative of the Sitian Council."

The man failed to look impressed.

"Either fetch your boss or I'll fetch a squadron of soldiers," Leif said.

"Jay, get Walsh," he barked to another person beyond our view. He kept his gaze on us.

We didn't wait long. Soon another man arrived. Walsh perhaps. He was a few inches taller than the guard, and a lot thinner—almost skeletal. His white tunic and pants hung on his frame. The sun had bleached his long blond hair almost white.

"What's going on here?" he demanded.

"Are you in charge?" Leif asked.

"Yes."

"Then I need to speak with you. In private."

"Jay said you're from the Sitian Council?"

"Yes."

"I'll need proof. We don't...associate with many people outside our family."

Leif opened one of his saddlebags and brought out a scroll. He handed the document through the bars to Walsh. The man unrolled it and scanned the paper.

"Open the gate," Walsh said to the guard. "I would apologize, but we don't usually receive *unexpected* visitors. Since we harvest pearls, we are naturally suspicious of foreigners. If you had sent me a message and arranged a meeting..." He swept a bony hand out as if to imply none of this would have happened.

"Our business is urgent. We didn't have time for protocol." Leif walked Rusalka through the gate.

Skippy and I dismounted and followed. Walsh led the way. Right past the wall were cottages made of bamboo. They were lined up with such precision, it looked as if they had been planted there. Farther out, near the tip of the peninsula, wooden buildings hugged the beach. People scurried between the water and the structures. A few carried buckets, while others pushed wheelbarrows.

Walsh guided us to a stable, then to a smaller building nearby. Inside was his office. Gesturing toward a round conference table ringed with wooden chairs, he invited us to sit down. He asked his assistant—a young girl around fourteen years old—to bring tea and fruit.

When she hurried away, he finally introduced himself. "I'm Walsh Bloodrose. Elected representative of my family."

"Bloodrose isn't a clan name," Leif said.

Walsh's laughter rasped in his lungs and transformed

into a coughing fit. "Sorry. I forget. My family has so many Bloodgoods and Jewelroses that we stopped keeping track long ago and just use Bloodrose." He wiped the corner of his eyes with a handkerchief. When he composed himself, he studied me and Skippy. "You haven't introduced your companions."

"This is Opal Cowan and Hale Krystal."

He nodded to us, but his gaze lingered on my sais. So far, Leif's predictions about our reception hadn't all come true. We kept our weapons and we were still together. His assistant returned. She carried a trayful of fruits and tea. Putting her burden on the table, she poured a cup of tea for everyone, then bolted.

"Now, what is this urgent business of yours?" Walsh asked.

Leif explained about searching for a magician.

"Then you have found him." Walsh spread his arms wide. "I'm Keep trained. I graduated about twenty years ago."

"A *new* magician. Someone who might not even realize they have power," Leif said.

Anger flared in Walsh's eyes, but he blinked it away. "No. Not here. I would have sensed him or her."

"Do you mind if we have a look around?" Leif asked.

Walsh's hesitation lasted a mere heartbeat. "Of course not. I'll give you a tour of our oyster farm." He swept out of the office, leaving us to follow in his wake.

He headed toward the beach on the northern side of the tip. Coarse yellow sand mixed with gray rocks that extended into the sea. The building nearby wasn't as solid as it appeared from a distance. The side facing the sea was open, letting in the cool breeze, while the roof kept the sun off the workers.

"It's a simple operation. The younger members of our family harvest the oysters from the sea and bring them here." Walsh gestured to the women and men sitting at long tables, prying open shells.

Pearls were placed in small containers and the oysters were scraped out into another. The children carted buckets filled with oysters from the sea and dumped them onto the tables. They returned to the surf and waded into the waves.

"What's going on over there?" I asked, pointing to the southern side.

"Same thing," Walsh said. "We use both sides. The pearls pay for supplies. A person can only eat so many oysters."

"How many people live here?" Leif asked.

"Two hundred fifty-three and two halves."

"Halves?" I asked.

"Two ladies are expecting babies in a few months. We count them as halves until they're born." He beamed with pride.

I noticed a few men standing around. Unlike the workers, they were armed.

Walsh noticed my gaze. "Guards," he said. "Pearls are expensive. We've had thieves and pirates steal them from us." He tsked. "It's why we built the wall and have armed men on the beach."

His comments were reasonable. Leif walked ahead of us. I guessed he sniffed for the wild magician. He wandered onto the beach, then turned south.

Walsh intercepted him before he moved too far away. "The best way to meet all my family is for you and your companions to stay for dinner. Everyone comes to the dining hall. And you're welcome to stay overnight if it gets too late. We have a few empty cottages just in case." He smiled, revealing stained teeth.

Skippy and I looked to Leif. He nodded, agreeing to dinner.

"Wonderful. Everyone will be so pleased." The skin around Walsh's mouth stretched wider, resembling a grinning skull. "You can tell us news from the Citadel. We haven't had visitors in..." His gaze drifted to the guards as if the memory of the last visitors hadn't gone well. "A while. Brand," he called. One of the guards left his post and joined us. "Please show them to our guest cottage. Also point out the dining hall and washhouse. We ring a dinner bell, so you won't miss it. Make yourselves at home." Walsh gave us a jaunty wave and returned to his office.

Brand played tour guide. Another cluster of buildings was located behind Walsh's office. He jabbed a thick finger at them. "Food's in the blue one and the baths are in the yellow."

Good thing he mentioned the colors as all the structures looked the same—one-story tall, wooden and a basic rectangular shape. In other words, boring.

"What's the red one?" I asked.

"That's the school."

"And the green?" Leif asked.

"A recreation room and common room. The gray one is storage and an infirmary, which is mainly used for the children's cuts and scrapes. There's a birthing room, though. We have our own midwife."

The stark compound lacked personality. Pure function. No gardens or flowers or artwork. At least none visible. Perhaps they decorated their cottages. As we entered into the guest quarters, I thought perhaps not.

Plain walls, drab-colored blankets and practical table and chairs.

"The dinner bell will ring in two hours," Brand said. He left.

We waited a few minutes, making sure he was out of range before saying anything.

"This is…" I cast about for the right word.

"Weird," Leif said. "I'm getting all kinds of emotions from these people. But they don't feel right."

"Did you sense the wild magician?" Skippy asked.

"No, but I haven't gotten close to everyone yet."

"What did you mean by right?" I asked.

"When outsiders arrive, the reaction is usually curiosity mixed with a little apprehension and a bit of excitement. These people are afraid and worried. Also there's a sense of urgency and secrecy. They could be hiding the magician, and we could be causing the fear.

But no curiosity. No excitement. Not even from the children."

Another oddity struck me. "Did you notice their clothing all matched? It reminded me of Ixia where they are required to wear uniforms. Except in Ixia, they use color. Here it's all tans, grays and white, as if the life has been bleached from this place."

"Why does it matter?" Skippy asked. "They're not doing anything illegal. We're here to find the magician. How this family chooses to live and dress is their own business. Not ours."

I hated to agree with him, but he had a point.

"I could be reading more into their reactions than is there," Leif said. "Just keep an eye out during dinner and listen."

Dinner was a quiet affair despite the full tables. The dining room lacked ornamentation. Walsh's family lined up and pushed plates along a long counter. Servers standing over containers of food spooned helpings onto the dishes.

Walsh had greeted us at the door and escorted us inside. He sent his assistant to fill plates for us even though we protested. The taste of oysters tainted all the food, even the bread. We sat at Walsh's table with his brother, Fallon, Fallon's wife and two daughters.

The youngest, Gia, sat next to me. She looked about eight years old. Her long blond hair had been woven into many thin braids, which were pulled back into a ponytail.

Walsh prattled on about the family and their accomplishments. The rest of the diners spoke in low tones.

I asked Gia what was her favorite subject in school.

Her eyes bulged like a fish out of water. She shot Walsh a terrified glance.

He gave her an indulgent smile. "Answer her, she won't bite."

With reluctance, Gia said, "I like math, but I like swimming the best."

"Do you dive for oysters?" I asked.

She nodded.

Walsh said, "She's a little fish. We can't keep her out of the water. She dives deeper and stays down longer than most of the boys."

Gia dipped her head as if embarrassed.

"That's wonderful," I said. Then I leaned close and whispered, "I'm not a good swimmer at all. The last time I was in the sea, the waves pushed me around like a bath toy."

A smile flashed on her face. It was gone in a second, and I realized that none of the so-called Bloodroses smiled except Walsh. But even his felt fake as if he tried to sell us something we didn't need.

"What do you do for fun?" I asked her.

She sought Walsh's approval again. "We bake bread. We sew clothes. We tend the garden."

All chores.

Before I could ask her another question, Walsh said, "Tell us news from the Citadel. Is Master Featherstone still First Magician or has some young hotshot passed the Master-level test?"

Wow. They've been out of the loop for at least five years. Leif filled him in on Roze Featherstone's attempt to overthrow the Sitian Council with her Daviian Warpers. No one in the whole room said a word. Even Walsh remained silent for a few moments after Leif finished the story.

"My, my," Walsh said. "And this...Soulfinder is a Zaltana? One of your cousins?"

"My sister," Leif said.

"That's impressive." Walsh turned to me. "Were you there for the Warper Battle?"

"Not the battle, but I helped with the...cleanup."

"How about you?" Walsh asked Skippy.

"No. I was on assignment in Fulgor." Skippy sounded petulant, as if he'd rather have been at the battle.

"Lucky you," Leif said. "It was close. Twelve magicians died fighting the Warpers." His sobering words failed to change Skippy's expression.

"Are you also a magician?" Walsh asked me.

"Yes."

"Opal's a glass magician," Leif said. He pulled one of my messengers from his pocket.

The sea horse glowed with an inner blue fire. Its happy song vibrated in my chest.

"Interesting. What makes it shine?" Walsh asked.

At least he'd told the truth about being a magician.

"Magic," Leif explained. "Trapped inside."

Gia crinkled her forehead in confusion. "But I don't see a light, Uncle."

Fallon, his wife and other daughter couldn't see it, either.

"Only magicians can see the glow. May I show it to the rest of your family?" Leif asked.

A calculating coldness slid behind Walsh's eyes. "Please do." He watched Leif present the sea horse to the others.

Aside from the general bewilderment, no one admitted to seeing the magic.

When Leif returned, Walsh said, "Now do you believe me?"

"It was never a question of belief," Leif said. "It's just that in the past few years, we've discovered magical powers in people who would have been passed over. For example, Opal's magic. She was assessed by Master Jewelrose, and Fourth Magician found no indications of potential. But Opal's power is rather unique, and these—" he held the seahorse up "—glass creations can find those with...latent magical powers."

"They must speed up the process of finding the fledglings," Walsh said. He stared at the sea horse with a speculative purse of his thin colorless lips. "It would be a handy device to have."

"You don't need one now." Leif gestured to the rest of the dining room. "I've assessed all your family members. Unless some are missing?"

"No. All are here." Walsh straightened for a moment,

then leaned back. Lacing his fingers together, he rested them in his lap. "You're right. I've no need for it."

His body language contradicted his words. Considering how worried he was about pirates and thieves, I suspected he lied to us about his people. A few guards must have been out patrolling the grounds.

While we finished dinner, I glanced around, counting tables. I estimated two hundred and forty people were in the room.

Walsh escorted us to the guest cottage. "It's been a lovely evening, but we wake at dawn to harvest the oysters. Please feel free to avail yourselves of the bathhouse. I'll instruct Brand to stay nearby in case you need anything." He said good-night and left.

Leif waited a few minutes before calling us over. We discussed the odd dinner.

"He lied about everyone being in the room," Leif said.

I agreed, telling him my estimate.

"Shoot. Wish I'd thought of that." Leif shook his head. "I used magic and he knew it."

"What's next?" I asked.

"We'll avail ourselves of his hospitality and take a look around."

Leif's plan didn't account for Brand being so... helpful. The guard led us to the bathhouse, gave us towels and robes to use and waited for us to finish. On the way back to the cottage, he talked about how self-sufficient the family was and how they only bought a few raw materials from the market. He lit the lanterns inside. Telling us good-night, he left. I doubted he went far.

"And now?" I asked Leif.

"Plan B." He crossed to the bed and wiggled under the blankets.

I combed my wet hair. Wishing my clothes were cleaner, I prepared to go to sleep.

Skippy glanced from Leif to me and back. "Plan B?" he asked.

"Wait until the middle of the night, and sneak out to investigate," Leif said, but kept his eyes closed.

"What about Brand?"

"Opal, do you have your goodies with you?" Leif asked.

"Of course."

"Then we'll send Brand a little present to keep him occupied. No worries, Skippy. Opal and I have done this a million times."

"A million. Right." Skippy didn't sound convinced. "Just so I know. How many *real* times?"

Leif's answer was a soft snore.

I thought back. We had used my glass spiders and bees when the Storm Thieves attacked us. And one of my spiders had saved my sister. "Two."

"Wonderful."

I detected a lack of sincerity in Skippy's reply.

Leif shook my shoulder. "Opal, wake up."

I peeked through heavy eyelids. Darkness filled the cottage. I swatted at his hand. "Go away."

"Come on. We need to move. Now."

The urgency in his voice roused me. "What happened?"

"Walsh has done more than lie to us."

"How—"

"Didn't you feel it?" Skippy asked me with an incredulous tone.

"Feel what?"

"The wild magician flashed with an unbelievable amount of power so close I can taste it," Leif said.

18

BRAND NO LONGER hovered near our cottage, but two new guards circled the building. I crushed six glass spiders and sent them to distract our guards.

A yelp followed a cry. "...see the size of that—"

"Over there! Huge sand spiders! We'd better..." The ring of steel sounded, masking the guard's words. "...poisonous bite. Get the one on the left, I'll take right."

As soon as the guards were lured away, we slipped out. Leif headed straight for the long building on the south coast—the one Walsh claimed mirrored the oyster operation on the north side.

We snuck around from the back. Leif held his machete and I clasped the orb Kade had given to me. Trepidation pulsed in my chest. The memories of how horrible Crafty had felt when I siphoned her magic replayed in my mind. Would I be able to inflict such pain again?

The building did indeed resemble the other, but instead of the oyster tables a long wooden chute occupied the work space. Scattered around the floor were boxes with wire-mesh bottoms. The structure was also thicker than the northern one, with an enclosed section running the entire length.

Leif bypassed all the equipment and aimed for a door near the southeast edge of the building. Lantern light shone from a row of small windows near the roof. We pressed against the wall. Loud voices arguing inside were punctuated with sounds of a scuffle.

The door burst open, spilling light and people. Two men dragged a struggling young man out. Walsh followed them. He spotted us and seemed more resigned than surprised.

"I found the magician you seek," Walsh said. "He's been hiding from me, and has, until tonight, flashed his wild power when I was away."

"We need—"

Walsh interrupted Leif. "I know. You've come to terminate him. Let me talk with him first. See how bad it is."

The young man stopped fighting his captors. He gaped at Leif in sudden fear.

"We don't need to kill him," Leif said. "We have... another way to neutralize his power."

"Really? How?" Walsh asked eagerly.

"I need to assess the situation. Perhaps we can go somewhere private?"

He snapped back to business. "I'll talk to him, then you can assess all you want." Walsh turned to the guards. "Take him to my office."

The men pulled the adolescent away. At least his terror had transformed into confusion.

"Join me after breakfast," Walsh said to us.

"What if he escapes?" Skippy asked.

"He won't."

Walsh didn't lie this time. The young man sat in a chair in front of his desk. He rested his head in his hands, but snapped it straight when we entered.

We arrived just after breakfast. The dining room had buzzed louder than at dinner. I had wondered if the change was due to Walsh's absence or the news of last night's excitement.

Walsh invited us to sit down as if we gathered to discuss the weather. I studied the wild magician. His shaggy black hair hung over his eyes and ears. He wore only a pair of gray short pants. No shoes. Tanned skin covered lean muscles. I guessed he was one of the swimmers and perhaps sixteen or seventeen years old. Wariness, fear and a bit of defeat emanated from him.

If Walsh was tired, he didn't show it. "Quinn has been telling me quite the story. He made a *big* mistake not coming to me right away, but I think, with some hard work, he can control his magic."

"Last night—" Leif tried.

"He pulled a lot of power, but no ripples. He released it back into the power source without using it," Walsh said.

Leif considered.

"Look what I have already taught him. Quinn, show these magicians what you can do."

Skippy braced. Leif signaled me to be ready. I removed the orb from my pack. Quinn drew in a breath as if he prepared for a deep dive. The teacup in front of Walsh rose into the air, hovered a moment and then returned to the table with a rattle.

"Not bad," Leif said. "But when he flashed fourteen days ago, he was on the verge of flaming out."

"He's managed to gain control since then. And now that I'm aware of his powers, I can teach him."

"I need to contact the Master Magicians." Leif pulled out the sea-horse messenger.

"That will take weeks. As the Council's representative, surely you can make a decision."

Walsh didn't know about the messengers. He watched in confusion as Leif peered into the glass.

"But, isn't that—"

"The magician finder? Yes." Skippy interrupted Walsh. "Opal's glass has a dual purpose." He explained it to the leader.

I squirmed. As more people knew about my powers, the more uncomfortable I grew.

"Amazing," Walsh said. He studied me as if appraising the quality of a pearl.

Averting my gaze, I met Quinn's. He too watched me. And a sense of familiarity flushed through me. Odd.

"What else can you do, Miss Opal?" Walsh asked.

The unpleasant feeling of being examined crawled along my skin. I lied. "Nothing else."

"Really? Then why are you holding a Stormdancer's orb?"

Caught, I cast about for an excuse.

"She was helping the Stormdancers' glassmakers when we received the order to find Quinn," Leif said. He'd just finished his mental communication with the Master Magicians in the Keep. "Master Bain is most impressed with Quinn's display last night." He changed the subject. "He would like Quinn to come with us to the Keep to learn more about his powers."

A brief joyful expression lit the young man's face before settling back into anxiety.

"Absolutely not," Walsh said. "We are a close family."

"It's not your decision," Leif said.

"Oh yes it is. Quinn isn't eighteen yet."

"Doesn't matter. If the Council believes it's in his best interest to train at the Keep, then it's theirs." Leif's posture stiffened. "But, I'd rather ask Quinn first."

Everyone turned to the young man.

His gaze darted to Walsh. "I—"

"Your *sisters* will miss you," Walsh said. "And who will teach the children to swim? You know how strong the current is around the peninsula's tip and you're the best instructor."

Quinn's shoulders drooped in resignation. "I'm needed here, sir. I want to stay."

"And he will have a personal tutor. Much better than being one of many at the Keep." Walsh put a chummy arm around Quinn.

Leif didn't appear happy. "I'd rather you train at the Keep, but I don't want to upset your family. However—" an ominous tone deepened his voice "—if the Master Magicians feel another uncontrolled flash of magic, they will send me back to finish the job."

"To neutralize him, but not kill him?" Walsh asked.

"Yes."

"Exactly how? Because the last time I heard, the only way to defuse a wild power was to terminate the person." Walsh's gaze slid to the orb in my lap.

"We have discovered a new way, but the Master Magicians are keeping the specifics quiet for now," Leif said.

"Interesting. Were you staying with the Stormdancers on the coast?" Walsh asked me.

"Yes."

"Quinn's confession last night included a variety of events he's been keeping from me. Go on, Quinn, tell them about the sea glass in case they find it on their way back." Walsh's anger flashed at the young man before he smoothed his features.

Quinn kept his gaze on the floor. "I...collect sea glass." He swallowed. "And I did something to my collection with my...uh...wild magic. When my...brothers began fighting over them, I tossed them into the sea."

"Did something?" Leif asked.

He grimaced. "I think I made them more...desirable. My brothers used to make fun of me for collecting it, but they were...crazed by them."

That's why Quinn felt so familiar to me.

"The glass is dangerous," Walsh said. He pressed his lips together, controlling his fury. "With the currents and tides, they may wash up onshore near The Cliffs. The Stormdancers should be warned."

Leif glanced at me with a question in his eyes. I nodded.

"Thanks for the warning, but it's a little late," Leif said. "One of the Stormdancers found most of the pieces, and when she brought them back to the cave...well, crazed is a good descriptor."

Quinn looked horrified.

Walsh asked if anyone was hurt.

"Minor bumps and bruises. But if Opal hadn't broken the magic, people would have died." Leif swept his hands out to emphasize his point.

"I didn't mean..." The poor boy put his head in his hands. "I'm so sorry."

Walsh, however, focused on me. "You seem to have an affinity for glass. How did you manage to break the spell?"

Leif saved me from answering. "It's complicated," he said. "Hopefully, Quinn won't do it again."

"Of course not," Walsh said. "I guarantee it."

Quinn shuddered.

I wanted to ask Quinn about the markings, but held my tongue. It was probably a way for him to keep track of his collection, and I had an odd feeling it might get Quinn into more trouble.

With nothing left to discuss, we returned to our cottage to pack. As soon as we were alone, Leif said, "That manipulating sack of seagull droppings!"

"I assume you're referring to Walsh," I said.

"Yes. I feel sorry for that boy. He should come with us."

"Why didn't you force him to?" Skippy asked. "It's within your power."

"There wasn't a good enough reason. Quinn's control with the teacup was impressive. Master Bain wanted him to come to the Keep, but he respects people's right to choose how they live as long as they're not a danger to themselves or others. The whole incident with the sea glass was an honest mistake. Since Quinn said he'd rather stay, I couldn't force him. But I can rescue him."

"What do you mean by rescue?" I asked.

"I gave him an out. He can pull a big hunk of power and alert the Masters."

I had trouble following Leif's logic. "But then we siphon his powers. How's that an out?"

"The danger of flameout is gone. If he yanks on the power blanket, it's because he needs our attention."

"And you think this boy is smart enough to pick up on your offer?" Skippy asked.

"Time will tell."

* * *

After we left Walsh's compound, my mind kept returning to the Bloodrose family. The family's bland faces haunted my sleep. Nothing they did or said raised a red flag of warning, but their resignation and apathy still left a rancid taste in my mouth. It felt as if they'd given in, letting Walsh decide their lives for them.

Perhaps the bad flavor resulted not from the Bloodrose family, but from my own worries. I had given in to the Council's wishes, allowing Skippy to guard me and producing enough messengers to earn permission to leave the Keep.

Quinn stayed because of his sense of obligation and guilt from Walsh. Was I doing the same thing?

At least Quinn had control of his magic. I clung to the one positive result of the whole trip, hoping it would drive out the unsettled feeling.

We headed north toward Stormdance land. Skippy protested that there was no need to return to The Cliffs, but I wanted to ensure the orbs would hold a storm's energy before I left the Stormdancers.

The trip south had been seven days of almost nonstop riding and six days searching the small costal towns for Quinn. Even though we pushed the pace, it took us eight days to reach The Cliffs.

Along the way, I found a few pieces of sea glass. They were scattered over a wide swath of beach. I managed to spark them before Leif or Skippy could fall under their spell. My hands throbbed for a while afterward.

We arrived two days into the heating season. The bright sun warmed the air during the day, making us sweat. But I still used my cloak to keep the chill off at night.

Kade and Heli greeted us first. They had been hiking on the beach seeking treasures. I dismounted with the utmost speed and crushed Kade in my arms.

"I'm glad to see you, too, but I need to breathe," he said.

I relaxed, although I didn't let him go.

"What happened? Did you…?"

"No. It's just the family…" I shuddered when I thought of the Bloodroses. "I'll tell you about it later. Will you promise me something?"

"Anything."

I smiled. "You should ask what it is first."

He shrugged. "The last one netted me a day on the beach with a beautiful woman. How bad could it be?"

"Not bad at all. Just promise me the next time I'm complaining about my family and their embarrassing stories, you'll remind me of the Bloodrose family."

"Bloodrose. Got it."

I pulled away to give Heli the sea glass I'd found. I explained about Quinn. She deflated, but agreed about my guess to the purpose of the markings.

"It was fun. I love puzzles. They're pretty," she said. "Do you think Quinn wants them back?"

Remembering the strange tension about the sea glass, I said, "No."

"Then I'll add them to my collection."

"Can we go now? I don't want to miss dinner," Leif said.

We walked the rest of the way to the stables. I rubbed Quartz down and groomed her. Moonlight banged his stall door. As soon as Kade opened it, the horse circled us, then leaned against Quartz.

Skippy worked on Beryl, but he seemed distracted. His attention focused on the sky instead of his horse.

Kade also contemplated the gray clouds over the sea. "I believe our first heating-season storm is headed this way."

"How bad?" Skippy asked.

"It's sullen and annoyed. It could blow for a while," Kade said.

"What do you mean?"

"This time of year, it's mostly thunderstorms. A few will pop up and sweep over us with nary a rumble, others grow into large chains with pouring rain, wind and lots of noise, and a couple will build into huge systems, sucking in moisture. Those monsters produce hail and tornadoes." Kade's eyes lit up at the prospect of monster storms.

Skippy swallowed. "Where is this one on your scale? A popper or a monster?"

"A popper or a monster?" Kade repeated. "I like that!"

"Thanks, I guess. But you didn't answer the question."

"This one is in between the two. Large, but not huge, with wind gusts and plenty of lightning."

"When?" Skippy combed the same spot on Beryl. She flicked her tail at him.

Kade studied the sky. The sun dipped behind the distant cloud bank. "Tomorrow afternoon. Maybe early evening."

"Do we need to bring the horses up to the storm cave?" I asked.

"No. It doesn't have enough force to push the water that far onto the beach." Kade smiled. "Besides, I'll be out there, taming that sullen storm into a nice shower."

Raiden and the others seemed glad to see us. Dinner bubbled on the fire and chairs ringed the flickering flames. The glassmakers asked if they could make the rest of the orbs for the season.

"Wait until after this storm. We need to make sure the orbs will hold the storm's energy," I said. Anxiety swirled. Kade insisted he dance the storm alone tomorrow just in case the orbs shattered. If that happened, the force of the flying glass would kill him.

Skippy claimed he had no appetite and went to bed early. Leif, Kade and I joined the group around the fire. We took turns filling them in about the hunt for the wild magician.

"I like it when a story ends well," Raiden said.

"How can you call that a happy ending?" Prin demanded. "The boy is being forced to stay."

"No one died and no one got hurt," Raiden said. "Besides, I said it ended well. Not happy."

Conversation drifted to the approaching storm. The Stormdancers analyzed and compared their thoughts and theories. With small frowns and little pouty huffs, Tebbs showed her disappointment about not dancing. Wick conserved his strength by falling asleep in his chair.

When my eyelids wouldn't stay open, I said goodnight and dragged my tired body up to Kade's cave. He followed soon after, joining me on the narrow cot.

I melted against him.

He wrapped his arms around me. "You're worried about tomorrow." It wasn't a question.

"A little. I wish I could be out there with you."

"Too dangerous."

"I know." Memories of the last storm season played in my mind, when Kade was faced with a similar situation to test new orbs. His strength had failed before he could harvest enough energy to calm the killer storm. "I helped you before."

"And I'll never forget it. You saved my life."

We had connected through Kaya's orb. "I would love to do it again."

"What? Save my life? You're up to two times now to my one."

"No. You've saved me twice. You forgot about blowing Devlen away."

"He didn't want to kill you."

"It still counts." Besides, if he had taken me, it would have been worse than dying. "What I want is to link with you again. I felt so powerful and in control." Two things I lacked. The Council told me how many messengers to make and when. I could use my powers, but only if the Council approved or assigned me the task.

"We could try linking through an empty orb," Kade said.

"I guess we could, but I think it was Kaya's power that connected us. If it doesn't work, I'll come out with you for the next storm."

"Why?"

"To see if I can channel the storm's energy like I siphon magic." A sudden realization jolted me.

"What's wrong? Your ribs?" Kade relaxed his arms.

"No, Crafty! I forgot all about her." She had been a member of Sir's group. A magician who could weave a null shield into a net. She should be locked in an Ixian dungeon, but could have escaped with Tricky. I made a mental note to ask Leif to message Yelena and find out what happened in Ixia.

"What about Crafty?"

"You taught her how to dance. Why can't you teach other magicians like Leif or Skippy?"

His muscles tensed. "Oh. Well." Reluctance clung to each word.

I pulled back. "What are you keeping from me?"

A slight cringe. "Crafty—I wish we knew her real name and Tricky's, as well. I'm sure the Ixian authorities—"

"Kade, tell me." Unease rolled at the back of my throat.

"I didn't want to upset you, but Crafty's magic was… unique."

"Why would that upset me?"

"Unique as in probably one-of-a-kind. I learned

from Sir that her father was a Stormdancer and her mother was a magician from the Krystal Clan. They had a brief liaison before she returned to her people. Crafty was the result of that encounter. She had both magical power and Stormdancer power, although she didn't know how to dance."

"And I stole her one-of-a-kind abilities, robbing Sitia of another Stormdancer."

"I knew you'd be upset. She never would have danced for us. Her mother's opinion of us wasn't...complimentary. Besides, she joined Sir and didn't have any problems with sabotage, kidnapping, torture and murder. You saved Sitia from a criminal."

He had a point. I relaxed against him, letting his warmth and the beat of his heart lull me to sleep.

The storm arrived right before dinner as predicted. Lightning sizzled across the dark gray sky. The sea churned, turning the water's color to an old bruise. Thunder vibrated and echoed off the walls of the main cavern. Gusts of wind fanned the fire, and small sand devils swirled in the corners.

Skippy flinched with every boom. He held his body so taut, I thought we would have to pry his hands from the chair's arms so he could eat. Leif chopped a pink fleshy sea creature, helping Raiden cook. I averted my gaze when I spotted tentacles. A certain amount of ignorance was required for various...meals.

Kade carried a mesh bag filled with four orbs. He

kissed me, then dashed off to his favorite rocky post before the rain. Prin and Tebbs tried to play cards. They spent more time focused on the storm than their hands. Between deals, they both stood and paced to the entrance to peer outside.

Ziven and Zetta stacked tiles and threw dice for an unfamiliar game. Their tosses seemed listless, as if they were bored. How could they be so indifferent while Kade tested their orbs? I was pretty sure the glass would hold, but tweaks of nervousness still pinched my stomach.

Wick carved small holes into Heli's seashells with a knife so she could string them together to make jewelry. She worked on making a bracelet. At one point Heli paused and cocked her head. "Kade's harvesting the storm's energy."

I checked on dinner's progress. Leif stirred the contents of the pot with loving strokes while Raiden grilled fish over the fire.

No one paid any attention to me. Skippy kept his death grip on the chair and his gaze trained on the entrance. I guessed if water washed into the cave, he would be out of his seat and up the path in the blink of an eye.

I pulled my orb from my saddlebags. Carrying it over to a quiet corner, I sat down and concentrated on the glass under my fingertips. Vibrations traveled through the bones in my hands. Potential quivered. I sensed the magic beating inside the Stormdancers, Skippy's icy pulse and Leif's green aura. If I desired, I could draw it to me and trap it inside the orb.

So why didn't I feel all-powerful? Feel in control? I had dreamed of wielding more power and not being a One-Trick Wonder. So why wasn't I thrilled?

Because this ability was useless. I'd rather be able to light a fire or heal someone, not rob them of their magic. Would Quinn have been grateful to me for saving his life? Doubtful. Once a person tastes magic, he desires more. I was the perfect example. I trapped magic in glass. My messengers helped Sitia. I should have been content with that one skill. And I wasn't.

On the other hand, Pazia seemed to be dealing with the loss of her magic, moving on with her life, and Devlen acted happier without the addiction. *Acted* being the key word. His reformed-man performance had to be part of a grander scheme.

Now, the Council feared me and, in order not to be thrown in jail, I'd bent to their wishes, striving to gain their trust. Pathetic.

Forcing my dour thoughts away from the Council, I reached toward Kade. His magic flashed with red energy. I quashed the desire to draw it to me. Instead, I tried to link my essence with his.

Nothing happened. No connection. No sharing of strength. I returned the orb to my bags and sat near the fire, waiting for the storm to end.

Kade brought back four filled orbs. The storm's energy swirled inside with an iridescent glitter of light. Their morose song thumped in my chest and scratched at my skin. Not at all like Kaya's orb. Even though she longed to be free, hers had sung with a positive energy.

Raiden placed the full orbs on a special shelf in the supply cave. "If they hold until tomorrow, they're good to go."

As predicted, Leif and Skippy made plans to leave after breakfast. Exhaustion clung to Kade and he headed to bed. Later, when I crawled under the blankets with him, he didn't move.

Sleep came in snatches. Sad dreams of death and separation plagued my mind. I tossed and turned. Eventually, I abandoned the effort and slipped from the bed. I dressed and lit a lantern. Kade remained in the same position, still sound asleep.

"Opal?"

I jumped.

"Are you awake?" Ziven asked through the screen.

I peeked around the curtain. "What's the matter?"

Ziven stood outside, holding a lantern. Concern creased his forehead. "I hate to bother you, but we're making more orbs and need some guidance."

"No problem, just let me leave Kade a note." I searched for paper and jotted a quick message before joining Ziven.

He quirked a smile. "What did you write?"

"Just that I'm at the kiln. He worries too much."

He led the way. Water coated the narrow path. I followed him with care, keeping my right hand on the rock face to steady me. Below, the storm-tossed waves crashed to the shore with angry whacks. Lingering clouds streamed past the moon.

Light spilled from the kiln's cave. Before we reached the entrance, Ziven stopped and turned around. "I understand why Kade worries," he said. "Even though you have powerful glass magic, you need glass in your hands for it to work. And you can't live your life holding glass all the time. Right?"

I agreed, but slowed as uneasiness brushed my skin. Ziven was never this chatty.

"I'm surprised the Council even allows you to leave the Citadel."

Alarmed, I stepped back. "Why?"

"They think your messengers are indispensable."

"And you don't?"

He shrugged. "Doesn't matter what I think." He continued up the path.

I relaxed, but kept my distance from him. Paranoid? Who, me?

"You mentioned needing guidance. What's the trouble?" I asked.

He paused and half turned. "The trouble is you're dangerous, and you cause problems. The Council refuses to do anything because of your messengers, but there are others who aren't so inclined."

Anger flared. "I meant with the orbs."

"The orbs are fine."

"Then what—"

Hands connected with my back, shoving me over the path's edge and out into midair.

19

I SCREAMED as gravity pulled me down.

I screamed as the beach rushed up to meet me.

I screamed until I realized I hit a cushion of air.

I stopped and bobbed about five feet above the sand before sinking to the ground. Reveling in the feel of solidness underneath me, I gasped for breath for a few quiet minutes.

The crunch of sand broke my euphoric paralysis. I scrambled to my feet, preparing to fight. Instead of Ziven coming to finish the job, Kade ran toward me, followed by the others.

He crushed me against him, the thumping of his heart audible. I soaked in the moment of peace before the inevitable questions.

I explained what had happened, guessing Zetta had snuck up behind me. Raiden, Leif and Heli raced up the path to confront Ziven and Zetta. Kade moved to follow, but I clung to him. We waited on the beach. The others conferred and speculated. Their voices buzzed in my ears, but I didn't bother to listen.

"Now we're even," Kade said to me.

"No, you're one ahead. How did you know?" Small tremors zipped through my muscles.

"I heard your scream and reacted without thought. I pulled the air before I even opened my eyes, hoping I covered enough of the beach."

I had felt a little embarrassed about yelling so loud, but not anymore. "Thank you."

"I couldn't bear to lose you." Then he scowled. "Besides, we'll need you to train another set of glassmakers."

"I'd like to talk to Councilor Stormdance about his interview methods before he hires the next ones."

"I'll make sure he receives your request."

Gnawing on my bottom lip, I waited. Leif and the others should be back by now. Kade stared up at The Cliffs. His muscles tightened as if he fought to stay still.

"Go on," I said. "Check on them."

He sprang from my side. To distract myself from imagining various horrors, I thought about the murder attempt. Ziven had said I was dangerous. He claimed there were others. Who were they?

The list of people who knew about my siphoning powers was ridiculously long and probably growing longer each day. Just like null shields. At first, only a handful of people knew about the counterattack, but now it was common knowledge. Word about Curare had spread. Good thing the limited supply kept the drug from being the new weapon du jour.

Although... How had Tricky gotten it? The drug came from a vine growing in the Illiais Jungle. Yelena's mother, Perl, extracted Curare and diluted it, creating an effective pain reliever. Daviian Warpers had stolen a shipment of the drug, and had been the first to concentrate it to use as a weapon.

Warpers again. Devlen must have given Curare to Tricky or told him where to find it. The temptation to test my Greenblade bees when I returned to the Keep played in my mind. I could send one after Devlen and another to Tricky. Imagine their surprise.

Leif returned, interrupting my evil thoughts. "They're gone," he reported. "We checked all the caves up to The Flats. I caught a whiff of them at the top, but we didn't see them. I've contacted security in Thunder Valley and a few nearby towns. They'll watch for them, but if Ziven and Zetta are professionals I doubt they'll be caught."

"Where are the others?" I asked.

"Searching their sleeping caves and the kiln, looking for clues."

I should go and help, but had no desire to leave the ground.

Despite the attempted murder, the sun rose. We filed into the main cave and roused the fire. Kade and the others returned. They had found a stash of weapons and a few personal items. No evidence or clues to who had hired the pair to kill me.

Raiden carried a white metal box and a scoop, handing both to me.

"What are these?" I asked.

"You tell me. We found a bunch of those boxes in their cave, and the scoops." He filled a pot with water and started breakfast.

The cube-shaped box was big enough to hold an orb. Two semicircular openings were centered on the top. Three latches held the box together, and on the opposite side were three hinges. I popped the clasps. The box spread apart like a book.

Inside, both halves looked like the reverse half of an orb. Confused, I ran a finger along a gap around the half orb-shape. Fishy-smelling oil coated the space.

Then it hit me. Those boxes were the reason for the orbs' perfection. Ziven and Zetta used molds to make the orbs, not their own skills. Using the scoop, they poured molten glass into the closed box. When the glass had properly cooled, they opened it and removed the orb. The gaps at the top, where the inner form connected to the box, could be closed with heat.

Ziven and Zetta went to a considerable amount of trouble for their cover stories. Perhaps they planned to remain with the Stormdancers after they killed me. It would explain why they didn't try another method to take my life. If the attempt had been successful, they could have claimed I had slipped on the wet trail and fallen by accident.

No matter what their reasons or orders, the Stormdancers still needed orbs for the season. After breakfast, Raiden checked the filled ones from last night. No cracks or any signs of weakness were visible. Though nontraditional, the molds worked. And I would have to use them since I lacked the ability to blow air into glass.

Kade estimated they would need a hundred and fifty to two hundred orbs for the season. I recruited Leif and Skippy to help me and started right away.

In the afternoon, Leif paused after filling the cauldron with sand. "How long will it take to make them all?"

We had ten molds, and I planned to have Leif blow in the blowpipe to craft ten more. The annealing oven could only hold twenty orbs. "Ten or eleven days."

Leif gasped in horror. "Ten days being forced to eat seaweed and clams." He placed the back of his hand to his forehead, exaggerating the dramatics.

"Forced to eat? *You?* The person who drools as soon as Raiden picks up his cook pot? I'm more likely to believe someone forced you to *stop* eating."

He shuddered. "*That* would be cruel."

After spending all day working, I dragged my body to Kade's cave. My arms ached from wrestling with the heavy molds. I collapsed on the cot, planning to take a nap before dinner.

Kade woke me when he added wood to the brazier until the inside glowed hot. "You missed dinner."

I mumbled a reply, making room for him on the cot.

"What's this?" He picked up a piece of paper from the floor.

"My note." It must have fluttered down when Kade heard my scream.

He read the words by firelight and laughed. "I see how handy those little check boxes can be. 'Kade, I went A, fishing, B, surfing, C, treasure hunting or D, to the kiln.' If you had checked B, I would have suspected foul play."

"Guess I need to add on a few options. E, cliff diving and F, dodging assassins."

"I hope you'll wake me up for those two."

"Don't worry, I won't let you miss out on the fun."

Leif woke us the next morning. At least, I thought the darkness didn't seem as thick. Kade told him to go away or he would zap him.

Undaunted, Leif said, "I received a message from the Council—"

"And I'm not going to like it," I finished for him.

"How'd you guess?" He acted shocked.

"I haven't liked anything the Council has ordered—why should today be any different?"

"Bitterness isn't healthy, Opal. Perhaps we should send you to the Sandseeds to work out your issues."

"Kade, could you zap him now?" I asked.

He pushed up to his elbow. "Sorry. He's too close to my screen. It would catch fire and I like that screen. Took me weeks to find it."

"Gee. I'm not feeling very welcome." Leif pouted.

"The man's a genius. Why don't you go celebrate on the beach." Kade plopped back.

"The Council has ordered us home." Leif waited. "'Why?' you ask. The Council is worried about your safety and wants you well protected until they find out who ordered your assassination."

"I think I've been insulted," Kade said.

"Do you think you could zap the Council from here?" I asked.

"No."

I considered. "Leif's a representative of the Council. If you zapped him, would it hurt them?"

"Maybe, but don't forget my screen."

"As much as I enjoy basking in your love and affection, we need to pack," Leif said.

"You go ahead. I'll catch up once the orbs are finished."

"Opal, you can't ignore a direct order again. You're gaining their trust. If you don't return, you'll lose it."

"So what! Maybe I don't want their trust. One of the Councilors is probably behind the assassination attempt."

"Whoa. That's a big leap without any evidence," Leif said.

I shrugged. "The orbs are more important than the Council's orders."

"You're using molds. Can you teach one of the Stormdancers?"

"No. Too many variables. Ziven and Zetta did their homework. Their skills with glass were rudimentary, but they had plenty of knowledge."

"How about the other glassmakers who interviewed for the job?" Kade asked.

"You want me to go?"

"No, but I don't want you to get into trouble with the Council, either."

I couldn't trust those glassmakers. There could be another assassin hiding among them or worse—they could be unskilled!

The solution popped into my head. Helen, the glassmaker in Thunder Valley. An accomplished craftswoman, she wouldn't even need to use the molds.

"Would the Council be agreeable to a compromise?" I asked Leif.

"Does it involve zapping?"

"No."

"That's a good start."

I calculated travel times. "Ask them if I could stay for five more days. That will give me enough time to train Helen to my satisfaction."

"Helen? Who's Helen?" Leif asked.

"A skilled glassmaker in Thunder Valley."

Leif looked at Kade. "Are you okay with this?"

"If Opal says she's qualified, that's all I need."

While I waited for Helen, I continued to make orbs. I also created a few of my glass messengers for Kade to use to test his clan members for potential magical abilities, and I designed one for Leif. The magic inside his sea horse had faded.

Three days into my five allowed by the Council, Helen arrived in the early morning with her mother. Helen's joy at being selected radiated throughout the main cavern, sending a sizzle of energy to the sleepy Stormdancers. She introduced her mother, Chava, to everyone, except Kade and Leif. Kade had gone to his spot on the rocks to scent the wind, and Leif was at the stable.

"I needed an assistant for such important work," Helen said. She had twisted her long brown hair into a bun, exposing an elegant neck. "And since the orb makers are always family members, I brought my mother."

"Has she worked with glass before?" I asked.

"A little. But she isn't good with taking orders."

Chava pished her daughter. "You aren't good with *giving* orders." She appealed to me. "She tells me to hand her a pontil iron. There are four different sizes. How am I to know which one she wants!" The stocky woman threw up her arms in mock disgust. "But don't you worry. This is the greatest thing to happen to our family ever, and we're not about to ruin this opportunity. If she needs a pontil iron, I'll bring all four over and let her pick."

Smiles erupted on everyone's faces, including Wick. This pair would be an excellent addition to the seaside community.

"Can we get started?" Helen asked me. "We're nine days into the heating season. There's no time to lose."

I led them out to the beach as Kade returned from the rocks. I presented the mother-and-daughter team to him.

Helen's ginger-colored eyes filled with awe. Her long, graceful fingers grasped his hand, and she shook it as if dazed.

"I'm glad you could come on such short notice," Kade said.

"It's an honor," Chava said. "You won't regret inviting us. My daughter will create the most beautiful orbs you've ever seen."

"Mother," Helen scolded. She kept Kade's hand in hers. "She exaggerates. I'll do my very best, of course. You're the ones risking your life for all of Sitia. Thank you so much."

She finally released him. I studied her oval face to determine her sincerity. Her acting skills could be well honed, or she might actually be genuine. I didn't remember her being so striking at the market. Her large almond-shaped eyes and small nose complemented her full lips. A few inches shorter than my own five feet seven inches, she appeared to match my age, though her curvy figure made my athletic build look scrawny. Jealous? Who, me?

I showed Helen and Chava the stockpiles and the kiln.

"Those...things can be thrown into the sea," Helen

said with distaste, referring to the molds. "How many orbs have you made so far?" she asked me.

"Twenty-five."

"Then we have lots of work to do." Helen examined one of the finished orbs, then gathered a slug of molten glass with a blowpipe.

With her mother's help, she produced an orb in record time. Her skills amazed me. I felt relieved I had picked an outstanding replacement, but at the same time, suspicion churned in my mind. She seemed a little too qualified, too confident. Her comments at the market about molds had hit too close to the mark.

During the next two days, Helen and Chava gave no evidence of being anything other than a mother and daughter determined to prove they possessed the skills to be the new orb makers. When a squall raced by, her orbs passed the test, containing the storm's energy without breaking.

I still didn't like the way Helen fawned over Kade, but I couldn't blame her. He melted my heart when he smiled. My blood sizzled with his touch.

My Council-approved extension expired, and I packed for the trip back to the Citadel. In such a small cave, my stuff had managed to spread all over the place. It didn't help that the mess of blankets covered most of the floor.

I paused and touched my lips. They tingled from last night when I made sure Kade wouldn't forget me. The desire to stay here with him pulsed in my chest. But I would be obedient and return to the Keep. I could endure forty-nine more days until graduation, assuming I would graduate and not be murdered or bled dry in the meantime. Then what? Prove the truth to the Council about Devlen and stop Tricky?

The illicit knowledge of blood magic spread like embers in the wind, igniting more areas. Soon everyone would know how to use it. It might already be too late to stop it. Yelena and I couldn't imprison so many souls in glass.

I sighed and continued packing. Checking under the cot, I bumped my head when Helen's voice sounded behind me. I scrambled to my feet, reaching for my switchblade.

"Sorry to scare you," she said.

My hand hovered near my weapon. "No problem."

She glanced around the untidy cave. "Is this Storm-dancer Kade's quarters?"

"Yes."

"Then you and he—"

"Yes."

"Then I picked the perfect one," she exclaimed. She pulled one of her glass statues from her pocket and handed it to me. "To thank you for your recommenda-tion."

The four-inch figure held an iridescent globe in his hands. A Stormdancer exalting over a successful harvest. His gold-streaked hair reminded me of Kade.

"You don't have—"

"I wanted to."

"It's exquisite. Thank you."

She bounced on the balls of her feet at the compliment. "Please feel free to show it to your friends. I take orders." She winked. "After all, I need something to do during the off-season."

"I will."

"Safe travels, Opal." She waved and headed up to the kiln's cave.

I realized my right hand rested on my switchblade. Before, I would have regretted being so untrusting, but not today. My reaction pleased me.

Carrying my heavy saddlebags along the trail, I stopped to catch my breath near the main cavern. Voices floated on the warm breeze. Prin and Tebbs stood on the beach, chatting and throwing small shells into the waves. They didn't notice me.

"...I like her. She's sweet and... Her mother...hoot," Tebbs said.

The sound of the surf obscured parts of their conversation. I guessed they discussed Helen.

"She would be...for Kade," Prin said.

I hefted my bags, preparing to move on, when a lull in the waves allowed me to hear them better.

"It's ridiculous," Prin said. "He should be with another clan member. We need more Stormdancers. If he stays with Opal, they'll probably have children with weird glass powers."

Uncertain how to react, I moved past them without saying a word. It didn't matter what they thought as long as Kade remained happy.

He waited for me at the stable. He had saddled Quartz for me. Leif grumbled and worked on getting Rusalka ready. Skippy sat on Beryl. She danced with impatience, sensing her rider's mood.

Kade grabbed my bags and secured them on Quartz. I glanced at Moonlight. Even though the stall's door gaped wide open, he pressed against the far wall of the pen, presenting his rear to us. His taut muscles and laid-back ears warned us to keep away.

"He won't come out," Leif said.

"He wouldn't let me bridle him," Kade said. "I'm sure the Stable Master at the Keep wants him back. Do you think he knows I'm not going with you?"

Leif and I just looked at Kade.

"Oh."

"Looks like you got yourself a horse," Leif said. He swung up on Rusalka. "Let's go, we're burning daylight."

Kade stepped close to me. He placed his hands on my shoulders and rested his forehead on mine. "Be very *very* careful. Post a watch at night, and don't let your guard down. Promise?"

"Yes. Will you be able to come for my graduation?"

"Sorry. Storms tend to trickle into the hot season. And I received a threatening letter from my mother. My parents haven't seen me since Kaya's flag-raising ceremony—almost a year ago."

"I understand." I remembered my parents had kept my sister's grief flag over her bed for five years before they could put it away.

"They want me to stay with them until the next storm season. Why don't you come visit me after graduation. I'm sure they would love to meet you."

"I would enjoy that. I'll send you a message."

"Come on and kiss already," Leif called to us. "I want to put as much distance behind us before dinner."

"Is he always ruled by his stomach?" Kade asked.

"Yep."

Our eight-day trip back to the Keep contained no ambushes. No signs of Tricky. And no assassination attempts. One of my better treks.

I should have suspected my luck wouldn't last. But no. Surrounded by magicians at the Keep, I felt safer than on the open road. I returned to my classes, gossiped with my sister, endured a stern lecture from the Stable Master about Moonlight, produced glass messengers and trained at least six hours every day, including lock-picking sessions with Marrok, the Weapons Master. Skippy and my babysitters no longer followed me around the Keep.

My parents arrived for my graduation ceremony. Every time my mother embarked on an embarrassing tale about my childhood, Leif leaned close and whispered, "Bloodrose."

Graduation day was the first day of the hot season.

Fifty graduates dressed in formal robes sweated in the heat as Master Bloodgood congratulated us on our achievement. Yelena sat with the spectators, but disappeared soon after. I hoped to have a chance to talk with her before she left the Citadel.

I met Pazia's father, Vasko Cloud Mist, at the post-graduation celebration held in the dining room. A tall man with black hair and mustache, he oozed power. Political power. Magical power. Wealthy power. Two of his associates stood behind him at all times.

"Thank you for the messengers, Opal," he said. "They've been a tremendous help with my business."

"You're—"

Too impatient for small talk, he asked, "What are your plans for the future?"

"I'm not sure. I have an appointment tomorrow morning with the Sitian Council to discuss my assignment." Although it sounded impressive, the Council really wanted to assess me before they went on hiatus for the season.

"Before you hear what they have to say, I'd like to offer you a business opportunity with my company," he said. "Pazia's coming home to work with me, so you'll already know a...friend."

Surprised, I asked, "What type of opportunity?"

"With your glass messengers, of course. I'm offering to support you financially. You'll have enough funds to set up a glass factory, hire workers and sales staff. All in the beautiful foothills of the Emerald Mountains." He gestured to the small group of Councilors who had attended the ceremony. "Committees and government red tape has slowed and complicated the process of sending messages. Relay stations. Pah! We'll do it right. Fast, efficient and fair with you calling all the shots."

And too good to be true. "What's the catch? How do you benefit from supporting me?"

"Smart girl. All I want are messengers. I want to be able to come to your workshop and request five messengers without having to fill out a single form. Hell, I'll even limit my requests so I don't take all your stock. We'll draw up an agreement. What do you say?"

His rapid-fire proposal overwhelmed me. I tried to pull my scattered thoughts into a coherent sentence. "I'm flattered you'd like to do business with me. I need to think about your offer first. Can I give you an answer later?"

"Sure, sure. We'll be here for a few days." He peered at me for a moment. "Don't let the Council scare you. You graduated. As long as you're obeying the laws of Sitia, they don't have any legal right to dictate what you can or can't do."

After a sleepless night of wondering and worrying, I arrived for my appointment with the Council. All eleven Councilors were in attendance with their aides as well as the three Master Magicians and Yelena Zaltana.

I kept Vasko's advice in my mind, gathering the

courage to stand up for myself if needed. And not be scared.

The Council session started out fine. We assembled in the great hall early in the morning to avoid the afternoon heat. The members sat along their U-shaped table, reviewing my recent achievements and discussing the successful magical test I had endured before I left for The Cliffs. Skippy and Leif had made a full report on our adventures with the Stormdancers.

No suspects had been found regarding the assassination attempt. The Council speculated Commander Ambrose might be behind it. He feared magical power and my messengers gave the Sitians an upper hand.

"It's not the Commander," Yelena said.

"Why not? It makes the most sense," Councilor Tama Moon said. She wore a white silk blouse and long skirt. Gressa stood behind her.

"Because the Commander would have assigned the job to Valek and, no offense, Opal, you would be dead by now. He doesn't fail."

"Obviously he hired local talent. He is well known in Sitia—surely he couldn't do the job himself." Tama flicked her long blond hair away from her face as if dismissing Yelena's comments.

But Yelena shook her head no. "For Opal, he would."

So nice to know if the Commander decided I was a threat, Valek would personally kill me. I had met him during the aftermath of the Warper Battle. He had been very grateful for my role in bringing Yelena back from the fire world and had offered his aid should I need it. Anytime, anyplace, he had said.

The assassination attempt concerned the Council more than the fact that Tricky remained at large. Tricky's attack, they reasoned, was revenge for siphoning his magic. I still couldn't tell them about his immunity to me. The vision of the Councilors arguing about using my blood to protect themselves from me kept me silent.

"You're not worried he could be teaching blood magic to others?" I asked.

"No, because all those who know the final stages of the rituals are safely contained in your glass prisons."

Ahh...collective denial. Wonderful. I studied Zitora. As in the past, she kept quiet during the session. Her closed expression gave no hint of her emotions.

Finally the Council asked me where I wanted to work after graduation. I sensed the question was asked out of sheer politeness and they would tell me what I would do regardless of my desires.

"I'd like to be a part of the Messenger Committee," I said.

A little ripple of shock traveled through the Councilors. I suppressed a grin.

"We will consider it," Councilor Greenblade said. "In the meantime, we have decided to hire you as a staff member of the Magician's Keep. You'll be in charge of the glass factory and can train students to assist you while you craft the messengers. This way, you'll also be available to assist with any magical problems that arise, like an out-of-control magician."

Councilor Zaltana added, "And living in the Keep will keep you safe from any more attempts on your life or from revenge seekers."

"Thank you for the job offer, Councilors and Master Magicians. I will consider it."

Another wave of disconcertion rolled around the U. I didn't wait for them to form a response. "And, as you're considering my request to be on the Messenger Committee, I wanted to let you know there won't be any messengers made for you unless I'm on the committee."

The rumble grew louder as Councilors conversed among themselves.

"Are you threatening to stop creating the messengers?" Councilor Cloud Mist asked me.

"No, sir. I just won't make them for you. The messengers are my creations. Since I've been busy with my studies, I haven't had time to be a part of how they are distributed and used. I'm trying to rectify that oversight now."

Tama Moon studied me with a shrewd expression. She nodded in approval when I met her gaze. After all, this had been her idea.

"We could force you, Opal," Councilor Krystal said.

"You could try." I kept my voice steady despite the spinning of my heart.

Arguments erupted and discussions sounded, filling the hall with an angry buzz. Master Bloodgood restored order with a bang of his gavel.

"We will take a short break, and then discuss Opal's counteroffer. Opal, you're dismissed."

Pleased by my courage, I left. Footsteps sounded behind me and I turned, reaching for my blade. Yelena paused. I relaxed my stance.

"You're jumpy. Do you really think someone would attack you in the Council building?" she asked.

"Yes. Weren't you listening? I just gave the Council an ultimatum. I'd feel safer at a travel shelter than in here right now."

"I think you did the right thing. You should have been put on the Messenger Committee from the get-go."

"Good to know I have one person on my side." I smiled, but she remained serious, appraising me with her striking green eyes as if she read my thoughts.

"What's the matter?" I asked.

"I wanted to tell you before..." She frowned and spun her snake bracelet around her wrist. "I did some research..."

"And?"

She met my gaze. "Opal, it's impossible for anyone to switch souls. Ulrick is Ulrick Cowan. Not Devlen, a Daviian Warper."

20

"COULD YOU REPEAT THAT?" I asked Yelena, certain I'd missed a vital hint.

She touched my arm. "I tried switching souls. And it didn't work."

I gaped at her, failing to grasp her words. "What do you mean tried?"

She steered me to a bench and sat beside me. "You have many supporters, Opal. Leif and Bain volunteered to help me experiment. I moved Leif's soul to Bain. Both souls stayed in Bain's body, but when I moved Bain's soul to Leif, they automatically flipped back."

Her words bounced in my mind. I refused to grasp them. "There must be another way."

"I searched Bain's books, and read everything I found on blood magic, but I didn't see anything about switching souls. I talked with Zitora at length. Ulrick's telling the truth."

"Did you talk with Kade and Janco?"

"Of course. They both believe you, and reported Ulrick's horrendous behavior. They couldn't offer any proof, and I can't find any. And you know how good I am about finding things." She tried to give me a wry grin, but it resembled a grimace.

I finally understood. She no longer believed me, and neither did Leif and Bain. Pain burned deep in my chest. The same unrelenting torment as grief. I muttered a few words to Yelena, then bolted from the building.

I had no memory of where I went or what I did. Tricky could have caught me and I would have sliced open my wrist for him. I would have welcomed an assassin. I wandered and suffered. Conversations with Ulrick and Devlen replayed over and over and over in my mind. Had I been duped? How could Ulrick know those pressure points? How could he use them? What about my conversation with Ulrick in Ognap?

Darkness came and went. Then a thought surfaced. Strange things had happened with magic. Yelena's Soul-finding abilities for one. All the history books about Soulfinders had been wrong. Yelena discovered they had been Soulstealers. She trusted herself, and eventually accepted who she was, changing everyone's negative perception about Soulfinders.

I had been determined to prove Devlen had switched with Ulrick. Just because Yelena didn't believe me didn't mean I had to give up. I knew Devlen's soul resided in Ulrick's body. When I had drained him of all his magic,

I felt his essence through the glass orb. I believed in myself.

To help solidify my resolve, I envisioned myself as a piece of thick sea glass. Worn by the water and sand, I was no longer shiny and new. Innocence and naiveté rubbed off by life, I had broken off from the rest and tumbled in the waves by myself.

I banished all the doubts and the pain of betrayal, replacing it with cold, hard determination.

Standing before Councilor Moon's door, I imagined sea glass. When I expelled my emotions, I knocked. An aide answered. He fussed about my lack of appointment.

"Tell her I'm here and let *her* decide if she wants to see me," I said with authority.

He disappeared through another door. I paced in a modest living area. All the Councilors had offices in the Council building and a residence in the Citadel.

The door swung open and Tama Moon greeted me with a smile. "So good to see you. We were getting worried when no one could find you at the Keep."

"After the session yesterday, I needed time to think over the Council's offer."

"And?"

"I'm going to wait for the counteroffer."

She laughed. "The Council believes it's a good idea to have you on the Messenger Committee. In fact, we have ourselves almost convinced it was our idea in the first place."

"I'm glad."

"Are you going to stay at the Keep, then?" She kept her tone neutral, but cold calculation filled her eyes.

"No. I decided to go out on my own. Be in control for once."

"Good for you."

"Shouldn't you be trying to talk me out of it? After all, you're on the Council."

"In this case, I don't agree with the Council. As you should be well aware of. I made my opinions clear in Fulgor. Although, at the time, you were feeling rather... charitable toward the Council."

"Well, the charity is gone. And I like your idea. You had offered to support my business before. Is it still good?"

"*I* didn't offer. *Gressa* made the proposal. And yes, it is still good."

"Excellent. I would like to set up a workshop in Fulgor, then. Can you let the Council know my decision? Tell them I'm willing to help out whenever they need my special...services. Oh, and ask them to return my diamonds to me. I'm going to need capital."

She whistled in appreciation. "Considering the Council isn't going to be happy with you leaving, that's very bold."

Bold. I liked it. "I'm being proactive."

While the boldness still flowed in my blood, I knocked at Zitora's office. She had ignored me long enough.

"Come in, Opal," she called through the door.

I strode into the room. Little had changed since I was here almost a year ago. She sat behind her desk as the late-afternoon sun streamed through the window. I stopped before her desk.

"Can I help you?" she asked.

"Oh! You want to help me now? It's too late. I'm going to help myself."

Her gaze flattened and she pressed her lips into a tight line. "What do you want?"

A small voice in the back of my mind warned me to shut up, but I smashed it with a surge of emotion. "To inform you I'm leaving the Keep. I'm not going to work for the Council. Instead, I'm setting up shop with Gressa in Fulgor."

She kept her body rigid. "Why are you telling me? I'm not your mentor."

Cold. "I thought you might be happy, considering you and Tama Moon are friends. I'll be supporting the Moon economy."

"You can't trust Gressa or Councilor Moon."

"Why not?" I waited, maintaining an expectant expression.

"I can't tell you—"

"Of course not. Why would you tell poor deluded Opal? The one who embarrassed you in front of the Council."

"That's enough. Do you really think the Council will just let you go?"

"Why not? You did."

She stood, but I held my ground.

"Who do you think you are to question my decisions?" she asked.

"I'm Opal Cowan. I *used* to be your student until you turned your back on me."

"I distanced myself for *your* protection."

"Easy excuse. Tell me the truth for once. Admit it, you're mad at me for not telling you everything that happened in Ixia."

"Leave now, Opal. I have work to do." She settled back into her chair.

"No. I'm not letting you ignore me. I want answers. If not out of anger, then why else did you support Tama's claim that Ulrick worked undercover? You know it's a lie."

"Because Tama did assign him. I talked to her at length. He hadn't been hit on the head by his sister. Together they visited Tama." She drew in a breath. "Opal, do you know how ridiculous you're being? Yelena confirmed it's impossible for Ulrick and Devlen to switch souls."

"That's sweet. You talked to Tama and Yelena. But you never talked to me. We've been through a lot together. Don't I get the same courtesy?"

"Just drop it, Opal. I realize your pride has been injured, but just admit you've been tricked and move on."

"Guess I'm not worth the effort." I paused. "Since

I'm no longer your student, I can disregard your advice. In that instance, you taught me well."

"What are you doing?" Yelena demanded as soon as I opened my door.

"Packing," I said, returning to my living area. A few crates rested on the table, and my saddlebags hung over the back of a chair. Packs stuffed with clothes littered the floor. Bearing in mind that I had lived in the Keep for five years, I didn't own many things.

"Are you crazy?"

"According to you... Yes!" I sorted through a stack of books, making two piles. One to keep, and the other to donate to the incoming apprentice class.

"The Council—"

"I don't care what the Council says. They'll have to arrest me or let me go. I'm prepared for both."

"Why are you going with Councilor Moon?"

"Why not? She offered to support me. And since the whole Devlen/Ulrick mystery has been solved, I've no worries." I studied Yelena's expression. "Unless you have something else to tell me?"

Her face remained impassive. "The Council won't return the diamonds."

"Too bad." I wrapped Tula's fox statue and Helen's glass Stormdancer in a sheet.

"How are you going to afford to make your messengers? You'll need equipment and supplies. Perhaps you should go home to Booruby and work in your family's factory."

Her suggestion had merit. In a normal situation, I would heed her advice. Nothing about this endeavor was normal. "Gressa offered to let me use her glass equipment and supplies. I will reimburse her when I earn enough money."

"You're going to get hurt," she warned.

I shrugged. Not like I hadn't been hurt before. "Then I'll stay on snake alert."

"Snake alert?"

"When I lived at home, we used to have a snake alert the first cold night of the season. The hot kilns were guaranteed to draw in poisonous fer-de-lance snakes. Armed with machetes, my family would kill as many as possible. It reduced the number of snakes living close to us. We couldn't get rid of them all, but it helped." I returned to my packing.

"Isn't that how your uncle died?" Yelena asked.

"Yep. Uncle Werner went left when he should have gone right. But he was well aware of the danger and made an honest mistake. Much better than being surprised."

"What about Kade?"

"Smart man. I should have listened to him when he advised me to keep quiet about my new power. Once I set up my shop and stockpile enough messengers, I'm planning to visit him."

"Opal, you know what I meant." Her frustration had grown to a dangerous level. "He won't approve."

"I don't need his approval. Do you seek Valek's consent every time you embark on a mission?"

Her chagrined expression answered for her. After a few more attempts to change my mind, she left. I sagged with relief. If I could endure Yelena's lecture, then Mara's should be easier.

Wrong again. Mara sliced into me. I was being selfish. Chop. I was being greedy. Chop. I was being stupid. Chop.

"Mara, stop," I said. "If I stay here, I'll be miserable."

She inhaled a breath as if to reply, but released it in one long sigh. "You need to do this?"

"Yes."

"Will it make you happy?"

"I'm not sure *happy* is the right word."

She considered. "Will it help you return to my carefree, trusting sister? You remember the one? Before her trip to Ixia with Ulrick?"

My response lodged in the back of my throat. "Don't you mean Devlen?"

Her hands pressed together as misery twisted her face. "Didn't Yelena talk to you about her experiment?"

Obviously Leif had told Mara. I wondered how many more knew. "She told me."

"You don't believe her?"

"Nope."

"But she's the Soulfinder, she'd know."

"Maybe."

Mara stepped back as if my lack of trust was contagious. "Do you think she's lying to you?"

"No. I think she gave up too soon."

"Opal, she cares about you. Why wouldn't she put her full effort into helping you?" Outrage and disbelief warred in Mara. She rubbed her forearms in agitation.

"Don't know. Don't care. I'm no longer relying on her. This trip should put this whole nasty business to rest."

"And if it doesn't?"

"Then I've been duped. I'll concede the point and get on with my life despite being the world's biggest idiot."

"Opal, you're not..." Another huff escaped her lips. "I hate to agree with you, but you do need to take this trip. Just remember, you have me, Ahir, Mother and Father all willing to support you no matter what. You *will* message us if you need us. You *will* be very careful."

"Yes, sir."

"...since I'm not going to be employed here, I'll pay the Keep for Quartz, the saddle, tack and my weapons with glass messengers," I said to Bain Bloodgood. "I already talked to the Stable Master and the Weapons Master to determine an amount. And I met with the head of the Messenger Committee, Councilor Featherstone, about providing them with new messengers as long as they provide me with details regarding their use." I continued to babble at him. "If you need my other services, let me know and I'll return to help."

Bain remained quiet. He sat behind his messy desk in his administration office. He fiddled with a piece of parchment, letting it slide between his fingers over and over.

"I'll make sure the shipments are well guarded," I said into the horrible silence.

Finally, Bain let the parchment fall onto the top of a pile. He focused a troubled gaze on me. "You realize Gressa is ambitious. She will desire control of who receives your messengers?"

"Yes."

"Then why, child, have you agreed to work with her?"

The endearment grated on my nerves. My childhood was over. All illusions and dreams were worn away, exposing the ugly reality.

"No matter what she desires, I don't plan to give her control. This is just a temporary arrangement until I become solvent."

"Plans can change," Bain said. Sadness hung on him like one of his robes. "You surprised the Council into agreeing to this...arrangement. Once they reconvene in the cooling season, be prepared for them to enact a law or make a counteroffer to bring you back here."

"They would actually try a legal route and not threaten me?" I tapped my chest as if shocked by the notion.

He ignored my sarcasm. "Try, yes. But will use other...methods to get what they want."

"Ahh... That's more like it. I was beginning to worry my views of the Council had been wrong."

Bain stood without warning. He leaned forward,

bringing his face close to mine. "You are playing with dangerous people. The Council can be an ally for you to use if your arrangement with Gressa fails to work. But they won't support you if you make them your enemy."

I sorted through my encounters with the Council. "Since they haven't ever supported me, I think I'm okay without them." I waved bye and left his office before he could reply.

Bain's comment about allies reminded me of Vasko Cloud Mist's offer. I found Pazia outside her room, loading a wagon.

"I didn't realize how much stuff I bought this past year. I filled all the extra space with junk," Pazia said.

I helped her carry a few crates from her quarters.

"Did you have a chance to consider my father's offer?" she asked.

"Yes."

She stopped pushing a stubborn box. "Well?"

I explained my intentions. Barreling over her arguments before she could voice them, I said, "However, if the arrangement doesn't go well with them, I'd like to come to Ognap and work with you and your father. Do you think he'd be agreeable?"

"He's used to getting his way, so he doesn't deal well with rejection. He'll probably sweeten the deal and try to tempt you to work with us. I think as long as he can buy messengers from you there won't be any hard feelings."

"Think?"

She shrugged. "My father is difficult to read. If he feels a certain deed is a personal slight, he'll be very upset and vindictive. If he sees the action as just business, he's fine. The difficult part is knowing which way he'll go. He's not consistent and I haven't figured out a pattern."

Vasko's counteroffer arrived late in the day. I finished packing and saying goodbye. Councilor Moon's retinue would leave tomorrow at first light. Composing a note to Kade, I planned to send it overland—a cowardly deed. By the time he responded, I would be in Fulgor. Too late to change anything.

One of Vasko's associates knocked on my door. I debated arming myself with my sais, but decided to hide my switchblade in my pocket instead.

When I opened the door, he handed me a sheet of parchment. The expression on his wide face remained impassive as he said, "I'll wait here for your reply."

I scanned the document. Pazia was right. Vasko had sweetened the deal so much my teeth ached. "I need time to think it over."

The man didn't move.

"I'll need to sleep on it. I'll send—"

"I'll wait here."

"Fine." I closed the door.

Carrying the deal over to the lantern on the table, I read the offer. Straightforward and with no fine print, it listed all the items he would provide for me. Glass factory, workers, supplies and sales force remained the same, but he added a house for me and a stable for Quartz to live in, a generous salary and two of his finest rubies each year. All in exchange for glass messengers.

Every aspect of the business would be taken care of. My job would be to produce them. He even left a space for me to write in a yearly total of messengers. I could write ten or a hundred. My choice.

The room tilted and spun. I groped for a chair, feeling light-headed. Resting my forehead on my arms, I sucked in deep breaths.

The downside of the contract would be not having a say in who bought them, and not being able to give a few away for free, bringing me back to where I started. The Messenger Committee had decided who they sent messengers to and how they were used. Working for Vasko, I would be in the same situation except I would have a house, money and rubies.

Though tempting, I couldn't relinquish control of my messengers. They were all I had. On unsteady legs, I shuffled to the door. I handed the man—who hadn't moved an inch—the parchment. "Please tell Vasko I decided not to sign the agreement, but I might change my mind in the future."

He left without saying a word.

I thought saying goodbye to Mara had been difficult, but it resembled a party compared to this morning. Joining Councilor Moon's caravan just after dawn, I focused on the transfer of my crates and bags into one of Tama's wagons. When I saw my possessions nestled in with hers, I felt queasy.

My stomach continued to sour as we left the Citadel through the east gate. The trip to Fulgor would take six days, two days longer because of the slower pace of the wagons.

Tama appeared to enjoy the ride despite the rising heat and humidity. She led the caravan along with two guardsmen. She smiled and called out instructions with a light tone. Her white horse shone in the sunlight, almost matching Tama's hair. Gressa rode in a carriage behind Tama. I suspected the cushioned coach was meant for the Councilor, although Gressa had no qualms about making it her own.

I hung back with the wagons. Aides and servants perched on boxes or sat next to the drivers. Five guards on horseback completed the group.

We traveled through Featherstone lands. Rolling green hills and bushy trees dominated the landscape. Wildflowers bloomed in the fields. We passed a few areas where the trees had been chopped down. The Featherstone Clan members used wood to earn a living. Carpenters built houses, furniture and wagons. Wood-workers carved bowls and artwork.

The first night on the road, we stopped at the Azure Inn in a small village called Bluejay's Eggs. All the towns in the Featherstone Clan's lands were named for an aspect of birds. Owl's Hill, Robin's

Nest and Cardinal's Tree were three of many examples.

Tama secured lodging for us. I would share a room with two other women. As long as I had a bed to myself, I didn't mind. Having no desire to make small talk with strangers, I returned to my room after dinner, planning to enjoy a few moments alone.

I groaned when someone knocked. Hoping it was a staff member, I palmed my switchblade and asked who was at the door. A mumbled reply about supplies for the washroom. I cracked open the door. Devlen stood in the hallway holding a stack of towels.

21

"Go away," I said to Devlen, closing the door.

He stuck his foot in the jamb. "Opal, I—"

"Get out."

"But I—"

"I don't want to hear it." I knew he would lie.

"...to explain."

"I'm done listening to you. Go. Now." I kicked his foot.

He shoved his way into the room with his shoulder.
I backed up. Tossing the towels onto a bed, he crossed
his arms against his chest. "I'm not leaving until—"

Snick. I brandished my switchblade. He should have
come armed.

"Leave or I'll stab you," I threatened.

His lips curved into a half smile. "No, you won't."

The old Opal wouldn't. But not the new girl. Oh no,
she was tired of being pushed around. I jabbed the
blade toward his neck, aiming for his Adam's apple.

Even though I surprised him, he moved a hair faster than me, blocking the strike.

I stabbed again, he ducked. He blocked another thrust and a fourth, sidestepping away from me. My last strike forced him up against the wall and unable to dodge another attack.

"The doorknob is on your right. Use it," I said.

"No."

"Suit yourself." I shoved my weapon toward his stomach.

He grabbed my wrist with both his hands. We struggled. Using all my strength, I leaned my body into it. I might have won if he didn't cheat. His fingers pressed. Pain ringed my wrist and shot along my hand, numbing it. My switchblade clanged to the floor.

He gasped. "You really were trying to—"

"Yes." I yanked my hand, but he clung to it.

"But what about preserving this body for Ulrick?"

"You'll heal." I pulled my arm. "Let go."

"So you can grab your sais and try again?"

"Good idea." My sais were hooked onto my saddle-bags. I punched him in the solar plexus.

He hunched forward, grabbing my free arm. "Stop...it." He gasped for breath.

I rammed my knee toward him, but he turned his body, so I missed my mark and hit his upper thigh. Twisting, I tried again, but he dug his fingers into my wrists. This time I collapsed to my knees as the pain raced up my arms and through my legs.

"Promise you'll...stop," he said.

Wave after wave of burning needles pricked my skin from the inside. How could two little spots cause so much agony? "I'll stop...for now...I promise."

He released his grip. I lay back onto the floor, panting.

He sat next to me. "I only came to warn you."

"Then consider me warned." I shooed him with a tired arm.

"Don't you want to know why?"

"Doesn't matter. It's not like I'd believe you anyway."

He whistled. "You're nasty."

"Thank you."

"Tama and Gressa aren't doing you any favors by sponsoring you. They plan—"

"To use me to gain control of the supply of glass messengers. Once they have a monopoly of the messengers, they'll use them as political bribes and other...illicit deeds. Did I get it right?"

Devlen squinted in confusion. "If you knew all this, then why are you here?"

"Everyone wants to gain control of the messengers. The Council, Tama and Gressa, and Vasko Cloud Mist. The Council will pretend I have a vote, and Vasko will mask my lack of power with money and rubies." I paused. His offer still tempted me. "Tama and Gressa will just take what they want. They seem more...honest to me."

"You're insane. What happened to you?"

"You."

"No. You were still optimistic the last time I saw you."

I'd hardly call escaping an optimistic endeavor. "It doesn't matter. What matters is you warned me. Now run along."

He remained sitting. "Aren't you curious about why I would risk my position on Councilor Moon's staff to warn you?"

"No." I struggled to my feet.

"Do you already know why?" He stood, too.

"You want to save me from them so you can force me to lead you to one of the glass prisons. I'll release the Warper trapped inside and you can learn how to finish the Kirakawa ritual."

"That's not why. Although you don't appear bothered by that scenario."

I shrugged. "At least then the Council would believe a Warper still lives and others are using blood magic."

"But people would die," he said in shock.

I almost laughed out loud at how we had reversed roles. It was fun playing the heartless destroyer. "It would be the Council's fault. In fact, the idea is growing on me." I tapped a finger on my lips as if lost in thought. "If I release a Warper, I don't really need you at all. Unless we use you as a sacrifice." I studied him.

He backed up. "You really are insane."

I pished. "I'm being smart. Think how powerful I would be if I teamed up with a Warper. We'd have my messengers, blood magic and, with my ability to siphon power, we'd have diamonds to fund our takeover. I could release the others and be unstoppable."

Devlen's shoulders dropped in chagrin as he realized what I'd been doing. "I should have known. You may have changed, but you're not a ruthless killer."

"I can learn to be ruthless." I bent to retrieve my switchblade.

He grabbed my arm to stop me. This time I grasped his wrist with my free hand and clamped down on his pressure point. He fell to his knees.

"After all, *you* taught me well."

I enjoyed the rest of the trip to Fulgor. Devlen avoided me, and I had a nice chat with Tama regarding my new job. She managed to mask most of her ire about the previous commitments I had negotiated for my messengers. Though she brightened at the prospect of being consulted before any other messengers were delivered. Being consulted was different than being in charge. I wondered how long it would take Gressa to resort to strong-arm methods.

Gressa graciously offered me rooms above her glass shop.

"They're very nice. I used to live there, but since my appointment to Tama's staff, I'm living in the Councilor's Hall." She introduced me to her glass workers.

A few remembered my "break-in" from before and frowned. Their scowls increased when Gressa announced I had priority on the equipment.

"Assist her when needed. Her work is very important," she ordered.

The apartment on the second floor contained six rooms—two bedrooms, a kitchen, living area, office and washroom. Glass items decorated shelves and tables, and beautiful stained-glass murals hung on the walls. Tall windows brightened every room.

We opened the windows wide to let in fresh air. I felt the roar from the kilns vibrate the floor. The constant noise wouldn't bother me. In fact, it reminded me of home.

When the workers finished carrying up my things, she asked, "What do you think?"

"It's lovely. Did you design the murals?" The swoops and swirls of color mesmerized me. A pattern could only be discerned from a distance.

"Yes. There's a glass cutter in town that has a light touch with the solder. See how delicate the lines are? It makes all the difference."

As she prattled on about the inspiration for the designs, I marveled over her friendly act, considering the cold reception I had gotten the last time we met. I lost track of the conversation until she mentioned Ulrick's name.

"…uses the kiln on occasion. Will it be a problem?" she asked.

"Not at all," I said.

"I noticed you both…avoided each other during the trip."

"It's difficult for me to be near him," I admitted. "With the whole undercover operation and his ability to completely fool me…" I cast about for an explanation that would please her. "I'm terribly embarrassed by my overreaction to his fake identity. I think it's best we keep our distance. When he's here, I'll just make sure to stay upstairs until he's done."

"Good idea. Don't feel too bad about being duped. It could happen to anyone." She swept her hand as if brushing dirt away. Matter settled.

After she left, I unpacked a few of my clothes, then planned how I would gather information. Since Gressa let me use her rooms and factory, I doubted I would find any clues here, but not for lack of trying. I searched through her apartment, concentrating on her office. Nothing.

Her office downstairs would be harder to access. The factory employed three shifts of workers, so the four kilns were in constant use. Perhaps I could try during a shift change.

The afternoon sun's warming rays combined with the heat from the kilns, turning the apartment into an oven. I left for the market, wondering why she hadn't insulated the ceiling below her quarters.

Before heading toward the market, I walked by the Councilor's Hall. At this time of day people scurried up and down the entrance's grand marble stairway. The Councilor's suite and a number of apartments for her aides resided inside. I guessed the building also contained break rooms for the guards.

Fulgor's security headquarters was located across the street. From personal experience, I knew a small jail filled the basement. Circling both structures, I noted the number of entrances and windows on the lower levels. A training yard and stable had been built behind the security building. Guards practiced with swords. I leaned against the wooden fence, watching them train.

Eventually one of the men ambled over to me. "Can I help you?"

"Yes. Would I be allowed to train with you?"

He studied me. "That depends on who you are and why."

"I'm Opal Cowan, a glass magician." No reason to lie. "I just graduated from the Magician's Keep and would like to keep my skills sharp in case I'm needed to go on a mission for the Masters." I could name-drop with the best of them. Janco would be proud.

"Don't see why not, but I have to check with my supervisor. Wait here." He hailed another man and they talked.

I counted twenty men and four women in the yard. There would be more guards inside and more out on patrol.

The man returned. "Captain said it shouldn't be a problem as long as you bring your own weapons."

"Great. When do you train?"

"We have a two-hour session at dawn and another one in the late afternoon." He gestured to the men. "If anyone gives you a hard time, just tell them Captain Alden gave you permission."

"Thanks." I stayed by the fence until they finished the session. By this time, the sun dipped behind the white dome of the Councilor's Hall. Finding a hidden vantage point, I spied on the Hall. The evidence I needed would be in either Tama's or Gressa's office. And the best time for me to search them would be at night while everyone slept.

It was full dark by the time I finished my stakeout. The market had closed with the sunset. I walked to Gressa's factory. The apartment's empty rooms echoed with loneliness, driving the fact that I was on my own to heart.

No support from the Keep. No support from the Council. No Kade. Sleep eluded me. I tossed and turned all night, sweating in the heat.

In the morning, I dressed and joined the factory workers. Though annoyed and grumbling, they vacated a gaffer's bench and assigned me a reluctant assistant. The unhappy boy looked as if he'd just graduated high school, but he handled the pontil iron with confidence.

"Do you need a special mix?" he asked me.

"Not really. What's in the kilns now?"

"Cobalt, Crystal Fire, Industry Clear and Milk." He pointed to each kiln in turn.

Most mass-producing factories used Industry Clear to make plates, drinking glasses and bowls. "What's Crystal Fire?"

"Miss Gressa's special blend for her fancy bowls."

"Is it clear?"

"Yes."

"Then I'll take a three-inch slug of Crystal Fire."

He moved away with an iron.

"Uh... Boy," I called.

He turned. "My name's Lee." His voice sounded resigned as if giving me his name was a commitment.

"Lee, gather it on a blowpipe. Please."

"Right." He switched rods and returned with a proper-size glob. The molten glass pulsed with a bright orange glow, beckoning me to play with it.

When I blew magic into the glass, Lee asked, "Do you need me to thumb a bubble for you? Some glassmakers have trouble with it. It's nothing to be embarrassed about."

"No, thanks. It's part of my...routine."

"Oh."

I finished the robin and put in a jack line to crack it off the pipe. Lee took the pipe over to the annealing ovens. Opening a door, he tapped the pipe. The robin fell onto a shelf in the oven. He closed the door with his hip. I marked the date and time on the oven's slate so the others would know when this oven had started the cooling process.

"You don't have to label it, that oven is just for your use. Are you going to make more?" Lee asked.

"At least a dozen today."

"Let me know when you're done. We're supposed to lock the oven's door so no one can steal your animals."

Practical, but still an interesting requirement. I

returned to the bench and we began again. After a full day, I crafted fourteen messengers. While Lee cleaned up, I returned to the apartment to change. I hurried through the streets of Fulgor to join the guards for their afternoon training session.

My arrival caused appraising glances and a few welcoming nods, but no one questioned why I was there. I warmed up and practiced defensive moves with my sais. A female guard asked me about my weapon. She held a wooden practice sword, so I invited her to spar with me to observe how the sais blocked and countered.

"They're nonlethal," she said in surprise.

"If you hit the skull hard enough, you could cause death. Or if you poke deep enough into the eye, it would reach the brain."

"No. I meant if I arrested someone, and they resisted, I could use these instead of a sword to subdue them."

"True, but you could use a billy club, too."

"But a billy club won't disarm a criminal if they have a sword. I can only carry a certain amount of weight—I have to make the most out of the weapons I have," she said.

We discussed various strategies. I taught her a few defensive moves with my sais and she showed me a couple new self-defense techniques.

"Hey, I know you," a male voice called out.

I glanced up and up. An oversize guard loomed over me. I recognized him as the bully from the jail. Nic.

He squinted with suspicion. "You were with that

Ixian who escaped. And I believe you caused trouble in the Councilor's Hall."

Everyone in the training yard stopped and focused their attention on us.

I thought fast. "You're right. Sorry about that. We were undercover for First Magician and we couldn't tell you."

"Undercover?" His voice lacked conviction. Hostility emanated from the guards as the tension increased.

"Go ask Councilor Moon if you don't believe me. I'm here at her invitation." I met his gaze without fear. My courage amazed me. I liked this new Opal.

"What's the trouble?" another man asked. He walked through the yard. The guards parted for him. His captain's insignia glinted in the sunlight—Captain Alden.

Nic explained his concerns.

"Ah, yes. The Councilor has advised me about our new glass magician." The Captain's pleasant attitude rippled through the surrounding guards, dispelling the tension. "She is welcome here. Please continue your exercises."

He stayed next to me as the guards drifted back to their groups. Soon grunts, clangs and curses filled the air.

When Nic moved to leave, Alden gestured to him. "You'll need to hear this. You, too, Eve," he said to the woman who had been practicing with me. "Councilor Moon has asked us to keep an eye on Opal."

Again suspicion creased Nic's face.

"She's been the target of an assassination attempt, and the Councilor requested we guard her so any future attempts will be unsuccessful," Captain Alden said.

"There is no need for her concern," I said. "It's been over a season and I haven't been attacked again."

"Doesn't matter." Alden turned to Nic. "I'm assigning her to your team. Draw up a shift schedule, I want her guarded at all times, starting now."

I must have had a panicked look on my face, because he placed his hand on my shoulder. "Don't worry. Nic's team is one of our best."

"I trust your abilities," I said. "I'm worried about my privacy." And about my illicit nighttime plans.

"No need. After our guard ensures no one is hiding in your rooms, he or she will leave, taking a position outside." Alden nodded with satisfaction before returning to the station.

"Don't glare at me," I said to Nic. "I've been doing fine on my own. I didn't ask Councilor Moon for this." I gave her extra points for intelligence. She now had an excellent reason to keep track of me.

"Considering all the odd orders Moon's been assigning us, at least this is what we're *supposed* to be doing," Eve said.

Nic's face relaxed as he conceded. "Sorry." He jabbed a finger toward the ground. "Stay here until I set up a schedule. Eve, do you want day or night shift?"

"Do you frequent the taverns at night?" Eve asked me.

"No. I'm a morning person."

"Day shift," she said to Nic.

He strode away. I met Eve's gaze.

"I don't like the night shift unless there's some excitement," she explained.

"You won't get much more action during the day."

"I can always hope." She laughed. "I think I should demonstrate a few more self-defense moves for you. Just in case."

My life lapsed into a routine. Creating messengers in the morning, training with the guards in the afternoon and walking around Fulgor in the evenings. My "protectors" wore civilian clothes. After a few days, I met them all and noted their habits. I started a friendship with Eve, hoping to obtain information from her.

One afternoon about a week into my routine, I asked Eve, "You mentioned odd requests from the Councilor before. What did you mean?" We had been sparring and had stopped to catch our breath.

"She's been...overly cautious since Akako's campaign against her was exposed. A lot of her requests are probably due to worry about being usurped. She dismissed her entire staff, and hired all new security officers after her sister was..."

"Caught?"

She looked uneasy.

"Don't worry, I won't say anything."

"Akako wasn't apprehended by us. In fact, the Councilor exiled her. We haven't seen her since."

"Exiled where?" I asked.

"No idea. All the Councilor would tell us was Akako was in a secured location and won't be bothering anyone. We think Councilor Moon is keeping her whereabouts a secret so no one can try to rescue Akako."

"That fits with being cautious. After all, Akako had supporters. I'm sure a few of them escaped."

Eve gave me another queasy grimace. "That's the other odd thing. None of Akako's supporters were arrested."

"But... That doesn't fit. Where did they go?"

"Captain Alden believes Councilor Moon's new security staff handled the cleanup."

"Cleanup—as in execution?"

"Yes."

"Remind me not to get on Councilor Moon's bad side."

"It set the whole force on edge," Eve said.

"I noticed the tension before, when I...stopped by on my way to Ognap. Even the townspeople seemed apprehensive."

"Except for the Councilor, it's a whole new administration, with new protocols and requirements. Plus, they're very suspicious. When a local baker wanted to purchase a larger building, they questioned him for hours before granting him permission. Then they supervised the renovations. That caused quite a bit of anxiety."

"They aren't as worried now," I said.

"People adapted. And we're hoping the new staff will relax with time."

Gressa supervised the first shipment of glass messengers to the Citadel. She had kept track of each piece throughout the week. Another month's worth of messengers would finish the debt.

I sat in Councilor Moon's office with Gressa and the accountant. The man held a thick wad of parchment.

"I'm already getting orders," the man said. "The Council doesn't need all the glass messengers at once. We can send a monthly payment until Opal's debt is paid."

"No. I want to pay them back before we start selling them to others," I said.

"What about these orders?" He shook the wad.

"Here," I said. "I'll take them."

He glanced at Tama in alarm.

"Don't waste your time with paperwork, Opal," Tama said. "You're the talent. Let Fenton deal with the hassle of shipping details and time schedules."

Ah. The first reasonable request. If I balked, she would be suspicious, and giving in too fast would also be viewed with wariness. "I'd like to approve *who* receives the messengers. We don't want them getting into the wrong hands."

"I assure you that won't happen," Gressa said. "There are a limited number of people who can

afford them and who have a magician on staff. The
Council won't let their relay-station magicians moonlight. I'm sure once the word is out, graduating magicians won't apply for government positions and will
seek employment in the private sector." Her tight
smile failed to reach her eyes. "Opal would be considered a trendsetter."

"I'd still like to see the list," I said.

"Fine," Tama said. "When you're done with the
Council's order, Fenton will go over the list with you."

Dismissed, Fenton and I left. He hurried away as
soon as we crossed the outer door. I used the opportunity of unescorted freedom to explore the Councilor's
Hall. Eve had been banned from accompanying me into
the Hall. Security insisted I would be safe within these
walls. By her expression, I had known the slight was
another one of those odd developments.

The vast lobby occupied the ground level under the
dome, which hung ten stories above. Next to this open
area was the core of the building. A grand staircase connected all the floors. The landings on each level had a
magnificent view of the lobby.

A large kitchen and a variety of utility rooms filled
the rest of the ground floor. I remembered the kitchen
door Devlen and I had escaped through. It led to an
empty alley and would be perfect for nighttime use.

Tama's and Gressa's well-guarded offices spanned
the entire first floor. I had seen the third-floor offices
when Yelena and Master Jewelrose had been assigned

to protect Councilor Moon. My explorations therefore started with the second floor.

As I wove my way up to the tenth level, I found nothing but offices, conference rooms, washrooms and a few "guest" rooms like the one I had been locked in. Workers scurried and labored at desks. No one paid me any real attention until I reached the top floor.

Two guards stood on the landing, protecting Tama's and Gressa's suites. They broadcast their displeasure. I apologized, asked for directions and returned to the ground floor. When I left the Hall, security checked my name off a list, which meant I couldn't hide in the building until everyone left for the night.

Eve joined me as I walked toward the glass factory.

"I was beginning to worry," she said.

"Why?" I asked.

"There have been a few...people who have gone in and have never come out."

"Do they have holding cells?" My explorations hadn't been as thorough as I'd wanted.

"Not really, but there is a tunnel underground. It's supposed to be used by the Councilor and her staff to escape during emergencies."

"Do you know where it goes?" It could be useful.

"No one except the Councilor and Captain Alden should know where it starts and ends. It's to keep the staff from fleeing without her." She shrugged. "But if the Councilor wants to break her own rule and tell her aides, then so be it."

I considered. "All the Councilor Halls in Sitia should have tunnels, including the Citadel's."

"They do." Eve put her hand on my arm, slowing me down. "This information isn't well known, Opal. I'm telling you because..." She touched her sword's handle. "Because I have a feeling you might need to use it."

A twirl of fear spun up my back. "Have you heard or seen something I missed?"

She hesitated for a moment. "No. Call it soldier's intuition. This whole situation—" Eve gestured to me and the surrounding buildings "—reeks. And Nic agrees. But don't worry, we have your back."

I wished I believed her.

I practiced in stages. The first night, I climbed out the window and scaled down the wall to the ground, then returned to my room without alerting the guard outside the apartment. For the second night, I crept around the dark town, staying in shadows and avoiding the three soldiers patrolling the streets. I repeated ghosting on the third night, but I tripped climbing into my room and landed with a loud thump.

Yanking the blanket from my bed, I wrapped it around my black clothes. I pulled my hair tie out and mussed my hair.

The door flew open. Nic rushed in with his sword drawn. "Hold it right there!"

"It's me," I said. "Sorry, I knocked the table over."

He sheathed his sword. "I should look around just in case."

I followed him as he checked each room. Moonlight shone through the windows. Unless clouds blocked the sky, I would have to suspend my nocturnal activities for a few nights until the full moon passed.

"You came in quick," I said. "How did you unlock the door so fast?"

Teeth flashed. "Once you go to bed, I unlock the door. No sense wasting time if you're attacked."

It made sense. "Why do you wait until I go to bed? Why not just ask me to leave it open?"

"A locked door gives you a sense of security—helps you sleep. Besides, I've seen you fight. If someone ambushed you while you're awake, you'd do fine until I could get in."

His compliment about my fighting skills offset his assumption that I felt secure with a locked door. I've spent enough time with Janco to know better. A pang of loneliness touched my chest. He would love all my nighttime excursions.

Nic returned to his post. I left the door unlocked, changed into my nightclothes and slid into bed. My whirling thoughts kept sleep at bay. A partner would help. The only other person I trusted was Kade.

His reply to my letter had been carefully worded, but his unhappiness and concern over my decision had been clear. He offered to join me in Fulgor, but I responded with an optimistic assurance that I would visit him before the storm season began.

When the moon waned, I continued my practice sessions. Each night I added a few more steps until I managed to break into the Councilor's Hall. Fisk's lock picks and Captain Marrok's patient instructions paid off as I crept through the kitchen door. With the utmost care, I ascended the stairway and peeked down the hall to the Councilor's office. Sure enough, a guard stood by her office door.

Hiding under the stairs, I waited. Eventually, another guard crossed the lobby and marched up the steps, relieving the one by the door. I counted footsteps as he climbed to the top level. The thud of boots on stairs grew louder as someone came down. This guard checked the kitchen door. I almost fainted in panic until I remembered I had relocked the door.

He looped around the lobby before joining another next to the main entrance. At least four guards were on duty at night. There could be more assigned to watch Tama's and Gressa's suites, but as long as only one remained next to their offices, I should be able to handle him. *Should* being the key word.

The next three nights, I repeated my nighttime observations, tracking the patterns of the guards. My practice excursions had spanned a total of twelve nights. I had lived in Fulgor for twenty days already—half the hot season. I decided not to waste any more time. The night of the new moon would be ideal to put my plans into action.

* * *

As I expected, the moonless night covered the streets with a thick darkness. Loading my pack with my blowgun, darts and various supplies, I headed to the Councilor's Hall. Once inside, I dipped the darts into a sleeping potion and attached them to a holder strapped around my upper arm. I smiled, thinking of Fisk. He had suggested I buy all the extras.

Swinging my pack over my shoulders, I waited for the guard change. A few minutes after the rotation finished, I crept up the steps. The lobby's shadows concealed me from the two men by the main doors.

Crouched on the top step, I reached into my pocket, grasping the glass rat inside. Keeping the bag's opening tight around my arm, I crushed it. A muffled huff sounded. I froze, waiting for an alarm. A cold wet nose pressed against my hand and fur brushed my fingers. I bit my tongue to keep from yelling.

When nothing happened, I pulled the rat out and placed him on the floor.

Run around the man's feet twice, then return to me, I instructed in my mind. He scurried to obey.

The guard recoiled, cursed and drew his sword, following the creature. When he came within range of my blowpipe, I shot him with a dart.

"What the…?" He sagged to his knees and collapsed on the floor.

Again I waited as long as possible. Did the guard's cry reach his colleague? The sound of my heart dominated all my other senses. With no time to waste, I hurried down the hall, popped the lock to Tama's office and slipped inside. I lit a candle and searched her desk, file cabinets and piles of folders, looking for anything unusual. Scanning budget reports, security reports and inventories, I found no evidence of Tama's plans.

I abandoned her office and relocked the door. Crossing to Gressa's door, I paused to listen for footsteps. Thirty minutes remained until the guard change and I planned to be gone in twenty.

Gressa's office contained the same dull accounting of money and resources. I found the stack of messenger orders. She had gone through them and marked approved or denied. I imagined she stamped the denials with vicious glee, but I wondered if the rejected orders would be presented to me, as well.

With time almost up, I pulled a file of receipts from her desk drawer. Flipping through invoices for glass supplies, sand and equipment, I scanned typical bills for running a glass factory. Except the quantity seemed rather large for four kilns. Perhaps she stockpiled the material at a different location in town or built another glass shop. I searched the sand invoice for an address. The delivery location was in Hubal. I memorized the street name and number before stuffing the file back into the drawer.

I straightened the piles and fixed her chair before leaving. Slipping down the stairs, I reached the kitchen without being seen. But on the other side of the swinging door, I startled a guard.

"Hey!" he yelled, reaching for his sword.

So much for my clean getaway. I ducked my head and rushed him, ramming my shoulder into his solar plexus. He stumbled back with a whoosh. I kept moving forward, but he tackled me to the ground. With his arms around my waist, he leaned all his weight on my back and legs. His gasps to regain his breath sounded in my ear.

My arms were free, but I couldn't pull away. Pinned, I halted for a heartbeat in panic until I remembered my darts. He called for help as I reached and tore one off, then blindly jabbed. Once asleep, he relaxed. I wiggled out from under him just as the door crashed open. Two guards paused to assess the situation. I didn't wait. Bolting through the door, I raced out into the night.

Yells and the sound of pounding boots followed me. After a quick glance behind me, I increased my pace. The guards chased me through the streets of Fulgor.

After a nerve-racking flight, I managed to lose them among the empty market stands. I returned to the factory and climbed the drainpipe to my rooms, shaking from the adventure. That was too close. If I had been caught, the consequences would have been...horrible.

And for what? Nothing. Another dire thought shot through me. What if the guards recognized me? Should I run away now? I prowled around the room, trying to decide. And I still needed to search Gressa's and Tama's apartments, which would be impossible since the guards would no doubt be on alert.

I plopped onto the bed and reviewed the evening's events. It was time to admit I needed help. Two people came to mind.

Kade. He was handy in a fight, but had no experience in sneaking around. Besides, he'd promised his parents he would visit for the season. I decided not to bother him.

Janco would have loved the chase through Fulgor's streets and would drool with happiness at the challenge of getting into the Councilor's residence. He had offered to help if needed. I decided to send Janco a message in the morning.

When my heart slowed to normal and the buzz of anxiety drained from my mind, I dressed for bed. Before drifting off to sleep, I realized the break-in hadn't been a complete waste of time. The address in Hubal where the extra glass supplies were delivered could be informative.

22

A COMMOTION in the outer room woke me. Gressa barged into the bedroom with Nic on her heels.

"...here all night," Nic said. "See?"

Anger simmered in her eyes as she studied me.

I sat up. "What's wrong?"

"*Someone* broke into the Councilor's Hall last night. *Someone* matching *your* description."

I had prepared for this. At least, the Hall's guards weren't with her. Jumping from bed, I let concern fill my face. "Is the Councilor all right? Did she get hurt?" I ignored the accusation for now.

She hesitated. "Tama is fine. No one was hurt."

"Thank fate." I relaxed with mock relief, then pressed my lips together. "What did they steal? Not that beautiful vase you made for her? That's priceless!" I stroked her ego.

Confusion replaced anger. "Nothing was taken."

"Oh." I blinked at her for a moment before putting a hand to my breast in horror. "You said the intruder looked like me. You don't think I...?"

Nic opened his mouth, but snapped it shut when she glared at him.

"No. Of course not. I'm checking to make sure no one tried to break in here. The person could have been after your messengers."

"Did you examine the cabinet? Lee always locks them inside after they're done annealing."

"No. I wanted to ensure you were safe first."

Her quick recovery and fast lies were impressive. I met Nic's gaze. He seemed awed, as well, but smoothed his expression before Gressa noticed. We went through the motions, inspecting the cabinet, counting glass messengers in the annealing oven and speculating on reasons why someone would break into the Councilor's Hall and not steal anything.

Eventually she left and I started my day. After sending a message to Janco by courier, I worked in the factory. As I crafted messengers, my thoughts kept returning to the address I found last night. Gressa had been ordering enough supplies for eight kilns with half going to Hubal. Why? No logical reason popped to mind. I would have to visit Hubal. It was a small town located about twenty miles northeast of Fulgor.

One problem. I needed to ditch my escorts for a couple of days. Plus, I would need to wait. If I disappeared right after the break-in, Gressa's suspicion would return to me. It would also be prudent to be here for Janco or his reply.

On horseback, the messenger should reach the Ixian border in a day, delivering the note to the border guards. Assuming Janco was at the Commander's Castle, he would receive my request in five days. If he left that day, the earliest he would arrive was ten days from now. Too bad the Commander banned all magic in Ixia. Otherwise, I could have contacted Janco via my glass messenger and halved the time.

Though sensible, my plan to wait produced an anxiety-inducing edginess. I imagined Tricky spreading his knowledge of blood magic like a stain, tainting everything it touched with red.

I followed my routine and tried to mask my impatience for action. After ten days of waiting, I twitched at every noise. By day twelve, I decided to go to Hubal without Janco.

Determined to pack and slip out the window that night, I fidgeted while Nic swept the apartment for intruders. He gave me the all-clear signal and left, guarding the door.

I barreled into the bedroom and skidded to a stop. Janco lounged on my bed with his hands laced behind his head and a smug smile on his face.

Recovering from my surprise, I said, "About time."

He huffed. "Not quite the welcome I expected."

"Thanks for coming. Is that better?"

"No. I imagined you would be so impressed by my ability to get past your watchdog, and so grateful for my arrival you would throw yourself at my feet and promise me your undying gratitude."

It was nice to know he hadn't changed. "If you can get free ale at the pub with that story, you can go ahead and use it."

"Is this an official damsel-in-distress call? 'Cause that would help me with Ari. He's going to be pissed I left. Especially since we had to explain to Valek how we managed to lose a smuggler."

"Yes, it's an official D-I-D call."

"Ooh...I like." He patted the bed, inviting me to join him. When I was comfortable, he said, "Spill."

I explained everything. It felt as if the story lasted hours. Janco asked a few questions, then scratched the scar under his right ear. A queasy expression settled on his face.

"What's wrong?" I asked.

He grimaced. "Well... If Yelena says souls can't be switched, I'm inclined to believe her. There's no reason for her to lie."

I rushed to assure him. "I don't think she's lying. There are aspects of blood magic that we don't know about. Just because she can't switch souls doesn't mean it can't be done."

"And you want to find proof?"

"Yes."

Mischief danced in his eyes. "How can I help?"

"Just an overnight trip," I said to Gressa. "Quartz needs the exercise and I could use some fresh air."

"But you haven't finished the messengers for the Council yet. And we have orders waiting." She tapped her fingers on the inventory list.

Time for a concession. "Why don't you keep half the messengers for our clients. The Council should have enough for now."

She brightened at the idea and agreed to my day off. I hoped my trip to Hubal would net us information. Janco had made many forays into the Councilor's Hall and Tama's and Gressa's apartments without finding a bit of evidence. Disheartening unless they kept their files in another location.

The next morning, I packed a few things. Eve arrived to relieve Nic and I told her about my plans.

"Let's stop by the station and I'll grab my stuff," Eve said.

"No offense, Eve, but I need some time to myself. No one has attacked me and no one knows where I'm going. I'll be safe."

"What about on the roads? You could be followed."

"I could, but I doubt they'd catch me. Quartz is a Sandseed horse. Besides, I don't plan to stop at any travel shelters or camp on the road. There's a half-dozen small towns within a day's ride. I'll stay at an inn and be back by tomorrow afternoon. Promise."

Her frown didn't ease. "What if they trail you to the inn and ambush you there?"

Damn. Since she didn't know about Janco, she had a good point. I thought fast. "How about if you watch me and see if anyone follows me from Fulgor. If no one does, then you don't have to worry."

"And if someone does?" she asked.

"Then please catch up."

She laughed. "Where are you going?"

"South to Chandra. I'll walk Quartz the first hour. If you don't show up, I'll assume no one is trailing me."

She agreed with reluctance. Quartz squirmed as I saddled her. She was as anxious as I to be on the road. She trotted at the slightest movement from me, and holding her to a walk was difficult. I headed south, trying to keep a lookout for a tail, but didn't notice anyone. After an hour, I touched Quartz with my heels. She broke into a gallop in an instant.

After a few miles, I turned her east, then northeast. I realized how easy it had been to lie to Eve. She trusted me, yet I wondered if the ease had come from me. My stomach used to get upset when I needed to go under-cover. New Opal lied without remorse, playing Gressa and Tama's game like a professional. I'd had a number of setbacks, but I'd learned how to be deceitful and ruthless.

Unfortunately I failed to factor in cheating.

The trip to Hubal was uneventful. I enjoyed the quiet hush that only a hot-season day could produce. The heat pressed down like a blanket with an occasional cicada's rattle piercing the stillness.

No clouds marred the sky and few travelers walked on

the road. Quartz burned off her energy until her coat gleamed with sweat. She slowed and I let her choose a pace. I glanced behind us from time to time. Janco trailed me, but he remained hidden.

We arrived in Hubal in the early afternoon. The downtown area spanned three blocks and included a handful of businesses. Most of the residents worked in the nearby quarries, digging out the white marble used to construct Sitia's government buildings. There was little activity on the unmarked streets, making it near impossible for me to find the Boulder Street address listed in Gressa's files.

I looped around the factories, searching for stock-piles of sand, smokestacks and the smell of molten glass. None of the structures indicated a glass shop might be inside.

I stopped at the Dolomite Inn and woke a stable boy from his afternoon nap. He stretched and yawned, helping me with Quartz's saddle and tack. I fed her grain. She drank water as I groomed her. After making sure she had a comfortable and clean stall, I rented a room.

I chatted with the innkeeper, an older man whose hair had migrated from the top of his head to sprout from his ears, eyebrows and nose.

"What's the main industry here?" I asked him.

"Engravers and carvers, mostly," he said. "The slabs of stone from the quarries are cut to size, polished and then customized, depending on the order. The big gov-

ernment projects always want some fancy columns or
statues. Date stones are popular." He touched the top
of his head as if he still couldn't believe his hair was gone.
"We also carve tombstones. Name, date—the works!"

"Any glass or pottery factories?"

"Nope. We import that stuff. We're focused on stone,
granite and marble."

"I didn't see a market."

"Of course not, it's not market day. You'll have to
wait three more days."

I didn't have the luxury of three more days. "Do you
know where Boulder Street is?"

His wheezy laugh turned into a hiccup. "Half the
streets in town are named Boulder, the other half are
Stone. Masons are not known for their imagination."
When he regained his breath he asked, "What are you
looking for?"

I debated how much to tell him. He seemed harmless,
but I'd made that mistake before. "A friend wrote me that
he found a job at a new factory here. I thought I'd visit
him."

"New?" The innkeeper pulled at his bushy white
sideburns as if trying to yank the information from his
brain. "I don't know about new, but someone bought
the old Donner place on the eastern edge of town. It's
tucked into the woods hidden from view. We haven't
seen much activity besides a few deliveries. Figured they
were renovating the inside and would be looking for
workers when it was ready."

He gave me directions to the Donner place. I decided to let Quartz nap and walked to the site. I almost missed the narrow lane leading back to the factory. Paralleling the path, I crept through the woods. Surrounded by trees, the two-story building looked ordinary at first glance. However, the stone construction and smokestack hinted a kiln might be in use. I circled the structure and spotted oversize doors. Sand and lime littered the ground as if spilled from wagons being wheeled through the doors.

"What took you so long?" Janco asked.

"I asked for directions."

He scoffed. "Amateur."

"Am not."

"Oh, yeah? Then why did you let your soldier friend follow you?"

"Eve's here?" I looked around. No wonder it was too easy. She'd played along to see where I was going.

"She's at the inn. She tried to trail you from there, but a clumsy man with a slab of marble almost knocked her out." Janco tsked. "By the time they untangled, you were gone."

"Guess I am an amateur."

"You're more a rookie," Janco said. "You need to learn how to spot a tail."

Muffled voices reached us and we ducked down. I glimpsed movement through the windows of the building.

"Is that our target?" Janco asked in a whisper.

"I think so."

"Tonight, then."

He traveled through the woods with silent steps. I felt like a pregnant cow in comparison. Did I really want to spend hours and hours and hours learning how to be a professional sneak? No. I'd rather be lying on a beach with Kade, with all this furtive nonsense behind me and with the Warpers all safely locked away.

I crouched in the darkness. Crickets chirped and an owl hooted above me. No sounds emanated from the factory. No light glowed from the windows. When I was confident the place was empty, I snuck to a side entrance and picked the lock.

The door swung inward with a tiny squeak. Heat puffed in my face, smelling of white coal and molten glass. I lit a small lantern. The ground floor contained two standard kilns, annealing ovens, benches and tools. Glassware and vases with Gressa's unique design lined a shelf. Why did she make them here and not at her factory in Fulgor?

In a back room I found a dozen of my messengers. The messengers still glowed with magic. Gressa had tricked me and sent my batch here instead of to the Citadel. Unexpected. Points for her.

I glanced out a window. Janco should be in position by now. After he had distracted Eve, he planned to wait outside just in case.

As I searched the mixing room and storage room, my

mind tried to reason why the messengers were here. Then I almost knocked over a table filled with pyramids made from opaque glass. I picked one up.

Magic pulsed through my hands. My stomach twisted. I recognized Ulrick's magic, and even though the opaque glass concealed the glow, I felt my own magic. They were mixed inside the pyramid.

Why? Unknown. An icy wave of dread slammed into me. I set the pyramid on a table before I dropped it. What I did know was Ulrick worked here and could be nearby. Ulrick's warning back in Ognap replayed in my mind. *I can sense you from a distance.*

Which would explain why Gressa had this hidden factory. Devlen was a wanted man for his involvement in the ambush on Zitora and me long ago. Since everyone was convinced switching souls was impossible, Ulrick would have to keep a low profile in Devlen's body.

I yanked off my backpack, tore it open and fumbled for my orb. Potential throbbed as I hugged the glass to my chest. I stood and scanned the darkness.

"Did you enjoy the tour?" Ulrick asked. He stepped from a shadowy corner. A wide smile spread on his face. "Took you long enough to put it together. You're still oblivious to magic. You walked right past my concealing illusion without noticing a thing."

"I can feel magic now."

"So you can," he agreed without concern. "What do you think of my shop?"

"Your shop? Don't you mean Gressa's?"

"It's more like a family business. We're working together."

"And Tama is involved, too."

"Of course."

"Why are you experimenting with my messengers?" I asked.

"Come on, Opal. You're not stupid. And neither is Gressa. She knew you'd eventually stop working for her."

"Have you been able to duplicate my messengers?" I asked.

"Not yet, but we're close."

"Then what?"

Ulrick sobered. "Businesses are more profitable without competition."

Meaning they planned to kill me once they figured out how to make the messengers. Wonderful.

"I must admit, you surprised me this afternoon. We didn't expect you to find this location or me. Gressa's going to be upset." He shrugged. "But now that you're here, you might as well stay until I figure out our next move."

"You can't force me to stay." The glass orb in my hands vibrated.

"If I use magic, you'll just channel it into your orb. But I don't have to use magic. Can you defend yourself while holding an orb?" He moved closer.

"No, but remember I can siphon all your magic before you get near me."

"Go ahead." He stepped.

Through the glass, I reached for his magic and pulled. It resisted my efforts. It wouldn't budge.

Ulrick pried the useless orb from my fingers. I tried to fight, but he backed away and let his magical power hold me immobile.

Pleased by his surprise, Ulrick leaned close to me and said, "I lied when I said it was a family business. We expanded to include a few old friends." He turned to the side and swept his arm toward the door. "You remember Tricky. After he offered to share the most wonderful present with us, we welcomed him to the family."

23

MY SINGLE LIFESAVING SKILL BLOCKED, I was...outma-
neuvered, outsmarted and outwitted. I would like to say
they cheated, but that would be if they played fair. In
this situation, no rules applied. However, all was not
lost, as I had my own surprise.

Ulrick searched me for weapons, removing my sais,
lock picks and glass creatures.

"She has a switchblade tucked into the small of her
back," Tricky said. He stood next to Ulrick with his
three goons flanking him. I recognized Boar, Len and
Aubin from the attack on The Flats.

Ulrick confiscated the weapon.

"Now what?" Boar asked.

"We should kill her," Tricky said.

"Don't be foolish," Ulrick admonished. "Until we
have our own, her messengers are going to make us
rich and her blood will make us powerful."

"She's dangerous," Tricky said.

"Not anymore." Ulrick held out his arms, showing the network of black tattoos. "We're all protected."

But Tricky shook his head. "We thought we had her before. Devlen and Crafty lost their powers, and I ended up in an Ixian prison. Bleed her dry now before her Stormdancer boyfriend shows up and blows the place to splinters."

"No one knows she's here. We'll wait for Gressa's orders. Until then, lock her in the basement," Ulrick said.

Aubin and Len glanced at Tricky. He nodded. I staggered as Ulrick's magic released me. They each grabbed one of my arms.

"We'll go with you," Tricky said, gesturing to Boar. "She's been training."

They dragged me down a flight of stairs. I wished I could fight four men and would have at least tried except I knew Tricky's magic would paralyze me in an instant.

The basement was all concrete, cinder block and thick wooden doors. A whole row of them—five in all. Tricky pushed the third door open. Aubin and Len shoved me into darkness. I landed hard on the floor.

"Should we chain her?" Len asked.

"Not yet," Tricky said. He slammed the door shut.

A muted snap of the lock sounded, then nothing. The weak light under the door faded and disappeared. Complete blackness surrounded me.

I remained on the ground, letting various emotions roll through me. Imagining myself as a piece of sea glass caught in the tide, I swayed with each wave. Panic. Fear. Despair. Anger. Chagrin. Hope. Determination.

When I calmed, I pushed all the negative thoughts away and concentrated on the positive. One—Janco would help me. Two—I wasn't chained. Exploring with my hands, I discovered the room contained a sleeping mat, a chamber pot and chains—four short lengths with cuffs at the ends and attached to the wall. I pulled hard, hanging my weight on a chain. It didn't move.

I touched every inch of the room within reach and found nothing more, not even a window. The door's hinges were on the outside and the door lacked a knob. My fingers felt a keyhole—positive number three. I paused to thank Janco before reaching for my shirt's hem. Another set of lock picks hid inside.

Sitting back on my heels, I hesitated. Both Ulrick's and Tricky's magic would sense me. They knew I was here, but could they determine my distance? I didn't know. What if they posted guards? I doubted one of Tricky's goons stood in the darkness, but someone could be watching the door at the top of the steps. Only one way to find out.

I extracted my diamond pick and tension wrench with care. No sense leaving a gaping hole as evidence. The lock had a large number of pins; hurrying only hindered my efforts. Time passed. Sweat ran. The pins slipped.

A tremble of relief washed through me as the cylinder finally turned and the door opened. I waited for a cry of alarm, but when nothing happened, I returned my picks and felt my way into the corridor.

At the bottom of the stairs, I paused. Why did Tricky choose the third door and not the one closest to the steps? I tried all the doors. The first and second were locked, but the others swung open. I debated: picking the locks would take more time, but I couldn't leave people here. Or could I? If I escaped and met up with Janco, we could return with help. Unless Ulrick moved everyone while I tried to convince the authorities. Considering my record, I doubted anyone would believe me.

I crouched next to the first door. "Hello? Anyone there?" I whispered through the crack underneath. Nothing. "Hey. Are you awake?" I called a little louder.

Shuffling noises, then a frightened female voice asked, "Who's there?"

"My name is Opal. I was a prisoner here, as well. I just escaped. Who are you?"

"Faith Moon, First Adviser to Councilor Moon."

First? Then I realized she was the former adviser, and one of the main people who'd conspired against Tama. A dilemma. She was supposed to be here.

"Hello? Are you still there? Please help us," she pleaded.

"Us? Is someone with you?" I asked.

"Yes. Councilor Moon is locked in the room next to mine."

The poor girl had lost her mind. Tama's sister Akako must be in the second room. I thought fast. "I'm going to get help for you both. I'll be back."

"No! The authorities won't help you. Come back! Are you there? Everyone believes Tama is safe at the Councilor's Hall, but she isn't there. Hello? She's trapped in Akako's body." Sobs emanated.

I felt as if I'd been slammed flat by a heavy slab of marble. My lungs refused to work as shock gripped my entire being.

"Are you there? Please answer!"

Her harsh cry pierced my paralysis. "I'm here."

"Thank fate!"

"Calm down, you're getting loud."

Faith sucked in a few gulps. In a low, intense voice, she continued, "I know it sounds insane, but you've *got* to believe me. Akako and a magician did...something to Tama's blood and they switched...bodies."

"I believe you."

She gasped in surprise. I understood all too well. Before she could say more, I told her my plan to check the door at the top of the steps. If no one guarded the door, I would come back and free her and Tama. No way would I leave them behind.

"Can you unlock cuffs? They've chained her to the wall," she said.

"Why?"

"To punish her. She tried to escape." Pride filled her voice.

"Why didn't Akako kill her?"

"She has information they need. They killed all her other supporters. I'm alive for only one reason. To ensure she cooperates."

With that gruesome image in my mind, I crept up the stairs, feeling for the door. I counted fourteen steps before I touched the wood. The knob turned without a creak and I pushed. Unlocked, it swung open. No cry of alarm sounded.

I waited. Darkness pressed on the windows. When I was satisfied, I returned. The lock on Faith's door resisted, but with more time than I could afford, I popped it, figuring out the trick to keep the pins aligned. Tama's lock popped within seconds.

Faith quickly explained to Tama as I worked on the Councilor's cuffs. The woman sagged in my arms when I finished. She whispered a thank-you in my ear before straightening.

"Let's go," Tama said.

We held hands, forming a line. I led the women to the steps. At the top, I instructed them to run as soon as we left the building. The presence of three people would no doubt alert Ulrick and Tricky, who, I hoped, slept on the second floor, since I hadn't seen bedrooms on the first level.

"Faster is better," I whispered. "If we get separated, meet up behind the Dolomite Inn's stables."

They nodded in determination.

It was a real shame we didn't even make it to the door. Tricky and his men poured from the shadows, creating a barrier between us and freedom.

"I thought you were smart," Tricky said to me. "Then again, you probably didn't realize just how much power

I've amassed since our last encounter. Your blood has given me a boost, and I'm well on my way to Master level." He gestured to his men. Boar and Len grabbed Faith and Tama. They dragged the women back toward the stairs. Faith's cries pierced me.

"You would have gotten farther without them," Tricky said.

I shrugged, projecting nonchalance even though my heart crawled up my throat. Janco was being smart. If he tried to rescue me, Tricky would have him, too.

"Not much farther," Tricky added. "As soon as you touched the basement door I knew. I'll give you extra kudos for popping all those locks. I guess Ulrick didn't do a proper search." His gaze swept my body.

Oh no.

Boar and Len returned.

"You boys go to bed. I'll see to our guest." Tricky advanced.

The goons leered, made rude comments and left.

Not good.

"Time for a proper search. Take off your clothes."

No way. I bumped into a gaffer's bench. Scrambling around it, I kept backing up. He continued to advance until I hit a wall.

He stopped inches from me. "Last time. Strip."

I fumbled with my shirt, yanking out the lock picks. "Here." I thrust them at him. "They're all I have. Honest!"

"Excuse me if I don't trust you." He reached for my collar.

I knocked his arm away. Big mistake. His magic wrapped around me, holding me immobile. He ripped my shirt open, then tore my undershirt off. His hot hands burned my skin as he pretended to search my upper body for weapons.

"Sir?" Aubin said from behind him.

He stopped. "It better be important."

"You should wait for instructions from the Councilor before...harming her. Her cooperation is critical."

He laughed. Tugging at my pants, he said, "This will ensure her cooperation. After I'm done, she'll do anything I ask."

"You just need to wait a day at most. The Councilor and Gressa may be upset."

"I don't care. Go away."

Satisfied with the ensuing silence, he pulled my pants down to my knees. I strained, wanting to scream when he touched my leg, but I was unable to make any noise.

Then he lurched forward as a horrible thud sounded. Bouncing off me, he dropped to the floor. His magic released its hold on me.

Janco held a blowpipe. "Come on."

I yanked my pants up and wrapped the remains of my shirt around my chest. "Are you insane? There are powerful magicians here."

"Which is why we're leaving."

We ran from the building and headed toward the woods. And slammed into an invisible barrier. It knocked us backward.

"You Sitians with your magic," Janco said in exasperation.

He helped me to my feet. We turned around. Ulrick, Len and Boar approached. Janco pulled a pipe from his pocket and loaded a dart. But before he could aim, the pipe flew from his grasp.

"Damn Sitians." Janco drew his sword, but Ulrick raised his hand. The weapon sailed from his grip to Ulrick.

"Damn magicians," Janco cursed.

Regret pushed out my fear. I shouldn't have asked Janco to help me. Ulrick reached us. He pointed Janco's sword at the Ixian. "Who are you?" When Janco refused to answer, Ulrick poked him in the chest with the sword's point.

Janco cringed but remained silent. Ulrick turned to Len. "Did you know he was hanging around?"

"No," Len said.

Ulrick cursed. "Who are you working for? Who knows you're here?" He jabbed Janco twice.

Even though blood soaked his tunic, Janco kept quiet. I recognized his demeanor. He had shut down, displaying no emotion. He had done the same thing when Ox's whip caught him.

"Check his pockets," Ulrick ordered.

Len and Boar frisked him. They piled an impressive number of weapons on the ground.

"He's an Ixian," Boar said.

"We should kill him," Len said.

"Not yet. Once Tricky is conscious, he can extract all the information we need from his mind. Take him down to the holding cells for now. Chain him up. I'm not taking any chances. You." Ulrick pointed to me with the sword. "Come."

No choice. I followed Ulrick back inside while Boar and Len escorted Janco to the basement. We entered an office on the ground floor.

Ulrick found a pair of gray coveralls and tossed them at me. "Change your clothes."

"Here? Now?"

"Yes. I don't want any more surprises." He sat behind the desk. "You've been full of them, Opal. Picking locks, finding this place, escaping twice, and now your friend." He ran his fingers through his hair. It had grown longer since our encounter in Ognap. "If you hadn't been such a pain in the ass, I would be proud."

"Those escape attempts failed and now a man's life is in danger. Real inspiring," I said.

"You're stalling. Get changed or I'll make you."

I turned my back to him and put on the baggy coverall. It was sized for a man. I piled my clothes. No real loss, since I gave the last of my picks to Tricky. If I lived through this, I would have to conceal more weapons on my person. Big if.

When I finished, I met his gaze. Those blue eyes appraised me with cold calculation, which was better than lust. With his increase of blood magic, his soul now matched Devlen's body and seeing him no longer shocked me. I wondered if Devlen's soul had also transformed.

"What are you thinking?" he asked.

"I miss Ulrick. The *real* Ulrick who wanted to assign a battalion of guards to protect me."

"That lovesick puppy dog?" He spat the words out. "Good riddance to him." Ulrick leaned back in his chair. "I guess I should thank you. If it wasn't for your rejection, I'd still be that weak whiner."

Wonderful. Another screwup courtesy of Opal. Lives ruined while you wait. How many people had I harmed so far? Too many to count. "I made a mess of things."

"Yep. Sit down."

I plopped in the chair in front of his desk. Talking to him was better than being locked in the dark.

"Who's your friend?" he asked.

I saw no reason to lie and wanted to spare Janco from being interrogated with magic. "An Ixian named Janco. He's working for me. No one knows he's here."

He huffed in amusement. "Right. I shouldn't have bothered. No worries. Tricky is very good at reading minds." He appraised me. "You know what's going to happen next. Don't you?"

"You'll take my blood and force me to make messengers for Gressa."

"Force how?"

I stared at him. "You need ideas?"

He laughed. "Guess not. Although you could tell me which one would be most effective?"

"No."

"Why don't we skip it. You know you'll give in. You might have changed, but you still care."

"I don't care," I said. "Not anymore. Everyone has either lied, betrayed or hurt me."

"If you didn't care then why did you spend all that extra time rescuing Tama and Faith?"

"Because I thought I'd use them. Put them in the line of fire so I could escape." I swept my hand out as if dismissing their deaths as an unfortunate side effect.

"Nice try. If I really believed that, I'd try to recruit you." He tapped his fingers on the desk as he considered. "You know Gressa will send Devlen."

Instinctively, I shuddered.

"He doesn't need to threaten the ladies or your Ixian friend to get you to cooperate."

"I know."

"Then why endure the torture?" Ulrick's curiosity seemed genuine.

My reasons faded when exposed to logic. I had been producing the glass messengers for Gressa for the last half season. Why would this be different? Because then I thought I had control and now I wouldn't? But I really wasn't in charge. This whole mess with Ulrick and Gressa went deeper than I imagined. I had deluded myself into thinking I could beat them at their own game.

"How about a deal?" I asked.

He raised his eyebrows, inviting me to continue.

"I'll make the messengers for you, if you don't kill Tama, Faith or Janco."

"Janco's too dangerous to keep alive," Ulrick said. "Unless…"

"I'll bite. Unless what?" I braced for the ultimatum.

"We've reached a dead end with blood magic. Devlen claims he doesn't know any more. We need guidance from one of the Warpers you imprisoned."

I laughed. "Couldn't you come up with something original? Devlen tried it before and it didn't work. This greed for magical power will only get you killed. Look at Roze Featherstone. She was a Master Magician, the strongest of the strong. Even adding to her power, she still failed. There are too many others to stop you."

As soon as the words left my mouth, I knew I'd made a gigantic mistake. Colossal. If I had felt guilty before, it was a mere scratch compared to what I had set into motion. At least when I screwed up, I triggered major disasters. No sense doing things halfway.

With numb horror, I watched as Ulrick's expression went from concern to contemplative as he chased the logic.

"You're right. The Master Magicians and Yelena would eventually get in our way." Ulrick smiled. "Unless…"

I kept quiet. No sense helping him.

"Unless, we neutralize them. Which would be impossible if we didn't have you."

24

A POWER-HUNGRY smile spread on Ulrick's face. "You can—"

"No. No way," I said.

"If you don't, we'll kill Faith, Tama and Janco."

"Still no."

"Heartless," Ulrick said. "I guess we'd have to find someone you *really* care for. That Stormdancer, perhaps?"

As much as I desired to agree in order to spare Kade, I couldn't. "Not even him."

"You're serious. Wow." He studied my face. "But they won't be harmed—not physically anyway."

"Doesn't matter. The answer is no."

"I know I can't force you to use magic with my magic. That trick only works for the Soulfinder." He clapped his hands together as if making a decision. "Devlen's been the most effective so far. After all, his methods convinced you to prick Yelena with Curare. You had to know Alea planned to kill her. This time, no one's life is at stake."

Still didn't matter. The new Opal wouldn't cave in. This time all of Sitia and Ixia were in danger.

"I'll message Fulgor right away. But first…" He stood and gestured for me to precede him to the door.

Ulrick guided me to my room in the basement. But this time he cuffed me in the chains hanging on the back wall. He locked my arms above my head, but at least I could stand, taking my weight off my wrists. He left, sealing me in darkness.

Alone with my thoughts wasn't fun. Not at all. The list of stupid things I had done circled through my mind. Janco. Delivered myself into Akako's group's hands and failed to have a backup plan. Kade's advice to always think the best replayed. I should have waited and listened to Yelena's advice. Then again…she should have trusted me and let me know what was going on. Unless she didn't know. And what about Zitora? Did she really believe Akako's story about Ulrick's undercover mission?

I leaned against the wall. Considering how much of the last year I had spent in the dark, I should be comfortable. Perhaps Yelena never trusted me. Probably not since the day I had pricked her with Curare. I'd been naive to believe she forgave me for deceiving her. And my tendency to give in to Devlen's pressure torture increased my untrustworthiness. I led him to the northern ice sheet to find his mentor. Yelena had to know Valek hid one of my glass prisons in a snow cat's lair. If my escape plan hadn't worked, I would have taken Devlen to the prison. I was weak—even I wouldn't trust myself.

Perhaps I should just join the team. Help Ulrick and save myself days of pain. No. Ulrick was right. I cared.

My abilities and knowledge were dangerous to Sitia. Looking back, I was surprised the Council hadn't locked me up when I wasn't crafting the messengers. This exact situation could have been avoided.

I needed to take myself out of the equation. When Devlen arrived, I would endure as long as possible, and give in. The first opportunity I had, I would find a piece of glass and slit my throat.

My despondency lifted. It was the answer to everyone's problem. A lump formed in my throat when I thought of Kade; being with him was the only reason to live. But it was a selfish reason. Very selfish.

I laughed suddenly. This situation wasn't unique at all. I had thought of the same solution half a year ago on the northern ice sheet when I told Kade to use the blizzard's energy to rip the station to shreds, killing everyone in it, including me. He should have heeded my advice.

Really. What did I do in the past three seasons? Craft messengers. Sitia could survive without my messengers, but not without Yelena and the Master Magicians.

A couple days, weeks or seasons passed—hard to tell when trapped in the dark. The opening door remained the only break in the constant blackness. Usually it was Len or Boar, bringing food, water and a few moments of exercise. Each time, I squinted into the bright lantern light unable to see who held the lantern at first.

When Devlen arrived, I smiled, knowing he brought a change of pace.

"Not the reception I expected," he said as he closed the door and set the lantern on the floor.

"Your presence is another step toward the end point."

"The end point as in you will agree to all of Ulrick's demands?"

"Yep."

"Then why not skip this?" He flourished the clamps in his hand.

"Pride."

He shook his head. "I warned you about Gressa."

"Yes, you did. Why?"

"You said you would not believe me."

"Then. Now you don't have a reason to lie," I said.

"What if you escape?"

"Has Janco escaped?" According to Len, Janco tried three times without success. The only reason they kept him alive was for the information in his head.

"Point," he said. "I warned you because I knew it would come down to this. Me, you and the clamps, torturing you to obey us. Tama and Gressa have been plotting to lure you to Fulgor. Gressa paid for the mock-assassination attempt. All part of the plan."

"The attempt seemed rather extreme."

"It worked. Tama convinced all the Councilors you were in danger. They ordered you home and assigned a guard to watch you at all times."

"I didn't see—"

"You were not supposed to."

Information swirled around my head until I felt dizzy. He might have no reason to lie, but it didn't mean he told the truth, either.

Sensing my disbelief, Devlen rolled up his sleeves and showed me his bare arms. "No tattoos. See? Tricky offered me a vial of your blood to regain my magic and protect myself from you. I turned him down."

"There are other places to put tattoos."

He stripped off his shirt and yanked his pants down, leaving his undershorts on. He spun around. "Should I take everything off?"

"No. I believe you." No ink stained his skin. I glanced away as memories of lying with him bubbled to the surface of my mind. He kept in shape. Not an ounce of fat clung to his well-defined muscles.

"I thought you wanted your magic back," I said. My voice rasped. Embarrassed, I cleared my throat.

"At first, I did and I do miss the magic. But I do not miss the obsession. The craving for more power that dominates every thought and action. I would rather be without the addiction."

"Why are you still working for Gressa?"

"To protect you."

I laughed. Who was going to protect me from him?

Offended by my outburst, he said in his defense, "I did rescue you from the Councilor's Hall."

I sobered. "Are you here to rescue me again?"

His shoulders sagged. "I cannot. Ulrick and Tricky have too much power. They will detect us before we leave the building." He sounded upset.

I bit my lip, hoping the pain would zap a measure of sense into me. Devlen was a master manipulator. He had a plan. It involved using me. I needed to remember that. "Whatever. Let's get on with the torture, then."

"No. I am not going to hurt you."

"What?"

"I will not torture you."

He was a master liar. This was a trick. He hadn't put his clothes back on. Perhaps he thought I would be so relieved I would sleep with him.

"What game are you playing now?" I asked.

"No games."

Yeah, right. "What do you want?"

"Nothing."

Hard to believe. I thought about the implications if he failed to follow orders. "If Ulrick and Tricky find out, they'll kill you. Or use you as a sacrifice."

"Probably."

"You don't seem very upset."

"I do not have any control over what they do, so why should I worry about it?" He pulled his pants back on and found his shirt.

"Maybe they won't find out." I snapped my mouth shut, clicking my teeth. Why had I spoken aloud? Because I was an idiot.

"What do you mean?"

I figured out his plan. It was official. I was an idiot. "You know *exactly* what I mean. You're being lazy. You know I'll give in after a few days, so you're saving yourself time by playing this I-won't-hurt-you card. I'm supposed to fall for it and be concerned you'll be killed. Then I'll offer to pretend to be tortured and give in so you aren't hurt." And why was I distressed? I had been planning to break anyway. At least this way I would avoid days of pain.

His eyebrows shot up in amazement. "You still do not trust me."

"And you're surprised?"

"I have not lied to you or done anything to hurt you since we left Ixia. I told you Ulrick agreed to switch bodies—you know that is true. I helped you escape Gressa, and I am trying to help you now."

"What about at the Bluejay Inn? You used pressure on my wrists."

"You were trying to kill me."

True. Kade's words sounded in my mind. *When forced into a desperate situation, you will defend yourself with the weapons available to you.* But I still didn't trust him.

He huffed. "People can change, Opal. I am free of the blood magic and have chosen not to go back. *You* have changed, too. And not for the better."

"That's supposed to convince me?"

"Okay. Fine. If my death will prove I speak the truth, so be it." He strode to the door and yanked it open. His boots pounded on the steps. Silence filled the room. My breath rasped through my nose, sounding loud.

Distant voices reached me, then the heavy tread of feet.

"Damn it, Devlen. You left her door open," Ulrick said.

"Do not worry, she is chained."

"We have thought that before and she managed to escape."

The two men entered my room.

Ulrick scanned my body. "You haven't even started! What's going on?"

What indeed?

"I am not going to torture her." He braced for Ulrick's response.

Son of a bitch!

Ulrick stilled. "Why not?"

"I—"

"He doesn't have to," I said before Devlen could finish. "I've been thinking..."

"And?" Ulrick prompted.

I drew in a deep breath. My thoughts raced. "And, you're both right. I'll give in after a couple days so why waste my energy? Besides, I'm not going to hurt anyone." I sounded as if I tried to convince myself, pretending to be a cowardly rat. Pretending?

Eyeing me with suspicion, Ulrick failed to appear convinced. "I figured you'd fight it for a while. Too easy."

"He brought three clamps, Ulrick. Three points! Have you ever felt the pain of one point?"

"No."

"Show him," I said to Devlen. "Please." I let panic fill my voice.

The men glanced at each other. Ulrick shrugged. "I've always been curious." He held out his arm.

Devlen grabbed his wrist, pinching the joint. Ulrick dropped to his knees. Surprise and agony flashed on his face. Devlen held the point a moment longer, then let go.

"That was...impressive." Ulrick touched his wrist and considered. "Why did you bring three?"

"I used two on her before and she lasted two days. I hoped three would speed up the process."

Ulrick stood. "Two days..." He absently rubbed his arm, then turned to Devlen. "Are you sure she'll cooperate?"

"Yes."

"Good. We've gotten word Master Cowan is heading our way. We must prepare for her arrival."

"Zitora? Why is *she* coming?" I asked.

"Another one of your surprises, but this time it worked for us."

"My surprise?" Now I was confused.

"Your soldier friend from Fulgor. Janco told her

about the factory before he came here to rescue you. She took off. Instead of reporting your disappearance to her commanding officer or to Councilor Moon, she sent a message to the Magician's Keep. I'd wanted more time to get ready, but the situation is perfect. I'd rather pick off one Master at a time than be attacked by all three at once."

They left. Once again, my thoughts plagued me. Zitora headed toward a trap, and I had leaped to Devlen's aid. Either Devlen told the truth or I had been manipulated. At this point, it didn't matter.

Time moved. I marked days by meals. Three meals equaled one day. Devlen visited, explaining Ulrick and Tricky's plans for surprising Zitora. I ceased to care. She would be safe from me.

My muscles ached from standing. Blood ran down my arms from donating to Tricky's protection. At least he stayed on task and his hands didn't explore.

I had failed miserably. My goal to prove Devlen and Ulrick had switched souls would never be achieved. I did hope my efforts would save Zitora. Once she knew about Tricky and the blood magic, she would put a stop to it.

After six days of counting, Devlen arrived to escort me to the kilns. My legs cramped and I held on to his arm as we climbed the stairs.

"Ulrick, Tricky and I will be in the mixing room," Devlen said. "They have grafted a null shield onto the wall so Zitora will not be able to sense them. But they have drilled holes and can blow a Curare-laced dart at her if they need to. Len and Boar are your guards. There are orbs nearby."

"Where is Aubin?"

"He has been sent away in case they are not successful. The plan is for you to siphon her power as soon as she enters the kiln area."

I stopped on the top step. "Why would she come in? Won't she be suspicious?"

"Yes, she will be. She believes you have been caught by Tricky and Devlen." He gave me a wry smile. "She is here to rescue you. They have staged leaving the building and going to town, presenting the perfect opportunity for Zitora." He hesitated. "You are not going to drain her, are you?"

I refused to answer.

"They will shoot her with a dart. They are protected from her magic." He wrapped me in an embrace. "Whatever you are planning, I will help you."

At that moment, I believed him. Why not? I closed my eyes, soaking in his warmth and musky smell. "You managed to fool me again."

"No. You are starting to trust yourself. I would not have been able to fool you as Ulrick if you trusted your instincts."

I created a mess when using my instincts. Logic failed to work, as well. My plan looked better and better. I only wished Kade held me for my final moments instead of

Devlen. But at least I would be able to ask Devlen a few more questions.

I pulled away to meet his gaze. "How did you switch souls? Yelena said it was impossible."

"A complete blood transfusion. Remember the device Tricky used on The Flats to siphon your blood?"

I nodded.

"My invention. Except I used a bigger and faster device to drain all the blood from Ulrick."

"But he would have died."

"Yes, except for magic. I told you I was a Story Weaver, but I also had a little healing magic. Enough to keep us alive while we exchanged blood."

Like he had said, *Blood magic with a twist.* "You did the same for Akako and Tama."

"Yes."

"Why?"

"I wish I had a more noble reason, but it was for money. I needed money and Akako paid me well."

The door to the basement jerked open.

"What's taking so long?" Len demanded. "The magician's getting close."

"Opal is weak. She almost passed out." Devlen hauled me up the final step. "Help me with her."

I pretended to swoon.

Len grabbed my arm. "Damn. Will she be able to—"

"Yes. She will be fine once she sits down."

Our little parade ended at the gaffer's bench. I "caught" my breath and took stock of my surroundings.

Boar loomed on one side, and a couple of orbs rested on the floor next to the bench.

"Does anyone know how to gather?" I asked the men. Devlen moved toward the kiln.

"No," Boar said. "Tricky warned us not to give her molten glass."

I huffed. "How are we going to convince Zitora I'm working for you if I don't have a slug?"

"Here," Len said, handing me an orb. "Pretend you're inspecting the glass. Devlen, you'd better go."

The orb throbbed under my hands, and I tried to sense Boar's magic. Nothing. Odd. If he was protected by a null shield, Zitora would believe I was alone, which would blow the whole captured ruse. In fact, all she needed to do was read my thoughts and know everything.

Unless they had grafted null shields on the other walls. My head hurt. Too many possibilities. All that mattered was I held glass and I felt magic. I didn't need to wait for Zitora. Break, cut and let my blood run.

I lifted the sphere, aiming for the edge of the metal rod holder on the bench. The crack rang louder than the kiln's hum. A perfect piece with a sharp edge remained in my hand. I pushed it against my throat.

"Opal, stop!" Zitora stood at the door, pure fury radiating from her. "What do you think you're doing?"

Boar and Len moved closer to me. Their weapons were drawn.

"Run away," I shouted. "It's a trap."

She entered the room, but kept her distance.

"Didn't you hear what I said?" Now fury claimed me. "Of course you wouldn't listen to me! Poor deluded Opal." I gestured at her with my glass shard. "Who can't be trusted. Go away. I can take care of all the problems I have caused right now." I placed the shard on my throat. Yet I hesitated.

A cold wash of sudden knowledge drenched me. I realized Zitora had come. If she didn't care for me, she wouldn't be here. She trusted me with her life and that was considerably more important than a few secrets.

Taking control of my situation hadn't caused the trouble. The real trouble started long ago because I had let others decide. Those small rebellions over the glass messengers were a child's temper tantrum compared to how I should have reacted. I should have demanded to be involved from the beginning. Should have trusted myself. Devlen was right. I almost laughed.

Zitora sensed my emotions, yet she pretended otherwise. "What are you waiting for?" she asked. "Slit your throat and take the coward's way out." She stepped forward. "Or do you want me to do it for you?"

I understood. "You would enjoy that, wouldn't you? Payback for not letting you know about my siphoning powers. I knew you were angry."

"You're right." She closed the distance between us.

By this time, we were almost nose to nose.

"Well, I'm sorry I didn't tell you everything, but you didn't have to shut me out!" I shouted.

"I was _trying_ to protect you, but I realize now it was the wrong thing to do."

"Too late." I scooped up an empty orb. The glass pulsed under my fingertips.

"Feel better now?" she asked.

"Yes. Thanks."

"Anytime." She spun. Hooking her ankle behind Len's calves, she yanked his feet out from under him. She backed toward the wall as Boar lunged for her.

The wall! I forgot! "Watch out for—"

Two puffs sounded as Zitora dived for the floor. The side door opened. Tricky, Ulrick and Devlen rushed in.

"I hit her on the arm," Devlen said. "She's not getting up."

Ulrick rounded on Devlen. "You said she would cooperate." He punched him in the stomach.

Devlen doubled over. Tricky pulled his sword and pointed the tip at him.

Confused, I wondered why Tricky hadn't used his magic. Since no one paid any attention to me, I assessed the others through the orb's glass. I felt no magic from Tricky or the other men. Again with the null shields... yet Zitora's magic burned hot, which meant Devlen lied about hitting her.

"You can't drain her now," Ulrick said to me. "The Curare in her will block your magic."

Devlen straightened and tugged his shirt down. Snap. I understood. The null shields had been woven into their clothing to protect them from Zitora's magic just in case I refused to cooperate. If I ripped their shirts open, I wondered if the shield would break.

Len scrambled to his feet.

"Len and Boar, carry Zitora downstairs. Tricky—"

"Kill Devlen." Tricky stepped forward as the other two bent over Zitora.

She gained her feet and yelled, "Now!" She tossed me a switchblade, then targeted Boar and Len.

I caught the weapon in midair, triggering the blade. Ulrick brandished his sword and Devlen dodged Tricky's attack.

Ulrick advanced on me. A switchblade was no match against a sword.

"Put the knife down," Ulrick ordered. "We'll wait for the others to finish."

"No." I bolted for the line of pontil irons and blow-pipes, grabbing an iron as I ducked his swing. I countered his next stroke with the iron. The harsh clang vibrated through my hands.

I managed to protect myself from his blade, but I knew my arms would soon tire from wielding the heavy rod. I glanced around. Zitora knocked Boar to the ground. Impressive. I didn't know she could fight. An unmistakable thump meant Len joined his friend. Devlen and Tricky wrestled for the sword.

Countering a lunge, I spun to the side. Zitora rushed to help me.

"No. Help Devlen," I said.

She shot me a confused look.

"Help Ulrick, then." I backed away from another strike.

But the real Ulrick stopped trying to disarm me and pulled off his shirt. "Time for magic."

Tricky shoved Devlen, letting him take the sword. He ripped his shirt off. Len and Boar stayed on the ground, but they yanked at their clothes. Tattoos covered all the men's torsos. Magic saturated the air. Zitora's magic cooled and disappeared as a null shield surrounded her.

The orb almost leaped from my hands, yet my blood in the men's skin protected them. I couldn't siphon their power.

Four magicians against one were terrible odds—even for a Master Magician.

25

THE CONFIDENCE FADED from Zitora's expression as her lips parted in surprise. Another trick, I hoped.

Devlen pulled at his shirt. "A null shield has been woven into the fabric," he explained.

"Clever. Did you know null shields could be manipulated like that, Opal?" she asked.

I squirmed a bit. "Yes. They attached one to a net to capture Kade."

She turned to me and I wanted to melt into the floor.

"Why didn't you tell us?" she asked. Her icy voice shot through me.

"Well...um...we didn't want it to become...you know." I made a vague gesture, but she stayed silent. "Become like null shields and Curare. Where everyone knows about it and can use it." Weak excuse. I stifled a groan.

She waited. At least she didn't point out the obvious. If I had told her, we wouldn't be here.

"If you believed me about Devlen..." I clung to a

slippery surface. Finally I let go. "All right, I admit it. I made another terrible mistake. At least I'm good at something!"

"You should be proud," she said.

"No more fake fights," Ulrick said. "Are you going to surrender or do we need to force you?"

"Such choices. I'll go with the forced option. I have my pride." She slid her feet into a fighting stance.

Tricky shook his head. "She's too dangerous. Kill her now and be done with it."

The four men shared a look.

"Now's a good time to spring your surprise," I said to Zitora.

"What surprise?" she asked.

Not good. "Your backup plan."

"Sorry, Opal."

Why didn't she pretend to have backup? Her pointed gaze said it all. *I* would have to be her backup.

The men advanced on her. She looked tiny and fragile in comparison to the muscular men. Devlen moved to help her, but froze, ensnared by Tricky's magic.

Tricky smiled. "You're next, traitor."

I kept still to avoid being trapped like Devlen. Zitora defended herself, but, without magic, four proved to be too many for her. She didn't last long. Three held her. Tricky gestured at me and the switchblade flew from my hand and into his.

Genuine panic flashed in her eyes. I kept expecting

a miracle or an army to break through the door, but Tricky drew his arm back to strike.

"Wait!" I screamed, gaining everyone's attention. "Don't kill her. I'll siphon her powers. I promise."

"I'd rather die," she said. The truth.

"I'll do it and I'll even promise to drain the rest of the Master Magicians and Yelena."

"No." She bucked and thrashed, but they held tight.

Ulrick laughed. "Almost, Opal. You almost had us. We would have to remove the null shield for your plan to work, giving Zitora access to her power."

"It would only be for a spilt second," I said.

"But then you wouldn't go through with it," Ulrick reasoned. "Tricky."

He stabbed her in the stomach with the switchblade.

He buried it up to the hilt.

He twisted the knife.

Blood spurted out.

The world faded. Sound disappeared. Color drained. Blackness crept into the edges of my vision.

The glass in my hands burned my fingers, seared my palms as magic potential sizzled along my arms. One thought slammed into me. *Break the null shield and Zitora can heal herself.*

Anchored by my blood, their magic resisted my efforts. *Break the null shield and Zitora can heal herself.*

Her face paled to ghost white. Red liquid puddled around her. I clamped down on an hysterical giggle. Died from blood loss. Killed by blood magic.

Not enough blood. Too much blood. Blood transfusions. Blood protection. My blood. Everything connected to blood.

My heart choked and coughed in my chest as the answer hit me. My blood.

I used my glass magic on the men. Instead of reaching for their power and drawing it into the orb, I reclaimed *my* magic. My blood in their skin linked us. Our magic intertwined. They collapsed to the floor in agony as the power flowed from them and into me. But I couldn't hold all the magic inside me. As soon as I relaxed, it would return to them. I would have to purge it. All of it, including my own magic.

I didn't hesitate. I had been willing to give my life. My magic was an easier price to pay. Diamonds filled the orb, ringing out with a clear and steady sound. They rained onto the floor. A hailstorm of diamonds.

I closed my eyes, gathered the last of our powers and purged it. A searing pain shattered me, reducing me to tiny shards like crushed sea glass.

After a few more pings sounded, I opened my eyes. I lay on the ground surrounded by diamonds. My last thought dwelled on the beautiful sparkles.

Much prettier than slitting my own throat.

My world ceased to exist.

I expected peace. I expected to float free—unconnected and unconcerned. Unfortunately, the unexpected and annoying chatter of voices kept intruding on my peaceful afterlife.

I peered through a slit in my eyelids. My entire family sat or stood around the room. They talked. They argued. My mother interrogated Kade. By the poor guy's panicked expression, I knew her questions had to be of a personal nature. Mara whispered to Leif. Ahir and my father discussed glass.

No Zitora or Janco. I hoped their absence was due to anything other than death. I closed my eyes, letting the voices flow over me. Though pleased to be alive, I had no energy for the inevitable questions. In my mind, I calculated how many travel days my parents needed to arrive in Hubal, assuming I remained in the town. Nine days on horseback at the minimum, and Kade would need ten.

Too tired to muster any energy to be concerned over the length of my sleep, I dozed. The next time the voices interrupted, I remained awake long enough to tally a list of woes. My muscles ached and my head throbbed.

Later Kade's voice roused me enough to open my eyes all the way. He sat on the edge of my bed, holding my hand. His other fingers stroked my cheek. Deep lines of concern creased his haggard face. "...eat or you'll wither away."

My heavy eyelids drifted shut.

"Come on, Opal," he pleaded. "Don't leave me."

I struggled to meet his gaze. I'd caused so much trouble. "Zitora?"

"She's fine," he rushed to assure me.

"Janco?"

"A pain in the ass, but otherwise fine."

"Did I...die?"

"No. Just utter and complete exhaustion. But you will if you don't start eating solid food. Yelena can't sustain you forever."

"Yelena?"

"She came as soon as she heard the news."

She shouldn't be here. She had more important things to do. "What happened—"

"I'm not telling you any more unless you eat." Kade reached for a bowl on the table next to my bed. "Your mother's soup." He waved the spoon under my nose. "It's your favorite."

"You're mean." But I let him feed me because I was unable to move my arms. The simple act of swallowing exhausted me. I would have to ask my questions the next time I woke.

Each time I opened my eyes, Kade fed me and answered a few questions. I only "roused" for Kade because I didn't have the strength to deal with anyone else.

"You were unconscious for twelve days. You're in a room at the Dolomite Inn. The owner has given us all rooms and the use of the kitchen while we're here," Kade explained for a full bowl of soup.

"Once she recovered from her injuries, Zitora contacted the Council. After Yelena helped you, she switched both Devlen and Ulrick and Tama and Akako back to their rightful bodies," Kade said for a bowl of creamy chowder.

"Ulrick, Tricky and the others have been arrested. Janco tracked down Aubin. The Council will decide their fate," Kade offered for soup and a slice of bread.

"The Council is awarding you a commendation for your help in exposing Akako's illicit deeds and the blood magic," he said for soup and apple butter smeared on toast.

"The Council has voted to let you keep all the diamonds. You won't have to worry about money anymore. You can languish on a beach and surf for the rest of your life," he said for half a bowl of beef stew.

A full serving of stew netted me permission to stand up and move around. Finally ready to face them, I asked about the rest of my family.

"Your mother—"

"I'm sure she isn't being very patient."

He tried to keep his expression neutral. "I have to update her on your progress hourly. And she isn't... happy with me at the moment."

"Why?"

"Actually, she's annoyed at Mara and Leif, too. All because we let you run off to Fulgor."

At that time, no one would have stopped me. "But you didn't—"

"Oh, and by the way," Kade added as if just remembering, "we have to spend half of my next off-season with your parents and half with mine."

I gave him a pained look.

"Not my fault. I had to promise my mother I'd be back when I left to join you in Fulgor. Imagine my surprise when you weren't there."

"Sorry. You should have sent me a message."

"And be told to stay away?"

A valid point. And I didn't have to be told why my mother wished me home.

A touch on my forehead revived me. Zitora cupped my face in her hands and warmth invaded my body.

"You look much better," she said. "You should be out of here and causing trouble in no time." A tired amusement lit her eyes.

"Not anymore. No magic left, so no more trouble."

She sobered. "True. You can't access the power source. Your glass magic is gone." She covered my hand with hers. "Does that upset you?"

"No. I'm relieved. Now I'm just a regular nobody. No longer a problem. No longer a danger. No longer useful to Sitia."

Zitora squeezed. "I won't agree to any of those statements. You will never be a 'regular nobody.' Your deeds for Sitia have extended beyond the regular and into the extraordinary."

I opened my mouth, but she shushed me.

"You may speak when I'm done," she said in a stern voice.

"Yes, sir." I pressed my lips together.

"Even when the entire Council, all your peers and I didn't believe you about Devlen, you persisted—an admirable quality. And you will always have people concerned about you. You haven't seen everyone who has gathered in this small town, waiting for good news."

"Of course, my family—"

"Hush! I'm not done. Although I didn't know you were related to two soldiers from Fulgor. They risked a court-martial to be here. Are Nic and Eve distant cousins?" She paused to drive the point home. "I'll address the 'no longer a danger' and 'not useful' at the same time. Because you *could* be both." Zitora held my gaze, making sure I paid attention. "You could be a danger to all magicians in Sitia *and* you could be very useful. The question is, *will* you?"

"Will I what?"

"When you siphoned the magic in the room, you grabbed it all. Yelena hasn't been healing you."

I sat up horrified. "I stole your magic too!" Kill me now!

"No. Not at all. You didn't touch me," she hurried to assure me.

I collapsed on my pillows with relief.

"Sorry. I'm trying to tell you gently and not doing a good job of it."

I gasped dramatically. "You mean you aren't perfect!"

"Far from it." She sat on the chair by my bed and stared at her hands. "You're not the only one who makes mistakes." She rubbed her stomach.

We were quiet for a moment.

"Why hasn't Yelena been healing me?" I asked.

"She can't. Leif earns the credit with keeping you alive. All those tonics he forced down your throat sustained you."

"But Kade said—"

"Kade doesn't know. No one except Leif and Yelena knows. We didn't want to tell Leif, but he is way too smart for his own good and he guessed."

At this point I wanted to shake her. "Know what!"

"You're now immune to magic."

I blinked. My mouth opened. Questions lodged in my throat. "How..." The word squeaked out. No others followed as I recalled a distant memory and answered my own question.

The last bit of magic I had channeled had been the null shield surrounding Zitora. It had come to me, but I must have collapsed before sending it through the orb.

"But I can't access magic. I don't know how to maintain it," I said.

"According to Yelena, you don't need to worry about maintaining your immunity. She wouldn't explain why, but she said it's a part of you like your soul. No effort required. However..."

I braced myself for horrible news.

"...you need to decide if you're going to tell the Council. They will be upset and wary over the news, but your recent good deeds should go in your favor. As long as you don't go rogue and turn into an assassin like Valek, the Council will have need of your immunity. Eventually, Kade and your magician friends will figure it out. Magic will no longer harm you, but it will no longer heal you, either."

"What should I do?" I asked.

She looked up in surprise. "You want my advice?"

"Of course."

"Don't listen to me, Opal. I've messed up and ruined your life. I couldn't even rescue you. You saved yourself." She retuned her gaze to her lap. "Some Master Magician, I fell for Tama's...Akako's lies."

"You weren't the only one."

She played with the fabric of her sleeve, bunching it and smoothing it over and over. Finally she looked at me. "I resigned my position."

I sat up. "Why? Everyone was fooled—even Yelena."

"You weren't."

I waved it off. "I had the unfortunate benefit of knowing Devlen before. If he hadn't used those pressure points when disguised as Ulrick, I would have agreed."

"Doesn't matter. You were my student. I let my anger overrule logic by not talking to you."

"I knew you were angry!"

A wry smile touched her lips. "You were right. Learning about your siphoning powers through Tama...Akako Moon upset me. Plus, your accusations against Ulrick sounded crazy. The Council turned to me to sort it out. So when Akako informed me of a secret mission, I knew I had lost control of the situation. To cover, I supported her claims. Her explanation made perfect sense." She slumped in the chair.

"I was more than relieved when Yelena confirmed the impossibility of switching souls by blood magic. Then you visited..." She threw her hands up as if surrendering. "Look what happened to you." Her arms dropped into her lap. "Everything I did was wrong. If I had listened to my heart, you would still have your glass magic. My actions harmed Sitia, not helped."

"No. You can't take all the blame."

"Too late. I assumed the responsibility and resigned." She pushed her chin out in stubborn determination.

"You're taking the easy way out by running away."

"I am not."

"Lying to yourself is easy, too. I know. It's much harder to stay and deal with consequences. The Council and other Masters will make it difficult to regain their trust."

"The hardest part was confessing my lack of judgment. And admitting I have a blind spot. I can't sense a null shield. I tried to hide it, but I started second-guessing myself, making matters worse."

Did she know I had also kept information hidden?

"If you still want my advice on what you should do about your immunity, my suggestion would be to tell the Council. Thank fate, I won't have to deal with the debate your news will trigger!" She smiled.

"What are you going to do then?" I asked.

"Oh." She blinked as if I threw her off. She probably expected another round of arguments. "I'm going to search for my sister. Spending time with your family has made me determined to find her. Without any obligations, I can put forth my full effort."

Zitora's sister had taken her to the Keep over eleven years ago and then disappeared.

"Good luck," I said.

As Kade nursed me back to health, I requested more visitors. My family filled the room with happy noises, stern lectures, embarrassing stories and lots of laughs. Mara glowed next to Leif and they announced their intentions to wed. I mouthed a silent thank-you to Mara as my mother's intense focus turned to her.

Yelena stopped in before she left on another mission. "So nice to see color in your face again," she said, grinning.

"I'd rather thank you than Leif. He's going to gloat for...ever, and I'll never be able to refuse one of his wretched potions."

Her smile faded. "You're going to need Leif's expertise. I'd suggest you be extra careful from now on."

The reality of my new situation hadn't sunk in yet, and I was sure a whole set of interesting consequences would reveal themselves eventually. "Good thing Leif will be a member of my family."

"Opal, he was always a member of your family. So am I and Zitora. I know we let you down with Devlen..." She shuddered. "But that's what families do."

"What happened with Devlen?" I asked.

"He helped me with Tama and Akako. A complete blood transfusion, using magic to keep the body alive. Nasty and painful and unnatural. I had to see it to really believe it. The second set was as bad as the first. But they're all healthy and back to normal."

"Swell."

Yelena cocked an eyebrow at my sarcasm.

"What's going to happen to them?" I asked.

"The Council needs to decide their punishments. Akako's list of crimes spans pages. Ulrick and Devlen will go to prison."

"Prison won't stop them from teaching blood magic to others." At least they couldn't regain their magic. Unless they used my blood.

"You think they should be executed?"

"Yes and no. I don't want them to die, but I don't want anyone else doing blood magic, either."

"The knowledge is out there. It can't be stopped now. It's just like null shields, Curare and Voids. All things to be used and abused by others. Everything has two sides. A good and a bad."

"Including people," I said, thinking of Ulrick and Devlen and how they had switched more than their souls. "No one is truly trustworthy."

"I don't agree with you. There are certain people I trust no matter what. Even when it seems like they've turned into monsters, you need to stay true to them. Because, in the end, they'll be the ones backing you up."

"Even when they believe in something impossible?"

"*Especially* when they believe in the impossible. A mistake I hope I won't make again. I'm still learning that it's all part of the relationship. Those you trust will make bad decisions and cause trouble and heartache." She quirked a smile. "Bad decisions like not telling the Ixian authorities Tricky still had magical abilities that helped him to escape, and failing to tell the Council why he kept them when everyone else was drained of magic."

I swallowed my weak excuse. She was right—poor judgment on my part.

"But as long as you know their *intentions* are trustworthy, that should be enough to support them."

"How do you decide who you'll give this loyalty to?" My biggest problem, knowing who to trust. "I'm sure you don't bestow it on just anyone you meet."

"Of course not. There are only a few who've proven to me that I can count on them," Yelena said. "It's a matter of time and experience."

Great. My experiences have been horrible. "Who are the people you rely on?"

Her gaze grew distant. "Valek, Kiki, Leif, Ari, Janco, Irys, Moon Man, my parents and you."

"Me?"

Yelena gave me that flat don't-be-so-stupid look.

"Okay. Okay." I reviewed her list of names in my mind. It was longer than mine. "I guess in time I'll add a few more to my list."

"Who are on your list?" she asked.

"Kade, Janco, Leif, my family and you."

"You're missing a few names."

"Who?"

"Think about it." She gestured to the bed. "You'll have plenty of time." She laughed. "I'd better go before Kade kicks me out for tiring you." She waved and slipped out the door.

With nothing else to distract me, I replayed our conversation. My list had improved from before the events in Hubal. I would have to trust Yelena's assertion of time and experience and expect to add more names as I dealt with the next round of trouble.

Nic and Eve stopped by before leaving for Fulgor.

Nic explained what happened in Fulgor after Akako's deception had been revealed. "Captain Alden couldn't believe the message at first. If it hadn't come from First Magician, he might have consulted the Councilor...the impostor and ruined the surprise attack. We stormed the Councilor's Hall." Nic punched a fist into his other hand. "They didn't know what hit them. We nabbed Gressa first. She tried to sneak out through the tunnel. The impostor hid under her office desk." Nic snorted with disdain.

"The whole city's changed," Eve said.

"The citizens are giddy with relief. Lots of drunk-and-disorderly-conduct charges," Nic added.

"Nic and I volunteered to escort the impostor here so the Soulfinder could switch her back." She folded her arms. "And we wanted to check on our charge, who did not go to Chandra like she said."

"You weren't supposed to follow me." I tried, but twin stern expressions aimed at me. I felt instantly guilty. "Um...aren't you supposed to be back in Fulgor?"

"Not until we were sure of your survival," Nic said. "Do you know how much trouble we'd be in if you were assassinated on our watch?"

"But my condition is my fault. No one harmed me," I said.

"You planned all this?" Eve asked.

"Not really, but—"

"Suspect's story is changing—we should haul her ass in for further questioning," Nic said.

"We'd need more backup and rain gear. Otherwise we won't get her past the Stormdancer."

Nic scowled. "All right, Opal. We'll let you go with a warning. *This time.* However, if you come to Fulgor again, you're to check in with us. Understand?"

"Yes, sir." I felt like I should salute. He was serious.

"And if you need assistance on another one of your...adventures, send us a message. We'll be there," Eve said.

By their posture and demeanor I knew they would keep their promise. "Thank you, I will." I shook both their hands and the mood lightened.

"We'd better go and face the Captain's wrath," Nic said.

"I'll bet you two silvers he gives us the 'Chain of Command' lecture," Eve said.

"No way. That's a given. I'll bet four silvers he says, 'Don't delay, just obey,' five times."

"You're on. He'll never say it five times. You're so going to lose."

The two soldiers continued their banter as they left. I wondered if Yelena referred to them when she had mentioned more names for my list. Remorse filled me as I thought of how I had started a friendship with Eve just to gain her confidence and gather information.

I huffed. Two sides to my relationship with Eve—one good and one bad. But I had the choice for next time, and I could atone for my deceit by being an honest friend.

This simple realization dispelled the crushing guilt I had carried with me since I had pricked Yelena with Curare over six years ago. It didn't matter that she forgave me, I needed to forgive myself. To know there would be terrible times, but I could balance those out or even tip the scales by my actions.

It was all a part of being trustworthy—of being a piece of sea glass. High tides, low tides, storms, sand and mistakes all contributed to the polishing process. Though difficult to endure at the time, the demanding elements helped smooth the surface, transforming one into a better person, not worse. A person who learned from the harsh environment, who knew the storm would end, and who felt confident she would still be in one piece.

* * *

Janco swaggered through my door with his usual smug smile. "I'm not supposed to be here. Kade has you on a strict one-visitor-a-day diet."

He settled into the chair with an athletic grace. No bruises or cuts marred his face. Even though the smile remained, a shadow lurked in his eyes.

"Janco, I'm sor—"

"Don't you dare say it." He poked my arm with a finger. "My choice to help you. My fault for being caught. No regrets. I'd do it again without thought." He cocked his head to the side and scratched his scarred ear. "Which isn't that big of a revelation. Ari says I do everything without thought." He shrugged. "Thinking is overrated."

"How about I throw myself at your feet and pledge my undying gratitude?"

"Better, but how about plain old gratitude? Undying sounds creepy. Like it would live on after you're gone. Ghost gratitude. Too much like magic." He grimaced. "Now I have another reason to hate magic."

His gloominess lasted a second before he hopped to his feet. He bowed with mock formality. "If you should need aid again, send me a D-I-D call."

"I will."

Finally given permission to travel after a total of twenty-five days in Hubal, I packed my saddlebags. It was the first day of the cooling season. Kade needed to be on the coast and I needed to make a decision. Should I tell the Council about my immunity or not? What would I do if I didn't tell them? How would I be useful if I did inform them? Questions without answers chased their tails in my mind.

A knock on the door interrupted my thoughts and I shouted, "Come in," without checking who was on the other side, my confidence due to the knowledge everyone had been arrested.

However, there were gaps in my knowledge. Not everyone dwelled in a locked cell. The door swung open and Devlen entered my room.

Instinct caused me to reach for my sais, but I stopped when I met his gaze. Ulrick's soul no longer lurked behind those blue eyes. Devlen had tied his long hair back. The dark features of his strong face held concern.

"I'm surprised you haven't been arrested," I said.

"Me, too." Standing by the door, he kept his distance. "The Council is discussing my future."

"And they didn't incarcerate you while they debated?" A slight, peevish annoyance crept into my tone. He'd used blood magic and could again, yet *he* remained free. I calmed my ire with the reminder of Akako's dishonest influence on the Councilors at the time of my trial.

"Yelena spoke for me."

"Why?"

He smiled in self-deprecation. "Because I tortured her with pressure points."

"Not funny." I waited.

Devlen rubbed his arms as if warding off a sudden chill. "When she helped...transfer my soul, she examined me. I never felt so...vulnerable. Every facet of me—my desires, needs and beliefs were exposed. Helpless, I saw them all in their raw form. Not pretty."

"Being helpless and in pain is never pretty." From the distress on his face, I knew he realized how much I'd suffered at his hands.

He hugged his arms tighter. "She returned me to my body and—" he pushed one of his sleeves up "—purged the ink and blood from my skin." He ran a finger along his muscle as if he still didn't believe it belonged to him. "I expected to be arrested, but she claimed my efforts to help you and Zitora went in my favor. I will probably have to spend a few years in prison for my prior deeds." He let his arms drop. "I plan to cooperate fully."

"How did you help Zitora?"

Devlen shrugged. "It was not much. I was the only one conscious after you siphoned the others. I put pressure on Zitora's wound to staunch the blood, but she struggled to heal herself and was close to losing the battle. I acted on instinct. Scooping up a handful of your diamonds, I poured them into her palm and held her fingers around them. Her powers are impressive."

The diamonds were charged with magic. He saved her life. The effort must have sapped her strength. He could have escaped.

"Then what happened?" I asked.

"When I was sure she would live, I checked on you.

No signs of life." The memory of horror touched his eyes before fading. "When I did find a pulse it was barely there. I freed Janco, and we ran for help."

He could have run away. I pushed away the dreadful memories of him and considered his deeds since we returned from Ixia. He'd had plenty of opportunities to disappear.

"Why did you stay?"

He shot me an incredulous look. "I told you before."

To protect me. "But why?"

"To make amends."

He had decided long ago what I just figured out. Not to let guilt rule him by atoning for his past actions.

"I know you will never forgive me, but this way I can live with myself."

I gaped at him. A response bubbled and popped in my throat. Could I forgive him? It would take time and experience. "Never say never."

He laughed. "A glimmer of hope." With a hitch in his step, he walked toward me. "I have something for you."

Pleased I didn't flinch as he neared, I asked, "Did you get hurt?" I gestured to his leg.

"No. I have to get...used to this body again. I am taller than Ulrick."

And the scar on his neck gave him a rugged, handsome appearance, adding to his lean and muscular build. With the tattoos gone, I wondered how he looked without a shirt. I berated myself for my thoughts. At one time, his visage haunted me.

He handed me a narrow box. "Go on. Open it."

I lifted the lid, revealing a black leather holder. Inside the sheath was a pearl-handled switchblade. Palming the weapon, I pressed the button. The blade shot out with hardly a sound.

"It is crafted by the Bloodgoods using the finest steel," Devlen said. "You can clip the holder to a belt or strap it around your arm or thigh."

I examined the metal blade. Symbols had been etched into the steel. "What are these?"

He grinned with devious glee. "Ixian battle symbols. Janco helped me with them."

"Janco? Are you friends now?"

He laughed. "Hardly. But he claimed he would suffer my presence since I no longer had magic."

Sounded like Janco. I brandished the weapon. "What do they say?"

"I am not telling you. You will have to ask your annoying Ixian friend." He turned serious for a moment. "If I am going to be spending time in the Fulgor prison, I will not be around to help you. With your tendency to find trouble, I wanted you to have a sturdy blade."

"I'll ignore the trouble remark and just thank you for the gift. Besides, I've been training. I'm not so easy to beat anymore."

He touched my arm. "You never were easy. Not even when you were fourteen."

My mouth felt dry. When did he get so close?

"I had men sobbing in less than two hours. You lasted days. I admired your resistance and tenacity. Later in Ixia, I admired your intelligence and resourcefulness. Even disguised as Ulrick and with the addiction to blood magic burning inside me, I never pretended with you."

"But—"

He pressed his fingertips to my mouth. The heat from them spread throughout my body. "My feelings toward you were genuine. Those days we were together as a couple were the happiest of my life."

I swallowed a lump of dust. He replaced his hand with his lips and kissed me. Devlen stopped before I could...what? Kiss him back? Push him away?

"I have not made enough amends. So expect to see me again." He trailed his fingers along my arm and squeezed my hand as if swearing an oath. Turning, he left without saying another word.

I groped for a chair. Sinking into the cushions, I struggled to understand my conflicting emotions. An epiphany failed to settle the questions. Time and experience would have to suffice for now. However, Kade's arrival helped banish the confusion to another part of my mind where I could dwell on it later.

He glanced around. "You haven't finished yet. Opal, I know you don't like to pack, but—"

I wrapped my arms around his shoulders and kissed him.

He smiled. "If you're trying to avoid pack—"

I covered his mouth with mine and didn't let him speak for a long long time.

He pulled away. "What was *that* for?"

"To thank you for saving my life."

"Not me. Yelena—"

"Not exactly. Leif earns the credit for keeping me alive. You deserve a kiss for giving me a reason to eat."

"How romantic. Is that how you're going to introduce me? 'Councilor Greenblade, I'd like you to meet the man who gives me a reason to eat.'"

"Sounds like a plan." I sorted through my meager possessions, packing what I needed for the trip.

"Wait a minute. Did you say *Leif* gets the credit?"

"Yes." I explained about my immunity.

He frowned, mulling over the information. "Zitora said you sacrificed your magic for her, but she didn't mention anything else."

"She's letting me decide who to tell. Right now you, me, Yelena and Leif are the only ones."

"Who else will you tell?" Kade asked.

"For now, no one."

"What are you going to do next?"

Decide what to tell the Council, figure out my role in Sitia, deal with my mother and try to become comfortable with the idea of Devlen being one of the good guys.

Instead of listing all my future problems, I focused on the man in front of me.

"Next, I'm going surfing. I know this handsome Stormdancer, and he promised to teach me."

Kade grinned. "I thought you were afraid of the water."

"Not anymore."

★ ★ ★ ★

Another adventure lies ahead for Opal.

Don't miss SPY GLASS*!*